Modelland

Modelland

TYRA BANKS

DELACORTE PRESS

This is a work of fiction. Names, characters, places, and incidents either are the product of the author's imagination or are used fictitiously. Any resemblance to actual persons, living or dead, events, or locales is entirely coincidental.

Text copyright © 2011 by Tyra Banks
Jacket and endpaper art copyright © 2011 by The Tyra Banks Company Books, LLC.
Jacket art and design by Perry Harovas and James Schmitt/Tribeca Flashpoint Media Arts Academy. Endpaper art by Hebru Brantley.

Delacorte Press is a registered trademark and the colophon is a trademark of Random House, Inc.

randomhouse.com

Educators and librarians, for a variety of teaching tools, visit us at randomhouse.com/teachers

Library of Congress Cataloging-in-Publication Data is available upon request.

ISBN 978-0-385-74059-3 (trade)
ISBN 978-0-375-98956-8 (lib. bdg.)
ISBN 978-0-375-89944-7 (ebook)

The text of this book is set in 11-point Berkeley Oldstyle Book.

Printed in the United States of America
10 9 8 7 6 5 4 3 2 1
First Edition

Random House Children's Books supports the First Amendment and celebrates the right to read.

To Ma and Daddy.

Thank you for being absolutely, positively

nothing like Mr. and Mrs. De La Crème.

YOU WANT *to be there. You know you do. Don't lie, dahling. It's okay. I know what you're thinking when you look up at that splendorous place atop the mountain. I know what fills you, spurs you on, fuels your dreams. You're obsessed with being chosen. Everyone is.*

The Land you thirst for has loomed at the top of the mountain in Metopia for as long as you can remember. But for most of the year, it's covered in fog, its color changing with each passing day as if it's a gargantuan mood ring. You begin your mornings staring at the fog, longing for the fateful evening when it will turn a golden yellow and then, finally, like a push-up brassiere, lift.

Oh, how you long for that moment, with bated fresh breath, I hope.

For it signifies that the luminescent eye will soon blaze in the sky, bathing the whole world in gold, touching every one of its inhabitants . . . including you.

But dahling, it is no ordinary golden light. Once it tickles you, you are suddenly . . . transported. You hear the softest of sighs or faintest of giggles in your ear, even if you're standing alone. The once-stale air around you becomes both sweet and tart, making your nose tingle and sending a charge of excitement through your brain. The finest silk, the softest velveteen, or the supplest suede will brush your skin, but whatever you thought was touching you is nowhere to be seen.

Basking in the light is such a naughty tease, like getting a single lick of the most delicious butter-pecan gelato you've ever tasted: it inflames your obsession, increasing your desire a hundredfold. You lust to go to this Land to become one of the only famous people in the world. You ache to be a 7Seven.

But very few ever get the chance.

Nevertheless, you and every young girl in the world vie for an opportunity on The Day of Discovery, which is grander than every global holiday combined. Making the delirium even more intense, the Land sends seven talismans called SMIZEs into the world. (What an arcane word! Who thought of such a thing?) These SMIZEs, which boost your odds of being chosen by ninety-one percent, are propelled through the world's waterways. Naturally, the week before The Day of Discovery, bathing, showering, pool use, and even sewer diving increase, threatening a drought. Chance meetings erupt into fisticuffs on occasion. Every girl wants to find a SMIZE, dahling.

But not nearly as much as you do.

You ignore the slim odds and disregard the warnings you've heard since birth, like how it's easier to grow three inches in a month than it is to score a spot in the newest class. You turn a deaf ear to the cautionary tales whispered in your hometown and throughout Metopia: in dingy alleys and side streets of PitterPatter, during shift changes in Shivera, and on assembly lines of Peppertown factories. Like the rumor that the school often takes inhumane and irreversible disciplinary action. Or that certain "disposable" civilian girls are brought to the Land to be tortured and then killed, used as human sacrifices for ungodly experiments and animalistic rituals. "It's obvious why they torture them," the gossipmongers whisper. "Those in the Land bathe in civilian blood to maintain their breathtaking beauty."

Goodness great-shoes! A literal bloodbath, dahling? That crimson elixir must leave a nasty ring round the tub.

And then there's the reality of the Pilgrim Plague, a form of sadness-meets-madness that compels unselected hopefuls to embark dadless on an unauthorized pilgrimage to the Land. It's a sickness that comes with a quickness and afflicts the most determined . . . and desperate. And the trek through the dangerous Diabolical Divide always ends in dismembering death.

Ouch.

As The Day of Discovery dawns, however, you and every young girl around the world tune out the horrifying negatives and concentrate on the glitzy, gaudy, dream-come-true positive. You dredge up every ounce of self-confidence from deep within. This is my year, you say to yourself. And so does every other girl. They'll choose me for sure.

Every girl feels the same way . . . except one.

Tookie De La Crème.

I

† O OKE

Have you ever seen her?

The girl whose face not even the meanest person you know would describe as yuck but who you'd never in a million—no, a trillion years describe as alluring either. The girl whose eyes are three centimeters too far apart and whose mouth is four centimeters too wide. Not that you'd break out a ruler, but when you look at her, it's enough to make you say that something is definitely . . . off.

Come on now, you've seen her.

She's the girl whose hair has multiple personality disorder and can't decide if it's supposed to be quasi-curly, silky-straight, frantic-frizzy, or wet-and-wavy—or maybe a "Power to the People" 'fro.

The girl whose body is a contradiction of itself: a slightly hunched

5

back (*from years of poor posture, one must presume*), *feet the size of snowshoes, and stick-figure arms and legs so fragile, you think you hear them screaming "Feed me an entire grilled cow, now!" The girl with the humongous, punch-bowl-sized head, with a forehead that goes on and on and on, making her look like the weight of her cranium will topple her over and break her into a thousand pieces.*

And not only is her clothing painfully mismatched, so are her eyes, dahling. You heard me right. She has one green eye and one brown one.

Have you ever seen Tookie De La Crème?

I bet you have.

Maybe you've even met her.

You just don't remember her.

No one ever does.

For as unusual-looking as she was, Tookie was a Forgetta-Girl, one of the most forgettable girls in the entire world.

But maybe not for long.

Ж

Our tale begins on a Thursday afternoon, the most ordinary of ordinary afternoons, a few days shy of the most unordinary day of the entire year. Tookie De La Crème was splayed on her back on the hallway floor of her school, the Bangle, Bauble, and Bead Institute—B3, as it was commonly called. Her large, mismatched eyes didn't blink as she stared at the stained ceiling. Her gangly legs shot out at odd angles, as though she'd fallen from a six-story building. Her enormous feet pointed straight up. An internal clock counted down the time in perfect cadence. *T minus six minutes and forty-nine seconds. Forty-eight . . . forty-seven . . .*

As Tookie waited, she lifted to her face a cold canister of

whipped cream, inserting the nozzle straight into her mouth. She pressed the trigger that delivered the airy sweetness directly onto her tongue. A bit of cream accidentally dropped from her mouth and dripped from her chin to her neck. With each squirt, more and more of the cream fell to her snug-fitting hand-me-up blue blouse, which had once been her younger sister's. Another squirt landed in her hair. She then licked her tiny baby fingers from thumb to pinky and prepared for the next squirt.

How was Tookie able to lie in the middle of her school's hallway, during class time, enjoying whipped cream from the can, and not get herself into any trouble? Well, Tookie was the Institute's best "skipper." No one, not even the most cunning teachers, noticed she was gone when she skipped out of class way before most of her lessons ended.

T minus four minutes thirty-three seconds . . . thirty-two . . . thirty-one . . .

As Tookie stretched her legs, the backs of her calves touched the bitingly cold marble, making her shiver. Most people would have found it uncomfortable, but Tookie was happy she felt *something*—at least she was still alive and breathing. Sometimes Tookie was so used to being a Forgetta-Girl that she thought she really *was* invisible.

T minus five seconds . . . four . . . three . . . two . . .

A loud but familiar clanging made Tookie jump. The school's bell was actually an old-time buzzer that had long ago signaled factory shift changes. In days gone by, before the Institute had taken over the building, B3 had produced three things: bangles, baubles, and beads.

Once the bell stopped, a familiar rumbling made Tookie

cringe. An oily belch followed, sending a thick cloud of greenish smoke through the vents. A stench filled the air. It smelled like a mix of gasoline, mold, melted plastic, and methane gas emanating from the bowels of the building. Excruciatingly loud school bells weren't the only relics left over from when B3 had been a factory—the administration had done very little in the way of renovation to convert the safety-code-deficient building into a proper institute of learning. The school let out belches and eruptions all day and leaked fumes from every crevice.

Groaning, the students emerged from their classrooms.

"Ugh," Ariella Burtona wailed, fanning the odors from her face.

"Nasty," Tatiana Sharonne said, pressing a sachet of dried flowers to her nose.

"The B4 Institute tooted again," Jason Milano chortled, trotting out the school's oldest, tiredest, but aptest joke. Everyone called the school B4, for Bile, Barf, Belches, and Butt Bombs.

More doors were flung open and the sound of footsteps thundered through the halls. Tookie quickly closed her eyes. She then peeked to see just how far the approaching mob was from her prone body. Nine feet away, she estimated.

The conversations of passersby began to wash over her. Tookie felt like a fly on the wall.

"Zarpessa says she's spending fifty thousand on her prep," said an annoyed female voice over Tookie's head. "Hag."

"What do you think the look will be at T-DOD this year?" a girl with a forehead tattoo whined. "I hope my tatted face will be in."

"Don't hold your breath, Inky . . . ," a male voice answered.

Another voice floated over from the other side of the corridor.

". . . if they don't choose me, I don't know what I'm going to do with my life. I'll die if I end up working in a belt-buckle factory like my mom. I've been crying for a month straight. I hope my eyes aren't going to stay all puffy like this."

Many of the conversations had to do with the big event that was taking place in two days, The Day of Discovery, which most people shortened to T-DOD. It was the grandest of holidays, and B3 was even letting its students have Friday off this week to prepare—an absolute rarity. Not that Tookie really cared.

"Where do you think the rest of 'em will be this year?" a girl with a nasal voice asked. "I heard that a girl found one in a pot of boiling sweet potatoes and burned up her hands real bad trying to get it!"

Tookie shifted on the floor. Now they were talking about SMIZEs. Girls had been searching for the magical charms for days, fighting at water spigots, sloshing through sewers, splashing in the Peppertown pool, which everyone knew kids peed in.

"I found the pipe where the gunk water from the Shivera hospital dumps out," a hopeful girl whispered. "No one is going to be looking for SMIZEs there!"

As more people passed, as more girls chattered about T-DOD, Tookie began to feel lonelier and lonelier. It was yet another day when no one, not a single person, looked down on the floor and cried, *Oh! Check out that girl down there!* All the students rushed past Tookie like water in a stream flowing around a rock. Rubber sneakers *almost* crushed her fingers. Heavy boots *nearly* bumped her shins. A piece of paper fluttered out of someone's notebook and landed *close* to Tookie's left hand. The paper's owner, a dark-haired girl, bent down to snatch it, not even noticing that Tookie was there.

Irrelevant. Expendable. *Forgettable.* All Tookie wanted was for someone to notice her. Anyone. Just a simple kick in the ribs or a sneaker sole that squished her hand or a textbook that slipped from a student's grip and fell on her large forehead. She wasn't picky.

Spin, thud, spin, thud, spin, spin, spin, thud.

Tookie looked up at a spinning dervish approaching, taking in her long, thick, curly wheat-blond hair, her silver-dollar-sized aqua eyes, and her perfectly symmetrical face. It was as if Tookie's wish had come true—sort of. For here was her sister, Myrracle, someone who did notice her. Except, well, Tookie didn't really want her to.

Spotting Tookie sprawled on the floor, Myrracle began to sing. "You. Are. Not. My. Deeee. Nay. Nayyy." She gave one spin for each word, making the hem of her blue dress flutter. It was a dress, Tookie guessed, that would pass to her as a hand-me-up in a matter of days.

Tookie rolled her eyes at her sister's mispronunciation of DNA. Beyond her looks and fancy flights of footwork, what was most disturbing to Tookie about The Myrracle, as Tookie's mother called her, was not that she was Tookie's younger sister. The most disturbing fact was that The Myrracle was distinctly, indisputably, flat-out . . . dense. As dumb as a lobotomized turkey—and turkeys were said to raise their heads to the sky during rainstorms and drown themselves. Oh, Tookie tried to give her sister the benefit of the doubt—Myrracle had memorized every intricate dance step of the twenty-two verses of "The Shivera Shuffle," after all, and at least she understood the *concept* of DNA, even if she got the pronunciation wrong, but in all honesty, Myrracle wasn't the brightest tube of lipstick in the makeup caddy.

Luckily, Myrracle pirouetted out of sight almost immediately. Problem gone . . . for now.

Tookie sighed and reached for a small, thick yellow book wedged under her lower back. It wasn't just any regular yellow, but the color of a taxicab that had been freshly painted and spit-polished. And it wasn't just any regular book, but a collection of letters Tookie had written to people she'd encountered throughout her life. Not that she would ever dare send them.

She called this book *T-Mail Jail*. Tookie found it ironic that the book's initials, *TMJ*, also stood for an ailment that impaired a person's ability to open her mouth. The front cover displayed Tookie's first name, handwritten in beautiful calligraphy. The spine of *T-Mail Jail* read *DON'T KEEP OUT!* The back cover urged, *INVADE MY PRIVACY—PLEASE!* If one were inclined to follow these instructions, the inside cover challenged, *I DARE YOU TO TURN THE PAGE.*

But no one dared . . . or, more accurately, cared.

As the crowd continued to move around her, Tookie opened *T-Mail Jail* to a blank page. She closed her eyes, selected one of the dozens of colored pens tucked into the pocket of the book's back cover, and held it in front of her face. Blue, in her color code, was for the English language. *Boorrrring,* Tookie thought.

Tookie uncapped the pen, held the journal in the air over her head, and began to write to her only friend in the world. She had been missing for over six weeks now, and Tookie feared she'd never see her again.

Dear Lizzie,
  It's day thirty-nine of my great SPLD campaign and everyone is still ignoring me.

SPLD stood for Silent Protest by Lying Down. Tookie pronounced it "spilled." As an oblivious classmate almost whacked Tookie's head with a rusty fencing épée, Tookie licked the tip of her pen, gripped it in her right hand, and continued to write. She wasn't a natural right-hander, but her mother had slapped her wrist so many times for writing with her left that Tookie had begrudgingly made the switch.

It hurts. And it hurts that you can't be here and I can't tell you this for real. It hurts too that you disappear for weeks and I have no idea where you've gone. Girl, you're my only friend! Can't you at least tell me where you've been? Anyway, everyone is caught up in The Day of Discovery happening this weekend. But even if they weren't caught up in all the hoopla of the coming event, they still wouldn't see me. Perhaps I don't want them to notice me. I mean, this is SPLD Number Thirty-Nine. Why not go for the world record? Forty days of lying on this cold hallway floor, waiting for someone to speak to me...but no one saying a word. Forty days of being invisible.

Lizzie, there must be an association that honors achievements like this. I can hear my acceptance speech now: "I'd like to thank the SPLD Academy. There is nothing more beautiful than a Forgetta-Girl being

recognized by her own Forgetta-Peers! And let's not forget my dear family.
"On second thought? Let's."
Miss ya, girl. Hopefully, I'll see you today.

Tookie FG

Over the *i* in her name, Tookie added a tiny *FG* for Forgetta-Girl. But before closing *T-Mail Jail,* she thumbed through its previous entries, admiring the rainbow of colors. Every color represented a different language: flamingo-pink for Gowdee'an, cabernet-grape for Très Jolie, mandarin-orange for BayJingle, and skyscraper-gray for Colorian, the language spoken in the distant land of SansColor. Tookie had a knack for quickly picking up foreign languages, and wrote whole letter entries in them. By the age of eleven, Tookie knew twenty-eight languages. Now, at fifteen, she spoke nearly every world tongue. The nagging truth, though, was that this incredible linguistic gift of Tookie's seemed wasted—it was almost a cruel cosmic trick. Why give this ability to a girl with whom no one wanted to speak?

The thundering crowd in the Bangle, Bauble, and Bead Institute hallway started to thin. Tookie nervously smoothed out her shorts, closed her *T-Mail Jail,* and straightened her body out of its position suggestive of traumatic injury—and then she heard the bowlegged footsteps she'd been waiting for:

Step-pause-step-pause-step.

Coming. Her. Way.

There was only one person at B3 who had spoken to Tookie besides Myrracle: class president Theophilus Lovelaces, the very *step-pause-step-pause* figure quickly approaching. It had been one year ago, almost to the day, but Tookie hadn't forgotten it—in truth, it was why she had invented the act of SPLDing in the first place. There were many letters in *T-Mail Jail* written to Theophilus, all expressing unrequited admiration and affection. Tookie longed to slip one into his locker, but she knew she never would.

A year ago, Tookie had taken a *real* spill, tumbling down the narrow spiral staircase to the cafeteria. All she clearly remembered about that moment was one foot touching that first step and then both enormous feet flying into the air. She was falling . . . falling . . . there was the floor . . . *boom!*

Tookie had landed so hard the world had gone black for a few minutes. Spots began to appear before her eyes. Bodies swept past her, but not one person tried to help. Tookie had just lain there while the day continued as usual for everyone else at the Bangle, Bauble, and Bead Institute.

But then a figure in a pin-striped jacket had appeared. Tookie's vision was still blurry, but she could make out a small, round button on the figure's lapel.

VOTE FOR LOVE

"Are you okay?" Theophilus Lovelaces stood above Tookie like a royal guardsman coming to the aid of his queen. The pin on his lapel was one of the good-luck charms he passed out to B3 students in hopes of getting reelected every school year. He'd never given one to Tookie, though.

The noises in the cafeteria ceased to exist. Tookie was groggy from her fall, her ears rang to the point of leaving her deaf, and her mouth felt like it had been anesthetized, but that didn't stop her from noticing his imperfectly perfect features: sun-kissed, tightly curled hair, a left cheekbone that was sharper and more defined than the right, and sympathetic golden-brown eyes the exact color of two salted caramels, Tookie's favorite candy. He wore a camel-colored suit of the finest fabric, an indication of his family's prestige—they were the wealthiest in all of Metopia—and yet he didn't carry himself with an air of privilege or self-righteousness. In fact, he chose to attend B3 over a private school in his own neighborhood because he wanted to be "among the regular people." And now he was smiling at Tookie kindly and generously, as though they were equals.

Yes, she had wanted to tell him. *I'm* better *than okay!* But her mouth wouldn't work.

Theophilus tilted his head to the side, his lip curling over a slightly chipped tooth. "That was quite a spill."

And then, amazingly, he had reached down and taken her hand. Tookie's tongue was frozen solid. She had imagined what she must look like to him—like a rag doll without most of its stuffing, and with trace lines of drool on both of her cheeks. *Disgusting.*

After a few moments of Tookie lying there, just staring, Theophilus stepped back, an apologetic look on his face. "Okay. Um . . . sorry."

And then he had turned around and left. They hadn't talked since.

Now Theophilus was fast approaching. *T minus ten, nine, eight.* Albert Talbert, the most disheveled student at B3, walked alongside him, his unlaced shoes flapping against the hard, shiny floor.

T minus three seconds, two . . .

Maybe Theophilus would see her today, splayed out in the SPLD. Maybe he would do as he did last year, standing above her, extending his hand, asking, *Are you okay?* And then Tookie would stare into his salted-caramel eyes and tell him exactly how she felt.

Theophilus crossed in front of Albert and stumbled over Albert's shoelace as if it were a trip wire. His body pitched forward. Tookie reached up her arms to catch him. Unfortunately, Theophilus caught hold of an open locker and steadied himself. Something plopped onto Tookie's chest, and she did a half sit-up to peer at it.

VOTE FOR LOVE

Theophilus's button.

Tookie stared at the button for a long time. Finally, she tentatively reached for it, thrilled to touch something that had so recently been so close to Theophilus's skin.

Tookie's hand was two centimeters from reaching VOTE FOR LOVE when *whoosh!* A field-hockey stick grazed her abdomen and sent the button flying across the hall.

Tookie sat up fast, panicked. There LOVE was, rolling right up to Manny Manuel's locker. *It's mine!* Tookie lurched to her feet and charged through the stomping crowd, nearly knocking Manny over.

She scanned the floor for the button. *Where is it? WHERE IS IT?!*

Then she spied it. *There! Near that pair of hairy legs!* The legs belonged to Abigail Goode, who wore her superthick long, wavy black hair with pride—even from her armpits. Abigail took a step forward and her sharp heel squished the VOTE FOR LOVE button, which shot out from under her shoe. Tookie cried out in pain, as if the button were her own tender skin.

LOVE careened down the stairs. Tookie bolted at top speed down the steps, taking two, then three at a time.

Follow the LOVE, Tookie, follow the LOVE.

A shiny black boot kicked the button and sent it sailing through the stale cafeteria air right into a trash can. Tookie pursued it like a lion after a zebra. She wanted that button. It felt like the only new thing anyone had ever given her in life—not that Theophilus had exactly *given* it to her, but Tookie wasn't one to quibble over semantics.

She reached the trash can, took a deep breath, and plunged her hands into it. She felt slimy banana peels, congealed macaroni and cheese, crusty heels of bread, and sticky soda cans. Finally, her fingers curled around the button, and she pulled it out with glee. The poor thing was badly damaged, dented, and slimy from its voyage. In fact, it no longer said VOTE FOR LOVE. Instead, the *V* and *O* and *E* of the first word were gone, the *F* and *R* of the second were totally erased, and of the last word, the *L* was knocked into nonexistence and the *V* was scratched so badly it resembled a *K*, but the *E* remained intact. Tookie almost threw the button back into the trash before her eyes focused again and she saw that it now spelled its own version of . . . her.

T O OKE

"Me!" she gasped.

And then she looked up. To her astonishment, Theophilus

stood at her side, staring at her gunked-up hands above the trash can. He was quite short, only coming up to Tookie's chin, and there was a whisper of a bemused smile on his lips. "You find what you were looking for?"

It was astounding. Amazing. The second sentence Theophilus had ever said to her. Tookie stared at the button in her hand. Maybe she could show it to Theophilus. *Look how your slogan changed into my name,* she could say. *Don't you think it's a sign too?*

"Theophilus?"

Tookie's and Theophilus's heads swiveled to the left. Zarpessa Zarionneaux strolled into the hallway. With long, single-textured, bone-straight auburn hair, flawless skin that didn't need an ounce of concealer, eyelashes that required not a stroke of mascara, and a tall, lean body kissed with subtle curves, she made every head in the B3 hall whip in her direction. And just like that, Tookie's heart drooped to her hand-me-up shoes, which were two sizes too small. Zarpessa was Theophilus's girlfriend. They'd been an item for the past three years.

"There you are!" Zarpessa trilled, swinging her goldenrod-hued Dream Bag, this year's five-thousand-dollar *it* purse, in her hand. She glided toward Theophilus with the grace of a swan and held up a massive poster written in gold glitter pen. ZARPESSA ZARIONNEAUX PRESENTS THEOPHILUS LOVELACES FOR PRESIDENT . . . AGAIN! "This is made with real gold dust," Zarpessa boasted. "My father had some to spare. And our mayor's sister's psychoanalyst's neighbor's BFF told me that posters written with precious metals like this definitely get you reelected," she added.

Theophilus turned his attention from Tookie and looked at Zarpessa. "Oh. Um . . . great, Zar." He unconsciously reached to the area of his chest where his VOTE FOR LOVE button used to be. The empty spot made him pause for a moment, flustered, but then he kissed Zarpessa gently on the lips.

It was hard for Tookie not to stare. Oh, how she wanted it to be *her* lips Theophilus was kissing right now. She had imagined it so many times: she and Theophilus alone together in the dry Peppertown forest, their lips moving closer . . . closer . . . closer . . . and finally touching, to give Tookie her first and only kiss.

Zarpessa would be forgotten. Tookie would be remembered.

The happy couple walked away arm in arm, leaving Tookie alone by the stinking trash can. She slipped the button into the pocket of her shorts, the fabric so tight she could feel T O OKE digging into her hip. All sorts of emotions flooded through her—hope, then disappointment, then embarrassment, then shame. Even if Theophilus had spoken to her, it wouldn't have meant he wanted to know her. It would take a miracle—no, not Tookie's sister, but a real miracle—for Theophilus to notice her in the way she wanted.

And for Tookie De La Crème, miracles were impossible to come by.

2

EXODUS

Oh, the smell! The dreadful smell! Poor Tookie, covered in the wretched decay of other people's refuse.

How I wish I could hand her a pair of loofah mitts or offer her a scalding bath with the essential oils of eucalyptus, bergamot and ylang-ylang with three boxes of baking soda, a gallon of laundry detergent, twelve capfuls of all-purpose bleach, two squirts of antibacterial hand soap, and a dash of ammonia.

Oh, dahling, I can feel the burn now. But you know what they say . . . no pain, no removal of funk stain.

M

Screech. As Tookie was exiting her last class of the day, a course called Autology, which stressed that students must look *inside* themselves to determine what kind of factory work best suited them, the speaker over her head bleated out five seconds of screeching feedback.

"'ttention, 'angle, 'auble, and 'ead students!" Principal Robby Cosby boomed over the horrendously unreliable PA system. "We have 'emporarily shut off all water due to the heightened misuse 'ecause of the SMIZE craze. So if you have to use the 'estroom, you must hold it until you are off school premises."

Perfect, Tookie thought, looking at her hands, still mucky from her date with the trash can.

She walked down the bank of battered lockers, rusty and chipped, some with doors nearly off their hinges and all with students' names written on strips of paper, and finally arrived at a space without a locker. At this crevice in the wall was a small door split across the middle. As Tookie pushed down hard on the bottom half of the door, both halves retracted, one into the floor, the other into the ceiling, revealing a dangling rope. She pulled the rope to raise a hidden shelf. It was a dumbwaiter, another relic from when B3 had cranked out baubles, bangles, and beads. Factory workers had used it to pass items like jeweler's tools, food, and garbage between the floors of the building. Today, this old relic was Tookie De La Crème's locker.

On the first day of high school at B3, all of the lockers had been taken. Left to fend for herself, Tookie improvised with the dumbwaiter. But she didn't mind it at all: beside the usual piles of textbooks and novels, Tookie had installed a miniature, fully stocked cooler.

She opened the cooler, pulled out a box of wipes, and cleaned the grime from the trash bin off her hands as best she could. Then she considered her snacking options—Tookie was *always* hungry, so she liked to have an arsenal of food on hand. There were buttermilk biscuits, plastic containers of sausage gravy, vanilla sandwich cookies, every condiment from spicy ketchup to Dijon mustard to mesquite, honey, and chipotle barbeque sauces, her favorites. She pretty much liked all food except chocolate—she'd once gorged at a chocolate festival her mother had dragged her to in the district of LaDorno, home of some of the finest chocolatiers in the world. She'd eaten so much she'd gotten sick on the drive home, but her mother hadn't shown her any sympathy when Tookie had demanded they pull over so she could throw up. So she had thrown up in the car. For punishment her mother had grounded her. Literally. Tookie had been forced to sit and sleep on the floor for one month solid.

Finally, Tookie selected a canister of strawberry-flavored whipped cream and shot a spurt of cold, delicious, whipped-berry yumminess onto her tongue. Then she grabbed the books she needed for homework, slammed the dumbwaiter shut, and continued toward the double-door exit.

Most of her classmates were still burbling excitedly about T-DOD.

Kylie, a bronze-skinned girl wearing bamboo earrings the size of her head, read aloud from the *Peppertown Press*. "'The Mayor of Metopia, the Honorable Devin Rump the Sixth, predicts the biggest turnout ever. Spectators who have traveled to Metopia from all over the world are paying record prices for prime spots. Rump has launched an aggressive campaign to arrest scalpers who are selling tickets to VIP sections. "I'm making it my personal mission," declared Mayor Rump, "to protect every young girl's inalienable right."'"

Not every *young girl's inalienable right,* Tookie thought as she pushed through the school's double doors.

A huge sign across the street confronted her:

WELCOME TO PEPPERTOWN, ACCESSORIES MECCA!

Metopia was split into four quadrants, each with its own weather system—there was frigid Shivera, tempestuous Pitter-Patter, lovely LaDorno (only the elite lived there, and it was where T-DOD was always held), and finally, sweltering Peppertown, as hot as—you guessed it—a Scotch bonnet. That was where Tookie lived and where B3 stood.

Each quadrant butted up against the others like the seams of a garment, and oh, what a shock it was to travel from one quadrant into the next! The thing was, because of Metopia's expansive range of environments and wealth of natural resources, the city's politicians realized that a great many things could be produced there—and a great deal of money made. The city grew into the global center of the fashion and beauty industry. The majority of Metopia's residents worked on inhumane fashion- or beauty-factory assembly lines—in fact, the majority of B3 students who weren't selected for the grand Land on the mountain would end up doing the same. There were always job openings.

The WELCOME TO PEPPERTOWN signs were on the corner of every block of the quadrant—the Quadrant Council had thought the signs would be cheerful beacons for tourists, not that tourists ever visited. Accessories weren't the only thing associated with

Peppertown, though. The thing most people associated with Peppertown was the . . .

Whoosh.

As soon as Tookie stepped out of B3's double doors, her eyes squinted almost closed from the searing sun. The heat wafted at her like someone had just switched on the world's largest, strongest turbine-powered heater. Students covered their faces as though they'd stepped into a dust storm. Sunglasses immediately rose to eyes, and hats clapped atop heads. When her eyes had adjusted, Tookie saw Abigail Goode yelling and marching by, wielding at the heavens a picket sign that read DOWN WITH RAZORS! And as usual, Tookie's hair exploded into expando-mode, each individual follicle swelling and swelling until . . . *pop,* her multiple-personality hair was about six times its original size. Groaning, Tookie reached into her bag, groping for a bottle of CheveuxMal gel, the only gel that kind of worked on her hair.

The sun's wrath determined Peppertown's landscape as well. The leaves on the trees were crisp and brown. No birds nestled in nooks or branches, no butterflies fluttered by, not even the tiniest insect scuttled past on the sidewalk. And you didn't dare touch the sidewalk in Peppertown—it would burn your fingerprints off. Only a few people trudged dazedly down the broiling streets that day. A fair-skinned, eggplant-shaped woman stepped out of a toe-ring factory. Before she could clap a sun hat on her head, her skin had turned an angry red. A man in a bowler hat weakly—and uselessly—fanned his face with a copy of the *Peppertown Press,* wet ink staining his sweaty palms. The headline on the front page said *Baroness Still on the Run.* It was a story that had ravaged Metopia for several years now: apparently, a famous, wealthy baroness had run a Yonzi scheme of sorts, investing people's money unwisely and bankrupting them all. Instead of making good on her payments, she had gathered her family and fled.

Dominique and Monique, two girls with large Très Jolie braids coiled around their heads, bent over a fire hydrant, watching water spray from the spout. "*Two* SMIZEs have been found already," Dominique squealed. "Only two! Which leaves *five* still out there somewhere. If a SMIZE comes out now, we'll cut it in half and we can both wear it to T-DOD!"

Monique squealed happily. "Our chances will improve by forty-five-point-five percent! Not bad!"

"Look!" A girl at the bottom of the B3 steps pointed at the sky. Everyone looked up. Some of the fog at the very top of the mountain had parted, revealing the top tips of what they all knew was a bright eye shining in the sky. "Ooh!" everyone cried.

The grand mountain poked between Peppertown's wilted trees. Even though Tookie couldn't see them from here, she knew that camera crews were camped out at the mountain's base, anxiously waiting for that golden fog to vanish and Scouts to start shuttling girls up to the peak.

"Is this it?" Dominique shrieked. "Is it happening?"

"Not yet," Zarpessa, who was standing at the curb, said knowingly. "My leg waxer's father's sister told me this fog peek-a-boo is just to get us all excited so we'll buy more souvenirs on T-DOD."

Then, as if following Zarpessa's command, the hole in the fog closed, obscuring the mysterious mountain once more. The pandemonium quickly turned to reverent silence. Tookie's heart slowed its pace.

"Hey, Zar, need a ride home?" Lorelei, one of Zarpessa's friends, asked. "I'd love to see the gorgeous mansion you live in."

"Uh, thanks, but no thanks." Zarpessa twirled her hair. "See, my therapist's yoga teacher's meditation guru's son-in-law told me that my walk to and from school is, well . . . it's my time to be by myself. Especially in prep for the big day. Maybe another time." And then she turned and marched off down a sweltering side street.

Tookie sighed and turned too. She had to walk home as well—but not because some meditation guru told her it was her *alone* time. As she trudged along the charbroiled sidewalk, she kept a running count of the cracks and the overlapping messages paint-stamped onto the concrete at street corners. Faded stamps read WHERE IS Ci~L? Newer ones painted on top of that said WHERE THE HELL IS Ci~L?

The messages puzzled Tookie. They referred to Ci~L—whose name was pronounced "see-el"—the most magnificent 7Seven ever to grace the earth, a Triple7, a majestic woman with caramel-colored skin and the most intoxicating eyes. For a long time, Ci~L's visage was everywhere, and monopolized every fashion campaign and runway in every major style capital of the world . . . until only a few months ago, when her images had abruptly disappeared from billboards, magazine ads, and the sides of buses worldwide. A special news bulletin had announced that Ci~L was no longer accepting work and wouldn't be the face of her own Ci~L by Jurk perfume, the bestselling fragrance in the world. But there was no explanation.

Tookie walked on past the long lines of accessory factories. Workers rushed in and out, their heads down, their faces permanently creased into frowns. Several children stood on the sidewalk, their eyes hollow, their hair cut short, their bodies swimming in workers' uniforms. These were the Factory Dependents, children sometimes even younger than Tookie whose parents could no longer, or chose not to, care for them. Greedy industry overlords took them in, housed them in slums, and paid them nothing—servants for life. Whenever Tookie saw them, she felt a rush of pity and dread.

Then she approached a sunglasses factory whose façade was made of long sheets of glass. Her image swam into the reflection, and she winced. She still had that fore—no, five; no, six—head. The slightly too-small weak chin, the multiple-personality-disorder hair, and the woolly-caterpillar eyebrows. Her eyes still spread wide like an antelope's, one the color of dirt, the other of snot. *Yep. Same old Tookie, different day.*

A few blocks later, Tookie turned down an alley between two factories and waited in front of an old oak tree. No matter how hot it was, or how tired and dejected she felt, Tookie walked down this narrow corridor and stopped at this tree every single day. It was a special place. The place her friend, Lizzie, called home.

It wasn't a home in the normal sense. The day Tookie met Lizzie, the nervous red-haired girl had been fleeing an invisible assailant and had dragged Tookie up this very tree with her. Nestled in the top branches was a tree cottage of sorts, with piles and piles of clothes inside. Nurses' uniforms and firemen's boots and mechanics' jumpsuits. Bags of scones and jugs of water sat in the corner. A twin mattress—who knew how Lizzie had dragged it up there?—sat in the middle, shaded by heavy branches. This was where Lizzie lived. Alone.

Now, as Tookie approached the tree, she thought she saw a branch rustle. She hadn't seen Lizzie in almost six weeks, which was a little strange. Sure, Lizzie kept an erratic schedule, not going to school, disappearing at night, but six weeks was an awfully long absence. Tookie was worried about her.

Then Tookie spotted a shock of red hair. A figure peered down from a high branch.

"Lizzie!" Tookie cried out. Her heart lifted.

The girl darted down the makeshift ladder that hung from the tree cottage, grabbed Tookie's hand, and pulled her upward.

When they reached the top, the girls extended their palms out, pointed to the sky with both hands, sniffed each armpit, and then curtsied. This was their silent expression of their secret greeting, *What's up, Hot Queen?*

"Is anyone with you?" Lizzie whispered, her left hand twitching.

Tookie snorted. "Is anyone ever? You know you're always safe with Forgetta-Girl."

"I hate it when you say that. Stop it!"

Tookie shrugged. "Just stating the truth."

Lizzie sighed. "Well, I remember you, as clear as this day is hot, so shut up." Then she peeked down at the ground. There was an unhinged, terrified look in her eyes.

"We're not being followed, Lizzie," Tookie insisted. "I swear. There's no one with me or near me."

Lizzie exhaled a long-held breath and flung her arms around Tookie, squeezing hard. "I've missed you so much!"

"Me too," Tookie said, feeling both grateful Lizzie was back and frustrated that she'd been gone in the first place. She pulled away and stared at her friend. Lizzie's skin was oddly smooth, nothing like its normal acne-prone, pockmarked, sunburned state, and she wore a blue hospital gown tied at the back and a pair of doctor's scrub pants that bagged at the ankles. SHIVERA

COUNTY HOSPITAL was stitched on the gown. This always happened when Lizzie returned after a long period away.

"So tell me everything!" Lizzie flopped down on her mattress. "What have I missed?"

Tookie shyly reached into the pocket of her shorts—which were now quite sweaty from the humid walk—and pulled out the button. T O OKE. "I found this today."

Lizzie stared at it carefully. "Is it . . . one of *his*?"

Tookie nodded. She'd told Lizzie about Theophilus countless times before, describing him in great detail, down to his VOTE FOR LOVE pin. "And he spoke to me too." She filled Lizzie in, except for the part about how Zarpessa had swooped in and ruined everything.

Lizzie ran her fingers over the dented metal. "Look at how the letters have worn off to spell your name! It's a sign!"

Tookie loved that Lizzie got her so quickly. No one else did. "Yes, but then *she* appeared."

"Zarpessa?" Lizzie guessed.

"Yup." Tookie groaned. "That girl has *everything*—gorgeousness, money, Theophilus. Every time Zarpessa touches my Theophilus, it digs at my heart."

A conflicted look crossed Lizzie's face, and then she smiled. "Actually, your heart's not the only thing Zarpessa's digging."

"What? What are you talking about?" Tookie prodded.

Lizzie raised her eyebrows. "C'mon. I'll show you."

She grabbed Tookie's hand and the girls climbed down the ladder. Lizzie pulled Tookie along a series of streets until they arrived at Juan Jorge's, the only fancy restaurant in Peppertown, which catered to the quadrant's politicians.

"What are we doing here?" Tookie whispered.

"Shhh," Lizzie whispered. She led Tookie to a Dumpster at the back of the restaurant. Its lid gaped open, the lock broken.

Tookie looked at Lizzie. "Lizzie, are you hungry? Do you need food?" Lizzie usually Dumpster-dove even though Tookie tried to provide her with as much food as she could.

But Lizzie shook her head. "Look."

A group of shabby people stood around the Dumpster. Some of them wore masks: the tallest man wore a gas mask, a shorter woman wore a tribal mask, and a what looked like a girl Tookie's age had on a tattered comedy-tragedy mask. The girl carried a familiar yellow Dream Bag in the crook of her elbow. Tookie frowned.

The woman in the tribal mask pushed in front of the rest and grabbed handfuls of untouched fish filets, half-drained bottles of wine, and loaves of day-old Très Jolie bread. "Zar, baby. I'm so sorry. You don't deserve this. Take the sea bass. It's still warm."

"Zar?" Tookie whispered.

Lizzie nodded feverishly, trying not to twitch.

The woman pulled more items out of the Dumpster. "Zar, baby, here's some sparkling apple cider that's still cold. Take it, honey, please."

The girl in the masquerade mask dropped the bottle into her Dream Bag. The same gold glitter that adorned Theophilus's presidential posters dotted her fingers. Could it really be Zarpessa under there? B3 Zarpessa? The stunning, wealthy girlfriend of Theophilus Lovelaces?

Tookie turned to Lizzie. "But Zarpessa is an heir to the Zarionneaux Peanut Empire! I just saw an ad for their peanut oil in the paper!"

Lizzie shrugged. "I guess they lost their fortune."

Just then, the masked girl's head shot up. The dark eyeholes in her mask aimed straight at Tookie and Lizzie. They both ducked, but not quite in time. Zarpessa's shoulders stiffened. The cider bottle fell out of her Dream Bag, shattering on the ground.

"Run!" Lizzie cried.

They bolted away from the restaurant and sprinted through the sweltering Peppertown streets. Once they were safely out of range, Tookie stopped and bent over, out of breath. "Do you think she saw us?"

"I don't know," Lizzie answered.

"I can't believe it." Tookie shook her head. "How long do you think she's been digging through trash?"

"I think it's been years," Lizzie said. "She just made the mistake of crossing over into my territory. At the used-clothes dump super-early this morning, I got into a tussle with her over a killer dress. It was deep yellow and it was made with this crazy shimmery fabric. Man, I coulda snuck into some serious black-tie blowouts in that thing. But Miss Zarpessa, she won the tug-of-war. I guess she wanted it more. So, I threw some matching yellow shoes at her. Her shameless butt scooped 'em right up and didn't even utter a thank-you."

"Wow," Tookie whispered. "She's living one big fat lie."

"One big fat *homeless* lie. And—"

Suddenly, midsentence, Lizzie's expression changed, clouding and contorting into a look Tookie knew all too well. Something else had overtaken Lizzie's mind. Her body twitched. The muscles in her face stretched and contracted. She glared blankly into Tookie's eyes.

"Tell them to stop," Lizzie pleaded in a strange, garbled voice. "They always say it won't hurt, but it does."

"Lizzie, come back," Tookie urged, grabbing Lizzie by her shoulders and shaking her.

"I can take it when they hurt me. But when they hurt Robyn, I feel it more."

"Robyn again? Lizzie, who *is* Robyn?"

Lizzie casually rolled up her sleeve and Tookie's gaze fell to her friend's bare arm. Three inflamed red marks marred the crook of her elbow, right at the center. A burn scar traversed her bicep. A larger patch of seared skin bubbled on the inside of her wrist. The burn looked fresh. Tookie winced.

Then Lizzie began to search the ground. "Lizzie, don't," Tookie said, knowing what was coming next.

Lizzie ignored Tookie and continued her search, finally locating a sharp rock. She picked it up and then brought its jagged edge down to her inner arm, near her wrist. Blood flowed from the fresh slice in her skin. Tookie grabbed her arm. "Stop it! Why do you do that?"

Lizzie lowered her eyes. Her face was a ballet of twitching and wincing. "Because it hurts so much and I feel better when I do it," she said desperately.

Tears came to Tookie's eyes. She felt helpless seeing her best friend so tormented.

"Lizzie, what hurts so much? You can tell me," Tookie begged. "I can handle it. And you know I'm not going anywhere. Ever. You know you can trust me. Does it have something to do with . . . that place?" She pointed to the embroidery on Lizzie's gown. SHIVERA COUNTY HOSPITAL. She both wanted to know the answer—and feared it.

"It's better you don't know," Lizzie whispered.

Tookie took a step back. *The Melancholia Ward,* she thought. That had to be where Lizzie had gone—that was surely where she always went. Officials probably repeatedly hunted down the paranoid orphan girl and dragged her off to the infamous mental ward in Shivera County Hospital, since she was too unstable to work in a factory. People in Metopia whispered that the staff at Melancholia ignored the atrocities that went on between the patients. Some said it was worse than the Shivera prison, which housed Metopia's deadliest criminals. There was never any way Tookie could look for Lizzie in Melancholia either—the Shivera hospital kept no records, as though it didn't exist.

During the five years they'd been friends, Lizzie had taught Tookie many things: not to be afraid to spelunk into the hidden Peppertown caves, which offered a stunning view of the undiscovered Peppertown platinum mine. How to sneak into the ritzy, no-tourists-allowed areas of LaDorno without getting caught—"It's all about attitude," Lizzie had said, donning a hand-me-up dress from Tookie's closet. And what with Tookie's strange SPLDs and writing-but-never-sending-letters habit and Lizzie's screams and paranoia, it was like they were the only two happily crazed screwballs in a sea of sanity.

"Try not to think about where I disappear to, Tookie," Lizzie whispered, pulling the gown's sleeves back over her arms. A wistful look floated across her face. "Think about Exodus instead. Sleeping on the beach every night."

Tookie smiled weakly. "And swimming whenever we want to."

Lizzie poked Tookie's thigh. "The whipped cream factory we could build for you, right on the shore."

"So we'd be in the dreaded factory business, huh?" Tookie

said playfully. "Grow what we know. We'll build a grilled-cheese-dipped-in-strawberry-jelly factory for you." Grilled cheese dipped in strawberry jelly was Lizzie's absolute favorite food. Tookie snuck Lizzie sandwiches whenever she got the chance.

"And we'd own the factories, not just work in them," Lizzie added. "Our workers would be part owners too. And we'd treat them with respect, not like the workers are treated here."

"And Theophilus would be our mayor!" Tookie swooned.

"And we'd give our leftover lunches to Zarpessa as she waited outside every night in the cold ocean air for our staff's scraps," Lizzie said with a devilish grin.

"And there'd be *no* sharp objects anywhere near our factories," Tookie said strongly, forcing Lizzie to look into her eyes. "Right?"

Lizzie locked eyes with Tookie, then looked down and rubbed her arm. "Right," she said. "Okay, so . . . when?"

Tookie looked off into the distance and her mind flashed with the memories of what she and Lizzie had talked about so many times—leaving Metopia together, forever. Who knew where they'd go? Who knew how they'd get there? But they'd figure it out. They'd be two Forgetta-Girl peas in a pod. They called it their Exodus plan. Their secret code for it was X-O-2; Tookie would write this symbol on the front door of her home when it was time to go.

"I don't know, Lizzie. I don't think I'm ready." Tookie had never been out of Metopia. How could she live in a tree and scavenge for food as Lizzie did?

"Of course you're ready," Lizzie said. "You're stronger than you think."

Tookie looked away. She didn't really believe that. Then Lizzie scanned the alleyway, probably looking for pursuers again. It was empty.

Tookie touched Lizzie's shoulder. "Lizzie? If I go away with you, will you tell me the truth? About what happened to you?" Her gaze fell to Lizzie's arm, the hospital sleeve now concealing the burns. She thought about how she both wanted and didn't want to know this dark secret of Lizzie's.

Lizzie's lips parted. She blinked silently for a moment, thinking, running her fingers slowly along her forearm. "No. They'll kill you if I tell you. You have to trust me." Then she shuddered and wheeled around. "I have to go. They're getting close."

"But I just got here, Lizzie. And you've been gone for so long! Don't go yet!" Tookie pleaded. "Where are you going? Do you need water, more clothes? I can steal some blankets from my house. You know how she gets rid of stuff that's hardly been used."

"I'll be okay. I'll wait for you to be ready, Tookie. And I know you will be soon. Exodus. Think about it. For real this time. I love you, Tookie."

Giving Tookie a hurried wave, Lizzie quickly ran down the hot Peppertown sidewalk. Tookie's eyes tracked Lizzie as far as she could see. Her last view of her troubled friend was of Lizzie stooping to pick something up from the ground. Tookie shut her eyes, devastated, when she realized what it was.

Another sharp rock.

3

Da-tahhhh!

3434 Pepper Lane, the home of Tookie De La Crème. Ah, the De La Crème residence! A splendiferous, luxurious palazzo of a dwelling with a marble façade, grand archways and columns, wrought-iron balconies at its second-floor bedrooms, and a fountain in the center of the yard, complete with a nude male statue with rippling musculature. Truly glorious! The crème of the De La Crèmes! We all wish we could abide in such a grand abode!

But be careful what you wish for, dahling. All that glitters is sometimes gold-plated.

What's that? There, in the corner, in the foundation near the koi pond and the birdbath made of bronze. That zigzagging line shaped like a witch's profile. Is that . . . a crack? And there, next to the crack, that silvery mass crisscrossed on the stucco—that can't possibly be duct tape? Watch your head! Did a chunk of slate just fall off the roof?

Surely your smoky eyes have deceived you. Surely these patterns of fissures in the foundation are just decorative elements. The De La Crèmes have nothing to hide.

Or do they?

М

Tookie walked up the seven stairs that led to her front door, tripping on the crooked third step. Another piece of slate broke off from the roof and fell to the ground, nearly slicing her skull in two. "Oh my God," she murmured. She'd have to tell her parents about how the roof almost tried to kill her.

After steadying herself, she stood with her fingers on the door handle, hesitating before she entered, wishing she didn't have to cross the threshold but knowing she had nowhere else to go. This was her home.

She opened the door and tripped again, first over a cardboard box that said CREAMY DE LA CRÈME on the shipping label. When she shut the door, goose bumps immediately rose on her skin, and her sweaty locks nearly turned into coil-shaped icicles. Tookie's mother insisted that their home's thermostat be kept at almost subzero temperatures at all times to combat the blazing Peppertown heat. Plus, she said people looked "fresher" when they were cold. Tookie then heard the banging of pipes and the whoosh of water spewing through taps. It sounded as though all the sinks, showers, and bathtubs were running simultaneously.

"Brown spot," her mother's voice rang out. Then a hollow

clunk. "Brown spot," her voice called again. "Ach! Another brown spot!" Clunk.

Tookie swept into the kitchen, which looked gleaming and new if one didn't peer very closely. The unused appliances shone. The pots and pans hanging over the island had price tags on them. The teapot was resting on a stovetop burner, tape covering the spout. A knife set still lived in its shrink-wrapped packaging. But if one were to go around the room with a not-very-strong magnifying glass, it would soon become clear that duct tape, electrical tape, caulk, industrial-strength glue, and other binding agents held the walls upright.

"I am having a panic attack right now!" Mrs. De La Crème exclaimed. Tookie's mother loomed over the kitchen counter, holding a bunch of bananas by the fingertips of one hand, examining their skins with a photographer's loupe. Her other arm held Bellissima, a lifelike baby doll dressed in a multilayered butter-yellow dress with lace trim, complete with a pacifier in her mouth. Bellissima was Mrs. De La Crème's favorite doll from her extensive collection. "I thought this banana was spotless, but it has one tiny brown speck! Yuck!" She tossed the banana into the trash.

Today, Mrs. De La Crème—or Creamy, as she insisted everyone call her, including her children—wore a perfectly tailored white one-piece pantsuit with dramatically pointed shoulder pads and a cinched belt to accentuate her small waist. A badge hanging around her neck said REGIONAL MANAGER, followed by the logo for Perfecta-Fecta, the beauty department store for which she worked. It was a very good job for a Metopian, a million steps above working in a factory.

She'd pulled her dark hair into a Très Jolie twist that was so severe it stretched the skin around her forehead and eyes, making her look startled. And though her body and soft, lineless, tan-skinned hands were remarkably well preserved, her face was a different story. Thick makeup clumped heavily in permanent lines on and around her mouth. Deep crow's-feet fanned out from the corners of her eyes all the way to her ears. Even her nose was covered in wrinkles.

Tookie hoped that whatever her mother's affliction was wasn't hereditary.

"And this one? Too yellow!" Mrs. De La Crème went on. "I need green ones only!"

Her gaze fluttered to Tookie. For a moment, she looked through her daughter the same way everyone at school did. Then she blinked, bringing Tookie into focus. "Ah. Hello, dear. You haven't been picking bananas out of the garbage bin and putting them back onto the counter, have you?"

Tookie blinked, her mind struggling to shift directions. "Um, n-n-no . . ."

"Well, someone has." Then Mrs. De La Crème thrust a small jar of pickles at Tookie. "Can those baby fingers of yours dig out a gherkin for me? I'm starving."

Tookie wiggled her small, slim fingers. Her mother was always talking about how delicate and dexterous they were, perfect for sewing small stitches or digging items out of tight jars. Tookie eyed the lush fruit in the waste bin. Bananas weren't the only items in the trash pile. There were mouthwatering grapes, two perfectly ripe avocados, and three tomatoes whose skins had just turned from green to red.

Then Tookie moved over to turn off the sink faucet, which

was indeed gushing brownish water. "Don't you dare!" Mrs. De La Crème screamed, and Tookie froze. "I'm keeping all the taps open until T-DOD! Water must flow continuously into this house! And when our SMIZE comes, we must catch it!"

Tookie stepped away from the faucet. Every year, on the eve of T-DOD, the world's reservoirs ran dry because *everyone* kept their taps open, looking for a SMIZE.

The television was on behind them, and a reporter, coincidentally, was reporting on the hidden SMIZEs. "Now *four* SMIZEs have been found," the man said excitedly. "A gang of hooligan females spotted the device floating in a condemned swimming pool in PitterPatter today. They rushed the barbwire fence and dove into the murky, stagnant, unfit-for-human-contact water. An underwater riot broke out, severely injuring three girls. One is in critical condition at Shivera hospital." The screen showed the girl who'd battled for the SMIZE and won. She was covered in pond scum and had a mix of black muck and blood all over her face and body, but she held a glittering, golden glasses-shaped object over her head and whooped with glee.

"Hmph," Mrs. De La Crème said, folding her arms across her chest. "That disgusting creature does not deserve a SMIZE. Not like The Myrracle does."

Then the news shifted to a different story. "There is still no word on what has happened to the world's most famous Intoxibella, Ci~L," the anchor said. "The official word is that she's gone on hiatus, but rumors have surfaced that something darker has happened to her. Abduction. An airborne terminal illness. A mental breakdown. Keep in mind, this is a woman who has been very forthcoming about how her childhood was spent in a place without a single mirror. One can only assume how that might psychologically impact a person as they reach adulthood. But let's pray that our formidable Triple7 is soon on the mend!"

Mrs. De La Crème glowered at the picture of the effervescent Ci~L that had popped on the screen. "*Uch,*" she said, wrinkling her nose. "Let's pray that she stays missing forever."

Mrs. De La Crème suddenly started to applaud and Tookie's stomach dropped. She knew what was to follow. Sure enough, Myrracle spun into the house, followed by her best friend, Brian. Myrracle and Brian bobbed in unison to music only the two of them could hear.

They jumped and spread their feet out, arched their heads back, rolled up through their torsos, and pointed at Tookie and Mrs. De La Crème. Every limb on Myrracle's body, every joint, moved gracefully and fluidly and with the utmost confidence. It was impossible for anyone, even Tookie, to take their eyes off her. Even though she was thirteen and Tookie was fifteen, she was more womanly than Tookie in every way—she'd even developed faster, getting her period earlier that year. Tookie still hadn't gotten hers yet.

With a couple more hip rolls and knee dips, Myrracle and Brian slid to the floor with their arms spread out as Myrracle exclaimed, "Da-tahhhh!"

Mrs. De La Crème applauded tepidly. "Myrracle, baby, it's not *da-tah*—it's *ta-dah*. And what have I told you? Every hallway is *a runway,* not a dance hall! What you need to be doing is practicing your walk!"

"But I love dancing." Myrracle pouted.

"Yes, honey. I know. But you don't love it *better* than becoming an Intoxibella, do you?" Mrs. De La Crème shrieked.

Myrracle looked torn, like she didn't know how to answer.

"I think dance will help Myrracle on T-DOD." Brian wrapped his arm around Myrracle's shoulder. His voice was both feathery and sharp. "Right, doofus?"

"It's true, Creamy," Myrracle whined, not noticing Brian's insult—she usually didn't. "What I have to do first to prepare is to get my dancing to perfectness-*ness*. That way, I can pose the best of the rest in a vest and pass the test and be the guest and walk with zest un*lest* they want me to walk from the east to the west and . . ." She launched into a tap number.

"Stop it!" Mrs. De La Crème yelled.

"So my baby girl wants to be a professional dancer like her daddy," boomed a voice from the doorway. "*I* thought your routine was fantastic."

In the doorway stood Mr. De La Crème. He was much younger than Tookie's mother. A stained black unitard cut deeply into his flesh. His once-powerful muscles sagged. He swept across the room, scooped Myrracle up, and spun her around. He closed his left eye, which was made of glass, an unfortunate souvenir of an acrobatic performance gone awry many years ago when he was The Incredible Chris-Crème-Crobat and not just Christopher De La Crème.

"Are you excited, pumpkin?" Mr. De La Crème asked Myrracle, sweeping past Tookie like he didn't even see her. Usually, he didn't.

Myrracle lowered her eyes. "I guess. But I'm *frightening* too."

"Scared?" Brian snorted. "Honey, I didn't know your li'l ol' brain *could* be scared. And anyway, girl, they're gonna choose you for sure."

"My baby girl, finally walking in The Day of Discovery." Mr.

De La Crème wiped an imaginary tear from his eye. Indeed, now thirteen years old, Myrracle was finally participating in the grand event. There wasn't an official minimum age for who could compete during T-DOD, but no one younger than thirteen had ever been chosen.

Then Mr. De La Crème pulled a chair out from the kitchen island. "Sit down, Myrracle, baby. Rest your feet."

"Oh, Christopher, will you stop smothering her?" Mrs. De La Crème said brusquely. Then she leaned down and brushed a stray hair from Myrracle's forehead. "My, my. We need to get you to the salon so Perry can do something with those atrocious split ends!"

Mr. De La Crème shot his wife an icy glare. "Woman, how stupid do you think I am? You just want to get her to that damn salon so you can do whatever you do with Perry while Myrracle is under the dryer! I see how you look at him."

Mrs. De La Crème thrust her nose in the air. "How dare you insult me and accuse me of such filth! And who are you, mister one-eyed ex–circus star who spends his nights boozing?"

Mr. De La Crème roared back, "At least I don't cheat on your ol—"

"Stop it!" Myrracle whined, and both parents froze. "Back to me, everyone! I'm the most important girl in the room, 'member?" Her voice and face were so adorable that the tension was momentarily forgotten.

Tookie popped another baby gherkin into her mouth, feeling as irrelevant as the bananas in the trash can. She spied the *Peppertown Press* and picked it up, a welcome distraction from being invisible in her own home.

"Give me that, Tookie!" her mother said, snatching it from her hands. "I haven't read the paper yet, and you know I cannot stand touching it after anyone else has had their dirty hands on it." She thumbed through the pages. "Ha! The police are moving in closer on that fugitive baroness!" She read the article aloud: "'Authorities believe the baroness may have fled to Terra BossaNova, although they have no firm proof. They are working with BossaNovian local authorities to track down this evildoer, who has ruined the lives of tens of thousands and scarred the image of the annual Intoxi-stakes event, in which second-year students travel to Striptown and gamblers bet on which girls will become Intoxibellas upon graduation.'" She looked up. "I hope they find that shady wench. We lost most of our savings trusting her!" Then she flipped to the next page. "Oh, look! There's a sale on teakettles at—"

"Woman!" Mr. De La Crème said through clenched teeth. "You still have a brand-new unused kettle on the stove! And you don't even drink tea because you say the leaves are dried-up and stale."

Mrs. De La Crème stared at him. "Tookie, make me some tea."

Tookie flinched. "B-b-but Creamy, you d-d-don't like—"

"D-d-duh," Mrs. De La Crème imitated nastily. "Spit it out!"

Tookie glanced at the floor. For as long as she could remember, the sight and sound of her mother had caused her heart to flutter, her palms to sweat, and her tongue to stammer. Mrs. De La Crème dragged Tookie to every speech pathologist in LaDorno, but the mother-specific stammer could not be cured.

Mrs. De La Crème rolled her eyes, exasperated. "What did I say, Tookie? Make. Me. Some. Tea. Now."

Tookie shrugged and took the tape off the teakettle's spout. She placed it under the gushing tap, filled it, and placed it on the stove. Suddenly, a tiny yellowish bubble spewed out of the running faucet. This wasn't unusual; off-color water was a common sight in the De La Crème household because of the home's broken water filters.

Tookie scampered to the cabinet, snatched a mug, and dropped a bag of mint tea into it. Moments later, she ran back to the boiling kettle and relieved it of its howling. She poured the scalding water over the bag and handed the brew to her mother, who scowled at the cup. Mrs. De La Crème defiantly looked over to her husband, then brought the cup to her nose.

"Smelling is not enough, Creamy," Mr. De La Crème taunted. "Drink it."

Tookie turned back to the tap. The small yellow bubble began to expand, filling half of the kitchen sink. Then it changed color, from spicy red to soothing blue to emerald-green and, finally, to a plethora of yellows. It was strangely beautiful. Tookie carefully picked up the bubble with her hands. And then, before her eyes, the bubble flattened itself and transformed into cellophane-thin, golden cat's-eye sunglasses without the frames.

"Oh!" Myrracle screamed, staring at Tookie. "Look!"

Mrs. De La Crème noticed it too, and dropped the teacup from her hand. It crashed to the floor. "Is it . . . could it *be*?"

"Our ship has come in!" Mr. De La Crème exclaimed.

Tookie looked from her sister, Myrracle, to the true miracle that had taken shape in her hands.

A SMIZE.

4

91% Chance

Tookie's body tingled. She was holding a SMIZE in her hands. Her. A Forgetta-Girl.

The SMIZE was made up of ornate eye-shadow-like flourishes in strokes of taxicab-, Dijon-, baby-chick-, banana-, and lemonade-yellow. Thinner than a sheet of paper, it was surprisingly heavy, and seemed to hum ever so slightly as it rested in Tookie's palms.

Mrs. De La Crème stalked up to Tookie. Mr. De La Crème was in perfect step behind his wife. Brian shoved Myrracle forward and joined the SMIZE parade heading in Tookie's direction.

"Slowly, Tookie, dear," Mrs. De La Crème advised. "Hand . . . it . . . over."

Tookie hesitated, then stretched out her arms, feeling a little sad to part with the beautiful membrane. Her arms wobbled. "Careful!" Mr. De La Crème roared. "Don't want those scraggy twigs of yours dropping our future!"

Tookie's mother's breath quickened and her wrinkled face started to turn blue.

Mr. De La Crème patted his wife's arm. "Calm down, Creamy. Everything's going to be okay."

"Excuse me!" Mrs. De La Crème shot him a look. "I cannot believe your flabby coach-potato ass has the audacity to tell my hardworking firm one that everything will be okay!"

Mrs. De La Crème placed Bellissima on the kitchen counter and scooped both hands into Tookie's palms. As the SMIZE was pulled away from her, Tookie felt a pang; her moment of being special in some way had vanished as quickly as it had arrived.

Mrs. De La Crème brought the SMIZE under an overhead light. Brian, Mr. De La Crème, and Myrracle gathered around and stared. Tookie had to stand on a chair to get a partial view of it. Soon the SMIZE began to shake. Waves of yellow of every shade popped out from all sides.

A miniature flag emblazoned with a SMIZE then deployed from the middle of the object, fluttering in its own mild breeze. Words began to scroll through the air.

Mrs. De La Crème began to read, in a clear, haughty voice: "'Congratulations, De La Crèmes!'"

"De La Crèmes? It can see us?" Mr. De La Crème wondered worriedly. He began to flit around the room, removing duct tape from various holes and cracks and tidying as much as he could. "We can't let them see the place like this!"

Mrs. De La Crème sucked her teeth and shook her head at her

husband before continuing to read the words that floated in the air. "'You hold in your tea-drenched hands the seventh and last Day of Discovery SMIZE. What girls everywhere dream of having! The wearer of this SMIZE has a ninety-one-percent chance of being discovered on The Day of Discovery . . .'"

"Ninety-one-percent chance? Ha!" Mr. De La Crème boasted. "My Myrracle will be batting a thousand!" He hobbled around, throwing out the tea bag, crumpling the newspaper, and crawling on his knees to glue the broken granite tiles back together.

"If you don't stop," Mrs. De La Crème said, glaring at him, "I'm going to poke out your other eye."

"'. . . which, we are elated to inform you, improves the De La Crème offspring's chances of fame and fortune. Perhaps you'd be able to rid yourselves of this ramshackle asylum should your spawn reach the pinnacle of success.'"

"We're going to be rich!" Brian yelled.

"We?" Mrs. De La Crème eyed him suspiciously. Then she continued. "'Might I bring your attention to the myriad of golden colors on the SMIZE. When choosing your attire for The Day of Discovery, pay close attention so that your ensemble complements and does not clash with this precious SMIZE specimen. Many of the left-behind nine percent of SMIZE holders during previous Days of Discovery deviated from dashing dress design decisions. You have been warned!'"

"Creamy, Creamy! I have the perfect dress!" Myrracle yelped.

Mrs. De La Crème read the last of the air message. "'May your clothes click, your hair shimmer, your face glimmer, and your stride glide. *Bonne chance,* De La Crèmes! And maybe, just maybe, we'll see you at Modelland.'"

A siren blared, and fine print with no spaces between words scrolled almost faster than Mrs. De La Crème could read:

"'Now for the rules: The wearer of the SMIZE must only wear it in the Day of Discovery Square. It must only be worn by a female. Do not inform others that you possess a SMIZE. Although the SMIZE comes from water, do not get it wet.

"'Violation of these rules may cause serious side effects: face-aches, nausea, vomiting, blurry vision, visions of fashion-police brutality, designer knockoffs knocking you upside the head, stinging bees in your hair bonnet, biting wolves in cheap clothing.'"

The words disappeared, the colored ribbons and the flag retreated, and the SMIZE let out what sounded like a contented sigh.

Tookie turned and stared at Myrracle, whose cheeks were pink with pleasure. So it was really happening. Myrracle was really going to walk on The Day of Discovery, that mysterious, elusive, galvanizing event that had driven everyone into frenzied mania.

Tookie knew she shouldn't be surprised—her parents had talked of little else all year. On the chalkboard in the corner of the kitchen was a training schedule, listing the times and dates for Myrracle's walking, posing, facial expression, pouting, and phonics classes. Trophies from Myrracle's dance competition victories crowded the mantel in the den. Eight crowns hung from hooks on the wall in Myrracle and Tookie's shared bedroom, each saying THE MOVER OF METOPIA in glittery letters across the front. Myrracle had won the Mover of Metopia contest every year she'd competed—it had become so predictable that few in Metopia even bothered entering anymore.

But still, Tookie felt like this moment had snuck up on her. With the SMIZE's help, Myrracle was almost sure to go to

Modelland, that misty, spooky, mysterious place atop the mountain. What actually *happened* there?

"So, listen up—on The Day of Discovery, we'll take Myrracle to the city square very, very early in the morning to get her ready," Mrs. De La Crème was saying to the group. She started counting things off on her fingers. "It will be me, your father, Tookie . . ."

"M-me?" Tookie interrupted, so startled that she straightened to her full six feet. "Wh-why do you need me?"

"Yeah, why does *she* have to come?" Myrracle wrinkled her nose, looking slightly . . . *jealous.* Suddenly, a tiny flutter of hope rose in Tookie's chest. Was it possible her parents wanted her to walk too?

Mrs. De La Crème sank into one hip. "Isn't it obvious? We need your baby fingers to fasten the buttons and zippers on Myrracle's dress. And to get my baby gherkins out of the jar for me while she's walking. You know my gherkins calm me down when I'm nervous."

"Oh," Tookie said quietly, feeling a little ridiculous that she'd thought for a moment that they wanted her to walk on T-DOD.

"I suppose it will be funner-er if you're there, Dookie," Myrracle said in a conciliatory tone.

"*Tookie,*" Tookie said, feeling a barb of anger.

"That's what I said!" Myrracle protested.

Yeah, right, Tookie thought. She noticed Brian snickering behind his hand.

"Don't laugh at me!" Myrracle said, frustrated. "I'm on my periodical right now! It makes me forgetful!"

"It's *period,* not periodical!" Tookie growled.

Myrracle smirked. "How do *you* know? You haven't even *gotten* yours yet!"

Tookie turned away, her face flooded with heat. Myrracle never resisted the urge to remind her that *she* had gotten her period already, even though she was two years younger.

Then Myrracle suddenly ran out of the room, perplexing everyone. She returned moments later, swirling and twirling, wearing an elaborate flamenco-style fuchsia costume.

"Here's my dress I'm gonna wear, Creamy! It moves like a chow-chow dancer when I do my model dance!"

"It's *cha-cha*, girl, not chow-chow." Brian stifled a snicker.

"And it's *walk*, not dance!" Mrs. De La Crème sounded like she was going to burst a blood vessel. "Besides, the dress is hideous and has nothing to do with couture. Take that thing off. Congratulations, Tookie, that dress is now yours."

Great, Tookie thought. *Another* that dress is revolting and will look marvelous on Tookie *hand-me-up*.

"Now, as for a Day of Discovery dress for my Myrracle," Mrs. De La Crème continued, "Myrracle, Tookie, and I are going to LaDorno tomorrow, and we will find a dress that is fit for fashion, not flamenco."

"But—" Myrracle whined.

"Me?" Tookie said again.

Mrs. De La Crème looked annoyed with both of them. "My decision is final. One of you will be trying on lots of dresses and the other will be busy picking them up."

Everyone marched out of the kitchen—well, Myrracle danced. Only after they had all dispersed did Tookie realize she'd forgotten to tell her mother about the piece of roof slate that had nearly sliced her head open on her way in. Tookie dejectedly walked to her room, sadly realizing that the Forgetta-Girl had actually forgotten about her own forgettable self.

5

Smacking into Mirrors

A few minutes later, Tookie stood in the doorway of the bedroom she shared with Myrracle. She was trying to enter the room, but a pile of leotards blocked her way, as well as a pair of toe shoes, two pairs of jazz shoes, and one stray sandal.

A long piece of duct tape bisected the room, separating Tookie's side from Myrracle's, but it made no difference—Myrracle's mess had invaded every corner in the same way mildew grew on tub tile. Dirty clothes were piled on the floor. Makeup trays and brushes and used cotton balls and a pair of dirty socks lay strewn about Tookie's otherwise neatly organized dresser. There was a sweat-stained leotard on Tookie's pillow; ample-cupped bras that certainly didn't belong to Tookie were draped across Tookie's

carefully made bed, and torn-out pages from *Modelland* magazines were scattered across the floor like leaves that had fallen
from a fashion tree. Tookie tossed the bras, three pairs of dance
shoes, and a variety of necklaces, bracelets, and leg warmers off
her bed and onto Myrracle's side of the floor. Every evening,
Tookie flung Myrracle's junk to her side. And every afternoon
when she came home, it had all migrated back to Tookie's side
once more.

Tookie slumped down on her bed. *Myrracle is walking on The
Day of Discovery with a SMIZE,* she thought once more. She wasn't
sure why it bothered her so much—*everyone* in her class was
walking. Abigail, Zarpessa.

Zarpessa.

The image of Zarpessa and Theophilus kissing in the hall
flashed in her mind. She closed her eyes and clenched her fists.
If only Zarpessa hadn't come up when Tookie and Theophilus
were having their moment! Had Theophilus *really* spoken to her?
Would she ever get a moment like that again?

She closed her fingers around the newly defective T O OKE
button. This piece of Theophilus fit perfectly in the heart of her
palm, the metal pin cold against her dry skin. She gazed at its
lacquered message.

T O OKE

Theophilus, oh, Theophilus. Tookie swooned. She closed her
eyes and licked her lips.

Your salted-caramel eyes, Theophilus . . .

She imagined Theophilus right in front of her. She leaned
toward him, her eyes closed, her lips caressing the air.

We can call our boy Tookophilus and our girl Thoodie!

She puckered and her lips connected with a solid, cold surface.

Theophilus, she thought. *Oh, yes, baby. I'm so happy you're giving me my very first kiss.*

"What are you *doing*?"

Tookie opened her eyes. She was face to face with herself. Her lips were in contact with Myrracle's full-length mirror. There, on the reflective glass, was the blurry outline of her broad, puffy lips. Tookie whirled around. Myrracle stood in the doorway with one hand on her hip.

Myrracle's eyes glimmered. "Are you making *in* with yourself?"

Tookie ducked her head.

Myrracle pirouetted to Tookie's perfectly made bed and flopped down on the mattress. "Who do you wanna kiss?"

Tookie turned away, clamping her mouth shut.

"Brian Quincy?" Myrracle teased.

"Ugh, no!"

"Who, then?"

"It doesn't matter."

"Don't feel bad about not doing kissing yet," Myrracle said in a teasing voice. "It feels like a little wormy man is crawling in your mouth, anyways."

A wave of humiliation rushed through Tookie. "Who says I haven't kissed anyone?" *Okay, so maybe it's true, but is it written all over my face?*

Myrracle sniffed. "Come *on*. But it's okay. Doing kissing with yourself is better than doing no kissing at all, Dookie." She giggled a little as she left the room, managing to drop a cardigan sweater, a tap shoe, and several gum wrappers on Tookie's side as she left.

ModelLand

M

Tookie's eyes popped open. Cold, chipped tile pressed against the bottoms of her feet. Icy wind gushed around her flannel hand-me-up pajamas. She wasn't in bed, as she was supposed to be, but standing in the doorway between the kitchen and the living room. *How did I get here?* She couldn't remember turning the knob of her bedroom door, walking down the stairs, or padding through the hall.

She then looked into the dark room in front of her and gasped. Balanced on one hand in the center of the living room's tattered carpet was her father, clad in a colorful unitard. His waist twisted in the air. His legs were bent at an awkward angle. His muscles strained and shook. An empty bottle of TaterMash, a colorless distilled beverage imported from Kremlingrad, lay tipped over on the floor. Next to it was a faded photograph of The Incredible Chris-Crème-Crobat, otherwise known as Christopher De La Crème. In the photo, Tookie's father still possessed both of his green eyes. And he didn't have the couch-potato paunch.

Tookie ducked behind the wall. When she was much younger, she'd assisted her father during many of his acrobatic practices; he'd even told her, lovingly, that they made a good team. And she had attended many of her father's performances with the Circo del Soul troupe before his tragic accident. She could still remember that day in almost perfect detail—the sparkling-gold cover of the programs, the plush red velvet seats, the set-your-mouth-on-fire taste of the bag of Gouda-and-habanero-flavored popcorn, and the sharp, five-foot swords that pointed skyward all along the perimeter of the stage. Three tumblers juggling fire with their tongues while jumping on humongous translucent trampolines suspended over the audience had been the first act. Next was a group of ten-year-old girls, contortionists who had backflipped into deep, hot-pink-dyed swimming pools full of crocodiles. And then the lights had dimmed, and mysterious music filled the air. A single spotlight shone down on Tookie's ripple-bodied father, the headlining star of Circo del Soul. Tookie had swelled with pride as her father looped and danced and climbed a dental-floss-thin wire.

Her father, the mighty Chris-Crème-Crobat, was going to execute a new move that evening. Circo del Soul had billed it as the first time any human had ever attempted such a feat. Mrs. De La Crème was full of pride that evening too.

However, right as Tookie's father had reached the seventh-story landing on the stage, Mrs. De La Crème pulled out her mirror to add a bit of Wrinkle Redux to her tanned and hideously lined face—"I want to look my best when the cameras all turn to me after his feat is done," she murmured. But the mirror caught a beam of light that shone right into Chris-Crème-Crobat's eyes, momentarily blinding him. In a panic, he lost his footing and fell seven stories. Most acrobats would have had extensive injuries or even died, but not Tookie's nimble father. He tucked his body and landed smoothly on his upper back, propelling himself forward into a smooth tumble. The audience erupted into cheers. Chris-Crème-Crobat then arched upward to stand from his backbend and face his adoring, applauding, whistling, screaming fans. Ever the devoted showman, he thrust himself forward into a deep bow, impaling his eye on one of the five-foot swords at the perimeter of the stage.

Tookie had wrestled past the security barricade and run to the stage. Pools of her father's blood splattered the stage floor, along with pieces of flesh. And there, staring up at her, was her father's eye. Disembodied, lifeless on the stage floor, gazing at Tookie accusingly as if asking, *Why?*

In the days that followed, Tookie was afraid her father would die. But when they'd gotten word that the blade had caused no brain or nerve damage, she'd rejoiced, which angered her mother. "Don't you see?" she cried in Tookie's face. "This is the end for him. He only has one damn eye. He's damaged. *Defective*. Done!" Her mother had then calmed down and held Tookie's shoulders. "It was a freak accident, okay. You and I do not have *any* idea where that beam of light came from that made him fall."

Tookie had been only eight years old, but she'd fully understood what her mother was telling her: *Forget what happened. Tell no one.*

Tookie let out a loud sniff, caught up in the memory. Mr. De La Crème's head shot up. His good eye squinted into the dark kitchen. "Who's there?"

Tookie bit down on her bottom lip and didn't move.

"I *said,* who's there?"

Tookie slowly padded into the hall and showed her face. Mr. De La Crème ran over to the couch, tore open the packaging of a new chenille blanket, and quickly covered himself with it. "What the—"

"I'm sorry, Daddy!" Tookie said. "I was sleepwalking again!"

"You scared the hell outta me, girl!" he slurred.

Tookie backed slowly away. She pointed at the photo on the floor. "You doing your old routines?" she asked. "You're still really good."

Mr. De La Crème harrumphed. "In some quadrants, spying on

people is punishable by death." But as he ducked his head, Tookie saw a tiny smile flash across his face.

"You want me to spot you?" Tookie asked.

Mr. De La Crème considered the offer for a long moment. "Like when you were a wee little thing?"

Tookie grinned. This was the first time since the tragic incident he agreed to let her help him. Mr. De La Crème got on his hands and knees once more and spread his palms wide. "All I need you to do is watch. For two things. One, if it looks like I'm going to fall, you gotta warn me before I do, so I can right myself. Two, watch out for that mean mother of yours. Understood?"

"Absolutely, Daddy," Tookie said. She watched as her father pressed into the handstand again, the veins in his arms bulging, his paunch shaking, sweat pouring down his face. Tookie stared at her father's flabby stomach and glass eye. Her mother obviously loved him less, or had fallen out of love completely, now that he was *defective*. In a way, it only made Tookie connect with her father more: they were two defectives in a world that was obsessed with perfection.

Suddenly, her father let out a groan and tipped over. Tookie jumped out of the way to avoid his heavy falling legs, which nicked the coffee table. "What the hell, girl?" he roared. His face had flushed as red as a spit-polished apple, and his hair was streaked with sweat. "Why weren't you paying attention? Why didn't you tell me I was out of position?"

"I'm sorry!" Tookie cried, instantly regretting her daydreaming. "I promise it won't happen again!"

Her father stared at her for a moment, carefully examining her. A startled, disgusted expression flashed across his face, as if a light had flipped on inside his head. It was a look Tookie had seen before—but one he'd never explained.

"Just *go*. For all of us," he said, waving her away.

Tookie's feeling of being needed was replaced by an emptiness that now burned deep inside her. She resisted the urge to plead with her father and instead turned away and went back to bed.

6

Stunning, Statuesque, Strobotronic Stars with Stupefying Stratospheric Struts

Now it's time to dish about LaDorno, dahlings, the most desirable quadrant in all of Metopia. Sunny skies. Pleasant seventy-eight-degree temperatures at all times—except on the beaches, where it's a wonderful eighty-five. Warm, sweet-smelling seawater. Low humidity, without a cloud for miles. And when you breathe in, you inhale only fresh, crisp, unpolluted air. You want to live in this place, right?

You and the rest of the world, dahling.

See, bliss comes with a price in LaDorno: only the richest and most successful Metopians get to live there. But how do you qualify to reside in LaDorno? Well, the quadrant's council puts you through a series of privacy-invading tests to prove your worth. Oh, they'll scour your bank accounts, examining every purchase. They'll interview your friends, your family, your employer, even the gentleman at the newspaper stand from whom you buy your Moneyed Metopian *magazine* every week. They'll visit your house and check the labels on all your belongings. If they discover a knockoff handbag? Stamp—a big red DENIED on your LaDorno residency application. If they notice that your prized Pekingese doesn't have the perfect pedigree? Stamp—DENIED.

One thing to know, though, is that there is a sect of people that does not have to be subjected to LaDorno's sadistic entrance challenges in order to be allowed to live within the quadrant's guarded gates. And who might they be? I'm sure you've guessed it by now, but let me clue you in: the names of these sacred souls begin with I and end with -ella. And guess what.

We're just about to sneak a peek at a few of them.

7Seven of them, to be exact.

Ж

The following morning, Tookie slumped in the back of the family car as her mother pulled into a space at the Sapphire Esplanade, LaDorno's premier mall. As she walked to the entrance with her mother and sister, Tookie was sure everyone was staring at the unusual De La Crème trio—one of them was a stunning blond girl who was so beautiful it was difficult to look at her for too long, another was a woman with a tanned-skinned, nubile body but the face of a pretty monster, and the third was a gangly girl with gargantuan hair and googly, mismatched eyes. Tookie often noticed how people stared at them, perhaps wondering whether they could possibly be related. It was as if, when her parents' DNA replicated at conception, all the subpar, defective strands had fused together to make Tookie.

The Esplanade contained every high-, medium-, and

low-fashion store imaginable, as well as a butterfly sanctuary and an entire wing dedicated to beauty products. Today it was brimming with shoppers, many of them dressed in T-DOD–themed gear. T-DOD posters covered every available surface. An enormous screen on an exterior wall showed Days of Discovery from years past, with thousands of girls walking frantically in LaDorno Square.

"Come on," Mrs. De La Crème said, dragging Myrracle and Tookie through a set of automatic doors. Tookie inhaled deeply. One of her favorite parts of the Esplanade was the smell: a jumble of *parfums* and *eaux de toilette,* fountain chlorine, and a variety of ethnic cuisines from the one hundred and six restaurants scattered among the stores. If she had her way, she'd sample barbeque sauces from the food court while her mother and Myrracle haggled over the perfect T-DOD dress.

T-DOD pandemonium assaulted them immediately. Hundreds of mothers and daughters pawed frantically through the mall, their foreheads beaded with sweat, the bags heavy under their eyes and on their arms. These lower floors of the mall near the main entrance consisted of bargain-basement seconds and clearance outlets.

Mrs. De La Crème pulled Myrracle and Tookie up six escalators, past the mid-fashion floors to the top level, straight to the Jurk flagship store, which carried couture frocks designed by Jeremy Jurk, the most lauded clothing artiste in the world. He refused to design any apparel but dresses.

The store was packed to the gills. Everyone spoke at once, their high-pitched voices mixing in the air and sounding like a squawking flock of wild geese. Dresses lay helter-skelter over the racks, on the counters, and on every inch of floor space: Feathered dresses; sequined dresses; tiered, bustled, and ruffled dresses. Dresses with sweetheart necklines, dresses with one shoulder; off-the-shoulder, strapless, and open-backed dresses. Halters. A-line and asymmetrical dresses. Sundresses and cocktail dresses. Prom dresses. Ombres. Metallics. A few girls ran around the department with three dresses on their bodies at the same time, for fear their final pick would get snagged by someone else.

"This is the perfect one!" one girl shrieked, holding a pale lavender frock in her hands.

The girl's mother pushed a ruched red dress into her hands. "Look, Janeef, I know what's best for you for The Day of Discovery. I was Miss Metopia twenty-six years ago. Hello! I know fashion."

Amid all the noise and the tussling, Tookie felt a pang of longing. Normal mothers helping their normal, single-color-eyed daughters. Tookie thirsted for a drink of it.

Mrs. De La Crème and Myrracle pawed through the dresses, clearly on the hunt. Myrracle pulled out a short green fringed frock. "Too flapper," Mrs. De La Crème deemed, wrinkling her nose. Next, Myrracle held out a crushed-velvet dress with black sequins and a tuxedolike white front with ruby buttons dotted down the center. Mrs. De La Crème shook her head. "Are these dresses for The Day of Discovery or the cabaret?"

"What kind of dress are you looking for?" Tookie ventured, trying to be helpful.

The rack let out an earsplitting screech as Mrs. De La Crème threw a score of hangers to the floor. "Something very specific. I'll know it when I see it. Myrracle must wear an original and it *must* not clash with the SMIZE."

"What about p-p-pants?" Tookie suggested. Now, *that* would be original.

"Pants?" Mrs. De La Crème stared at her in horror. "Pants are not majestic."

Then Mrs. De La Crème's gaze clapped on something across the store. *"There,"* she said, moving toward a nude-colored strapless gown with tons of tulle.

She pulled it off the rack. Though it had a Jurk label on it, there was another label that said *Vintage*. Tookie knew Mrs. De La Crème would drop it immediately—a vintage dress was as bad as a ripe banana, an object way past its expiration date—but instead she pressed the dress to Myrracle's body. "Yes, Myrracle, this is it. I can feel it in my gut."

After Mrs. De La Crème had paid for the dress, they left the Esplanade and exited onto a street teeming with vendors hawking Day of Discovery souvenirs. One cart was dedicated to T-shirts, hats, and a variety of trinkets bearing the WHERE THE HELL IS Ci~L? slogan Tookie had seen on the sidewalks on her walk home.

Tookie paused, staring longingly at the Intoxibella's face on the cheap T-shirt, beguiled by her hypnotizing matching green eyes. Ci~L was the only Intoxibella in history to grace the cover of *Modelland* magazine twelve times in a row, every month for an entire year. There were six top cosmetics brands in the world, and Ci~L had had contracts with all of them—simultaneously. One season, all of the designers during LaDorno fashion week had decided to have Ci~L be their only model. Ci~L starred—solo—on eighty-two runways that season.

So where had she gone?

The shady vendor eyed Tookie. "Hey there, funny-lookin' girl, wanna buy a piece of Ci~L?"

"Uh . . ." Tookie turned away nervously. Then she noticed someone familiar sitting on a bench only a few feet away from the mall's entrance. A man she'd seen on her walks home from school. He had broad, football-player shoulders, but today he was so drooped over that his body made a shrimp shape on the bench. His skin was faintly wrinkled, and his root-beer-brown eyes looked sad. He mumbled softly to himself, just like he always did, and held on to the laces of an enormous battered wingtip shoe slung over his shoulder. That shoe was why Tookie had given him a secret nickname: Wingtip.

Wingtip's head shot up. His eyes met hers for a brief second, suddenly clearing. Tookie froze. She wasn't used to being seen.

A disgusted snort sounded to her right. "Ugh, what riffraff they allow into LaDorno," Mrs. De La Crème scoffed, sneering at Wingtip. She pinched Tookie's arm. "What have I told you about making eye contact with the demented? Turn away! He's dangerous!"

Tookie shrugged. Wingtip didn't seem so dangerous to her— though the fact that he spoke to himself did frighten her a bit. Lizzie spoke to herself too, but only during her episodes, the moments when she went far, far, away to a scary place in her mind that Tookie couldn't enter.

She snuck a glance back at Wingtip. At his threadbare suit, his crusty clogs, his sad smile, and the single shoe slung over his shoulder. He was still looking at her too.

"You all right?" he asked.

Tookie's jaw dropped. Now he was *speaking* to her? But before she could say anything, a boom sounded, echoing off the tall buildings. A brisk wind stirred, whipping Tookie's hair into super-expando mode and fluttering her skirt. Tookie peered into the sky.

It had suddenly darkened, as if a storm was coming. The clouds weren't black, though—they were golden.

"Oh my God," Tookie whispered. Golden clouds could mean only one thing.

Everyone turned and gaped at the mountain in the center of town. All at once, huge waves of the mountain's golden fog began to vanish, and beams of gold light that transformed to golden shadows cascaded down the ridge and swept over every street. Tookie heard a soft, alluring giggle in her ear. She felt a swipe of satin brush up against her arm. The smell of blood oranges filled the air.

"It's happening!" a woman yelled, rushing out of the mall.

"The shadows!" cried a man who'd been washing windows on a high platform.

The fog on the mountain had completely evaporated, revealing the top of the mountain, which glowed like a metropolis at dusk. Hovering above the mountain was an illuminated eye with its SMIZE flourishes made up of millions of birds from a myriad of species. Tookie had seen the phenomenon before, but never this close. A sleek yet enormous hand of smoke looped around the entire mountaintop and proceeded to spell a word with its white plumes of smoke.

M-O-D-E-L-L-A-N-D.

Everyone spilled out onto the sidewalk to watch the spectacle. Cars stopped in the middle of the street, the drivers gawking out their sunroofs. An elevated train halted in its tracks. All the passengers stared out the windows, their mouths open.

"I see I have your attention!" boomed a familiar Gowdee'an-accented voice. It seemed to be coming from the sky itself. Lightning bolts shot from letter cloud to letter cloud, turning them from white to red to blue to green to yellow. "This is the Bella-Donna speaking," the voice continued.

Everyone oohed and aahed. The BellaDonna was the grand dame of the Land on the mountain and the final decision-maker about all candidates.

"The Day of Discovery is less than one sunset away," the Bella-Donna went on. "And so, the time has come to present to you this year's newly minted 7Seven. This is a glimpse at what your future might be, *if* you are so lucky, *if* you are so divine, *if* you're one of the most special girls in the world! Each and every girl on the planet has a chance to be one of the enlightened. Could it be you?"

"Yes!" Myrracle screamed, jumping up and down in the parking lot.

Clouds swirled in the sky. Lightning bolts danced and snapped. "In a moment you will lay your eyes upon this year's graduating class of Modelland," the grand voice explained. "As you all know, only seven girls graduate from Modelland each year, and those talented seven join the ranks of the only famous people, known throughout the world. The Intoxibellas."

Intoxibellas. The word sent an uncomfortable shiver up Took-ie's spine. They were so dazzling, so enchanting, so beautiful, so influential and magical that they were simply, well . . . intoxicating.

The voice grew louder and louder. "Without further ado, I present the Stunning, Statuesque, Strobotronic Stars with Stupefy-ing Stratospheric Struts! The 7Seven! Please worship them as the Intoxibellas they have now become!"

A swirl of smoke and blue fire swept around the bottom of the mountain and spiraled to the top. As it traveled, the swirl revealed a translucent three-dimensional image of a copper-haired girl with copper-colored eyes. Around her waist flapped her Sentura, the belt made of shimmering gold fabric that all the Intoxibellas wore. According to Modelland lore, Senturas allowed Intoxibellas to activate their inherent power. Young girls all over the world wore replicas of them as part of costumes and dress-up games. Even Tookie had, when she was ten years old.

"Feast your eyes upon . . . Evanjalinda!" the BellaDonna said over the cheering crowd.

The image of Evanjalinda expanded from the fiery bottom of the mountain to the misty top. The luminescent eye hovered above her head like a golden crown.

"Evanjalinda's power? Chameeleoné!" the BellaDonna explained. And then Evanjalinda's appearance changed a dozen times over the course of a few seconds—long hair, short hair, copper-colored, blond, brunette. Almond-shaped eyes, then doe-eyed. Plump lips. Bow-shaped. Her physique morphed too, from a thin frame kissed by an hourglass to one with defined musculature. Then Evanjalinda shook like a dog removing water from its coat and her copper hair and eyes returned, as did her original frame.

"If I had her, I'd have a different girl every night!" a man next to Tookie cried. "I could stop cheating!"

"I want to be just like all of her!" a girl exclaimed.

The BellaDonna's voice filled the air again. "Next, meet Simone!" The image of Evanjalinda shrank and the swirl of smoke and blue fire climbed up the mountain again, revealing another newly minted Intoxibella. This girl's hair was slicked into a chic chignon and her eyes were a piercing ink-black. "Simone's power? Multiplicity!"

Simone raised her arms and swept them gracefully through

the air. Two identical Simones slid out from either side of her body, sending a chorus of oohs through the crowd. Each Simone made a unique pose before being sucked back into the original Simone. The spectators applauded thunderously, overcome with excitement. Tears of joy rolled down some of their cheeks.

Tookie felt a shiver. This was the first time she had ever seen the Intoxibella ceremony in person. And it was even more magical than she'd ever imagined.

"Our third Intoxibella . . . Bev Jo!" the BellaDonna roared. A raven-haired Intoxibella with sky-high cheekbones and a sharp jawline appeared above the crowd. "Bev Jo's power? ThirtyNever. When Bev Jo ages to twenty-nine, she will begin her next year looking again like she is seventeen until she reaches twenty-nine again. That cycle will continue until she perishes!"

A gray-haired woman on the ground made a face. "She's so beautiful, she doesn't need it! Give me that power. It's wasted on her!"

"Tell me about it," Mrs. De La Crème muttered, clutching the side of her precarious face.

"Our fourth Intoxibella . . . Leemora!" The smoky mountain swirl revealed a dark-haired Intoxibella with seductive narrow eyes. "Her power? Excite-to-Buy . . . the ability to sell!"

Leemora made an inverted V with her hands and then thrust the point toward the spectators. Tookie touched her hair, acutely conscious of how wild it was. "CheveuxMal," Tookie suddenly said aloud, feeling like an alien invader had taken over her thoughts. "I need it! Now!"

Beside her, Mrs. De La Crème patted her face. "I should pick up some more Wrinkle Redux." And similarly, everyone around them murmured other names of skin products, clothing brands, and diet soft drinks that they suddenly craved.

"Gentlemen, get ready for our fifth Intoxibella . . . meet Sinndeesi!" The swirl unveiled a platinum-blonde with hazel eyes whose body swayed in a hypnotic dance. Sinndeesi's smile was blinding, and her Sentura undulated toward the crowd in a come-hither fashion. "Her power?" the BellaDonna teased. "Seduk-sheeon!" As Sinndeesi's hair blew in the wind, all the men in the crowd stared. "I'm ready to sin with Sinndeesi, right here, right now!" one of them yelled.

"Our sixth Intoxibella . . . Katoocha!" said the BellaDonna. A cocoa-skinned, large-eyed beauty with close-cropped hair spun in the air. Unlike the other Intoxibellas, who wore the most fashionable couture, this Intoxibella wore an outrageously mismatched tattered blouse-and-skirt combination. "Her power is SixxSensa, a remarkable supernatural sixth sense. Katoocha can see into the future of fashion—which means this unusual outfit will be on your body next year! Oh, and did I mention that Katoocha has enhanced sight, hearing, touch, taste and smell?"

"Wow," Tookie murmured. She wouldn't have minded having all those powers.

As Katoocha faded back into the atmosphere, the BellaDonna cleared her throat. "Unfortunately, once again this year, Modelland has not produced the ultimate Intoxibella, a Triple7, a girl possessing all seven powers. While this is disappointing, it by no means should dull the adoration you give our last newly or-dained Intoxibella of the evening. Completing our presentation of this year's Modelland graduates is a girl who possesses the power of . . . Teleportaling!"

An Intoxibella with a pixie haircut and aqua eyes whirled

into view. "Her name is quite fitting!" the BellaDonna narrated. "Exodus!"

Tookie shot up. Exodus? Was that a sign?

The sprightly Intoxibella fell backward into an immense hole that formed behind her and disappeared.

"Creamy, she banished right before our eyes!" Myrracle covered her mouth with both hands.

Then something rumbled a few feet away from Tookie. The ground split, making a jagged Z across the sidewalk. It widened and widened, making the earth rumble.

"Look out!" a woman to Tookie's right yelled. "Earthquake!"

The hole grew larger and larger. Everyone stepped away from it, fearing for their lives—everyone except Tookie, who tiptoed closer to the edge. Out popped a human-sized Exodus. The glorious creature posed triumphantly, then whipped her head around and locked eyes with Tookie and smiled. "Hi there. What's your name?" she asked.

Tookie stared at her, tongue-tied as usual. Myrracle pushed in front of Tookie. "Myrracle De La Crème!" she screamed, assuming the Intoxibella was talking to her. "You're so pretty!"

Then Exodus rose into the sky and flew back to the top of the mountain, reappearing seconds later in immense, translucent form.

The BellaDonna's voice boomed through the sky once more. "Every. Girl. In. The. World. Has. The. Power. Within. Her. To. Become. A. 7. Seven. Is. It. You?"

Fireworks burst around the Intoxibellas. The crowd cheered wildly. Several people fainted.

Tookie suddenly caught a glimpse of blue behind a bench. It was two feet clad in doctor's booties. She drew in a breath. *Lizzie?*

Tookie scampered over worriedly, not even bothering to tell her mother or Myrracle where she was going, since they were transfixed by the spectacle in the sky. Lizzie was half hiding behind a bush, twitching wildly. Her eyes were rolling back in her head.

"Lizzie!" Tookie cried, taking her friend's hand. "What are you doing here?" Normally, Lizzie didn't dare show her face in places so public or crowded.

Lizzie just stared ahead into nothingness, not at all unlike Wingtip. Then she spoke in a drone Tookie had never heard from her, as if she was a medium at a séance. "They took her last night. By her feet. The burning continued throughout the night. They cut open her blisters and poured liquid metal into her veins."

Lizzie then raised the cuffs of her pants, which were dragging on the ground, revealing feet that looked like they had been dipped in battery acid, with open sores that oozed pus. The area near her arches had a hundred little cuts ranged in straight lines, as if they were soldiers ready for battle.

"Lizzie!" Tookie cried. She looked around frantically, hoping someone could help her. "We have to get you to a hospital!"

Lizzie shook her head violently. "No! I don't need a hospital. They'll kill me! But . . . I do need *you*, Tookie."

Tookie clutched Lizzie's hands. "Need me? For what?" But Tookie knew what Lizzie meant.

"Exodus," Lizzie whispered oh-so-faintly.

Tookie widened her eyes. A shiver went through her. "Wh-when?"

"Tomorrow. Please."

"Tookie!"

Tookie turned at the sound of her mother's voice. Mrs. De La Crème was standing near the parked cars, looking annoyed. Tookie swallowed hard, then turned back to Lizzie—but she was nowhere to be seen.

"Oh my God," Tookie whispered, running her hands down the length of her face. Fresh tears spilled down her cheeks. Lizzie had braved this crowded part of Metopia to find Tookie. Whatever was happening to her must have been even scarier than her burns and scars themselves—it was dire. A life-or-painful-death situation.

Exodus. Lizzie was leaving. Had to leave. And she needed Tookie to come with her.

"You all right?"

It was Wingtip. He stood behind Tookie, his face crumpled with sadness, the shoe slung over his shoulder.

"Oh!" Tookie exclaimed. She tried to wipe away her tears. "Uh, I'm fine." Then she looked away, feeling awkward. It was so rare for her to speak to strangers. Usually, they didn't notice her. And her mother's warning rang in her head. What if there was something wrong with Wingtip? What if he was truly a dangerous man?

"What's got you so sad, little lady?" Wingtip asked.

Tookie shrugged. "It's nothing. Really. I'm not supposed to look at you, let alone speak with you."

He chuckled. "Nothing I'm not used to."

"Why do you talk to yourself?" Tookie blurted out, then clapped her hand over her mouth, fearing she'd been rude.

But Wingtip didn't look bothered. "Little lady, when your world has been ripped right from under you, you tend to not trust much of what anybody says. Anybody but yourself, that is. And I do a good job of keeping myself company."

"Okay. Confession time," Tookie said. "Sometimes I speak to myself too, since nobody else does."

"It'll stop you from going crazy," Wingtip chuckled.

"Crazy? Ha! My mother says *you're* crazy!"

"Oh, *does* she, now? Well, maybe you should listen to your mother."

"Nah, I think you're more sad than crazy."

"Smart little lady you are." The man fiddled with the laces of the shoe slung over his shoulder. "I know why I'm a sad sap of a man, but why are *you* crying?"

"Um . . . because it hurts."

"*What* hurts?"

"Everything."

"I can relate to that."

Tookie pulled her bottom lip into her mouth and bit down hard to keep from exploding into more tears. Wingtip leaned forward and pointed at her. "You've got more important things to do than hurt, little lady. You've got a beautiful light that only a few people can see, shining brightly inside of you."

"A *light*?" Tookie repeated, hardly believing her ears. Perhaps he'd said a *plight* instead. Or a *blight*.

Wingtip leaned closer, offering a genuine smile. "Go for your destiny, girl. Dream big. Take it from a sad and crazy man who talks to himself. Everyone's entitled to dream, you know. Even you."

Tookie looked away. "Dreaming is dangerous, though. It just sets you up for disappointment."

He gave her a shocked look. "Who gave you that idea?"

Tookie ran her tongue over her teeth. *My parents,* she almost said.

As more fireworks exploded in the sky, Wingtip sighed. "Little lady, if you don't dream, you'll wind up not just talking to yourself but answering your own questions, wearing last week's clothes, and walking around with a shoe over your shoulder." He rose, slung the shoe onto his back, and gave her a nod. "I'll be seeing you." And then he slipped through the crowd, the old wingtip shoe bouncing against his back. Tookie watched him for a moment, awestruck.

"How *dare* you abandon us?"

Tookie turned around and saw her mother standing behind her, Myrracle's Jurk garment bag in her arms. "You dropped Myrracle's dress on the ground and the crowd traipsed all over it! What were you doing all the way over here?"

Tookie quickly scooped the bag from her mother's arms. "I'm s-s-sorry, C-Creamy. I was just . . ." She gestured at the fervor around them, searching for an excuse. "It's just, um, h-h-hard not to get caught up in this."

Mrs. De La Crème blinked hard at her. A cruel smile spread across her face. "What does all this matter to a girl like you, Tookie?"

Tookie swallowed. Normally, she would have wilted, turned away, and told Creamy she was right, but it suddenly felt like she'd just put on a steely coat of armor. *Exodus,* she thought.

Everyone's entitled to dream, you know. Even you.

"You'd be surprised," Tookie said, emboldened. And then she turned away.

7

X-O-2

"Damn it, woman! Where were you?"

Tookie's head jerked up from her pillow with a start. She'd been exhausted after the shopping trip and had gone straight to bed. *How long have I been sleeping?*

"You came home an hour later than you said you would!" Mr. De La Crème continued with an acidic rage Tookie had never heard before. Then there was a sound of liquid sloshing from a jug, followed by the sharp, sour smell of TaterMash.

Mrs. De La Crème sighed. "You're drunk, Christopher. For the last time, we were at the mall buying a dress for your daughter and stopped to watch the 7Seven ceremony!"

"Woman, whether you disappear for an hour or days at a time," Mr. De La Crème scoffed, "you always have some clever excuse!"

Tookie peeked around the corner into her mother's office, which was next to the kitchen. Mrs. De La Crème was dressed in an ivory satin nightgown with a matching robe that cinched her waist so tightly, Tookie thought it might leave permanent indentations. Creamy sat in a lambskin chair at her massive desk. Brand-new books with shiny covers lined the shelves. Sitting on the long backless couch and the windowsills and in custom displays all around the room was her doll collection, which she'd started years before Tookie had been born.

There were swaddled babies. Dolls with eyes that opened and closed. Dolls that wet themselves and digested food and spoke. Each was positioned just so, an arm curled here, a leg crossed there. Their heads pointed straight at Tookie's mother, as though she were conducting a meeting with all of them. Tookie wished she could close every single pair of glassy eyes. Maybe if they didn't stare so adoringly at her mother, Mrs. De La Crème could resist their charms and would share some of her love with Tookie.

Mr. De La Crème stood in front of his wife, his hands balled into fists on his hips. "Oh, I know you stopped to watch the 7Sevens. But I also know you can see that damn show from anywhere in the world. Hell, I saw it right here from our front porch. You could have watched it here with me. But no, you wanted to watch it with your man friend, didn't you? I know people, Creamy! And I trust what they tell me!"

Mrs. De La Crème tossed her hair. "So now your desperate flabby behind is spying on me?" She laughed cruelly. "Oh, Christopher, you have reached an all-time low. I pity you."

"Spare me," Mr. De La Crème growled. "The only thing you should pity is that disastrous, petrifying mug of yours."

Mrs. De La Crème instinctively touched her face. "Oh, so the one-eyed unemployed monster has the nerve to talk about *my* face? Have *you* looked in a mirror lately, dear?"

Mr. De La Crème slammed his jug of TaterMash onto his wife's desk. "That's what all this is about, isn't it? You think I'm damaged goods." He grabbed Bellissima from Mrs. De La Crème's arms.

Tookie's mother groped for the doll. "Christopher, don't you *dare* hurt her!"

"Her?" He waved the doll in the air. "You say that like she's a human being. Like she's more important than *me*! Where do *I* fit in your life? Sometimes I think you wish that sword had killed me. So that you could continue your life with her father!"

"What?" Mrs. De La Crème asked, her eyes focused on Bellissima. "Whose father?"

"Your daughter's father, Creamy! Don't play dumb."

Mrs. De La Crème blinked confusedly. "Myrracle's father?"

Mr. De La Crème laughed heartily. "Oh, you wish I was talking about Myrracle! You wish it were Myrracle I had doubts about—that would make her all yours! But no, Creamy, she belongs to both of us, and we will both reap her rewards. You can't push me out that easily!" He pointed at her. "You know who I mean. The other one."

Tookie widened her eyes.

Mr. De La Crème prowled around the room. "Every time I look into that child's mismatched eyes, I see—or shall I say, I *don't* see it."

Mrs. De la Crème paled. "But Christopher, you *have* one green eye! Just like hers!"

Mr. De La Crème glowered at her. "There is nothing about me that lives within that girl. That circus freak. She is uncoordinated, unattractive, and unmemorable."

"You don't know what you're talking about! You are the only man I have ever been with!"

Tookie waited for her to say more, to deny that she thought Tookie was uncoordinated, unattractive, and unmemorable. But she didn't. It was the equivalent of saying she didn't love her. Tookie bit down hard on her inner cheek.

"I do too know what I'm talking about," Mr. De la Crème said calmly. "She's not mine, Creamy. I haven't felt like she was mine from the second she hit puberty. She went from adorable to atrocious almost overnight."

"What?" Tookie whispered, pressing her spine against the back wall. She felt dizzy. Was this a nightmare?

"Creamy, let's be real," Mr. De La Crème continued. "As soon as you got pregnant with her, you had to go off to some special medical facility to deal with all the complications you said you were having, scary things that could've made you lose the baby. I was on the road and couldn't go with you. Remember? I had to keep working to make sure we could put food on the table for our growing family. Then, nine months later, you had her—thousands of miles away from here. You refused to let me be with you to see her take her first breath. My *first* child, Creamy! You denied me that right. How come you never let me talk to the doctors who delivered her? Was there another man in the room while you gave birth? Her *real* father? Was that why you called me only *after* it was over?"

"You don't know what you're talking about!" Mrs. De La Crème spat.

But Mr. De La Crème barreled on. "You told me they didn't

know if you or the baby would live. And after that, you said you couldn't have any more children—your insides were ruined. But two years later, Myrracle came. Thank God. A *real* miracle. The spitting image of her father . . ."

Tookie's mouth dropped open. Did he really believe that? Was a child's life worth more the more they resembled their parents?

Mrs. De La Crème scoffed. "You have lost your mind! That sword must have sliced your sanity!" But she sounded less resolute than usual. Her face was pale. Her wrinkled lips pursed.

Mr. De La Crème shut his one good eye. "Woman, I cannot take your lies anymore! *Just stop it!*" He turned and faced the wall. And suddenly . . . *crack!* He pummeled his fist through the flimsy plaster. A cloud of dust billowed everywhere. Tookie shot back and ducked behind the curtain across the hall.

Tookie's mother whirled around. "Christopher, you have gone *crazy!*"

Mr. De La Crème's skin flushed puce. "Well, Creamy, if I'm *crazy,* you sure are breaking your number one rule, because you're making a hell of a lot of eye contact with a crazy person right now, aren't you?"

Tookie's mother shot to her feet, grabbing Bellissima from her husband. "I'll say it again: not one bit of your ridiculous accusation is remotely true."

"Oh, but it is, Creamy. And you know it. And I'm going to tell everyone I know after I prove my gut instinct to be a scientific fact." He removed a yellow toothbrush, its bristles worn and bent, from his pocket and waved it in front of his wife's face. Tookie squinted and realized it was hers. She had brushed her teeth with it earlier that night.

Mrs. De La Crème lunged for her husband and pinned him against the ruined wall. "Oh no you won't!"

"Oh yes I *will*!" Mr. De La Crème cried, trying to push her aside. "Right after Myrracle gets chosen tomorrow, I have an appointment at the DNA paternity lab. This very toothbrush of your daughter's will prove she's not mine. And once I find that out, I'm sending Tookie away. I don't want her in this house anymore. I'm sending her to the factories."

Tookie's eyes goggled. But that would mean she'd become . . . a *Factory Dependent*. She closed her eyes and thought of the shaved-headed, dull-eyed, miserable, penniless children trudging through the factory doors. That would be her life—forever. Did her father really want *that* for her?

Mrs. De La Crème shook her head slowly, but she said nothing. Once again, she didn't defend Tookie. Nor did she debate his decision to send Tookie away. *Maybe she wants to get rid of me too.*

Tookie couldn't help it. She let out a squeak. Her mother didn't hear her, but her father—or whoever he was—turned in the direction of the sound and locked eyes with Tookie. At first, he looked surprised—even panicked. And then he stood up to his full height, possibly relieved. "Just go," he said gruffly, staring at her with his good eye. "For all of us."

Tookie gripped the rough curtain fabric. She wheeled backward out of the house, leaving the front door wide open. The words vibrated in her brain like a clapper in a bell. *There is nothing about me that lives within that girl. That circus freak. . . . I'm sending her to the factories. . . . Just go. For all of us.*

Her chest seared. It felt like her father's hands were squeezing all the air out of her body. She staggered down the porch stairs into the evening's heat. Her bare feet skidded over the dead grass. The pain was so deep, tears did not even streak her face. *I have to get out of here*. To somewhere far away. *But where?*

And then she realized. Of course she knew where.

Exodus.

$$\text{\scriptsize M}$$

The zipper of Tookie's bag made a loud *scrittttch* as she tried to pull it closed. She winced, looked around to make sure no one heard, slipped her *T-Mail Jail* into the left pocket of her cargo pants and the T O OKE button into her right, and tiptoed out of the clothes-strewn bedroom. She paused in the doorway to glance at Myrracle, who was sleeping soundly, letting out a giggle-snore here and there. This might be the last time Tookie would see her sister. Ever. Tookie wondered how she'd be able to fall asleep once she was separated from Myrracle. Myrracle's signature giggle-snore had sort of become Tookie's sound machine, lulling her to sleep every night.

"I know you'll get in," Tookie whispered. "I hope Modelland is everything you and Creamy always wanted . . . and more."

Dawn was breaking as she crept down the stairs. Tookie had stayed awake all night, plotting and planning. She now knew for certain that this was her only option. This was what Wingtip was talking about—this was her "dreaming big."

Last night, after hearing her parents' conversation, she'd painted X-O-2 on the front door of her home, her secret signal to Lizzie. Less than two hours later, Tookie had heard a soft shriek outside her bedroom window. She looked out and saw a barren tree trunk bearing the same symbol: X-O-2. It was accompanied by a smiley face and the number seven, the time in the morning when they would meet.

Tookie was escaping Peppertown forever. Escaping her parents. Escaping with Lizzie to the place of their dreams and being in total control of their destinies.

She could start her whole life over . . . and become a Rememba-Girl.

Two more steps. One. Tookie curled her finger around the doorknob. She could taste the freedom.

"Where do you think you're going?"

Tookie jumped and spun around. Her mother stood behind her. She wore tight-fitting, iridescent bone-colored jeans with a matching one-shouldered top made of silk jersey that read MODEL-LAND NEEDS A MYRRACLE! Her cheeks shone with Wrinkle Redux. Bellissima, whom she'd tucked under her arm, wore the exact same ensemble, minus the face cream.

For a moment, Tookie couldn't move. This was the first time she'd faced her mother since overhearing the dreadful conversation the night before. Instantly, all the feelings of shame and betrayal and rejection rushed back to her.

"Well?" Mrs. De La Crème repeated, her gaze shifting from Tookie to the bag. Her face brightened. "Oh, Tookie . . . what a good sister you are! You've already packed the extra supplies for Myrracle for today. That's very thoughtful of you."

Tookie's heart pounded. How could her mother act like last night hadn't happened? Creamy had all but agreed that Tookie should be sent off to work in one of Metopia's horrible factories.

Tookie swiveled her head back to the narrow window at the side of the front door. The sun was over the tree line. "I j-just wanted to go outside for a m-minute."

"There's no time for anybody but The Myrracle today, Tookie." Mrs. De La Crème turned to the stairs. "And here she is now."

Myrracle bounded down the stairs and did a full body wave when she reached the last step. The SMIZE rested gently in her palm. It glittered and hummed. A small case was in her other hand. "Da-tahh!" she cried.

"Time to go." Mrs. De La Crème walked to the front door.

"No." Tookie dug in her heels. "I'm not going."

Mrs. De La Crème stopped short in the foyer, swung around, and stared at Tookie. "Have you lost your mind? Of course you're going."

The door gaped open. Mr. De La Crème stood by the car, Brian Quincy at his side. Mr. De La Crème wore his old Chris-Crème-Crobat costume, the exact costume he'd lost his eye in; he'd cut out the MODELLAND NEEDS A MYRRACLE! portion of his T-shirt and sewn it to the abdomen. There were even old brown spots on the fabric, evidence of the bright red blood that had stained the costume on the day his life had changed forever.

"We gotta go and we gotta go now!" Mr. De La Crème yelled. "I am not missing the countdown and the opportunity to change our sad excuses for lives. Plus," he added, "I have an important appointment to get to after Myrracle is chosen." He tapped his hip. Tookie could see the outline of her toothbrush underneath the pocket of his costume.

Mrs. De La Crème seized Tookie hard by the neck and walked toward the car. "No!" Tookie cried desperately, trying to wrench free. She swung her neck to the side of the house and saw the X-O-2 written on the tree. All she could think about was how desperate and scared Lizzie had seemed in LaDorno the day before. *They're going to kill me,* she had said. What if Lizzie was telling the truth? Tookie's gut told her that if they didn't escape today, something dreadful would happen to her one and only friend.

Mr. De La Crème bounded over. "Look, girl," he growled, grabbing Tookie roughly by the shoulders. "You need to get in the car and help your sister with the most important day of our lives." He walked Tookie toward the vehicle and shoved her into the back of the car as one might shove a pan of bread into the oven. "In you go."

Tookie was surrounded by garment bags, shoe boxes, makeup cases, hair sprays, and hair-straightening apparatuses. "Hold this," Myrracle said bossily, shoving the SMIZE into Tookie's lap while she buckled her seat belt. The SMIZE rattled inside its case, as if it were trying to escape. It was a feeling that Tookie understood far too well.

Tookie pressed her hands to the back window. As Mr. De La Crème started the car, Tookie's ache for Lizzie cut so deep, she envisioned Lizzie standing just beyond the tree line, her flame-red hair wild around her face.

Then she sat up straighter. That wasn't a vision. "Oh my God!" she screamed. "Lizzie!"

Myrracle swiveled around and followed Tookie's gaze. "Creamy, there's a dirty girl in our yard."

"Ugh." Brian looked too. "She looks like roadkill."

Lizzie took a few steps toward the car, as if she was considering chasing after it. Her shoulders drooped. Her mouth hung open. Her arms were heavy at her sides. She looked so small standing there. So helpless. If Peppertown ever had even the tiniest wisp of a breeze, it could have blown her away.

"Roadkill?" Mrs. De La Crème's eyebrows arched. "Where?" She swiveled around to look at Lizzie too. Her eyes narrowed darkly.

Lizzie's eyes popped wide, as if she'd just seen something

that terrified her. She took a couple of wheeling backward steps, her hands trembling. And then Lizzie let out a shrill, window-shattering, eardrum-piercing scream, a sound that sent tremors through Tookie's limbs. A sound Tookie would never forget as long as she lived.

"I'm so so so sorry!" Tookie called. Lizzie's screaming was intensifying as Tookie moved away from her. "Lizzie, I'll be back for you tonight! I promise!"

The car made a sweeping left turn onto the street, moving farther and farther away from the small red-headed girl. Lizzie's screams persisted. Tookie could hear those loud, shrill, betrayed wails for blocks and blocks, reverberating over and over as the De La Crèmes drove down the wide avenue full of cars, all on their way to The Day of Discovery.

8

WELCOME TO T-DOD

*Can you smell it, feel it, taste it? Oh, I can. And it tastes . . . ooooh . . .
so sweet. And the sound? Deafening. Think about the loudest, most riot-
ous crowd you've ever been in . . . and quadruple it. Then multiply that
by the power of ten!*

*That is The Day of Discovery. And yes, my dahling, that delightful
day has arrived.*

*The whole world is flooding to Metopia to see the delectable spec-
tacle unfold. It takes place all over the planet, of course—on the sexy
beaches of Terra BossaNova, on the strip of Striptown, round the Taj
Gardens in Chakra—but there's nowhere like Metopia for the most
authentic experience. Modelland is right there, after all! At the top of*

Metopia's highest peak. Everyone wants to see the Scouts' first descent from the mountain and their final flight back into The Land, their capacious carriages full of new recruits.

But some visitors don't trek from their corner of the globe just to see the Scouts' initial descent. Some come to experience something else.

The Aftermath. The madness that affects the forsaken, the rejected, the unchosen, and the denied once all the Discovery after-parties have ended.

There are always some rejected candidates who just cannot accept Modelland's decision. They are so sure they deserve a spot in the new class, so convinced that there has been a terrible mistake, that they embark on a pilgrimage up the Diabolical Divide in hopes that Modelland will see firsthand the grave oversight that has been committed.

Those intrepid females—the Pilgrims, as they are called—have tunnel vision so laser-focused that no one can convince them they're mistaken. People call this debilitating illness the Plague. The first telltale symptoms are profuse sweating, massive headaches, and bulging veins.

This plague is worse than the one you might already be familiar with—the B one. Bubonic, that is. That plague induces seizures, fevers, chills, gland swelling, the upchucking of blood, and the decomposition of skin while one is still alive. But I will take the bubonic plague any day—for if it's caught in time, it can be ousted from the body with a simple swallow of one of the two "mycins": genta or strepto. The Pilgrim Plague, however, is terminal, dahling. And I am not referring to an airline departure lounge. None who have journeyed up the mountain have ever made it to Modelland. And none have returned to Metopia alive.

Now, doesn't that send Shivera shivers all the way down to your sky-high stilettos?

By the time the De La Crème car pulled into downtown La-
Dorno, people had already spilled out onto the streets. Tourists
lined the curb, gawking at every car that passed. An unnaturally
bleached-blond, orange-tanned, middle-aged man sold pink,
purple, and turquoise cotton candy in the shape of Intoxibella
hairdos from the latest *Modelland* magazine fashion editorial—a
sugary asymmetrical bob, a mess of candy curls, and a flossy nest
of sharp-looking spikes. Everyone wore something Modelland
related—T-shirts with a photo of the mystifying mountain on the
front; hats with the eye logo; and dresses, shoes, and hats bearing
pictures of Ci~L. The ravishing Intoxibella's intoxicating eyes en-
tranced Tookie, pulling her in. Once again, the merchandise was
adorned with the slogan WHERE THE HELL IS Ci~L?

Tookie's stomach lurched when she saw the shoulder bags
a man was selling with photos of Exodus, the new teleportaling
7Seven, on them.

Exodus. Lizzie. She shut her eyes tight, Lizzie's scream echoing
in her mind.

Protesters also lined the sidewalks, holding up signs that
said WOMEN, DON'T WALK! IT'S ALL A SHAM! T-DOD'S A CROCK. A PHONY
EXAM! Overpowering all the spectators were the thousands upon
thousands of candidates making their way to LaDorno Square.
Homely girls, riveting girls, short and tall girls, droopy-eyed and
doe-eyed girls, shapely-hipped and pigeon-toed and slew- and
flat-footed girls, twig-limbed and ample-figured and athletic girls.
All of them marched into the square with confidence. Tookie had
forgotten that not all the participants were exactly Intoxibella

quality. She stared at them as they passed, envious of their guts and determination. Plus, none of them had to stand around helping their younger sisters realize her destiny.

As the De La Crème vehicle rolled toward a parking lot, Tookie's mother leaned over to apply a puff of bronzer to Myrracle's cheeks. "Now, Myrracle, you know that you must runway-walk the whole fifteen minutes the music is playing, right? No chassés, jetés, or pas de bourrées. You hear me?"

"I know, Creamy." Myrracle opened her eyes wide to allow Mrs. De La Crème to apply mascara to her bottom lashes.

"And when the Scout chooses you, be gracious," Mrs. De La Crème went on. "They appreciate good manners."

"Your mother has been preparing for this very day since before you were born," Mr. De La Crème said. He pulled into a handicapped parking space, beating another car to the spot. "Success," he murmured, pumping his fist.

The De La Crèmes and Brian clambered out of the car and onto the street. Mr. De La Crème held the encased SMIZE under his arm like a football.

Mrs. De La Crème shoved Tookie's large Exodus-slash-"accessories" bag into Tookie's arms. "We have lots of work to do." She held tight to Tookie's wrist, pulling Tookie toward the town square, which was paved in bleached marble as far as the eye could see. Three sides of the square pulsated with throngs of spectators jockeying for position and participants preparing for the event. The fourth side offered a perfect view of the mysterious mountain, almost butting up against it. Six glittering fountains decorated the square, spewing effervescent plumes of water that sent unwitting tourists scurrying for cover. An enormous, exquisitely carved eight-story clock stood on the north side, and screens flanked the perimeter, many projecting images of the approximately one thousand other cities hosting chaotic Day of Discovery events all over the world. One screen showed girls standing atop a frozen lake in the town of Palinian. Others displayed candidates milling excitedly in a cleared-out sugarcane field in Kwaito, pelt-wearing tribal leaders dancing ceremonially around them. A third depicted a massive crowd of young ladies gathered around an auto racetrack in the city of FiveHundred.

There was an opening that offered a panoramic view of the Modelland mountain. Three obelisks stood at the base, pointing straight up into the sky—one sparkling ivory, one golden, one bisque that was covered with spots. No one knew who had built them—they'd appeared overnight six months ago. But the Obscure Obelisks, as they'd come to be called, attracted their own gathering of spectators, many carrying religious icons, who believed that the structures were significant to *them*. Others posed, allowing friends to take pictures of them with the obelisks in the background.

"Those damn ugly-ass obelisks," Mrs. De La Crème muttered as she walked. "They block the view of the mountain."

I don't think they're ugly. Tookie gazed at them with wonder. *I think they're architecturally interesting. Unique. A mystery.*

The De La Crème family continued through the square. Tourists, television cameramen and reporters, horse-mounted riot police, and Modelland hopefuls jammed the space. More girls were getting prepped in the tent areas around the perimeter of the square called Walkers' Village.

"You're dragging your feet, Tookie," Mrs. De La Crème snapped.

Finally they arrived at Walkers' Village. They found a clear patch of grass and dropped their bags of gear. Most of the girls were changing in the open, their body parts exposed for the world to see.

"Not my Myrracle!" Mr. De La Crème boomed as he pulled a brand-new blow-up tent from the large duffel he was carrying. He pressed the automatic-inflation button and a white and cream striped tent staked itself to the ground. Mrs. De La Crème and Brian surrounded Myrracle, opening makeup cases and pulling out needles and thread and pins and scissors.

"Brian, open the duffel that Tookie brought," Mrs. De La Crème commanded.

Brian unzipped the bag crammed with Tookie's escape gear. "What the hell is this?" In each hand, he held a flashlight and a pillow. His eyes settled on Tookie.

"Oh, honey! Good thinking!" Mrs. De La Crème said, running to the bag. "Brian, bind these two flashlights to the tents ceiling for extra light. The pillows are perfect for Bellissima to nap on. And . . . green bananas . . . Tookie, you didn't!"

Yeah, you're right, I didn't, Tookie thought bitterly. Those green bananas were supposed to last for a week, for her and Lizzie.

Mr. De La Crème and Brian waited outside the tent while Myrracle put on the gauzy, strapless vintage dress that was the exact color of her skin. The skirt fanned out nearly three feet from her slim hips, and the folds settled in such a way that the dress looked like the surface of an elegantly rippling ocean.

Tookie crouched down beside her sister and began fastening the row of hundreds of tiny buttons on the bodice, her small fingers expertly sliding each button through its loop.

Mrs. De La Crème grabbed a stack of bobby pins and began

to fix Myrracle's hair. Tookie moved closer to her mother, thinking this might be a good time to talk.

"Uh, C-C-Creamy?" she said softly. "After Myrracle is chosen, n-nothing has to change, right?" *You're not going to send me away to become a Factory Dependent, are you?*

"Tookie, your father has made some hard decisions, but he is my husband, and I have to honor them," Mrs. De La Crème murmured absently, applying gloss to Myrracle's lips. "I should imagine things will change quite a bit."

Tookie gasped. "So does that mean . . ."

But Mrs. De La Crème had already turned away.

Tookie's mouth hung open. So that was it. They really were sending her away. Tears pricked her eyes.

Finally, when Myrracle was finished, Mrs. De La Crème opened the case holding the SMIZE. She slowly lifted the lid and a glow spilled out, bathing the tent's interior with multi-golden luminescence. She moaned in ecstasy.

"Come here, baby," Mrs. De La Crème breathed. "Come to Creamy."

Tookie wasn't sure if her mother was speaking to the SMIZE or to Myrracle, but as if on cue, Myrracle glided as if in a trance toward her mother and placed her chin right into her mother's cupped hands. The SMIZE sucked onto Myrracle's face, wiggling itself into place, and rested above her eyes, its undulating colors creating the most magnificent eye-shadow effect Tookie had *ever* seen. Tookie resisted the overwhelming urge to reach out and stroke the SMIZE.

A gasp rippled through the crowd as soon as they saw Myrracle and her SMIZE. One girl who was biting her nails began to cry and another looked as if she was about to pummel Myrracle, but she made eye contact with Mr. De La Crème and backed off.

"Oooooooooooh," Brian cooed, scuttling over to admire Myrracle's gold three-dimensional eye shadow.

"Gorgeous, baby," Mr. De La Crème seconded, lacing his fingers together. "Just gorgeous. With or without that thing."

Tookie had to agree. Myrracle was a stunning girl, but the SMIZE made her beauty otherworldly. A smidgeon more stunning than the 7Sevens Tookie had seen the night before.

Riot police began to move the crowd behind the barricades, clearing the square. A shrieking whistle filled the air and all eyes turned skyward. A bowling ball–shaped man with a full white beard and mustache, twinkling little eyes, and a jutting chin, wearing a white top-hat, swept straight down into the now-empty square, supported by a harness. Tookie recognized him as Devin Rump the Sixth, the mayor of Metopia.

"Greetings!" Mayor Rump said. His voice echoed off the hard marble surfaces. *Eetings. Eetings. Eetings.* Members of the Quadrant Councils of Peppertown, PitterPatter, Shivera, and LaDorno and their spouses stood on the side stage. Each councilmember's wife was decked out in the products his quadrant's factories were famous for.

"I have the great honor of welcoming all of you from around the globe to the fashion capital of the world, Metopia," Mr. Rump boomed into a microphone headset. "Today is the day you have all waited three hundred and sixty-four days for, The Day of Discovery—or T-DOD, as you young folk have come to call it. I want to wish all of you competing for Modelland admission the best of luck. Metopia has a long-standing track record of producing many Intoxibellas, which is why so many of you trek here from your far away homelands each year. And today, we hope to send many more of you to that special place on the mountain."

Cheers erupted in the crowd.

"What will be the look of this season?" the mayor asked no one in particular. "Is it the year of the blondes? The brunettes? Perhaps it's a ginger season."

"Ginger! Yes!" a strawberry-blonde in a pink gown cried a few feet away. "They never pick ginger!"

"Will it be tanned skin or rosy epidermises?" Rump went on. "Blue irises, cognac ones? Emerald or hazel?"

Tookie used to watch the mayor every year on television on The Day of Discovery, wishing, hoping he'd utter, *Will it be girls with one brown and one green eye?* But it had never happened.

"Will it be the slim-limbed, the slightly curved, the athletically built?" the mayor continued, his words echoing throughout the massive square. "Will it be . . . you?"

More cheers. "And if you are not chosen, don't fret. Metopia has many wonderful jobs manufacturing clothes, accessories, and beauty products. Holding a job in a factory is just as worthy of esteem as being an Intoxibella!"

The mayor paused for cheers. He was met with dead silence.

Suddenly, a hand slipped into Tookie's and squeezed. It was Myrracle's. Her wide eyes flitted back and forth nervously. "Do I look okay?"

Tookie looked at her sister, suddenly feeling a protective and loving rush. It wasn't *Myrracle's* fault their parents were horrible people. Myrracle might not have been the best sibling, but she was all Tookie had. "You look absolutely beautiful," she said. "Breath-taking. Really. Now, remember, Myrracle. Dance in your spirit but not with your body, 'kay?"

"I know, I know! You sound like Creamy!" Myrracle playfully groaned. Tookie had a sudden revelation: This might be it. The last time she would see Myrracle. "All Day of Discovery candidates. Are you ready?" Mayor Rump called.

A resounding, excited "Yes!" filled the air, so loud that it made the mayor and the Quadrant Council members clamp their hands over their ears. Cowbells clanged again. The crowd clapped in slow unison.

Mr. De La Crème crouched down to Myrracle and held the sides of her face. "Dance in your spirit but not with your body. You want this, baby, right?" Myrracle sucked on her bottom lip, eating off her lip gloss, and then stared blankly into her father's eyes. "C'mon now, baby. Wake up. This is our destiny."

Myrracle nodded, shaking out the tension in her arms and legs exactly like she did before her Maven of Movement competitions.

"The time has come!" Mayor Rump picked up a long striped tube and lit it with a match. Sparks began to fly. The tube shivered and bucked. "Lives are about to magically change . . . forever! Candidates, get ready!"

Rump let the sparking tube go. It shot into the sky and exploded into the clouds, creating a gigantic burst of blues and pinks and golds, visible even in the daylight. Tookie gawked at it, her hand to her mouth. When she looked back at Mayor Rump, his harness had yanked him up into the sky once more. Fireworks continued to explode around him. And then, from his dangling perch, the mayor uttered the very word everyone had waited for all year.

"*Begin.*"

9

Bzzz

Thousands of girls stampeded to the square all at once. Heels clacked. Dresses swished. Hairdos wobbled. The T-DOD theme song boomed a pulsating beat.

There was one rule and one rule only: a girl must be walking in order to be chosen.

Other than that, there was no prearranged runway on which the girls could walk, so everyone created invisible ones wherever they were standing. Violence was not encouraged nor was it condemned, and some girls' parents insisted on adding martial arts training to their walking lessons in preparation for the big day. T-DOD Square was an every-man-for-himself—or, more precisely, an every-girl-for-herself—event.

Scores of girls marched down their own stretches of the square, paused, posed for the cameras (real and imaginary), and then turned around. Trains of walking girls intersected with others. One area behind Tookie was so crammed with street vendors, it bottlenecked into a slow, shuffling line. Some walkers had only enough space to take a few steps before they had to stop and turn. Tookie's heart went out to a young girl in a ruffled pink dress who seemed way below the unofficial thirteen-year-old age requirement. She marched in place as if she were on a drill team.

Riiiip. A girl stepped on the train of a walker a few feet from Tookie and tore the fabric right off the dress. Both girls fell forward into a heap. The walkers behind them stepped over their bodies and continued.

Crash. The De La Crème white and cream blow-up tent went down as two brawling girls entered it. *Oof.* A girl who looked as if she had never walked in heels before stumbled, breaking the tips of both stilettos. Two girls got into a fight at the end of their makeshift catwalk, rolling to the ground. "Kenya, use the Gyaku Zuki move!" her mother screamed. "Reverse-punch the hairy hag! But watch *your* hair, sweetie!"

Tookie wheeled around. The hairy hag was Abigail Goode, sideburns in full glory, faint mustache above her upper lip, unshaven leg hair coating her calves, underarm hair swaying in the wind, and a DOWN WITH RAZORS! picket sign still in her hands. The girl she was fighting with tried out a karate move on her, but Abigail expertly evaded her blow.

Tookie's jealousy meter skyrocketed. Even *Abigail* was competing?

She looked around some more. Actually, not only were eligible girls walking, but lots of other people were too. An elderly man on a power scooter shot a gap-toothed smile to the crowd as he steered his vehicle with his hands on his hips. Two down-on-their-luck women dressed in trash-bag dresses and beat-up sweat suits walked while pushing everything they owned in shopping carts, heckling every girl who passed. "Honey, you *wish* you had it like I do." "Get back, spring chickens—age before beauty, ladies!" Tookie chuckled when she noticed that even some of the protesters ditched their RUN AWAY, DON'T WALK signs and sashayed energetically while chanting, *"Women, let's walk! Smile for the cams! T-DOD, it rocks. Crank the music, let's jam!"*

A few drunken boys from outside the gates got into the action, strutting next to the girls in exaggerated, long-legged lopes. One guy snaked an arm around a girl's waist, but she swatted him away. The photographers and cameramen scrambled to catch every moment, projecting various images onto the screens next to the stage.

Thump, thump, thump. The music beat on. The largest screen showed the remaining time left for walking. Twelve minutes, twenty seconds.

"Go, Myrracle, go!" Mrs. De La Crème shouted. Myrracle had staggered a few feet away from the fallen tent and was standing there staring at the melee, eyes bugged, frozen in place. "Don't freeze up! Wake up, baby. You *have* to do this!"

"Yeah, Myrracle. You can do this. Come on!" Tookie urged, holding her sister by her arms and staring into her eyes, trying to spark a connection. "Dance in your spirit, but not with your body," she repeated over and over. Then she turned Myrracle around, placed Myrracle's hands on her hips, and whispered in her ear: "Left, then right, then left, then right . . ."

Myrracle suddenly broke out of her trance and began to follow Tookie's instructions. Tookie jumped out of the way to watch her sister. Halfway down her imaginary runway, Myrracle began to wiggle her hips and shake her shoulders to the infectious music that swelled over the sounds of the crowd.

"Don't dance!" Mrs. De La Crème bellowed, giving Myrracle a pinch. "If you sway one more time, you'll get way worse than a little pinch! If I have to beat the last pas de bourrée out of you, I will! Now walk, walk, walk like an Intoxibella!"

Myrracle snapped back to focus. Her arms swung gently. She thrust her hips forward, as she'd learned to do in hours upon hours of walking class. She reached the end of her catwalk and came face to face with Abigail Goode. Both girls vied for the same spot to pose. Myrracle stuck out her pointy elbows, bumped her hip, and shoved Abigail hard out of the space. Abigail teetered over in her high shoes, hit her head on the footrest of the old man's motorized scooter, and passed out cold.

Almost immediately a siren sounded and Tookie heard someone yell, "Girl down! Girl down!"

Myrracle posed for a long three seconds, then raised a shoulder and swirled back around. There was a *don't mess with me girl unless you want to get hurt* expression on her face as she strutted back toward Tookie and her family.

"That's my Myrracle!" Mrs. De La Crème jumped up and down and clapped. "Claim what is ours, baby!"

"Uh, I know you, right?"

Tookie turned and nearly jumped out of her skin. Standing next to her was Theophilus Lovelaces. His eyes glistened in the LaDorno sun. He was seeing her, actually seeing her. His eyes focused right on hers. His words were meant for her. Tookie tried to smile, but she had a feeling her mouth made more of a grimace.

"You're not participating?" Theophilus asked, gesturing to the crowd.

Tookie opened her mouth but couldn't speak. She was dying to say, *Really? Me? Have you lost your mind?* But instead a cross between a yelp, a sneeze, and a burp came out.

"Good for you." Theophilus indicated the candidates in the square. "This is a little crazy."

They both turned to Zarpessa Zarionneaux, who strutted confidently right over an open manhole that three girls had just fallen into. Her long, straight auburn hair streamed behind her. Her skin glistened in the sun. She wore a bright yellow dress that seemed electrified, with matching yellow shoes. Tookie assumed it was the ensemble Lizzie had mentioned the other day, the one she and Zarpessa had fought over at the clothing dump.

"She even makes trash look beautiful," Tookie murmured.

"Hmm?" Theophilus glanced at her in surprise.

"Oh, nothing." It pained her that her very first conversation with Theophilus was about Zarpessa. She considered telling Theophilus about Zarpessa's Dumpster digging, but then she clamped her mouth shut. No matter how much she envied Zarpessa, exposing something that awful was just too mean.

"What's your name, anyway?" Theophilus asked, looking at Tookie again.

Tookie gaped at him. He wanted to know her *name*? Her mouth tried to form the words. She felt Theophilus's T O OKE button in her hip pocket.

Suddenly a piercing voice rose above the din. "Theophilus!"

Zarpessa's voice.

"I'd better go." Theophilus tipped an imaginary hat to Tookie. Then he whirled around and marched toward his beloved.

"Seven minutes left!" Mayor Rump bellowed.

A blinding neon-yellow flash filled the sky. The clouds vanished. The sun disappeared. Someone screamed. Everyone shaded their eyes or ducked their heads. Even the walkers paused for a moment and squinted upward. Another whoosh boomed through the air. "The Scouts!" a voice bellowed. "They're here!"

Scouts? Where? Tookie stood on her tiptoes, her heart beating like mad. People stepped back from a nearby lamppost that had started to vibrate, staring at it with a mix of wonder and terror. The lamppost began to lengthen, like a long telescoping pole. *Snap!* It broke apart and reassembled as a slender, mysterious-looking woman in a black metallic jumpsuit. Her head glowed as if it contained a lightbulb.

"A Scout!" Tookie whispered. She'd never seen one in person before.

The Scout's head began to blink, as if warning people that something amazing was about to happen. Then the woman marched to a thin girl with cheekbones so sharp they could slice a melon in half, and tapped her arm. The girl clutched her chest in disbelief. The Scout took her hand, and the bright light of her cranium flashed like lightning. And then . . . *poof!* They were gone, and the lamppost was back where it had always been.

"Oh, my baby!" the girl's mother cried, running up to the lamppost, hugging it tightly and covering it with kisses. "My baby, my baby, my baby! First-draft pick!"

More gasps and screams rose in the crowd as the huge clock

in the square ticked past the six-minute mark. Suddenly, Scouts from Modelland were everywhere. An asteroid rocketed to earth, throwing up chunks of marble all around the square and causing nearby runway walkers to flee in hysterics. A stunning Scout emerged from the rubble, with skin that seemed to be made of rough stone. She wore a bathing suit ensemble that appeared to be made of rocks. She tapped a tall, long-haired girl in a plain, dingy cotton dress. The dress wasn't nearly as fancy as most of the outfits the other girls were wearing, and its front was wet with tears. When the girl looked up and saw the Scout, her jaw dropped.

"Are you sure you have to pick me?" the girl whimpered incredulously.

A pointy-chinned competitor in a poufy-sleeved dress and studded boots pushed to the front. "Pick me, she doesn't want it!"

The plainly dressed girl's mother tugged the Scout's arm. "No, my Desperada does want it! Please take her! I don't have the money to feed her anymore."

The Scout nodded and grabbed the sobbing girl's hand, and they both disappeared into a hole in the ground. Immediately, all the broken marble flew into the sky, reassembled, and then dropped right back to exactly where it'd been before the disruption.

The clock edged past the five-minutes-left mark. The shopping cart of one of the homeless women flew from her hands and rolled wildly around the square. Girls near the cart ran away screaming. The cart flipped forward, and old food and tattered clothes spilled to the ground. A Scout in a dress with rips in all the right places materialized from beneath the decrepit belongings. She strutted to the middle of the square and stopped in front of a raven-haired girl who was wearing a dress with an enormous bustle. The girl's mother, who was clad in a muumuu, held out her own arm. "You want . . . *me*?"

With a slight, tired, *oh how the old ones always do this* roll of her eyes, the Scout touched the daughter's shoulder instead. "Oh!" the mother squealed. "Well, of course, of course!" She enveloped her daughter in her arms and cooed how proud she was of her and then let go. But as the Scout and the daughter descended into the worn clothes and rotten food within the cart, there was the tiniest look of disappointment on the mother's face.

"Three minutes, fifty seconds!" Mayor Rump announced from his VIP perch. Myrracle strutted on, posing and turning. Mrs. De La Crème bit her nails. Mr. De La Crème paced back and forth.

Eruptions occurred all over the square. The reporters swiveled their cameras and microphones, trying to keep up with the mayhem. Walkers to the left, right, front, and back bumped into Myrracle. She walked two steps, posed, turned, and walked again. Even Zarpessa was losing space, walking in a tight circle near the strange obelisks.

"Tookie, climb up here so your sister has more room to walk!" Mr. De La Crème commanded behind her. Tookie turned and saw her parents and Brian standing on the roof of the wildest car she had ever seen: a blinged-out golden low-rider with a pavé roof and hubcaps that spun in place, even when the car wasn't moving. The gaudy and glam automobile was parked on a piece of marble that had a huge crack down the middle that looked, strangely, like a question mark.

Tookie dutifully climbed onto the shiny bumper. Mrs. De La Crème anxiously compared the time on her watch to the time on the huge clock in the center of the square. Worry marred her wrinkled face. "We still have time," she murmured. "A miracle will happen for The Myrracle. I just know it."

More flashes filled the sky. More Scouts appeared. The candidates walked hungrily. Dozens of fights broke out, and at least six girls lay on the marble ground, nursing their wounds. As Tookie made her way up the trunk of the car, a strange vibrating sensation tickled her feet. *Bzzz.*

What was that?

"One minute left!" Mayor Rump called. Hundreds of people began to count down. *Fifty-nine, fifty-eight . . .*

Bzzz. Bzzz. Tookie looked down and gasped. A strip of the diamond-encrusted roof of the car had transformed into a thick layer of brilliant fabric. As she watched, even more of the roof disappeared and reappeared as cloth. The fabric looked as if it were being spontaneously woven by a giant loom. "Whoa," she whispered.

Mrs. De La Crème noticed the fabric too. She kneeled down to within an inch of the strange material and then bounced back up. *"It's a Scout!"* She jumped off the roof. *"Myrracle, it's a Scout!"*

Brian was right behind her. He shook Myrracle by the shoulders. "It's a Scout, doofus!"

"Where?" Myrracle halted midpose.

"On the roof of the car!"

Myrracle pushed past girls in her way and scuttled over to the vehicle.

Thousands of crowd members were now counting down the seconds.

Forty-five, forty-four . . .

Another row of fabric emerged. Then another, then another. Myrracle shrieked. "A Scout, Creamy! A Scout!"

Mr. De La Crème grabbed Myrracle from the square and pulled her toward the car. "Everything we've strived for. It's all coming true, baby!"

Thirty-nine, thirty-eight . . .

Tons of girls ran for the gaudy car, clamoring for the attention of the soon-to-appear Scout. Tookie surveyed the crowd, noticing how many people were watching the De La Crème family on the roof. Jealous girls, rabid mothers . . . even Theophilus was in the back of the crowd, looking amused. But strangely, he wasn't staring at Myrracle, as most of the mob was. His eyes were locked on Tookie. Her stomach flipped over.

"Tookie!" Mrs. De La Crème grabbed Tookie's ankle. "Get down from the hood! Myrracle needs her space! This is her moment!"

"Uh . . ." Tookie stared at the ground. The area around the car teemed with so many girls now, she was kind of trapped. Furthermore, Myrracle wasn't able to climb atop the roof to greet the Scout properly. *This is Myrracle's moment,* Tookie thought. She had to help her.

"Come on, Myrracle!" Tookie called. She reached out her hand for Myrracle to grab. It took all of Tookie's strength to pull Myrracle and her twenty-pound dress onto the hood. Once she was up, Myrracle pushed Tookie out of the way, nearly knocking her to the ground.

"I'm here!" Myrracle cried. She stood in the center of the hood, hands in the air, her chin thrust high. "Da-tahhhh!"

"Tookie, for the love of God, get off the roof!" Mrs. De La Crème screeched. "Give Myrracle room!"

But Tookie didn't want to move. She wanted to see this happen to Myrracle firsthand. The roof had finished its diamond-to-fabric transformation. There was a slight pause, and Tookie felt the world around her go silent. And then the whole roof began to tremble.

Suddenly, the fabric split violently in the very center, knocking Myrracle off the roof. She fell to the ground almost as if in slow motion.

"Nooooooo!" Mrs. De La Crème wailed. Tookie's father pushed Brian out of the way to catch his daughter. Tiers of tulle billowed into his face. Myrracle's legs kicked into the air.

"Get back up there, Myrracle!" Mr. De La Crème screamed, shoving a shoe back onto Myrracle's bare foot. He pushed her up on the hood.

Fifteen, fourteen, thirteen . . .

The tear in the fabric grew wider, until a human-sized hole appeared. And then a nearly naked woman emerged from the center of the tear and rose into the sky. She had long limbs and golden skin and wore shiny necklaces strategically placed over her chest and lower half. A gem-encrusted veil covered her face.

Tookie gasped.

The Scout's hair blew in its own wind. Her arms stretched wide. Her fingers gripped the very ends of the piece of fabric that had materialized on the roof of the car. It seemed as though the fabric had grown from her fingers, an extension of her body itself.

"Wow," Myrracle whispered. Tookie couldn't agree more.

Fireworks began to explode in the air, the sparkles showing the numbers as they counted down.

Six, five, four . . .

The Scout looked at the De La Crèmes and nodded majestically, looking both strong and feminine at the same time.

"Please take her!" Mrs. De La Crème gushed.

"We would be honored!" Mr. De La Crème cried.

Three, two . . .

And then the Scout reached out her long, slender, radiantly decorated hand and beckoned.

To *Tookie*.

10

Bou-Big-Tique Nation

The entire De La Crème family stood dumbfounded. Tookie stared at the Scout's outstretched hand. Was this some kind of cruel joke?

All sorts of possibilities flashed through Tookie's mind. Blood pulsed hard from her heart to her head. She glanced at the question-mark-shaped crack in the ground. It seemed very appropriate at this moment.

The Scout's hand reached closer.

Mrs. De La Crème scuttled onto the car's hood with the nimbleness of a mountain goat. "Oh no, no, no, my most honorable Scout," she spouted. "This is *not* the girl you came for." She pushed Tookie aside. "You want my Myrracle!"

A sparkling slip of paper appeared in the Scout's hand. Studying it, she first eyed Myrracle, arching her body toward the girl so that mere millimeters separated their faces. Then, in a flash, the Scout turned to look at Tookie. She returned to Myrracle, triggering a hopeful smile on Mrs. De La Crème's quivering lips. Then she scrutinized the paper in her hand again.

"What's taking you so long?" Myrracle blurted out. "You want *me*! I'm The Myrracle! I'm wearing the SMIZE! I'm on that list, right?"

Myrracle reached for the list in the Scout's hand. *Whap!* The Scout jerked back so quickly that one of her necklaces swatted Myrracle's hand away.

Myrracle let out a sharp squeak. "Ow! Creameeeee! She smacked me with her thing!"

Mrs. De La Crème squared her shoulders. "Oh no, you did not just whack my Myrracle. I may not know who the hell you are, but I do know you have lost your diamond-encrusted mind!"

The Scout's body tensed, and in the blink of an eye, Mrs. De La Crème changed her tune. "But, I mean, lovely bejeweled goddess, you do indeed know best. You can whack, slap, smack, clobber, knock out, even give my Myrracle a black eye. Do as you wish. *Just choose her!*"

Myrracle pointed accusingly at Tookie. "She's the one you should be smacking! She doesn't even care about Modelland!"

"Yes I do," Tookie said softly. "Not that any of you have ever asked."

But her words were drowned out by the howls of the crowd, the blares of car horns, and the earsplitting *bonnnnnng* of the giant clock in the middle of LaDorno's square as it marked the official end to The Day of Discovery.

The Scout consulted a glittering piece of jewelry on her wrist that resembled the top half of a crystal snow globe. It changed colors slightly with every second that passed. Then she extended both hands to Tookie, waving them impatiently.

"Oh, um . . . okay," Tookie said uncertainly. It felt like she was in a dream as she reached for the Scout. But just before they touched, two strong hands shoved her from the side. She tumbled off the car, falling straight into Mr. De La Crème's arms.

He quickly pushed Tookie back up on the roof. "Creamy, what are you trying to do, kill the girl? They want *one* of our daughters—isn't that good enough? If she wants Tookie, let her take Tookie!"

Mrs. De La Crème glowered at him. "Oh, so *now* the circus freak is your daughter?"

Mr. De La Crème looked up at Tookie. "Tookie, don't listen to her. You know I love you, right? Always have, always will. You're Daddy's special baby girl."

Tookie's chest burned. *Daddy? Special? Love?* She had a strong feeling he didn't mean it, but she couldn't help letting his warm words affect her anyway.

"Just go," Mr. De La Crème told Tookie. "For all of us."

As if it had been waiting to be released her entire life, a single tear dropped from Tookie's eye. Did he want her to go because he just wanted to be rid of her? Was he truly proud of her and thought she really deserved this? Or was he now willing to be her daddy because she was the Scout's choice?

Suddenly, something in the crowd caught her attention. There on one of the huge screens was her face. Her six-head. Her multiple-personality-disorder hair. Her mismatched eyes. This image was projected all over Metopia—all over the world. Hundreds of bewildered spectators in LaDorno Square stared at the screen. Thousands of hopeful girls wailed to their mothers, *Why does she get to go? She's crazy-looking!* Millions of people all over the world saw Tookie's image right now and thought, *What the . . . ?*

Trembling, Tookie remembered the words Wingtip had whispered to her outside the Esplanade the day before: *Dream big. Even you.* Perhaps this was what he meant. This was the biggest dream any girl could have. Especially a Forgetta-Girl.

Tookie swallowed hard, and her trembling hand finally met the Scout's bejeweled one.

A flash of golden yellow light surrounded them. A strong sucking sensation pulled at Tookie's feet, then her legs, and then her stomach and back. Her body tumbled into a brilliant, sheer fabric that spewed from the Scout's fingers. More fabric surrounded her, enveloping her bottom and legs, and the force of a billion hands lifted her up and buoyed her into the air. Suddenly, Tookie was in some kind of translucent mesh pouch.

She looked down through the gossamer fabric. LaDorno Square swung beneath her. Myrracle fell to her knees on the car's hood, letting out a scream so piercing Mr. De La Crème covered his ears. Mrs. De La Crème's brow was dripping with sweat. She gripped her head and the veins in her hands looked as if they were about to burst. She raised her hand in the air like it was a pistol aiming for the Scout. "You think you are flying high and mighty, but I will whack, slap, smack, clobber, knock out, and give your bedazzled ass a black eye!"

It was too painful to watch them anymore. Tookie shifted her gaze ahead. The Scout floated in front of her, her arms stretched out behind her in a V, the fabric of the pouch protruding from the tips of her shimmering fingers. The grand buildings around LaDorno Square moved swiftly past. As Tookie sailed up and up, people looked dumbstruck, as if they were wondering why on earth such an odd-looking girl was in a Scout's pouch.

Tons of parties were taking place: in a fifth-floor window, Tookie saw silver-haired men in shiny silver suits and young women in the finest gowns, all holding bright, bubbly concoctions in their hands. Higher up she waved to a group of grinning children with cake-smeared faces. One cherub-faced girl was pressed so hard against the glass that Tookie worried she might push through some unseen crack and plunge to her untimely death.

This is a dream, Tookie kept repeating to herself. *I've dozed off during the ceremony. I'm going to wake up and Myrracle will have been chosen.* She squeezed her eyes closed tight and then popped them open. But she was still in the strange pouch.

The streets of LaDorno spread out in a grid beneath her. Not surprisingly, every other part of LaDorno was virtually unpopulated at this particular hour, nearly all of its residents crowded around the square for T-DOD. It was strange to see no pedestrians, no buses trundling past, no cars waiting at the stoplights. But then Tookie noticed a red flash—a figure darting down a dark alleyway.

Tookie pressed her face hard against the translucent fabric. The figure ran crookedly down the alley, arms spread wide. Then the person abruptly stopped and looked straight at the pouch.

"Lizzie!" Tookie's jaw dropped. "We have to stop!" she yelled to the Scout. But the Scout kept flying.

Tookie grabbed a handful of the pouch's fabric and pulled with all her might, trying to tear a hole in the side. A horrible thought struck her: *What if Lizzie saw my face on those humongous screens? What if Lizzie saw me willingly take the Scout's hand? What if she thought I skipped out of Exodus because I wanted Modelland more?* "I didn't know about this, Lizzie! I swear!" Tookie screamed.

But Tookie and the Scout were too high in the sky for Lizzie to hear her. Lizzie's tiny body jerked to the side in a big twitch. After a moment, she lowered her head and began to run once more, the shadows swallowing up her crimson head. Soon she was nothing but a small dot.

"Lizzie . . . ," Tookie whispered, overcome with shame and guilt. She stood and curtsied, saying farewell to her one and only friend.

They moved fast through LaDorno, traversing the Resort Quarter, the Luxury District, and Platinum Row. As they neared the base of the mountain to Modelland, the Scout slowed in front of the Obscure Obelisks and stopped so abruptly that Tookie tumbled backward. Then the Scout took a sharp turn and headed straight down.

Tookie scrambled to the front of the pouch. The ground was approaching fast. A rush of air pushed against her body, the g-forces distorting her face and making her cheeks flutter. A horrible wail rang through Tookie's ears, and after a split second, she realized it was her own terrified scream. *We're really going to crash,* she thought hysterically. She squeezed her eyes tight and braced herself for impact.

But instead of hitting the sidewalk, they merged into it, disappearing beneath the streets. Tookie rolled to the back of the pouch, legs over head. When she opened her eyes, they were in a narrow, dimpled tunnel with pale green walls. It looked to Tookie like the inside of a plant stem. The air smelled like it did before a thunderstorm. A loud *whomp-whomp-whomp* vibrated in her ears.

Tookie and the Scout shot forward even faster, the pouch bouncing up and down. Just a few seconds later, the fabric darkened, turning black and shiny. Muffled music filled the air, growing louder and louder, until Tookie recognized it as the T-DOD theme song, set to banjos.

A green-tinged fluorescent light appeared at the end of a tunnel. It grew brighter and brighter, and soon Tookie found herself face to face with cash registers, credit card machines, *Modelland* magazines, and hundreds of checkout lines. In front of her the Scout's paper-flat, gem-studded and now shiny-black-patent-leather-clad body rolled out of an enormous black rubber mechanism. All at once, Tookie understood: the Scout had just unrolled from a conveyor belt! They must be in some kind of store! Then she looked around.

"Oh. My. God!" Tookie gasped aloud. "I'm in—"

"*Bou-Big-Tique Nation walking ladies!*" a chipper-voiced man boomed over the PA. "*It looks like we've got a zirconia-encrusted Modelland Scout on the loose!*"

Thousands of girls screamed with excitement. Voices bubbled through the air.

"Where is she?" a girl screamed.

"I think I see her in aisle 453 near the purple lightbulb section!"

"No, she's in the auto parts aisle!"

Tookie looked through the pouch, taking in Bou-Big-Tique Nation for the first time. She'd read all about the place—it was the most convenient of convenience stores, for everyone *lived* inside the giant store! Small houses peppered the perimeter as far as

Tookie could see, and a wide upper-level balcony filled with larger houses encircled the entire place. To her left was a large section of motor homes for sale. A bored salesman sat under a sign that read READY TO TAKE YOUR FAMILY ON A BOU-BIG-TIQUE VACATION TOUR? EXPLORE THE OTHER SIDE OF THE NATION IN STYLE! The rest of the square footage contained mile upon mile of merchandise. But no one was shopping.

Everywhere Tookie looked, girls were walking.

They were in a different part of the country, in a different time zone. *It's still T-DOD here,* Tookie thought.

Scores of girls sashayed through the aisles, shoving each other and screeching whenever they crossed paths. Every girl wore a single color from head to toe. A curly-haired strawberry blonde with a gap between her teeth was dressed in all mint-green. A bronze-skinned girl wore metallic gold from her headband to her false eyelashes to her shoelaces.

Tookie's Scout was the only one doing any shopping at the Bou-Big-Tique. Her head darted left and right. Then the Scout homed in on a girl about an eighth of a mile away. It was weird—whatever the Scout saw and heard, Tookie could see and hear too. Like the tiny ticks in the tick farm display way down aisle 135 and the tapping of a girl's foot at a messy counter marked THE NATION'S CUSTOMER SERVICE, which was clear across the store.

The girl stood behind the counter. Her name tag said *Dylan.* Dylan was shaped like a bottle of Bou-Big-Tique cola and had a heart-shaped face. Her lips were full and naturally raspberry-colored, and her lavender-blue eyes sparkled. Her thick, healthy, golden-blond hair stretched to her butt, and she wore it in two ponytails, one on each side of her head. Her monochromatic outfit was the exact hue of her lavender-blue eyes. An apron with strips of blinking lights displayed BOU in bold across her chest, BIG in block letters down her right thigh, and TIQUE in script across her buttocks.

A little girl ran up to Dylan. "Dyl, why can't I walk? I've been practicing my strutty-strut." She twirled around Dylan.

"DeeDee, you know you can't walk today, babycakes. You're only five years old. Plus, Mama would go *cuh-ray-zee* on me if she saw you anywhere near that loony-bin farm of desperate chicks."

The little girl pouted. "Can I walk with you, then? Right here? She won't know."

Dylan smiled good-naturedly at her little sister. "Okay, baby-cakes. Stand on my feet."

As if on cue, a crash sounded down an aisle. "You stole my walking style!" a girl in an ivory outfit screamed to the strawberry blonde, lurching for her and knocking over a display of motor oil. Gallons of slick ooze were now creeping across the tile floor.

"Strawberries and Cream are mixing it up in a blender on aisle number one ninety-seven," cackled a voice over the loudspeaker. *"I wonder what that juicy smoothie is gonna taste like!"*

A female Bou-Big-Tique security guard bicycled down to break up the brawl and to keep the flow of walkers moving. Strawberry promptly punched the security guard in the eye, and a new brawl ensued.

The speakers crackled again. *"Girls and ladies, chicks and dames, the Strawberry on aisle one ninety-seven is one sexy knockout! We need assistance! Can someone please back that thang up and get over here now?"*

Dylan sighed and whispered something in her sister's ear, then marched toward the altercation. Swinging her hips to dodge frantic walkers and lifting her arms to squeeze between displays, Dylan looked graceful and very sexy even as she slid in the oil spill.

"Come on, ladies!" Dylan shouted at Strawberry, who was swinging punches at anyone nearby. Six instigating girls continued to prance and strut around the ruckus.

Dylan's mere presence seemed to calm Strawberry. Dylan put her hands on her hips, cleared her throat, and spoke like a referee. "Okay, so since the day you were born here in the Bou-Big-Tique hospital, nursed on wombat milk, you've dreamed of going to Modelland. Am I correct?"

The girls nodded.

"And has *Modelland* magazine ever mentioned that it prefers girls with high hopes of bein' the next welterweight champion of the BBT Nation?" Dylan asked.

The girls shook their heads.

"Then let's get back to fulfillin' ya dreams, ladies. Y'all are all busted-lookin' now from your championship fight, but pull your confidence from your insides. That's gotta count for somethin'." And then under her breath she muttered, "Cuz whoo, chile, y'all look *cuh-ray-zee*.

"Let's put one foot in front of the other," Dylan continued. "Swing them hips . . . not too much . . . don't slip in the oil . . . there ya go." The girls formed a line behind Dylan like an army following its captain.

"Now repeat after me," Dylan said. "If I don't get chose for Modelland's fam, they can kiss my butt, I won't give a damn!"

Swoosh. Tookie felt a tug, and suddenly the Scout made a beeline for Dylan's marching lineup.

All the girls saw her at once. "It's happening! Pick me! Pick me!"

But the Scout swept past all of them and stopped at Dylan. Dylan froze in her tracks, looking confused. The Scout extended her neck, pushing her face within a millimeter of Dylan's, just as she had done with Myrracle and Tookie. Satisfied, the Scout stepped back and reached toward Dylan.

Dylan stared at the Scout, in a bug-eyed trance. "You're . . ."

She looked behind her.

". . . here . . ."

She eyeballed an immense crowd forming silently around her and the Scout.

". . . for me?"

"They're taking Dylan!" a distant voice announced. A rolling wave of murmurs headed Dylan's way and grew louder.

Dylan's mouth dropped open. A look of understanding washed across her face. "But what about my brothers and sisters?" Dylan gestured to a tiny house near the dental and feminine-hygiene aisles. "I got four of each. I look after them."

Suddenly, a woman who looked just like Dylan, only about twenty years older, pushed through the spectators and hugged Dylan's shoulders. There were proud tears in her eyes. "Don't worry, baby. This is your time."

"Um, seriously, Mama? I'm going to Modelland? Me?" Dylan ran her hands over her generous hips, then shrugged. "Maybe a little—or should I say a lot—of some Bou-Big-Tique booty is just what Miss Modelland needs!"

The Scout nodded and the whole of the Bou-Big-Tique erupted into cheers and applause.

And then Dylan fainted, crumpling to the ground. Everyone gasped.

"Don't worry!" Dylan's mother waved her arms frantically. "She does that when she's excited or scared or in shock!"

The Scout reached down and lifted Dylan in her arms. Blue, green, and red fireworks exploded above them inside the store. The music pumped louder. Then the golden light that Tookie had seen in LaDorno appeared again. Suddenly, a foot rammed into Tookie's waist. Dylan was in the pouch next to her, just like that.

The blonde jumped when she saw Tookie. "Hey, girl! I'm Dylan! Whoa! I never seen eyes like *that* before. Interestin'. Who are you?"

Tookie flinched. She wasn't used to people paying attention to her. "Um, I'm Tookie," she fumbled. She tried to smile.

The pouch lurched to the left, and the Scout lifted off. Both girls tumbled about as they shot up through the roof of Bou-Big-Tique Nation. The last thing Tookie heard was a crackle over the loudspeaker.

"*All right, little losers . . . ,*" the announcer resumed. "*Tissues for your boo-hoos and bandages for your boo-boos can be found in aisle two twenty-twos!*"

11

Shiraz Shiraz

The pouch swept through the green portal again. After a few minutes, a vanilla-scented breeze tickled Tookie's nose. In seconds, the pouch began to fill with thick white goo.

"What in the heck is happenin'?" Dylan yelled.

"Uh . . ." Tookie tried to move, but the goo had already reached her waist. It rapidly filled the pouch, soon submerging even their heads. But weirdly, Tookie could breathe in it as easily as a fish could breathe in water. The warm goo grew thicker and thicker until it was difficult for her to move. Then she and Dylan were frozen in place.

Crack! Suddenly, the goo released them. Tookie and Dylan

tumbled, turned around, and saw a seven-foot candle busted open down the middle. The veiled Scout was still in front of them, flapping away now in a waxy diamond-covered bodysuit.

Dylan wiped some remaining goo from her eyes. "Hey, Scout lady! Did we for real just pop out of a *candle*?"

But the Scout didn't answer.

The sky above was an inky black. The lights of a village glowed far below. Candles in all shapes and sizes lit the entire town. Every house had an immense candle where the chimney should have been, and thin candles illuminated every street. A stiff breeze blew, and all the lights flickered in a surge. Some blew out but relit just seconds later.

"Ooh, look over there!" Dylan pointed past a hill to an area much brighter than the rest of the dimly lit town. "It looks like a fire's blazin'!"

The waxy smell in the air got stronger, as if someone had pushed a candle close to Tookie's nostrils. Suddenly Tookie knew exactly where they were.

"Canne Del Abra," she murmured in a tiny voice. She'd read about it in a book once. Canne Del Abra was the world's candle manufacturing center, the source of waxy light for all.

"For real for real?" Dylan looked excited. "We sell Canne Del Abra candles in aisles three eighty-five to four hundred and one! Sometimes I trek on over there durin' my break and inhale the fudge-scented ones! Don't you just love fudge?"

Tookie grimaced. Chocolate was practically the only food she didn't like.

Dylan's eyes goggled. "Girl, you don't like chocolate? You must be *cuh-ray-zee*!"

The Scout soared through the town's crooked cobblestone

streets. A makeshift market of tents and tables sold fire-starter kits and fire insurance. Down a narrow alley, a man scurried along pushing a cart filled with the scrunched stubs of burnt-out candles. A tall, olive-skinned teenage girl with nervous eyes rushed alongside him. "Aéï ëì æîï áùáéì îìëú, éååùåüøååî ëì æîï," she urged.

Tookie sat up straighter. They were speaking Labrian, the official language of Canne Del Abra, which she understood perfectly. The girl had just told the man, *Daddy, I'm so nervous. The Day of Discovery walk-off is about to start and my dress has still not arrived.*

A petite, muscular girl with thick curly hair, a face covered with freckles, and full lips ran toward the man and his daughter. She carried bundles and packages under her arms and wore a loose beige top that gaped at the neck, gathered shorts that flapped with her movements, and gladiator sandals whose straps looked on the verge of becoming undone. In Labrian, the girl sang:

"Your frock needed steam—
I'm sorry I'm tardy.
You're a Labrian dream,
The belle of this party."

After she finished the song, the messenger girl dropped the dress into the arms of the teen girl, who looked extremely relieved. "Thank you, Shiraz," the father said to the messenger girl, handing her a coin. Then she took off again.

Darting in and out of the streets clogged with Day of Discovery aspirants, the girl approached a decrepit door and slipped an envelope underneath. Then she was off once more, stuffing envelopes under every door she passed. Her footsteps pattered rapidly against the stone streets.

"Man oh man, that chick is quick," Dylan murmured.

The Scout swooped down and positioned herself right in Shiraz's path. They collided head-on. Undelivered mail fluttered out of Shiraz's fingers, but she hardly looked fazed to see the Scout. "Of course!" Shiraz spoke in Labrian, confidently extending her hand to the Scout. "You have come for me!" But the Scout didn't react.

The girl tried again. "You are here for me, yes?"

The Scout remained motionless.

"Ah, the language barrier," Shiraz said in heavily accented English. "I try to speak in the English. I am Shiraz Shiraz! Seven inches and four feet tall! Perfect for studies at the Modelland, yes?" Shiraz shook out her hair, straightened her clothes, and stood as tall as her small frame allowed.

The Scout extended her hand, and Shiraz grabbed it with lightning speed.

"Hello to the Modelland and goodbye to the Canne del Abra," she sang, her voice rising and falling melodiously. The pouch bulged, and Shiraz tumbled inside. And . . . *snap!* Into the green hole once more.

Shiraz noticed Tookie and Dylan and widened her eyes. "Oh no! Do not say you are my others."

"Your others?" Dylan repeated.

"The other girls who are part of the Modelland . . ." Shiraz waved her hands around, searching for the proper word.

"Experience?" said Dylan.

Shiraz shook her head briskly.

"Excursion?" Tookie said shyly.

Shiraz shook her head again.

"Discovery?" asked Dylan.

"Discovery, yes, yes." Shiraz brightened. Then she frowned. "But you two, you are not the beauty exceptional like Shiraz."

Dylan pursed her lips. "Ex-cuh-yuse ME! You may be all cute and little and can run as fast as an exotic feline in the plains, but hold up a sec, Miss Thang, cuz Miss Modelland, or should I say *the* Modelland"—Dylan mocked Shiraz—"don't have girls lookin' like you up in there either! And besides, you weren't even tryin' out, honey! Me and her saw you!"

Shiraz sniffed huffily. "The jealousies in your big body are burning like big dripless candle. I blow you out now." She puckered her lips and blew in Dylan's face.

Dylan's nostrils flared. "Oh no, this little dot-faced thang did NOT just bl—"

"Stop!" Tookie blurted out, surprising even herself. "Don't you realize none of us look like Modelland girls? Not one of us!"

Dylan set her jaw, but Shiraz just peered at Tookie, confused. Tookie repeated the tirade in Labrian. "Please don't fight," she added. "I see enough fighting at home."

Shiraz smiled slowly at Tookie, clearly amazed that Tookie could speak her language. But then she sat up straighter. "Well, they pick us for some reason."

"Yeah," Dylan said toughly. Although when she looked down at her broad thighs, an uncertain expression washed over her face. She looked up at Tookie. "Do *you* got a theory?"

Tookie stared through the pouch at the electric lightning snapping around them in the tunnel. "I don't know," she said. "I just don't know at all."

12

First Princess of SansColor

The pouch emerged into a sea of thin white strands. Some of them even entered the pouch, covering Tookie's head and drifting past her mouth. It tickled a little. Everyone started to giggle.

"What are we gonna pop outta *now*?" Dylan joked. "A horse tail?"

Through the mesh wall of the pouch, Tookie saw a bear-cave-sized hole and peeked in. Sticky, pasty gunk with peach fuzz was lodged inside. She frowned. "I think we're inside an ear!"

"How can we be inside ear?" Shiraz frowned. "Ear of giant? That make no sense!"

"This whole journey ain't made no sense," Dylan said.

Then a loud scream erupted. The girls jumped and looked at each other. "Was that you?" Dylan asked Tookie. Tookie shook her head. "Was that you?" Dylan asked Shiraz next. But Shiraz shrugged.

The pouch accelerated without warning, popping out of the sea of white. Behind them, Tookie saw a pale-skinned woman with long platinum locks screaming at the top of her lungs. She was also scratching her scalp and poking at her ears.

Dylan squinted. "You know, I think Tookie was right. I think we just popped out of that gray-haired woman's head."

Once again, the pouch emerged from the portal, giving the girls a view of a giant city in the distance. It was different from any city Tookie had ever seen. A clear protective dome covered the entire metropolis. The city was laid out in what appeared to be a perfect grid and reminded Tookie of one of her algebraic graphs. Not a speck of dirt marred the city streets. The most modern, high-tech buildings hovered about two stories above the ground, allowing pedestrians and vehicles unobstructed passage beneath them. Tube-shaped elevators zipped up, down, side to side, and diagonally on the structures' exteriors.

The Scout, now translucent and sparkling, floated through the city toward the sound of thumping drums. As they arrived at the edge of the city's square, a vast crowd of girls, all with stark-white hair and nearly translucent pale skin, moved with drill-team precision. Tookie, Dylan and Shiraz scrambled to the walls of the pouch so they could get a good view.

Tookie gasped. "SansColor," she whispered. She'd only read about it in books. It was a place that few ever got the chance to experience.

"Sans-cuh-what?" Dylan asked.

"Um, SansColor," Tookie mumbled, unaccustomed to people asking her direct questions.

About eight hundred pale-skinned girls wearing different types of blue uniforms and caps marched in formation. Along one axis, girls in teal marched together, doing hand and head movements in unison. Another group in navy pranced in the opposite direction. A third group, this one in aqua uniforms, sped along the intersecting axis, and a fourth group, wearing turquoise, headed for the middle of the navy group. The overall effect was of four colorful trains running along intersecting tracks, each set going in a different direction.

Tookie was riveted by the show. The navy and turquoise groups nearly crashed into the aqua and teal groups, but they veered off at the last second, making a precise right turn.

"Is Day of Discovery for them?" Shiraz whispered. Tookie nodded. Here, the T-DOD theme song had a drum-major beat. The walkers wore the expression common to every Modelland hopeful—just a bit toned down.

Dylan squinted at the crowd. "How do they stand out, for goodness' sakes? It's the battle of the blands!"

Everyone had the same coloring. Alabaster-skinned onlookers sat on bleachers, watching the performance. A brigade of pale white-blond soldiers stood at attention. Sitting in a plush oversized cobalt-blue chair in the middle of the stage was a platinum-blond woman. A tall, bored-looking girl stood at her side. Even the birds in the sky were pale: a flock of pure-white birds swooped past, their eyes cherry-red.

"Everybody here sick?" Shiraz whispered.

"No, they have albinism," Tookie whispered back.

"You mean they albinos?" Shiraz blurted out.

Tookie was pretty sure it was rude to call them albinos, but she kept her mouth shut, not wanting to seem like a know-it-all. The Scout swooped through the crowd. All the marching girls on the ground looked up and started to scream and stomp their feet, turning the synchronized parade into chaos. The platinum-haired woman in the thronelike chair frowned, popped her tongue, and rasped at the highly decorated soldier to her right. The soldier then uttered a short popping sound, which was repeated in unison by all the other soldiers down the line. All the girls immediately jumped back into formation.

"It's Colorian," Tookie whispered, listening to the distinct rasping, gurgling, popping, and sucking sounds. To the untrained ear, the language sounded like someone swallowing a bucket of raw oysters, but to Tookie, each tiny sound was beautiful. Every language was.

"That sound makes me want to clear my throat," Dylan said, wrinkling her nose.

The woman on the throne, evidently some kind of dignitary, blurted out more Colorian gurgles, slurps, pops, and rasps, but this time, to the Scout. Tookie was a little rusty with Colorian, but she could understand well enough. "I am the prime minister of SansColor. This is an occurrence we have been awaiting. A chosen one from SansColor at your Modelland might prove to be an effective ambassador for us."

"What that woman saying?" Shiraz murmured.

"Sorry, I don't speak gobbledygook," Dylan said.

"Actually, I do," Tookie said, and then translated what the prime minister had just said. The girls goggled at her, hanging on her every word.

The woman continued, and Tookie translated: "'If you can

guarantee safety for whomever you choose, you may select anyone who declares herself willing. That is my pledge.'"

The Scout bowed to the prime minister, and the crowd cheered. The tall, bored-looking girl who had been standing behind the throne stepped out to get a better look at the Scout. She had keen bright rose-colored eyes and an intense expression that made her appear highly intelligent. She probably was, Tookie thought—all people from SansColor were supposed to be off-the-charts geniuses.

Slowly, the Scout scanned the hundreds of girls in the procession, then floated over the prime minister's head and landed in front of the bored-looking girl, who stood poised like a statue. The Scout extended her bejeweled hand. The crowd gasped even louder.

The prime minister whirled around. "Not Piper!" she shouted, a vein in her pale forehead glowing blue-green. "Guardians!"

The soldiers aimed their weapons at the Scout and the pouch. "You cannot take her," the prime minister declared, standing protectively in front of the girl. "She is my daughter."

"Uh-oh," Dylan snickered. "We're in the middle of a royal mama-daughter showdown."

The Scout bowed respectfully and turned away to scan the crowd of other pale T-DODers. But the girl ran around her mother to face the Scout. "Madame, please do not listen to my ridiculous mother the *queen!*" The girl rolled her eyes. "I am Piper, First Princess of SansColor, and I have rights. I hereby accept admittance to Modelland!"

Piper's mother hurled a menacing popping sound at her daughter. "*I will not allow you to go to that mindless school on the mountain!*" Tookie translated.

"She said all that with that one sound?" Dylan said.

Before anyone could stop her, Piper grabbed the Scout's hand. Suddenly the pale girl was in the pouch too.

The prime minister's face twisted with shock and fury. "Fire!" she yelled.

The pouch jerked hard as the Scout flew away. The girls were thrown left, then right as the Scout spiraled frantically through the air.

She's dodging the bullets, Tookie thought, her heart in her throat as the soldiers fired their weapons again.

Whirling sideways, the pouch burst out of the bubble dangerously close to a war-torn concrete jungle that surrounded Sans-Color.

Thousands of ten-foot spears pointed at the bubble now shifted their aim to the Scout. A horde of demonic yellow-eyed jungle inhabitants stared at the pouch, roaring savagely.

One wrong move and the pouch would be ripped to shreds.

13

The Express Lane

"What in the name of wombat milk are those thangs?" Dylan screamed as the Scout lifted the pouch high above SansColor.

Piper, who was huddled on one side of the pouch away from the others, covered her eyes and shook her head violently. "The Le . . . the Le . . . ," she stammered.

"The LeGizzârds?" Tookie guessed. She'd read about them in the only Colorian history book at the Peppertown library. The creatures encircled the SansColor bubble, desperate to get inside. "They can't reach you here," she said, speaking in Colorian to Piper. "We're safe."

"You know my language?" Piper said, switching to English. "Impressive. And rare. What's your name?"

Tookie lowered her eyes. "Her name's Tookie," Dylan spoke for her. "She don't talk so much, but she knows what everybody else is sayin'—no matter what the language."

"Those things . . . the Gizzards?" Shiraz widened her big brown eyes. "Big balloon over your city to keep the Gizzards out, yes?"

Piper nodded. "Yes. The bubble protects us from the sun and the LeGizzârds. They live outside SansColor and thrive off Colorian sweetbreads."

"Sweetbreads!" Shiraz exclaimed, rubbing her tummy. "Would be nice now. Stomach is doing the growling."

"Think less pancakes and piecrust and more pancreas and thymus. Glands," Piper stated with a shiver. "Hundreds of Colorians have been butchered by the LeGizzârds, including my father. Although my mother, the *queen*"—at this Piper rolled her eyes—"lies to our people and says he succumbed to a deadly dermal disease."

Tookie's mouth made a small O. Dylan and Shiraz fell silent.

"My papa die too," Shiraz volunteered.

"Really? My daddy passed when I was a wee li'l thing." Dylan looked off into the distance.

Piper turned to Tookie. "What about you? Is your father alive?"

Tookie thought about Mr. De La Crème. "Um, I lost my father too. Just recently." It was, in a way, true. The four of them had at least one thing in common.

Then Piper straightened up and gave Dylan a closed-lipped, narrowed-eyed, strangely striking glare. For a moment, as the light caught her, she looked like a muse in a painting. "I see you staring at me."

Dylan looked caught. "I—"

"My people have little to no melanin in their skin, hair, and eyes," Piper explained in a clipped voice. "It makes us susceptible to excruciating sunburns and various terminal diseases—not to mention stares from people like you."

"I—I'm sorry," Dylan blurted out.

"Yeah, right." Piper turned away.

Tookie couldn't bear more fighting. "So you are really, um, a princess?" she asked, changing the subject.

Piper turned to her. A small smile formed on her pale face. "Not exactly. I just call myself that to annoy my dear mother. She's an elected official but acts like a queen. I actually campaigned for her opponent during the election."

"Really? Girl, you got you some guts!" Dylan applauded.

The pouch popped out into a windy, thunderous sky and swelled and dropped dramatically. The four girls looked out every side of the pouch to see if they could tell where they were. Thick fog covered the ground below. Voodoo-style drumbeats sounded from the ground. In the distance, they saw what they thought were the Modelland gates. A wide expanse of bright orange and red flames shot from the top of the mountain.

"Are the gates on fire?" Dylan asked shakily.

"No, no, no!" Shiraz clutched her head. "Cannot be happening!"

Dylan looked at her. "*What* can't be happenin'?"

Shiraz trembled with fear. "This is the real reason we are chosen for the Modelland!" She began to sing in a sweet, haunting voice:

"*On The Day of Discovery,*
When new recruits arrive,

A plan of debauchery
Where all but four survive.
Deformed and Defectives,
They torture and connive
Till no bones are connective.
They blaze the four alive."

When Shiraz finished, she looked at them. "When I was little girl in Canne Del Abra, that song we sang," Shiraz whispered. "You know sacrifice rumors, right? They true!"

Piper frowned. "*I* haven't heard anything about sacrifice."

"Really?" Dylan raised an eyebrow. "Those rumors run rampant all up and down the Bou-Big-Tique aisles. It goes somethin' like, Modelland brings in four lesser girls to brutally experiment on 'em—and then *sacrifice* 'em to some sort of ancient Gorgeous Goddess or somethin'."

Shiraz nodded frantically. "Yes, yes! Exactly that!"

"So . . . you believe *we're* this year's fresh meat?" Piper asked.

"Yes!" Shiraz squeaked. "Four crazy-looking girl in sack. They will burn us in ceremony!"

A loud thud echoed through the pouch. Dylan had fainted. She was now flat on her back, a ghastly expression frozen on her face. Tookie scooted over to check on her. "Dylan? Dylan!"

Dylan batted her eyelids open and mumbled, "I need a cleanup on aisle one ninety-seven. Oil spill!"

"Dylan, you're in the pouch," Piper said.

"But what about my siblings?" Dylan asked. "I got four of each."

Tookie's heart pounded fast. She'd heard of the sacrifice

rumors too. Everyone in Metopia whispered about them, debating whether they were true. Intoxibellas were even asked in interviews if the torture and murders really happened. Every Intoxibella denied it, but maybe that was because they didn't know—or worse, were in on it.

Reality started to set in. Tookie had known this was all too good to be true. Of course Modelland didn't want her, a dirt- and snot-eyed freaky-looking Forgetta-Girl.

"Look!" Piper screamed, pointing at the Diabolical Divide.

Tookie shot up. Lightning flashed every few seconds in time with the beating of the drums. With each strike, Tookie saw the evidence of lives somehow lost: a filthy gray hooded sweatshirt caught on a dead tree limb; a patent-leather backpack, its pockets ripped open, abandoned near a small stream; half a girl's white sneaker propped against a tree stump. The shoe looked as though something had taken a huge bite out of it. Tookie swore she saw blood smeared on the toe.

"Those items must be from the expired Pilgrims who caught the Plague," Piper said quietly.

"Expired?" Dylan shook her head. "The princess of SansColor is also the princess of understatement! Those Pilgrims aren't just expired, honey—they're *dead*!"

"They no Pilgrims!" Shiraz cried desperately. "They killed through sacrifice!"

The Scout made an abrupt incline. Only the glowing eye at the very tip-top of Modelland was visible. The thumping of the drums grew stronger, vibrating through Tookie's chest. The flames shot higher into the air, setting fire to a giant wall made of a mishmash of unidentifiable items.

Then the Gates of Modelland came fully into view. They were made of blue and gold metal and deeply engraved silver, and they had gears on both sides that seemed to be some kind of high-security locks. The Scout flew lower and lower. Tookie chewed feverishly on the inside of her lip. Her heart was pounding so fast she was sure it might soon rip from her chest. Could Shiraz be right? Were they flying to meet their doom?

The pouch's walls begin to drip liquid, lightly at first, but then the wetness poured down in sheets.

"They're gonna use this liquid to electrocute us!" Dylan cried.

Tookie felt a wet hand slip into hers. It was Dylan's. Piper grabbed Tookie's hand from the other side and Shiraz gripped Piper. Tookie squeezed her eyes shut, bracing for impact.

The pouch skidded on the ground with a loud, jarring thump. There was a ripping sound, and the pouch split open, spilling out Tookie and the girls. Tookie leaned down and grabbed the empty pouch in a panic, rummaging through it, trying to locate the Scout. But the fabric remained lifeless in Tookie's arms; the Scout was nowhere to be found.

An immense umbrella appeared out of nowhere and plopped into the middle of the pouch. "Oh, thank God," Piper said, grabbing it and holding it over her head, surely to block her sensitive skin from the sun's rays.

Suddenly, the strange voodoo drumming stopped. The silence was deafening. The girls looked around. They were in a large clearing atop green grass. Tookie ran her hands over the green and in the dim light realized it was not grass but fine fabric.

"Now what we do?" Shiraz whispered.

Something shot toward them through the darkness. When

Tookie's eyes adjusted, she saw a tall creature with a head shaped exactly like a human hand, with four fingers and a long thumb. The palm of the hand contained pale blue eyes, two holes for a nose, and two full lips. Below the strange hand-head was the body of a normal human.

"Hello, mesdemoiselles! *Je m'appelle* Guru Applaussez, ze head of ze couture department," the creature said in a thick Très Jolie accent, smiling with its broad mouth full of perfectly straight white teeth. "I am beyond *excité* you have arrived early. Your lack of tardiness deserves a round of applause, *oui?*"

With a squeal of pleasure, the creature leaned all the way to the left and hit its hand-head to its left palm and then did the same on the right side with its right palm. Just looking at this bizarre ovation made Tookie dizzy.

"That thang gives new meanin' to the phrase 'talk to the hand,'" Dylan whispered. Tookie couldn't help but giggle.

"Ah! You are ze seamstresses I ordered, no?" The hand looked excited. "Ze Intoxistakes theme this year is Insects of the Bush, and I need all ze extra helping hands I can get. Seeing as I only 'ave three." It paused for effect, a coy smile on its face. "Now let's get to work, *oui?*"

Yellow smoke began to swirl around the girls' feet. Shiraz jumped back. "Sacrifice is starting! I too young and spry to die!"

The other girls yelped and grabbed each other's arms. Tookie could barely breathe she was so afraid. But as she grasped the girls hard, she suddenly felt one small note of reassurance: she wasn't going to die alone. The other three actually wanted to face death with her.

The smoke rose higher, fully encircling them. Tookie squeezed her eyes shut. *At least I had an adventure at the very end,* she told herself. She could feel the hot flames on her cheeks. The smoke tickled her nostrils.

Suddenly, the smoke flew away, coming to a halt in a wall-like clump a few feet from the girls. Slowly, the cloud-wall reassembled, forming a door of black smoke. The door flipped open. Behind it was a black chamber full of angry, swirling wind. Tookie's hair blew backward. Piper gripped the umbrella tightly, but it turned inside-out anyway. Dylan and Shiraz covered their eyes.

A nude figure emerged through the doorway, stalking toward them with a rhythmic pace. With each step, the tornado wind whipped even faster. Then the figure raised its arms. Tookie felt a tugging sensation under her feet. The pouch whipped out from underneath them and streamed into the figure's fingertips.

Dylan's mouth trembled. She looked like she was about to faint. "What in the heck is goin' on?" she murmured.

Smaller pieces of fabric shot from the figure's fingers and into the air, hanging weightlessly over the girls. The strips of material tumbled and lashed around their heads, ripping and combining violently into undergarments of every color and fabric. A white lace girdle whipped past. A purple merry widow floated by, followed by a chartreuse camisole, marigold briefs, and blue bloomers. The unmentionables floated in front of the dark figure that had appeared at the door. Suddenly, a long, bejeweled, tentacle-like necklace appeared.

"Our Scout!" Tookie breathed.

The Scout chose a pair of very unsexy blue bloomers and put them on her bare body. All of the other intimates were sucked back into the Scout's fingers.

And then, *thwap!* More garments shot out of the Scout's fingers: a one-shouldered, bias-cut burnt-orange chemise, a maroon eelskin jacket with severe shoulder pads, a fire-engine-red felt porkpie hat, a pair of metal-studded heather-gray ankle boots. It was like they were in a zero-gravity department store.

The items spun around and around. The Scout's jeweled appendages acted like hands and arms, moving the choices around into unconventional ensembles. When the jewels had settled on a preferred selection, they thrust the winning selection onto the Scout. The remaining choices were sucked up into the Scout's fingers once more.

The Scout was left wearing a plunging white V-neck blouse with so many odd angles to it, Tookie couldn't quite figure it out. A high-waisted, corseted indigo-blue fine-woven cotton skirt barely covered her butt. Boots with alternating strips of leather and canvas laced up just above her knees, chocolate-brown swirls decorating the material.

Then the bedazzled jeweled tentacles burned bright red. In a flash, they melted into one, forming a belt of golden yellow fabric that rested snugly on the Scout's hips.

"It's her Sentura," Tookie whispered.

"Amazing," Dylan managed to say.

The Scout lifted both hands to her face and peeled her veil slowly from the bottom up. The girls oohed and aahed.

For she had shimmering caramel-colored skin, the very skin that had made trillionaires of quite a few CEOs of skincare companies.

Full, soft-looking lips with the deep cupid's bow that had inspired so many girls to wear Glow-Glow lip gloss.

Large emerald eyes with mile-long lashes that seemed to look into your soul, knowing exactly what you desired—needed—at any given time.

Tookie gasped. Could it be? She looked around at the others, and they were awestruck too.

It was the celebrated, renowned, mythical Intoxibella.

Ci~L.

"Sorry, I was sweating buckets back there." The Intoxibella sniffed her armpits. "Yuckity yuck! I totally forgot to put on my sweat stopper this morning. I'm a girl who can't skip a day, if you know what I mean!"

"You—you're . . . ," Dylan stammered.

"The most distinguished . . . ," Piper began, but was too stunned to finish.

"The Ci~L!" Shiraz summed up.

Tookie gaped, feeling completely unworthy of having a conversation with a creature so regal and divine. Ci~L, the last Triple7, a real 7Seven-7 with all seven Intoxibella powers, was the one who had taken them to the ends of the earth. The one who had taken *her* hand instead of Myrracle's. And finally, the mystery was solved! WHERE THE HELL IS Ci~L? Why, she was right *here*!

"Yes, I'm Ci~L," the Intoxibella said, a calm, reluctant smile fluttering across her lips. She stared at Dylan, Piper, and Shiraz in amazement. It seemed like something clicked in her mind, and her expression totally changed from serene to something much darker. "Hendal, Katherine, Woodlyn! I can't believe it." She ran up to Dylan and put her ear to Dylan's mouth. Then she moved to Shiraz and placed her fingers on her wrist. Finally she touched Piper's chest, where her heart was. "You all made it."

The three girls looked at each other confusedly. *Huh?*

Ci~L noticed Tookie and coolly extended her hand. Her welcome was far less enthusiastic.

"*Excusez-moi!*" Guru Applaussez stood behind them. "I hate to break up this party, but *j'ai besoin de* these seamstresses. Ci~L, thank you for transporting them so swiftly. I will take them now."

Ci~L shielded the girls protectively. "With all due respect for the world of handmade couture, as well as for you, Guru Applaussez, these young ladies are not dressmakers, they are tastemakers—of tomorrow. Bellas of Modelland."

The girls exchanged a shocked glance. *Bellas?* Everyone knew that was the Modelland term for *students.* So they *weren't* sacrifices?

"*Comment?*" Guru Applaussez recoiled from the girls as if they had an airborne illness. "Look, sweetie dear, I am *fatigué* and am going to go nurse my hand-ache. So please stop this *jovialité* and have my new seamstresses report to my *couturier.*" And with a beauty queen wave of its hand-head, the Guru turned and left.

"Don't mind Applaussez, girls," Ci~L murmured. "The Guru's a bit frustrated to have been born with three hands while the rest of the fam has four."

Tookie's gaze was still fixed on Ci~L. She just couldn't believe this was happening. Beyond being awed by Ci~L's worldwide fame, Tookie actually *respected* her the most of all the Intoxibellas. She actually had substance behind her heavily made-up face and accessory-adorned body. Ci~L was a legendary spoken-word-poetry-slam champion, spouting many controversial poems that even some of the snobbiest literary critics praised. She gave keynote addresses at college graduations, speaking about her many interpretations of human beings' physicality. Ci~L was an icon, an Intoxibella unafraid to speak her mind.

But then Tookie realized something: Why was Ci~L a T-DOD Scout? Was it a demotion? After all, everyone knew that Scouts weren't 7Sevens—they were second-string Modelland Bellas who'd tried to reach 7Seven status but missed it by a hair.

The other girls were gaping at Ci~L too. "How did that cheer about Ci~L go?" Dylan asked, her eyes bright. She raised her arms overhead, fists clenched. *Give me a big C . . ."*

". . . *a little* I, *a TILDE!"* Shiraz joined in, executing the cheer-leading moves that went along with the chant. To signify the tilde, the squiggle character at the center of Ci~L's name, the girls made a wiggly shape with the flats of their hands.

"Come on, Tookie!" Dylan said, bumping Tookie's hip. "What's the next line?"

Tookie bit her lip, still feeling shy. "Uh, I think it's *throw me a lanky lanky lanky long L."* She remembered the rhyme from the playground of B3.

"Atta girl!" Dylan whooped. *"Simple and clean, no! But not a tongue twista. That's the way way way way way you spell SEE-EL!"*

"Please stop," Ci~L said flatly.

Dylan lowered to her knees in front of Ci~L. "I've recorded all of your speeches and poems. You're so . . . so . . . powerful."

"Please don't bow down to me. That worship stuff is uh . . . kinda not my thing," Ci~L said, pulling Dylan up. "Plus, you'll have plenty of kowtowing to do today, so spare your delicate knees. Oh, which reminds me. I have to recite the welcome crap."

She straightened up and cleared her throat. "Welcome to Modelland," Ci~L said in a monotone, as if on autopilot. "You nouveau Bellas are among the chosen few. But your place in the Land is not promised. It is yours to earn, every day, every minute, every second . . ."

Ci~L trailed off. "Ugh! You know what? I can't recite that mess with a straight face. Besides, you'll hear it all again momentarily. From a stone bitch."

The Intoxibella then started to scratch her arms and legs. "Ugh, this getup is itchy as hell, man." And with that, she shook her body and her avant-garde skirt, shirt, and boots instantly transformed into a T-shirt, ripped jeans, and dirty sneakers.

"Girl, you are so *real*. Recite a poem about us, Ci~L!" Dylan begged.

Ci~L raised a perfectly plucked eyebrow. "You want me to freestyle right here? Right now? Nuh-uh."

"Then perform one of your 7Seven powers!" Piper urged. "I'd love to see Excite-to-Buy . . . or maybe Multiplicity."

"Honey chile, you've already *seen* the powers at work," Ci~L said nonchalantly. "How do you think we got to Modelland? In a bus?"

"The teleportation and flying!" Shiraz cried, thrusting her chest out and stretching her arms behind her in a V.

"Anyway, there's no time for power show-and-tell or a slam now," Ci~L said. "But hopefully I'll be seeing you again if you pass the torture tests."

Tookie swallowed hard. *The torture tests?* What did *that* mean? Ci~L turned for the smoke door. The winds and swirling dust had subsided, revealing the colossal wall the girls had seen from the sky. It was a mash of antiquated musical instruments, ragged slices of art canvases, clothes and outdated accessories of seasons past, and an immense assortment of architectural pieces. Marble arms and legs jutted out from the bulkhead, making it difficult to stand too close. Beyond stood the carved gold, blue, and silver Modelland gates. Eight immense gears were at each corner of two gigantic doors. The gears were connected to steel arms—literally arms with forearms, hands, and fingers—that crossed in the center of the two doors, holding them tightly in place.

A chorus of unseen women's voices ululated, *"Hel-hell-helllllloooo. And wel-wel-welcome to Modelland. . . ."*

More people appeared around them. Other Scouts and their pods, pouches, and people-pockets landed on the soft fabric grass. Ci~L led Tookie and the others to a line of new Bellas standing in front of a peculiar mosaic-tiled face. Its features seemed to shift depending on where you were standing, much like looking in a fun-house mirror: to the left or right, the face looked distorted and terrifying, but when you stood directly in front of it, the face was three-dimensional and breathtaking.

"What we do here?" Shiraz asked.

"This is where you register," Ci~L explained.

The girls watched as an ash-blond Bella approached the mosaic face. "Veekay of NorDenSwee," she said, referring to an icy land.

The mosaic face abruptly sprang to life, its bulbous eyes opening. "Validated!" it yelled. A green light appeared, a striped barrier lifted, and Veekay advanced to a holding area beyond the gates.

"Franca of Cappuccina," the next girl in line said.

"Authenticated!" the face deemed. Franca joined Veekay.

"Kamalini of Chakra," said a girl wearing an intricately embroidered chartreuse wrap dress made of endless yards of the finest silk. One arm was full of gold bangles, and her eyes were decorated with a SMIZE, which fluttered every time she blinked.

"Documented!"

A girl with toned golden thighs stepped forward. "Bibiana of Terra BossaNova."

"Confirm-iated!" The face scrunched up, seeming to know full well that *confirmiated* wasn't a word.

Tookie, Piper, Dylan, and Shiraz moved up the line. In front of her, Tookie spotted a familiar girl with pin-straight auburn hair in a golden-yellow dress with matching shoes. She had brilliant white teeth and an attitude as thick as the afternoon air in Peppertown. Tookie sucked in a breath. *No. This can't be happening.*

"Zarpessa of Metopia," the auburn-haired girl trilled haughtily.

"Corroborated!"

"Zarpessa?" Tookie blurted out.

Zarpessa turned at the sound of her name. Her eyes clapped on Tookie's, and horror rippled across her lovely face. Then, without saying a word, she turned and marched to a holding area.

So she did *see me at the Dumpsters,* Tookie thought. *Clearly, Zarpessa doesn't want to relive that moment.*

A few more girls passed on through, one of them a tall raven-haired girl wearing way too much makeup and a sequined mini-skirt that was hacked all the way up to her butt cheeks; nothing but two giant faux diamonds covered her chest. "Chaste Runnings, from Beignet," she lilted seductively into the mosaic face. She shimmied a little, showing off her round, pert butt.

Then it was Tookie's turn.

"Tookie from . . . um . . . Metopia," she whispered at the mosaic.

"Louder!" the face boomed.

"Tookie . . . uh . . . Metopia? Peppertown?" she said a teensy bit louder.

The face paused. *Here it comes,* Tookie thought. *The revelation of the Day of Discovery administrative error!*

The painting smiled awkwardly and yelled, "Sub—um . . . substantiated." But it didn't sound so sure of its decision.

Before the face could change its mind, Ci~L ushered Tookie into the holding area. Then Ci~L walked back to the face, leaned down, and whispered something into where its ears would be if it had any. The other Scouts accompanying their Bellas stood on their toes to see what the famed Triple7 Intoxibella was doing.

At first, Ci~L laughed, as if the face had told her a joke, but then Tookie noticed that Ci~L's lips weren't moving—she wasn't really whispering anything to the mosaic at all. What was happening, however, was that one of her jeweled tentacles was making contact with the face. A surge of sparks traveled from the tip of the tentacle to the mosaic's mouth. The face looked temporarily stunned. All of its tiles were suddenly scrambled.

"Shiraz, Dylan, Piper!" commanded Ci~L. "Come up here. NOW!"

Shiraz approached the face. "Say your name, Shiraz," Ci~L urged.

"Shiraz, from—"

"Vindicated!" the face trilled, before Shiraz could finish.

Then Ci~L yanked Dylan up to the face. "Name!" Ci~L insisted.

"Dylan, from Bou—"

"Predicated!"

Ci~L pushed Piper forward and positioned her dead center. "Speak now!" Ci~L barked.

"Pi—"

"Justificated!"

The tiles fell back into place. Other Bellas stepped up, not even noticing anything was amiss. Ci~L shoved Piper, Dylan, Shiraz, and Tookie into the holding area. She pushed them so hard, Tookie tripped over her big feet, nearly tumbling to the grass. Dylan helped her up.

"What was *that* about?" Dylan whispered to Tookie.

"What, don't you like the express lane?" Ci~L snapped harshly . . . but then winked.

Tookie stared at her, puzzled. Was Ci~L on their side or not?

The last of the new Bellas marched into the holding area. Tookie counted one hundred girls in total. She also kept a running tally of the number of SMIZEs. Six. The seventh was Myrracle's. She was supposed to be here, not Tookie.

Suddenly, the giant gears on the gates began to turn, generating a deep rumble that Tookie could feel in her feet. Slowly, the gates opened inward.

Ci~L bent down to the girls. "All-righty then. My job here has been completed, for now. Back to the torture chamber for me. And the beginning of it for you."

Shiraz looked alarmed. "Torture for you *and* us?"

Ci~L shrugged. "Beyond your wildest nightmare. And as for me, I got myself into this mess."

"What mess?" Tookie inquired, hoping she didn't sound prying or rude.

But Ci~L just turned away. With a flash of golden light, a hole opened in the ground. Ci~L fell backward into it and was gone.

One by one, all the other Scouts melted or flashed away, leaving the new Bellas alone. The gates continued to roll open. Tookie squinted to make out her very first glimpse of Modelland.

Through the still-narrow slit, she saw that it was like nothing she could ever have imagined.

14

Arancia Rossa di Sicilia

The gates creaked open to reveal a path through a large entrance hall. Lining the entrance on both sides of the hall were about twenty statues of women, each more glorious and stunning than the one before.

Tookie, Shiraz, Dylan, and Piper slowly walked down the path, awestruck and a little frightened. The statues were massive, and all were in very distinctive poses. One with chin-length hair was doing a split midair. Another with a high ponytail that draped all the way to the ground had limbs that roped around her body like a pretzel. A sign above the figures read IF YOU DO NOT RESPECT US, WE WILL SHAKE, RATTLE, AND ROLL YOU.

Who are they? Tookie thought. What *are they?*

After they exited the hall of statues, they entered a large clearing. Laser fireworks zinged above them, forming the letters B-I-E-N-V-E-N-U-E one at a time, then W-I-L-L-K-O-M-M-E-N, and finally B-E-N-V-I-N-G-U-D-A. The words fluttered to dust, which tickled the girls when it touched their skin. The scent of rich, sweet citrus filled Tookie's nostrils, making her mouth water.

"I smelling something good!" Shiraz waved the scent in the air toward her nose.

"It's *arancia rossa di Sicilia*," Piper explained clinically.

"Arancha-what?" Dylan snorted at the air hard.

"I think it's blood orange," Tookie said tentatively. "The pulp looks like blood, but they taste so good."

"This place is so beautiful, it's blowin' my mind! Don't faint, girl," Dylan chanted to herself. "Don't faint."

A crystalline all-glass skyscraper stood before them. It towered high into the sky, shaped like a giant *M*. The building glowed from the inside, as though radioactive.

"Have you ever seen anything like this?" Shiraz sang out, stretching her arms and spinning around.

"I'll give ya my firstborn if ya stop singing everything," Dylan muttered, but then she shot Shiraz a good-natured smile.

A line of ten girls in matching attire waited in the distance. They looked older than the new Bellas and appeared to be from all different parts of the world—some had blond hair, others had hooded eyes, and others had ebony skin. Strangely, however, their different skin tones and hair colors aside, they kind of resembled each other. They wore two-tone-yellow pointy-shouldered vests and matching leotards over tight pants, their Senturas looped around their waists twice. Shiny diamond-shaped badges fastened to their chests read MODELLAND BELLA TOUR GUIDE.

The troop of uniformed girls surveyed Tookie, Dylan, Shiraz, and Piper as they neared, shooting questioning looks at each other. The question was obvious: what are those four doing here?

I'm wondering that myself, Tookie thought nervously.

"Come, come!" the tour guides called to the advancing girls. Tookie headed toward them. Smooth, seamless gold paved the plaza in front of the M building. As she began to cross it, the ground started to move a bit, wobbling and shimmering ever so slightly.

"Reflection inspection!" one of the uniformed girls bellowed. Suddenly, the gold surface bubbled and curved upward around the line of uniformed girls. With astonishing speed, the material melded into perfect three-dimensional gold versions of each of them.

"Oh my Lordy." Dylan clutched her breast.

The guides surveyed themselves in their gold reflections, fixing a hair out of place and a smudge of lipstick. The liquid-gold substance mimicked them exactly, a mirror image in three dimensions. Then the guides' reflections quickly dropped back into the ground, which reverted to a flawless, smooth, caramel-colored surface.

"Now you!" one uniformed girl said to the cluster of new Bellas.

Tookie stuck her toe on the surface. Solid. She walked slowly onto the gold. The other girls from her pouch followed suit. As the golden liquid rose before them, Dylan started to move and pose. *She's good,* Tookie thought. But then, instead of mimicking Dylan's body, the gold formed a giant question mark.

Tookie looked at her own golden shape. It had become a question mark too. So had Piper's and Shiraz's. Every other girl in the plaza had a normal gold doppelganger standing before them.

"Ha! The ground is more confused about them than I am!" Zarpessa snorted. The girl named Chaste, whose diamond pasties were threatening to slip off, snickered.

"I've never seen the Reflection Pool use punctuation before," said a voice behind Tookie.

Tookie and her three pouch-mates spun on their heels. Behind them stood a strikingly beautiful, incredibly tall girl wearing the two-tone leotard uniform. She had long, shiny reddish hair with lots of bounce and body, dark brown almond-shaped eyes that turned up in a friendly way, and a smile on her face that made her look as if she was on the verge of bursting into laughter—the kind that laughed with you, not at you.

"Excuse me," the pretty girl said. "I'm looking for Tookie De La Crème from Peppertown, Metopia." She had a BayJingle accent.

"Um . . . that's me," Tookie said shyly.

The pretty girl squinted, perplexed. "You're Tookie? You look . . . uh . . . well, anyways, hi! I'm so happy I found you!" She thrust out her hand. "I'm ZhenZhen. It is my destiny to be your Modelland Bella tour guide today." Then she smiled slyly and whispered, "Well, maybe not exactly my destiny. I swapped my group for yours. But hey, destiny's what you make it, right? I mean, you flew here in Ci~L, didn't you? I just had to meet you. I'm kind of obsessed with her."

Before ZhenZhen could finish gushing, Guru Applaussez, which was passing in a rush, yelled, "ZhenZhen, authenticity and originality are *très importants* to couture, as they are to identity! Return your *cheveux* to its color of origin or you'll be removed from Bella tour guide duties!"

ZhenZhen rubbed her forehead and blinked, as if she was creeping quickly toward a panic attack. "But I look best with *this* color."

Guru Applaussez's hand-head reddened. "If you do *not* return to your natural color, I will send you to the BellaDonna."

"Okay, okay!" And then ZhenZhen's hair morphed from soft reddish-brown waves to pin-straight, waist-length coal-black hair parted down the middle. "Ugh, I hate when they make me change my hair back," she said morosely. "Look, if Ci~L had long black hair, I wouldn't mess with Mother Nature, okay? So it's not about what looks best on *me*. It's about what looks best on *Ci~L*, which in turn looks best on *me*."

Dylan was eyeing ZhenZhen like she should be locked up in a mental facility.

"Ci~L select us too!" Shiraz said enthusiastically, pulling Piper and Dylan in for a tight hug.

ZhenZhen grinned at all of them, snapping out of her funk. "*Lucky!* You all spent intense, intimate time with Ci~L. You got to speak with her, to touch her, to be chosen by her. If I could roll back time and be newbie Bellas like you all and get swooped up in Jingle Square by Ci~L, oh goodness golly gracious, that would be amazing! When I was eleven, I actually tried to change my name to *Zhen~L,* but my parents refused to let me.

"Okay, on with the Bella tour." ZhenZhen pulled her shiny, diamond-shaped badge from her chest and peered at it. With a series of clicks and clacks, the badge unfolded until it was the size of a magazine.

ZhenZhen studied it intently. "So, Tookie, I've got your name here, but your buddies aren't on my list. That's weird." She rubbed the surface of the card as if that would somehow make the names appear.

Shiraz, Dylan, and Piper looked at one another nervously. Tookie felt a stab of worry too—she didn't want anything to happen to them.

Then ZhenZhen's eyes widened at something across the courtyard. Ci~L had appeared once more, standing next to a glowing building. She raised one jeweled tentacle at ZhenZhen and gave her an eerie, wide-eyed look.

"Uh, wait a minute." ZhenZhen held the card out. "There are three new names here: Dylan of Bou-Big-Tique Nation, Piper of SansColor, and Shiraz Shiraz of Canne Del Abra. Look at that!"

The girls let out sighs of relief. Tookie wondered if Ci~L had had something to do with it. But she couldn't think about it for too long; when she looked up again, ZhenZhen was halfway across the courtyard, leading them over to a group of new recruits.

This group of girls inspected Dylan, then Shiraz, then Piper, then Tookie. Their eyes grew narrower and their brows more furrowed. Whispers began.

"Oh, sister, we are getting BitterBalled by those girls," Dylan muttered.

"BitterBalled?" Piper raised an eyebrow.

"BitterBalls are in aisle five ninety-two at the Bou-Big-Tique," Dylan explained. "They clear up all sorts of gastrointestinal problemos, but Lordy, the expression your face gets stuck in while your belly is gettin' healed is a stinker."

"I see your point, Dylan," Piper admitted. "These young ladies probably think we cheapen the prize."

ZhenZhen and the girls stopped at the group Zarpessa and

ModelLand

Chaste were in, which didn't have a Bella tour leader. "I'm head tour guide," ZhenZhen said, "and I'll take you two groups from here. Stay with me! I wouldn't want you to get clawed on your first day." She laughed nervously.

Clawed? Tookie wondered.

ZhenZhen led the girls down a long, crescent-shaped path toward the left side of the M building. "The entire golden area in front of the M building is called the M plaza," she recited. "The M building houses the BellaDonna and all of the Modelland administration and who knows what else. One must never go inside unless explicitly invited."

She gestured to her left. "All the way down this path and directly on the other side of the M building is the O, where later the BellaDonna will welcome you. Can you guess what it stands for?"

"Ovaries?" Chaste called out slyly.

"Obi?" tried a girl from Fuji.

"Ox tongue!" Shiraz yelled.

"Oddballs?" Tookie whispered.

"No!" ZhenZhen grinned. "The O is for . . ." She drew it out, pausing for effect. "Opera!"

Shiraz's eyes nearly popped out of her head. "Opera? We get to do the singing here at the Modelland too? *Oohwee!* I sing lead!"

"Unfortunately, Shiraz," ZhenZhen lamented, "you will *not* be the star of *that* show."

Then ZhenZhen launched back into her tour script. "The BellaDonna is the latest generation of the Modelland royal line and has commanded the school for ten years. The statues that lined the entrance hall? Past BellaDonnas."

The group strolled down the path until they came upon a

circle of floating images of the world's current most famous Intoxibellas. There was a special section for the newest 7Sevens, the ones Tookie had seen at the demonstration the other day: Evanjalinda, Simone, Sinndeesi, Leemora, Katoocha, Bev Jo, and Exodus. Seeing Exodus's name sent a pang through Tookie's chest. *Our escape plan. Lizzie.* What was she doing now? Where had she gone?

"Why that one all staticky?" Shiraz whispered, pointing to one.

"Maybe I can fix it," Piper suggested. "Who is it?"

ZhenZhen bit her lip. "It's my glorious and most magnificent Ci~L. But I can't speak about why her image is fuzzy. It hurts my heart too much."

Tookie and the girls looked at each other. "Please tell us," Tookie said.

"God, don't you know anything?" Zarpessa piped up, catching up to them from the back of the group. "Ci~L went rogue. My colorist's aunt's sister's grandfather's daughter knows her, and she said Ci~L lost her mind trying to beat to her own crazy drum."

ZhenZhen winced. "Oh, please don't say it like that."

But Zarpessa breezed on, enjoying knowing something the others did not. "And my uncle's daughter's best friend's designer buddy told me that the reason Ci~L is back at Modelland is because she's being punished for being off message."

Chaste looked impressed at Zarpessa's knowledge. All the girls in the group chattered with this new bit of gossip. Tookie's ears burned with the sounds of different languages swarming around her.

Words from Kwaito, the land of safaris and tribal dance filled the air. "I wonder how they're punishing her. . . ."

Phrases from TooLip, the land of windmills, engulfed her. "Do you think she'll lose her Intoxibella status forever?"

Two girls muttered in Pyramidian, "Has Ci~L truly lost her mind?"

Chaste snorted. "Ci~L's gone loony. She brought *them* here." She gestured to Tookie and the others. BitterBalls for sure.

"Enough gossip!" ZhenZhen said angrily. She bolted ahead of the group, holding herself stiffly, and turned down a narrow sidewalk off the main path. The group stood in front of an enormous wall of twisted trees and plants with rapidly moving large bulbs and ivylike vines. All made of fabric, Tookie assumed. As they watched, the vine wall sprouted immense burgundy- and eggplant-hued metal thorns.

ZhenZhen dove straight toward the thorns. Right before they should have impaled her, the thick vines parted, revealing a new path made of mirrorlike stones. "Come on, girls!" she called over her shoulder. "You are now entering Beautification Boulevard! This is where all your classes will occur, assuming, of course, that you survive THBC!"

"THBC?" Tookie swallowed. "What's that?"

ZhenZhen turned around, her face reddening. "Actually, I'm not supposed to mention it," she whispered. "I really wish I could tell you, but Guru Gunnero likes to keep it secret. I'll give you one teensy hint: it's a special test not for the fashion weak or faint of heart."

Tookie dared a glance at the other girls. Shiraz, Piper, Dylan, and quite a few others in the group looked nervous. Zarpessa, on the other hand, shrugged nonchalantly, tossing her auburn hair over her shoulder.

Then ZhenZhen whipped around and continued to walk. "Beautification Boulevard consists of dozens of distinct structures, each designed specifically for one class," she explained. "Each structure's architecture directly correlates to the subject matter you experience within them. Ci~L was a master at all of her courses on this row. To this day, not one student has surpassed her extraordinary skill."

Zarpessa flounced the ends of her yellow dress. "That's because I just got here."

Tookie looked down the boulevard. At the far end was a large, open-work structure shaped like an immense egg. A narrow wooden plank traversed its center and there was a scoreboard. Spectator seats lined the inside of the frame.

What kind of game is that for? Tookie wondered.

"That," ZhenZhen said, pointing at the egg building as though reading Tookie's mind, "is the OrbArena, where pretty boys and gorgeous girls battle in ManAttack, the one class you'll have with our brother male modeling academy, Bestosterone."

"Bring it on!" Chaste crowed. "Can we do that today?"

"No, we never know when ManAttack will happen," Zhen-Zhen said. "It's always a surprise. And anyway, girls, males are accessories at Modelland. Don't ever forget: we're the stars, not the boys. Yeah, they do some modeling stuff, but basically we have them here to work for us: build our buildings, provide security and eye candy . . . that sort of thing."

They continued down the boulevard, passing more fantastical and unique structures. A windowless plaid cube, about the size of a department store, balanced on the very tip of one of its corners. To the left, Tookie saw a ship bobbing on a body of water that seemed to appear from nowhere. Through the round portholes, she could just make out a class in session. A group of girls stood in neat, even rows, making bizarre faces in unison.

"That boat building is where CaraCaraCara class takes place," ZhenZhen explained.

Tookie wasn't sure if she should feel excited or alarmed. She'd never been on a boat before—the only opportunity to go on the water in Metopia was on a yacht in LaDorno, and only the rich got to do that.

Then Tookie swiveled around and stared in the other direction down the boulevard, fixing her eyes on an immense octagon-shaped course broken up by high walls, gravel pits, flamethrowers, ropes that whipped indiscriminately, jutting corners, sections of runways, and, of all things, spinning dance floors. As if that wasn't confusing enough, thumping trance music began to pump loudly from the space.

Shiraz started bopping to the beat. Dylan smirked. "You really can't help yourself, can you?"

Tookie watched Shiraz, feeling a familiar pang. Shiraz's dancing reminded her of Myrracle. But then, Shiraz was much more pleasant to be around.

"So what is that place? Tookie asked ZhenZhen after the impromptu dance party had ended. "It looks like an obstacle course or something."

"You're very close." ZhenZhen smiled at her. "The final-year Bellas—that would be me and my class—train on that course for the 7Seven Tournament."

Dylan raised her eyebrows. "I didn't know the 7Sevens actually trained. I thought it was just about who was the prettiest."

"Which certainly wouldn't be you," Zarpessa said under her breath.

"The prettiest?" ZhenZhen giggled, addressing Dylan's

question. "Oh, Dylan, haven't you seen that pretty here is just a commodity, that every girl is easily exchangeable for the next Bella? There's so much more to the equation."

"Equation?" Piper looked excited. "If it deals with mathematics, specifically algorithmic statistics, I'll be an immense help to you all!"

Zarpessa rolled her eyes. "Where did Ci~L dig up this idiot savant?" she whispered, loud enough for everyone to hear. Chaste giggled.

"There's no need to worry about the 7Seven Tournament now," ZhenZhen assured them, ignoring Zarpessa. "You're years away from competing."

Then Tookie noticed a girl wearing a long, flowing giraffe-print gown and five-inch leopard heels running the 7Seven course. She dodged the flames, nimbly cleared the walls, expertly walked the runway upside down, and gracefully performed a dance routine before disappearing into a waterfall.

ZhenZhen's nose wrinkled. "Of course Kaitlyn would be practicing already. We aren't supposed to start until two weeks before the 7Seven announcement. I should report her." ZhenZhen checked the timepiece on her wrist. "Oh goodness golly gracious, I have to finish fast!" She started walking again. "This is only one section of Modelland. There is much more that you will be allowed to experience firsthand, should you survive THBC. Oops!" She clapped a hand over her mouth. "Pretend I didn't say that, okay?"

"Whatever THBC is, I can't imagine all of us surviving it," Zarpessa simpered viciously, eyeing Tookie's crew. Then ZhenZhen motioned for all the girls in the group except Tookie, Piper, Dylan, and Shiraz to gather together. The girls did so, eyeing Tookie and the others with snarky confusion.

"I have one last piece of knowledge to share with you." Zhen-Zhen leaned in close. "It's about Catwalk Corridor. Technically, I'm not supposed to warn you about it, but when Ci~L used to give these tours, she always broke the rules a bit and warned the girls. So beware Catwalk Corridor—you never know where it may appear. It's nothing stinging antiseptic and a tetanus shot can't fix, but still, it can give you a fright."

Tookie's stomach roiled with dread.

Then ZhenZhen giggled nervously. "Really, Catwalk Corridor isn't half as bad as the Ugly Room. You don't *ever* want to get sent there. And then there are some of the natural dangers around this place." She leaned even closer, her voice dropping to a whisper. "You all know about the Diabolical Divide, right? For sure, that's a big and scary *no, no, no*—don't you dare enter it! And there's more than one way to get to it, so be careful. Rarely, like every few years, but too often if you ask me, the Divide sends out fireballs at Modelland. Many years ago, a fireball landed right on top of the old 7Seven stadium! It burned the whole thing down, and a bunch of girls died! And—"

Screech!

A piercing alarm cut off ZhenZhen's tirade. Hordes of tour groups ran down the boulevard, stampeding past Tookie and her group in a blur of arms and legs.

ZhenZhen waved her arms around. "That's the buzzer! Run, girls! To the O! Back through the thorn bush! You know the way! Now!"

Shiraz took off instantly in a cheetahlike sprint. Piper was close behind her, her gallop precise and efficient, like she was speeding forward but barely moving at the same time. Dylan followed, her run a sexy swagger.

Tookie had not yet moved. She felt stuck, compelled to observe. Just for a moment.

She considered her place in this . . . place. The place every girl in the world wanted to be. The place that produced the only world-famous people on the planet. Where did she fit in here? From the looks of the nearly perfect bodies that ran ahead of her, minus the three misfits who accompanied her on her trek, she knew that she was living not her fate, but someone else's . . . Myrracle's.

Tookie wasn't sure if she should just run and hide or run to catch up with the girls sprinting toward their destinies.

"Run!" A kind-faced girl whose eyes were decorated with a SMIZE and who wore a headphone contraption tapped Tookie on the shoulder. "Come on! You can do it!"

It felt like a sign. Tookie lifted her right leg. Then her left. She started into a run. Four steps later, her large right foot got caught on the back of her left leg. She stumbled, suddenly airborne, then went straight down into a textbook Tookie De La Crème fall.

I5

THE BELLADONNA'S BURDEN

Tookie's right foot had hit her left leg with the power of a sledge-hammer, forcing her knee to give way. But before she could tumble to the ground, she dredged up all her strength. No. Tookie would not crumble. Not this time.

Screech! the buzzer wailed.

Tookie regained her balance and ran as fast as she could. ZhenZhen had told her to look for the thorn bush. But where was it? She spied a wall of prickly metallic brush. She hurtled herself into it, just as ZhenZhen had done minutes before. "Ouch!"

Wrong plant.

She ran down the street until she spied another wall of thorny vines. Tookie eyed it, not sure if it was friend or foe. But then one of the thorns arched up and seemed to . . . smile at her. Tookie gawked. Taking a deep breath, she jumped full force toward it. The barbed bush opened, revealing the passageway to the O.

"Thank you!" she yelled back. The thorny passageway closed with a thwack.

Tookie ran down the crescent path toward the left side of the M building. The buzzer screeched even louder and faster now, like it was counting down. *You're not going to make it, Tookie. You waited too long back there.*

Modern symphony music grew louder in her ears, the only indication she was making any headway. Tookie rounded the curve at the end of the walkway and came to a wall of . . . She squinted. *Are those . . . zippers?*

There were hundreds of them. Zippers of all sizes, some as tall as Tookie—perfectly polished ones, broken ones, zippers placed vertically and horizontally. It was obviously a dead end.

The music in the O swelled. The hideously screeching buzzer was almost a continuous noise. Tookie was running out of time. She whipped around, considering trying a different path, but she was met by yet another wall of zippers behind her. Unfastened zippers, zippers on the diagonal. She turned around once more, and there was another wall of zippers. She was surrounded. Now the only thing Tookie could see was the sky. A flock of rainbow-colored birds flew overhead, seemingly flapping in the direction of the music.

"Hello?" Tookie called desperately. What if she'd taken a wrong turn and was stuck in this weird zipper room forever? Maybe this was her Modelland fate.

"Hello?" she screamed again. Rustling made her turn. A stuck zipper started to wobble. The teeth parted and a figure jumped out. Tookie gasped.

It was Ci~L.

Ci~L was now wearing a silver and purple bodysuit and a silver circle headpiece framing her face. Dressy somehow. And she didn't look happy. Tookie cowered, not knowing what to expect. A reprimand? Would Ci~L send Tookie back to Metopia? She felt ashamed that she'd disappointed someone she so badly wanted to impress.

Ci~L strode toward Tookie and grabbed her arm roughly. "Come on, girl! We gotta move! If you don't make it to the O before she starts her anthem . . . Follow me!"

Turning on her heel, Ci~L scampered up the nearest zipper wall and put one leg into the halfway-stuck zipper through which she'd just emerged. She gazed down at Tookie, who still stood on the ground, dumbstruck. "Well, come on! It's like you're mountain climbing."

"B-but I've never mountain climbed before," Tookie stammered.

Ci~L looked exasperated. "That's no excuse! Fake it till you make it!"

Mustering up all her courage, Tookie struggled up the zippers, carefully watching her feet to make sure she wouldn't slip. When she looked up, the last of Ci~L's foot was disappearing through the half-open zipper. Tookie scrambled to that point herself and looked through the opening. It was pitch-black and as silent as a tomb.

It's now or never, Tookie, she thought, and tumbled in.

Immediately, she got the sense that she was sliding down, down, down. Screams echoed in her ears. After a moment, she realized they were hers.

"Stop overreacting!" Ci~L's voice echoed off the walls. "We're just in the ZipZap! We'll be there in a second!"

"Be . . . where?" Tookie asked. No answer came.

Instead of being an opening to the other side of a wall, like Tookie had expected, the zipper fed into a chute filled with fast-flowing air. The air pushed her around curves and down steep drops. It propelled her straight up, up, up, and then down, down, down. Finally, she landed on her butt on a cushy surface and opened her eyes. A jagged slit slowly opened, and daylight rushed in. When Tookie's eyes adjusted, she could see that she was next to Ci~L. The zipper had let them out in the O plaza. The rest of the Modelland student body stood in front of them, staring at an empty stage.

"Wow, um . . . thank you," Tookie said gratefully to Ci~L.

The statuesque Intoxibella shrugged.

Then someone snickered a few feet away. Zarpessa was watching Tookie, a big smirk on her face. Tookie hung her head.

Ci~L glared at Zarpessa, then grabbed Tookie's chin hard. "Listen to me. You're different. *Way* different. You know that. You're gonna experience lots of cuts and slices here, but you'd better suck it up—the girl who is sucking your blood is hurting way more than you. Never stoop to her level."

Tookie nodded, squirming as Ci~L's sharp fingernails dug into her skin. She was happy Ci~L was giving her advice, but also a little scared. Suddenly, Ci~L released her, pushing her forward. When Tookie turned, she saw that shackles had appeared on Ci~L's wrists and ankles. Ci~L staggered backward and fell into the ZipZap.

Tookie gasped. Should she go after Ci~L? But then she heard a cheer behind her and turned toward the O. It was actually an O-shaped plaza behind the M building. An immense waterfall cascaded to the ground from an invisible source in the sky. Past and present Intoxibellas played in the waterfall and then sprang to life in 3-D water forms. Ci~L's image was not displayed.

Ninety-nine Bellas, all still in their T-DOD garb, clogged the space. In front of them was a group of a few hundred girls dressed in the same uniform as ZhenZhen and other tour guides, the two-toned leotard-and-pants outfit, but there were subgroups, each wearing a different color, seemingly split according to their ages. Brilliant yellow Senturas encircled their waists. But what struck Tookie most was that the groups got smaller and smaller the closer they got to the front of the stage.

Tookie's eyes strayed to the left, to an assembly of about three hundred other girls. Some were not girls at all but older women. They were totally nude, and their flesh seemed to be made of hard plastic, with creases at every joint—the shoulders, elbows, and wrists, the neck, hips, knees, and ankles—which made them look like living, breathing mannequins. Their eyeballs were completely black, making them look soulless. They stood stiffly, staring blankly at the crowd. Just looking at them made Tookie shiver.

As Tookie approached the last line of the group of new girls, she noticed Piper, Dylan, and Shiraz. They all turned and saw her at the same time. "There you are, girl!" Dylan cried.

"Nice of you to make it," Piper said sarcastically, smiling a little.

"Tookie arrive!" Shiraz bleated. "We worry for you!"

A rush of warmth settled over Tookie. They cared about her well-being. Maybe they were even her new . . . friends. She let this moment sink in for a second. For the first time in her life, she actually used the word *friend* in the plural. She made a mental note to herself to start spelling *friends* with four S's, *friendssss*, in her *T-Mail Jail*. One *s* for each of the four friends she now had: Dylan, Shiraz, Piper . . . and, of course, Lizzie.

If Lizzie still considered Tookie her friend.

The music roared to a crescendo. All girls turned to the front. Something momentous was about to begin. The music changed abruptly to a funky military march. An authoritative female announcer then boomed, "WELCOME OUR PROTECTORS, OUR MASONS, AND THE BEST ACCESSORIES SINCE THE TONGUE STUD, OUR BRETHREN FROM . . . BESTOSTERONE!"

The Sentura-clad groups of girls applauded in a rhythmic clap, thigh-slap, and whistle serenade that offered a perfect complement to the beat of the music. A group of young men marched in, doing a highly powerful staccato dance. Each was more handsome than the next. They wore black billowing trousers stuffed into calf-high boots, leather suspenders crisscrossing their bare chests. Some had laserlike focus; others were pouting and surveying the crowd of gawking girls, aware of their handsome looks; and still others seemed distracted, their thoughts far away. But all in all, they were a sight to relish: cleft chins, strong brows, flexing muscles, eyes that looked not *at* you but *through* you.

"I'm claiming him first!" Chaste cried.

"Which one?" Zarpessa asked.

"*All* of them!"

Dylan snorted. "She *looks* like the type of girl who'd do all of 'em, doesn't she?"

"Remember what I said, girls." ZhenZhen scuttled back from her class at the front. "Don't touch the accessories—unless you're doing ManAttack or a photo shoot with them."

Suddenly, the melody dropped to an ominous octave.

"Ladies and gentlemen, please welcome . . . the Bored!" a female announcer said. A series of fireworks in the sky spelled *B-O-R-E-D*.

"They're spelling that wrong," Tookie told ZhenZhen.

ZhenZhen shook her head. "Nope. They spell it that way because that's how they always look, like people sitting in the front row of a fashion show. They're the highest level of instructors here. The powerful ones. It's mandatory to call them Gurus. They report to the BellaDonna."

Tookie counted six members of the Bored, one stranger than the next. Guru Applaussez marched with them, its hand-head waving to the crowd. Another Bored member, an ancient-looking troll of a man, had aged-parchment skin that hung loosely from his arms. Every inch of his body was covered in moving tattoos. Tookie read a message scrolling across his forehead: *Long, long ago, the battle raged between the Muses and the Nar . . .* But before the message could end, the Bored member frantically wiped his forehead and changed what was being spelled out. The scroll started over: *Long, long ago, the battle raged between the Muses and the nail polish remover.*

One Bored member had lizard skin and yellow eyes and a forked tongue that sprang out of its mouth. *That thing makes me feel normal!* Tookie thought. As she watched, the lizard's head turned white, and it morphed into an alabaster alligator with pink eyes.

Piper smiled. "I just know I'm going to be his teacher's pet."

A stunning figure that looked like it was three-quarters man, one-quarter woman pranced in next, generating a halfhearted smattering of applause. This Guru wore what looked like the mating result of a black leather jumpsuit and a bustier. He—or she— was muscular yet thin, with blond hair slicked back in a tight ballerina bun. When the figure's eyes connected with girls in the crowd, everyone jumped back a step. Then the Guru turned and stared at Tookie and her friends. A sickened expression washed over the Guru's face.

Bloodcurdling seconds passed. Tookie spotted a deep gash on the Guru's right cheek, directly under the eye. Tookie held her breath, expecting something awful to happen. But then, abruptly, the strange figure continued toward the base of the waterfall, disappearing from view.

"What was that?" Dylan murmured.

The music shifted again, this time to an enchanting classical melody. The deep timpani rolled. The music shifted, and on cue, each of the uniformed color-coded groups started dancing wildly. One group of Bellas did an intricate Viennese waltz; another belly danced and shimmied wildly; another trance-danced like they were at a pulsing rave; and another responded with acrobatics. They all seemed to be trying to outdance one another.

Shiraz grabbed Dylan's hands. "Come on! Is fun!"

Dylan gave in and swung her long ponytails round and round. Even Piper did a unique robotlike bop, every movement precise.

Suddenly, Tookie got a twinge of sadness that Myrracle hadn't been chosen. Her sister would love this.

Suddenly, the waterfall vanished, revealing an enormous statue standing directly in front of all the girls. The statue was as tall as a ten-story building and made of what appeared to be shimmering, flawless diamond. Atop its dazzling head sat a broad-brimmed headdress. Its chin tilted to the right, its hands froze artfully around its cheekbones, and its eyes remained half closed.

"It's—" Piper blurted out.

"Th-the—" stammered Dylan.

"Bella—" chirped Shiraz.

"Donna!" Tookie whispered.

Dylan bit her lip nervously. "She looks pissed off, y'all!"

One of the blank-eyed, soulless women took five giant, measured steps and stood at attention on the left side of the statue. She appeared to be in her midforties. She was the only one of the mannequin-bodied women who wore epaulettes.

"Who's that?" Tookie asked ZhenZhen.

"Her name's Persimmon, like the weird fruit," ZhenZhen replied. "She's the BellaDonna's chief Mannecant."

"Mannecant?" Dylan asked.

"Servants of Modelland," ZhenZhen explained. "They are failed Bellas who dedicated their lives to this place in exchange for never having to leave." She eyed Persimmon. The dark seams of her mannequin joints stood out in the light. "I wouldn't trust her. She always adds her own special spin when she relays a message to the BellaDonna. We call her Persimmon the Persecutor."

The music diminished to a steady drumroll. Persimmon turned around and faced the crowd. "New Bellas and old," she began, speaking without the help of any microphone Tookie could see, "male models and Mannecants, and the esteemed Bored, I present to you the most beloved of the beloved, the chicest of the chic, the definer of all things beautiful, and the esteemed leader of all Bellas lucky to be led . . . I present to you the BellaDonna of Modelland!"

Everyone in the O dropped to one knee and bowed their heads. Their poistions looked as if they were posing for a photograph. The new girls quickly followed suit awkwardly.

Then, as the music flared once more, the grand statue began to move. Tookie's mouth dropped. "The BellaDonna is a *statue*?"

"Might as well be," ZhenZhen said, her gaze nervously darting around the O. "We only see the *real* thing once a year. At the 7Seven Tournament."

The statue looked around the O. Its head moved in Tookie's direction, and Tookie's stomach clenched. *The BellaDonna is looking at me!*

Then the statue directed its full attention to the entire audience and, accompanied by the full orchestra, began to sing.

"My dear Modelland is a heavenly queendom,
Its walls rich with memories of yesteryear.
Our laws, antiquated, but must be respected,
Or I'll discard you like moth-eaten cashmere.
Listen to me now, my spanking new No-Sees,
You're infants, you're rascals, and oh-so-askew.
You've entered a world that most would slay for,
But amongst them all, I have chosen you. . . ."

Tookie tilted her head toward ZhenZhen. "No-Sees?" she whispered.

"New girls," replied ZhenZhen, before bringing a finger to her lips. "Listen up . . . this is my favorite part."

The BellaDonna began the chorus of her melody and the older Bellas sang with her.

Modelland

"Modelland is your new HOME . . ."
"Home . . . home," the older Bellas sang.
"Welcome to this superDOME . . ."
"Dome, Dome," sang the older Bellas.
"For you XX-chromoSOMED . . ."
"Somed, somed," the older Bellas echoed.
"Modelland is your new HOME."
And then the BellaDonna launched into the next verse.

"Regard your dear neighbor, the Bella to your near left,
Ambassador to Modelland, and you are now, too.
She'll excite the world to buy wares of design and splendor.
Here's a list of Modelland's curriculum menu."

ZhenZhen leaned in to Tookie and the girls. "Listen to all the great stuff you'll be learning how to entice the world to wear. It's really cool!"

"From footwear to freeze sprays, foundation, face powders
To corsets and camisoles and culottes and trousers,
Moccasins and miniskirts, mesh tops and bronzers,
Sandals, suspenders and sunblock with powers . . ."

"Sunblock?" Piper commented. "Your poster girl's right here, BellaDonna!"

"You'll wear waistcoats, wedding dresses, wet suits, and
   lingerie,

Leotards and yellow belts, deodorant every day,
Hosiery and houndstooth and rougy lips to chalets,
Bandeaus and bodices and LBDs at soirees.

"You'll exfoliate, emulsify, depilate, and moisturize,
Sell glycerins, jojoba oils, fragrances, and fluorides.
Cocktail dresses, cardigans, concealers for tired eyes,
And practice all your posing tricks from sunset till sunrise.

"Perform in petticoat-themed much-attended fashion-elite
    expos,
Safari-wear, tuxedos, tunics, tops, all types of clothes.
Kilts and cloaks and swinging coats and crocheted kimonos
With audiences making bets on who will fall upon their nose."

The older Bellas began to sing the chorus again, and this time some of the new girls sang along.

Ci~L, dressed in a sateen couture straitjacket, rose through the ground, imprisoned in a birdcage. Its bars were made of razors.

Tookie clapped her hands over her mouth.

The BellaDonna continued.

"Regard this renegade, this rowdy rabble-rouser.
This shameless charlatan, this skank scalawag.
A troublemaking malady, a traitor, defective.
While we all zig, this pest must zag . . ."

Ci~L cast a mournful look at the statue.

"You've all grown up dreaming, hoping to be her,
Now this Triple 7Seven is inferior to you.
So learn from her missteps, hello to your futures,
To Ci~L's: au revoir, adios, and adieu."

Beside them, ZhenZhen let out a whimper. "I feel her pain," she cried, tears forming in her eyes.

"I *knew* it!" Zarpessa yelped. "How the mighty have fallen! Maybe if Ci~L had a famous boyfriend, she wouldn't be in this mess."

The orchestra ended with a crescendo, and all that remained was a lone violin playing a haunting melody. The girls sang the chorus once more, but this time they sounded nervous and even a little fearful.

"This scary," mumbled Shiraz.

"Listen closely to this next part," ZhenZhen warned.

"*UNO!*" the upperclassBellas called in Gowdee'an.

"You will exit my gates through five distinct fashions.
Listen closely, one of five'll be your truth."
"The foolish, moronic, the feeble, the mindless
Will risk all and regift their coveted youth . . ."

"'Regift their coveted youth'? What does that mean?" asked Tookie.

"Close your eyes and imagine yourself fifty years older," Zhen-Zhen said. "If you leave Modelland without permission, you kiss your youth goodbye."

"*DOS!*"

"The meek and misguided muckety-muck flunkies
Will ride senso unico *through farewell tollbooths."*

"Tookie, what she mean?" Shiraz asked.

"*Senso unico* means 'one-way' in Cappuccinian," Tookie translated.

"You get a one-way ticket out of here if you continually suck," ZhenZhen explained.

"*TRES!*"

"Other castaways'll opt for Mannecant memoirs,
Perhaps better to pitiful pre-Modelland pursuits."

When the BellaDonna sang the word *Mannecant*, Tookie turned to look at Persimmon in time to see her head drop.

"*QUATRO!*"

"Second-string Bellas will opt for the silver screen,
Miming in the multiplex, so trite, so uncouth."

"The BellaDonna can't stand actresses," ZhenZhen whispered. "She says they're pitiful Modelland rejects who just want any kind of spotlight. I once heard her say actresses are a step below Mannecants."

"*CINCO!*"

"Prime few'll emerge 7Seven 'toxibellas.
For this reward, pathetics would sell their eyetooths."

After the last chorus, the newly recruited Bellas all cheered wildly. The agile ones did high kicks, backflips, and splits in the air. Shiraz did a cartwheel.

The statue began singing again, this time without music:

"Your premature merriment has come much too fast.
Disparity 'tween good and bad will be very vast.
THBC separates the punks from the class.
For some No-Sees, Discovery Day will be your . . . last."

16

THE THBC TAMASHA

The new Bellas' contagious jubilance at the start of the opera had abruptly turned to an awkward mix of hope and dread. Quickly, tour guides ushered the new girls back to the ZipZaps. Everything was taking place very hurriedly, as though they had somewhere very important to go next. No one spoke. The BellaDonna's song had been so . . . ominous. Piper had a very determined look on her face, as though she was doing math problems in her head. Dylan nervously straightened her outfit and combed her two long ponytails with her fingers. Only cheery Shiraz was still dancing and singing the music from the event.

Then Tookie detected someone else humming a different melody, quite out of tune. It was a girl with skin the color of toasted breadcrumbs standing one line over. She had long, wavy dark brown hair, honey-colored eyes, a tiny ruby decorating the middle of her SMIZE, and a decorative Headbangor—a newfangled invention from the far southeast that delivered music directly to a wearer's brainwaves—in her hair. Tookie realized this was the girl who'd rescued her in the plaza, telling her to run for the ZipZaps.

Tookie walked over to her. "Are you from Chakra?" she asked shyly. She'd never met a Chakran before.

At first, the girl didn't notice her, and Tookie was about to turn away when the girl touched her Headbangor lightly to pause it. "Oh, hi, I'm . . . *nervous*. Nice to meet you."

Tookie and the girl shared a laugh. The girl continued, "I'm also Kamalini. Kamalini Dara from Chakra."

"Tookie De La Crème. From Metopia." Tookie shifted back and forth, waiting for Kamalini to look at her strangely and re-mark on how odd-looking she was, how she didn't belong here.

Kamalini smiled. "*Tookie*. I like that."

"Quiet, ladies! Keep moving!" Kamalini's guide yelled.

"Bye, Tookie from Metopia," Kamalini said. "See you later, hopefully."

Clutching her Headbangor, Kamalini scuttled ahead to join her group, climbing through a ZipZap and disappearing down the hole. Tookie and Dylan turned back to the ZipZaps and noticed four nearly identical girls wearing identical outfits. The only way to tell them apart was by their pastel-hued hair.

"Well, lookie here. Who are y'all?" Dylan asked.

"I'm SheLikee!" the first girl announced. Blue hair.

"I'm HerLikee!" Green hair.

"I'm ILikee!" Pink hair.

"I'm MeLikee!" Purple.

"We're"—"from"—"Mini"—"Paul!" Each said a different word in the sentence. Then, one by one, the girls disappeared into the ZipZap like sand crabs sneaking down their little holes.

A girl named Angelīka from Icylann yapped like an excited Yorkshire terrier. "Yay, yay, yay! Isn't dis great?" She jumped into one of the ZipZaps so enthusiastically, she scraped the top of her head on its sharp pull-tab. Tookie cringed, seeing bits of blood and hair still hanging from it.

ZhenZhen then stepped up to Tookie and put both hands on her shoulders. "I have to leave you now, Tookie. You heard what the BellaDonna said, right?"

Tookie nodded.

"Be careful, okay?"

"Why?" Tookie whispered. "Should I be worried?"

"Um . . ." ZhenZhen looked uncomfortable. "Well, yes. Everyone should be worried about what comes next."

"Why? What's going to happen?"

ZhenZhen blew out a long breath. "I cannot tell you. One bit of advice, though: there's strength in numbers."

There were only ten girls left waiting to enter the ZipZap, including Tookie, her friends, and Zarpessa, who turned around, glared at them, and then started feverishly scratching her arms. "Ick. I'm allergic to dust, pollen, and *farm animals*."

Ci~L's words echoed in Tookie's head. *The girl who is sucking your blood is hurting way more than you. Never stoop to her level.*

Tookie walked up to Zarpessa.

Zarpessa flinched. "What?" she growled.

Tookie stared at the ground, unable to make eye contact. "I—I'm not going to tell," she murmured into her chest.

Zarpessa's face drained of color. She brought her nose close to Tookie's. "You're not going to tell about *what*?"

"About . . . *you* know. I saw you. At the Dumpster. Eating all that rotting food, and—"

Zarpessa cut her off. "You don't know *anything,* okay?"

"But—"

ZhenZhen's voice rang out from the back of the line. "Zarpessa from Metopia! Into the ZipZap! Go!"

Zarpessa strutted to the zipper, then turned and looked at Tookie. "Are you ready?"

ZhenZhen frowned. "What do you mean is she ready? Are *you* ready?"

"No, you heard me right," Zarpessa simpered, her eyes still on Tookie. "Are. You. Ready?" Then she grabbed the zipper teeth on either side of the opening and used them as handles. With a dramatic hair sweep, she gracefully launched herself into the ZipZap and disappeared. But Tookie could still hear her voice from the inside of the zipper. "For a lesson in how to shut the hell *uuuuuupppppppppp* . . ."

"What is she talking about?" Dylan sidled up to Tookie. "What did you say to her?"

Tookie shut her eyes, not answering. *The absolutely wrong thing,* she thought.

"All right, the Super Ci~L Foursome, you guys are the last ones. Step right up there." ZhenZhen pointed at the zipper opening.

They sat at the zipper's base. Dylan first, then Shiraz, with

Piper and Tookie pulling up the rear, a human train. They slid fast down into the hole, darkness enveloping them. "Woooohoooo!" Dylan screamed in the ZipZap, throwing her hands up in the air like she was on a roller coaster. In seconds, with Tookie now in the lead, they were spat out on the other end in reverse order, sliding across a cold metal floor and coming to a halt in a room lit by a single dim bulb swinging overhead.

They were the only ones in the room. The only other thing Tookie could make out were more zippers, but they were shut tightly.

"Hello!" Piper yelled. "Hello? Hello? Helllooooo?" She crossed her arms and squinted. "Hmmm. From the resonance of the sound, I presume we're in a fairly large space."

Just then, the ZipZap zipped open and spit out a girl with a kente cloth dress and spiral braided hair. She landed on top of Tookie. Then came another. And another. Dylan ran over and heaved aside the girls pinning Tookie to the floor, yanking Tookie out of the flow of traffic.

"You okay, girl?"

"Uh-huh," Tookie murmured, feeling a rush of pleasure. Dylan had come to her rescue! First Ci~L and now Dylan. Tookie was loving this being-cared-about feeling.

All the zippers coughed up their human cargo in reverse order of the girls' entrances at the O. They all tried staying in the lit area of the room, but as their total number approached one hundred, some had to venture into the dark parts.

"Oh my God!" a girl screamed. "The ZipZap KILLED her!"

The entire group turned to see a girl lying motionless at the mouth of a zipper. Blood pooled beneath her head. Everyone started to scream. Dylan turned quickly away. "I can't. I feel like I'm gonna throw up and pass out."

Shiraz stayed with Dylan while Tookie and Piper went to investigate. Angelïka from Icylann lay still, her head and shoulders covered in blood. Tookie and Piper kneeled down to check her. Piper felt around Angelïka's head.

"Not that big a gash," Piper said. "But even small head wounds can bleed profusely."

"Is she . . . dead?" Tookie whispered.

Angelïka sprang up to a sitting position and yelled, "Dead? *Who?*" Everyone screamed again. It was like seeing a body rise from the grave.

Tookie and Piper lifted Angelïka to her feet. Shiraz ran forward and ripped her gauzy sleeve from her shirt so Angelïka could wipe the blood off her face.

"Where are we?" a girl cried.

A voice emerged from the darkness. "You're in THBC."

The girls stared into the dark abyss. Dylan grabbed Tookie's hand.

"Thigh-High Boot Camp, ladies!" the same voice belted.

A spotlight shone down on a figure across the room. It was the stunning three-quarter man, one-quarter woman Guru the girls had first laid eyes on at the O ceremony. The Guru stood on an ornate metal platform with arms crossed and feet splayed in ballet's fifth position, surrounded by a halo of multicolored fireflies. The Guru's gray eyes glowed alarmingly, almost from within.

Suddenly, more lights clicked on, one by one.

"I am Gunnero Narzz. Guru Gunnero to you cheap nylon No-Sees!" the instructor yelled at the girls. "I am head of Modelland security. Head of Run-a-Way Intensive class. Head of the THBC, and the head man in charge of all of you slovenly scrubs."

"That's a *man*?" Tookie heard Chaste snicker.

"There is only one person more powerful in Modelland than me," Guru Gunnero continued. "But I'm not going to be singing you any songs." He glared around the room with piercing, snake-like eyes. The scar on his face made him look even meaner. The girls leaned back or turned away. Tookie felt the creep of goose bumps from her toes to her head.

"Your assignment, my ladies—your mission, if you will—is my specialty . . . a fashion show!"

"A fashion show?" Angelika exclaimed. "How fun!"

"I always want to do fashion show!" Shiraz jumped up and down.

Gunnero stared at them. "This *sfilata* will not be run*way*-of-the-mill. So if at any time you feel like you need a permanent breather, if the going makes you want to go on a go-see to go see your mommy and daddy, along this journey will be doors for the most delicate dames marked *Home*."

The girls' smiles faded abruptly.

"But remember," the Guru went on. "Once you step your trembling toes through any door marked *Home,* there is no coming back. Choosing the Home door is not like choosing a vintage designer gown that will indeed come back into fashion. You leave through those Home doors and you are forever banned from these gates, like Nehru jackets!"

Guru Gunnero's laugh sent chills up Tookie's spine. "Now. You will be experiencing a fashion show from start to finish, in five phases. So let's get started. Phase number one. *Measurements!*"

Shiraz turned toward Tookie and mouthed, *How bad can be it?*

Gunnero kicked his high-heeled boot hard on the floor, and the room instantly changed. Suddenly, all the girls stood in a stark white round room. There was only one visible door. It was marked HOME.

Mannecants poured in through a dozen hidden entrances, pushing carts full of various apparatuses—rulers, T squares, compasses, miniature scales, gauges, and meters. They marched to the girls and instantly got to work. A Mannecant forcefully held Kamalini by the shoulders to measure the angle of her chin and the distance between the ruby in the middle of her SMIZE and her eyebrows. "Supreme," the readout announced. Another Mannecant pinched Dylan's arm with a caliper. "Ow!" Dylan screamed. Yet another Mannecant yanked Shiraz by the top of her head, presumably trying to get her to stand a little taller. "I not growing taller!" Shiraz protested. And one more Mannecant waved a meter across Piper's cheeks. "Lack of pigment," a woman's robotic voice proclaimed. "Skin prone to burning, blushing, and flushing."

Piper wrenched away from the wand.

Then a Mannecant approached Tookie and carefully measured the space between her eyes. "Too far apart," the meter announced. It measured the length of her arm next. "Proportionately too long," the meter said. And then her neck: "Too ostrichy. Preferable fowl neck: swan."

And finally, when the Mannecant waved a comb-shaped device over Tookie's hair, the readout proclaimed, "Unfortunate condition. Both oily and dry, limp and frizzy, completely uncombable, uncurlable, and unstyleable."

"Phase one complete!" Gunnero roared.

The measuring Mannecants vanished just as quickly as they'd arrived. Tookie peered around at the other girls and they looked just as flustered as she felt.

Gunnero barked, "Well, your class seems to have near-perfect degrees of beauty supremacy, almost as becoming as I. Quite the rarity. All except four of you."

Everyone knew exactly which four Gunnero was referring to, without his even having to look in their direction.

Then Gunnero began to strut around the room. "But measurements are just the beginning of this acid-washed denim trip. It's time for phase two."

"Is this where we get our thigh-high boots?" Zarpessa interrupted. "My hairdresser's stepcousin's uncle who works in the marketing department for Zoozeeton, the thigh-high boot designer, told me the THBC boots are amazing this year!"

Gunnero's eyes widened at her outburst. His lips curled into a smirk. "Well, my mother's youngest and only son said that he heard you were a wannabe, kiss-ass, brownnosing Bella and that he wants me to tell all the girls here to tell you to shut the heck up!" He whipped around at the girls. "Well? Tell her!"

The group of girls awkwardly obeyed. Even Tookie sputtered, "Shut your hole, I guess." Zarpessa looked shaken.

"*Merci*, ladies," Gunnero said primly. "Now, moving on . . . *Cathedra!*"

One hundred salon-style chairs dropped from above. Each girl's first name was engraved in the back of a chair. Even Tookie's.

"*Spiegels!*" Gunnero roared.

On cue, one mirror for every chair appeared.

"Locate your seats and plop your firm newbie fannies into them!" ordered Gunnero. "Move!"

The flock of girls stepped down the aisle. Some girls who had found their chairs jumped into them excitedly. Tookie, however, was suspicious.

"What is all this?" she asked Piper as they walked to their designated seats.

"I don't know," Piper said grimly, seeming frustrated she didn't have the answer.

Once all the girls were seated and facing their mirrors, Gunnero screamed again: *"Maquillage!"*

A high-pitched sound like a missile approaching filled the room. Everyone looked up. One lone white lacquered cart plummeted from the ceiling and landed in the middle of the aisle with a crash. Amazingly, it was still intact after impact. The cart wasn't very big and contained five drawers that spilled over with every type of makeup and beauty tool Tookie had ever seen: thickening, lengthening, and multiplying mascaras. Lipsticks, lip glosses, and stick-on faux-lip attachments. Eye shimmers and shadows and lash curlers that promised to make lashes retain their curve for two years. Face shimmers, glitters, and pills that promised an instant inner glow once ingested. False eyelashes made from deceased daddy longlegs. Tookie spotted an area of the cart that held multiple hair-removal systems: tweezers, razors, and black wax that slowly dripped to the floor. The label on the wax jar said LP WAX: RECYCLED FROM VINYL ALBUMS OF YESTERYEAR.

Gunnero announced the next order in a wavering falsetto: *"ARRR-TISTES!"*

One hundred Mannecants fluttered out from behind Gunnero and made their way to particular chairs.

Tookie looked at the Mannecant who had come to her chair. Her black-filled eyes had many lines and wrinkles around them, reminding Tookie of the dry and cracked lake beds at home in Peppertown. They reminded her of Creamy too, and she winced. All she could think of was Creamy's horrified, enraged face as Ci~L lifted Tookie above the LaDorno square. And how her parents had fought, arguing to get rid of her. She swallowed a lump growing in her throat.

"*FLURRY!*" screamed Gunnero.

With that, the Mannecant-Artistes moved at superhuman speed. They all ran to the cart and grabbed handfuls of products, then dashed back to their designated girl and got to work. The Artistes tossed mascaras and sponges, eyeliners and lip glosses across the aisles to each other in a spectacular juggling display. Tookie's Artiste had five sponges and brushes flying through the air while applying a kohl blue-black liner to Tookie's lower inner eye. After she was finished with it, she passed the liner to Piper's Artiste, who then used it and passed it to Zarpessa's.

The Artiste slathered creams on Tookie's face and had a feather-light touch as she swept mascara across her lashes. The pampering and the attention lulled Tookie into a trance. She couldn't see herself because her Artiste was standing in the way of her mirror. But it didn't matter. Never before had Tookie been fawned over in such a way. The closest anyone had ever come to examining her face was when Creamy took her to the doctor last year for tests to figure out why her forehead seemed to be growing faster than the rest of her face. Tookie was loving Thigh-High Boot Camp. She thought the name was especially fitting because she felt like she was flying on a natural Thigh *High*.

Gunnero's voice broke Tookie out of her trance. "Two minutes left, Artistes! Use every muscle in your bodies on the dung you're working on. The transformation of shaggy No-Sees is no runway walk in the park."

After two more minutes, the lights went out. The girls let out a chorus of surprised screams, and then the lights snapped on again.

"BEHOLD YOUR REFLECTIONS!" Gunnero screamed.

The Artistes had disappeared. For the first time, the girls had unobstructed views of themselves in their mirrors. Tookie opened her eyes a crack, her old fear of mirrors flooding back. *This isn't going to make me look good,* she thought. *I'll be the same old kooky Tookie as before.*

But she had to look. Slowly, she opened her eyes and stared at the reflection before her. Her mouth dropped open. Who is *that*? There was a brilliant stroke of eye shadow above her eyes. A perfect swipe of iridescent lip gloss on the middle of her bottom lip. Those spider legs were glued to her lids, making her lashes look a zillion miles long. She almost looked . . . *good.*

Tookie glanced at her friends and gasped. Shiraz's berry-stained lips looked edible. With the help of periwinkle and sienna eye shadow, Dylan's eyes were now a bright, electric lavender. Piper's skin glowed as if lit from within. She looked even more like a marble statue than before, reminding Tookie of a saint.

Suddenly, Shiraz's eyes bulged. "Tookie!" Shiraz wailed, pointing shakily at her. "What *happening*?"

Tookie turned to see what Shiraz was pointing to. An older, unrecognizable person was staring at Tookie. It had a boil growing on its nose, letting out a smoke that smelled of rotten eggs and animal droppings. Much of its hair had fallen out in clumps, and many of the hanging strands had fused together into what looked like chunks of petrified wood. Its eyes were bruised, swollen nearly shut, and its ears were swollen into what looked like bulbs of cauliflower.

"Oh my God!" Tookie and the creature whispered. That was when she realized.

The gruesome creature . . . was *her.*

17

HOME, SOUR HOME

Everyone in the room screamed, their faces melting and warping just like Tookie's was.

Piper's skin was so raw it was transparent. Her blood was visible, pumping wildly through her face. She resembled a skeleton with muscles and veins, with a thin layer of clear plastic keeping it all together.

Dylan's ponytails had completely fallen out and she was cradling them in her arms. Her nose had become detached from her face and was sitting on top of the bed of hair. Shiraz's grapefruit-sized eyes bulged and bulged like they were about to pop out of her head. The spot where the ruby had been on Kamalini's SMIZE was now a gaping hole four inches wide, exposing her brain. Angelïka's ZipZap head injury had split open wide from the top of her head to the base of her neck. When she screamed, her exposed vocal cords, which lay in a spaghetti-like tangle at her throat, vibrated.

"My *heads* hurt so much!" both sides of Angelïka cried. Even Zarpessa and Chaste looked like mutants, their noses falling off and their lips turning into slugs.

Three monster girls instinctively ran toward the white door marked HOME. As soon as they went through, huge sighs ensued. "I'm beautiful again!" one girl said through the door. "I'm not melting anymore!" another cried.

"Last chance! Anyone *else* want to go through the Home door?" Gunnero teased. "It's dreadful to be hideously fugly, isn't it?"

Tookie's muscles twitched. She couldn't take this. *Is this what Modelland is about? Bringing lovely—well,* mostly *lovely—girls up here and turning them into ogres?* Who would be left to become an Intoxibella?

Suddenly, she sat up straighter. *Wait a minute.*

She turned to Shiraz, who sat to her left. "It's a trick."

Shiraz's lips, which were now also the size of grapefruits, parted. "What you mean?"

"It's a *trick,*" Tookie repeated. "We're going to be okay, I think. Stay in your seat. Tell Dylan and Piper too."

Shiraz looked uncertain but turned and gave Dylan and Piper Tookie's message. For a moment Tookie feared she might have been steering them wrong. But she stayed put. *It's a trick, it's a trick, it's a trick.*

Ten more harried girls ran through the door marked HOME. It

slammed shut once more and the room went dark. More screams filled the air.

"Oh dear, ladies," Gunnero's voice purred in the blackness. "I am very disappointed. A mere baker's dozen skinless chickens chickened out. I thought I could count on more of you No-Sees leaving by now. *C'est la vie.* Let this be a lesson to you, ladies. Here in Modelland, we have a golden rule about passed-around beautification apparatuses."

"What is it?" Kamalini asked.

Gunnero sighed deeply. "The first thing you must know about cosmetics, feebleminded females, is to forget everything Mommy and Daddy ever told you about sharing. Unless, of course, you want your face to fall off just like it has now—shared utensils give you creepy conjunctivitis, gory gangrene, bubonic boils, atrocious abscesses, styes, and staphylococcus! So from this moment on, you have my personal permission to be stingy, selfish wenches when it comes to your *maquillage.* Got it, No-Sees?"

Everyone said yes, and bright searchlights immediately shone in their faces, making everyone cringe. Piper yelped and shielded her face with her hands.

Tookie peeked at her reflection. The grotesque effects of the contaminated makeup had miraculously vanished.

"Moving on to phase three!" Gunnero crowed. *"Embellishments!"*

More Mannecants appeared, this time carts full of jewelry that sparkled like raindrops on clean windows—chunky rose gold necklaces, beaming bangles and bracelets, pairs of enormous hoop earrings that were connected to each other via a thin rope of platinum, and rings, rings, rings galore. The Mannecants draped layer upon layer of brilliant adornments onto the girls.

Shiraz leaned over in her chair. "You so smart, Tookie! You make us stay! And we pass first round!"

Her other friends grinned gratefully at her as well. "You guys would've figured it out on your own," Tookie said bashfully, ducking her head.

Then she looked in her mirror, marveling at the accessories chosen for her. Each bore a name that looked vaguely familiar.

"Receptacles!" Gunnero screamed.

Another group of Mannecants rolled in a much larger cart full of every kind of purse imaginable. Studded clutches, hobo-chic bags, drawstring styles, quilted ones with sparkling chain straps, antique leather satchels, rare over-the-shoulder treasures. The Mannecants went down the row of girls like a factory assembly line, placing the purses across the girls' bodies, shoving them into their hands and onto their shoulders. Tookie ended up with a snazzy black nylon backpack; a short-handled, boxy purse made of stiff but fine leather; and . . . a Dream Bag! The very same yellow tote Zarpessa had, the one all the girls at B3 envied!

"I got a Helly!" Chaste trilled, holding up a monogrammed tote.

"I got a Xizo!" Zarpessa cried happily, holding up a hobo bag that bore a logo of interlocking Xs.

The Mannecants scuttled out of the room as fast as they had come in. Almost instantly, the jewelry and bags began to revolt. Chaste's tote handles bound her wrists and squeezed. Dylan's earrings turned into two-pound weights, dragging down her earlobes. She screamed in pain. The necklace Tookie was wearing started to get warm, then scalding hot, and then it wrapped several times around her neck and squeezed and squeezed. Tookie clutched at her neck, barely able to breathe.

A door appeared across the room and a lantern swayed back and forth. HOME. Then it swung open, giving way to lush tropical scenery, golden sunlight, and the sound of surf hitting the sand.

Eleven girls made a mad dash for the exit. *"Ahh,"* they all said in chorus as soon as they crossed the threshold. The Home door closed with a boom.

With that, the necklace unwound from Tookie's neck. All the other accessories fell limply in the girls' laps, inanimate again.

Tookie looked around. Shiraz, Piper, and Dylan were still here, huddled under their maquillage tables. *Relief.*

Just then, Gunnero Narzz entered from a dark space in the room, swinging in his hand the lantern that had been the light source beckoning the now-departed girls to the Home door. He glared at Tookie and her crew. "Figures you four survived."

Then he turned, addressing the winnowed-down group of girls that remained. "Fraudulent. Phony. Forgery. Fake. Close your eyes and think about the time when an item you adored, cherished, took such pride in owning, was taken from you . . . without your permission. Swiped! Swindled! Snatched! Stolen! Your world crumbles around you! Betrayed! Bitten! Backstabbed! Bereaved! Being the victim of theft doesn't feel good, does it, No-Sees?"

The girls shook their heads confusedly.

"That's how my cronies feel whenever you purchase or accept a gift of a counterfeit couturier creation," Gunnero explained. "You may think you are sporting the latest fashions and fooling your pitifully clueless circle of friends, but you are merely concocting a deceitful world of pseudo luxury and corrupt make-believe, while the hardworking artisans who dedicate their lives to producing authentic wares are robbed blindly. And who produces these fake wares? Poor starving children who roam homeless in public squalor and live poverty-stricken in rodent-infested shanties."

Gunnero stopped right in front of Tookie and whipped the Dream Bag off her shoulder. Tookie hadn't even realized it was still there. "How. Dare. You."

He turned to the group, eyeing the fake bags that rested on their laps and the counterfeit jewels that sparkled at their throats. "How dare you *all*! So, the lesson for phase three is what?"

"For Gunnero designer friends, buying of the fake no good!" Shiraz offered.

Gunnero looked pleased. "At least one of you is listening. Even if it is a knee-high Lilliputian."

"Lilli—wha?" Shiraz blinked innocently.

"Oh, excuse me for being prêt-a-politically-incorrect," Gunnero simpered. "I believe the acceptable phrase is *Five P:* Puny Pocket-sized Petite Particle of a Person."

Shiraz looked crushed. Tookie wanted to defend her. But she'd never defended anyone before—she'd never had an opportunity to. And anyway, now wasn't the time.

"On to phase four!" Gunnero trilled. "This next part is— heh—*piercingly* funny."

His heel attacked the floor again. A panel in the wall tilted backward and fell to the floor with a loud bang. Gunnero ushered the girls forward into a new space. Tookie did a rough count. Only seventy or so of the recruits were left.

As Gunnero walked into the next area, he glanced at the girls over his shoulder. "Can any of you dimwits guess what the final phase is?" The Bellas just stared at him blankly, and he sighed. "Oh, I swear. The No-Sees are getting thicker and thicker each year. And I'm not talking about your hips." Then, eyeing Dylan, he said, "Well, maybe I am."

Dylan bit her lip and balled her fists.

"The final phase is the actual *defilé,* the *sfilata di moda,*" Gunnero trilled. He eyed Kamalini. "The *tamasha.* The *fashion show.* And ladies, you'll love this. It will allow me to *drill* into you all you need here at Modelland."

One by one, ten exits marked HOME lit up around the perimeter of the space. The ceiling opened, revealing a gigantic, loud, mechanical contraption. Tookie realized it was a giant sewing machine with an enormous needle that was as long as her dining room table in Peppertown. Slowly, the machine descended upon the girls, its needle slamming up and down.

"Have we all had our ears pierced, ladies?" Gunnero asked.

Most of the girls nodded shakily.

"Well, then this should be a piece of cake!" Gunnero shrieked. And then he was gone.

"This look like trouble," Shiraz whispered.

Some girls scuttled away. Some dropped to the floor and covered their ears. But Tookie had learned by now that running was futile, so she remained completely still. Her three friends copied her. Together, they watched as the needle drew closer and closer. . . .

Chaste was also standing still. Slowly, the needle bore down on her head, its tip piercing her skull and continuing all the way through her body to the ground. When the needle retracted, Chaste was . . . *gone.*

The machine quickly sought out the next girl, then the next, puncturing them into the unknown. Tookie recognized one of them as Desperada, the sobbing girl she had seen in LaDorno

Square at T-DOD. The needle punctured Desperada's head and she howled, but Tookie couldn't tell if it was from physical or emotional pain.

The Home doors glowed even brighter than before. Angelīka from Icylann spun and dodged the needle, then scurried to the door. And with that, she was gone. A few more girls avoided the needle's wrath and followed her through one of the Home doors.

Within seconds, the needle loomed just inches away from Tookie. Her heart thudded as the tip jabbed close to her skin. Then closer, closer . . . until the tip was aimed straight at her head.

She waited for a sharp pain. The moment the tip of the needle hit her skull, she suddenly felt like a million tiny appendages were tickling her skin. Her body tilted upside down and she felt her shirt, cargo pants, and underwear slip off. More fingers gently pulled at her limbs and clothed her body. The space she was in was incredibly dark, and Tookie rubbed her hands over the mystery fabrics that now touched her skin. They had dips and folds and tucks and felt extremely luxe.

The enclosure turned her upright and deposited her into a soundless room. Floating in the air, bisque-colored orbs glowed like full moons. Slowly, faces appeared in the orbs. Tookie recognized one of the faces as Kamalini's, her Headbangor still strapped firmly to her head. Zarpessa's face appeared in another orb, then Chaste's. By the startled way the girls were looking at her, Tookie realized that she must be inside an orb too.

Music thumped in the distance. As Tookie floated behind the other girls through an entryway, it grew louder and louder, making her insides vibrate. It was a familiar sort of music. Kind of like the type of music one would hear at . . .

A fashion show, Tookie thought.

More orbs bearing girls' faces floated behind her. Tookie spotted Shiraz, then Dylan, then a dirty-blond curly-haired girl she hadn't seen until now, and then Piper. "You made it!" Tookie cried. But her friends didn't appear to hear her. *These orbs must be soundproof.*

A door appeared ahead. It pulsed to the beat of the music as if the fashion show behind the door wanted to burst through it. *I'm going to be in a fashion show? Seriously?* She feared falling on her face. She feared Gunnero laughing at her. But more than anything, she was almost . . . excited. Forgetta-Girls weren't in fashion shows. Only Rememba-Girls were.

Tookie's orb approached the door, which began to glow a bright white. One by one, letters appeared.

T
H
I
S

W
A
Y

H
O
M
E

What? Tookie tried to pedal her orb backward, but it didn't work. Up ahead, girls' heads floated through the Home door: first Zarpessa, then Chaste. *Good! They're gone! Yes!*

But next to approach the Home door was Shiraz. "No!" Tookie cried. But her protests were futile: through the door Shiraz's floating head went. Then Dylan's head. Then Piper's, then Kamalini's. "No!" Tookie screamed. "Please! Don't leave me here alone!"

But to her horror, her own bubble was floating toward the Home door too. Tookie summoned all her might to turn herself around, but the bubble had a mind of its own.

She closed her eyes and tried to hold on to all the good things that had happened to her on her journey here. She recalled Dylan's sassy laugh, Shiraz's spunky broken English, Piper's intelligence and dry wit, and ZhenZhen's contagious giggle and nurturing kindness.

And finally, as she passed though the Home door, Tooke bid a silent goodbye to Modelland.

18

La Lumière

Tookie's eyes were shut tight. A stiff breeze made her face tingle. It smelled familiar, sort of like . . . tangerines? *No.* Blood oranges.

Tookie opened her eyes. She was wearing exactly what all the girls in the O plaza had had on, except it was two-tone green.

Her head felt foggy. *I don't remember how I got into these clothes. Where are Piper and Shiraz and Dylan? Am I sleepwalking? Was Thigh-High Boot Camp just a nightmare? Or . . . Oh no . . .*

Am I still IN Boot Camp?

Way off in the distance, the M building stood proud and tall. In front of her was a mishmash of cubelike houses, connected by slivers of jade and turquoise opaque stones. Huge faces carved into hedges decorated the grounds. Vines and flowers made up the faces' eyes and hair. One of the flower-eyes opened and stared straight at her.

"Admiring the D, are you?" a voice asked.

Tookie spun around. ZhenZhen scooped her into a huge bear hug. Then, over ZhenZhen's shoulder, Tookie saw Shiraz, Dylan, and Piper walking toward her in slow motion, all wearing the same outfit she was. *They're walking in slo-mo. It* is *a dream. Wake up, Tookie.*

More girls appeared behind them. Kamalini . . . Desperada . . . and Chaste and Zarpessa. *Yuck. No, it's definitely a nightmare.*

"You made it, girl!" Dylan cried, running toward Tookie. Shiraz and Piper barreled toward her too, and the girls crashed together into a sloppy, love-filled reunion hug.

Then Tookie looked at ZhenZhen. "Is Thigh-High Boot Camp really over?" Tookie asked.

ZhenZhen nodded, and the girls erupted into hugs and applause.

"But there was no fashion show," Piper stated, interrupting their celebration. "Guru Gunnero stated, rather demonically, that the whole THBC process would culminate in one big fashion extravaganza."

"You mean you didn't do the fashion show ending?" ZhenZhen frowned. She looked worried. "The BellaDonna is going to be so upset. Gunnero has been excluding the fashion show part of Boot Camp for the past two years. Word is he doesn't want any fashion shows happening before the new Bellas get their walking lessons from him. It's like he wants to take full credit for any walks." She rolled her eyes. "I'm really sorry you had to experience such hell without getting a payoff of heaven. But you made it. I hope your time here is worth the agony you just experienced."

"Oh, it was nothing. My hairdresser's personal trainer's manicurist's nephew has a friend who went through it before, so I already knew everything that was going to happen," Zarpessa said smugly.

Dylan rolled her eyes.

"So how many made it?" Kamalini asked.

"Fifty-four," ZhenZhen said.

Shiraz cocked her head. "Those who no make it? Where they go?"

"They're gone. *Forever.* Never to return." Tookie and her friends looked at each other with wide eyes. If they'd buckled under the tests, they would've been gone too.

Then ZhenZhen turned and faced the bizarre building. "So, guys, this is the D. Come, I'll get you settled."

Dylan planted her feet. "Honey chile, I just been invaded by bacteria, sliced and diced by earrings, stabbed by a monster needle, and had my head imprisoned inside a bubble. I'm not goin' in there until I know what that whacked-out place is."

ZhenZhen stepped up onto the porch. "It's where you're going to be living while you're here."

She motioned for the surviving six members of her original dozen to follow her into the D. Sun streamed through high windows into a vast living room with couches, tables, and pillows. It was decorated in a blend of styles—Gothic, midcentury modern, art deco with a hint of . . . laboratory, in some strange way. The place smelled, as most places in Modelland seemed to, of blood oranges.

"Modelland is now your home, home, home!" ZhenZhen

trilled, beaming with pride. "This is the *Un*Common Room, where you'll all hang out!"

"I get it!" Tookie announced, "The *D* stands for Dorms!"

"Exactly!" ZhenZhen said. Six stoic-looking youngish Mannecants entered the room and stood next to ZhenZhen, holding stacks of what looked like stiff scarves draped over one arm.

"Senturas!" Zarpessa yelped. "I'd know that shade of yellow anywhere!"

"Same color as the dress you wore here," added Chaste. "What a coincidence."

"Zarpessa's right—these are Senturas," ZhenZhen said. "The Senturas are very, very special. The more you wear them, the stronger your *pow-pow-pow*ers become." ZhenZhen accented the *pows* with a pointed finger, like she was shooting a pistol.

The Mannecants tossed the stacks of Senturas into the air. Miraculously, the strips of fabric circled above the girls in a brilliant air show. Some flew in formation; others did solo kamikazes into the crowd. The girls oohed and aahed at the performance, which ended with each Sentura nose-diving into the group, finding its recipient, and wrapping itself two times around the girl's waist. *Whap!* One wrapped around Zarpessa. *Zing!* One circled Shiraz. And finally, a Sentura even cinched Tookie's waist. She stared at it, barely believing her eyes. *Is this really . . . mine?*

"Listen, up girls. Keep tabs on these magic golden cummerbunds," ZhenZhen said. "You might have innate powers, but this is the only thing that can make the Bella magic happen." She shook her head. "You all should see some of my photo shoots when I don't have this darn thing on! Pitiful."

The girls gingerly touched their Senturas. Tookie held the

ends of hers like they were the wings of a wounded bird. Zarpessa and Chaste scooted to a mirror at the far side of the space to admire themselves. Tookie could see them yanking their Senturas tightly and trying to find the most flattering spots on their hips for the sashes to rest.

ZhenZhen clapped. "Okay, girls. Go up to the second level and look for your names."

The girls climbed the long suspended staircase that only had steps. No risers, no banister. And it floated in midair. Down a long, wide hall with immense fabric flowers and plants growing out of the artwork were a series of bedroom doors. Slowly, the names of the girls who would occupy each room appeared on the door graffiti-style, as though an invisible hand was doing the writing. Everyone ran to look for their names.

"Piper, you're here!" Tookie called, pointing to a door to her right and then waiting at the door for it to write the next name. "Dylan, you're with her!"

"Tookie, you here!" Shiraz beckoned Tookie from down the hall. "And . . . *K-A-M-A-L*—"

"Kamalini! That is me!" Kamalini scooted to the entrance of the room.

"Next one is . . ." Shiraz peered closely at the door. Her lips spread into a smile. "Shiraz Shiraz!"

Tookie and Shiraz ran through the purple door and gasped. The room was a large, bright square lit by floor-to-ceiling windows. But there was nothing in the room save for four square burlap bags on the floor.

Kamalini clutched her Headbangor. "We have to sleep on the floor? I guess we can make do."

Shiraz walked toward a window, but suddenly there was a loud clunk and she stopped short, as though she'd knocked into something. She lost her footing and fell forward. Instead of crashing to the floor, she stopped as something invisible broke her fall.

"Huh?" Tookie whispered. She scuttled over to Shiraz to see what was there. It seemed like a cushion of air was now suspending Shiraz three feet above the floor.

Shiraz grinned. "Is soft! Feels like a—"

"Bed," Tookie finished. The outline of a bed materialized before their eyes. A cushy white comforter and four fluffy pillows rested atop the mattress.

"Is fancy! Way better than Canne Del Abra cot!" Shiraz joyfully exclaimed, looking at the bed forming around her.

Then the sound of a pencil scratching against paper filled the room. Black lines traversed the white comforter, slowly forming a picture. Shiraz jumped off the bed to give it a closer look. In no time, the lines formed a large eye, then a nose, then another eye and a pair of full lips, and finally an abstract scribble made luxurious black hair flow from the head. When miniature dots began to cover the face, Shiraz gasped. "Is me!"

Tookie and Kamalini looked at each other excitedly. "Where's my bed?" they said at the exact same time.

"Jinx!" Kamalini teased, bumping Tookie's hip. Tookie smiled so hard, her cheeks hurt. No one had ever jinxed her before.

Tookie walked to the left of Shiraz's bed, Kamalini strode right. At almost the same time, their knees bumped into an invisible bedpost. They both allowed themselves to fall forward.

"Delicious!" Kamalini exclaimed.

"Like falling onto a cloud of whipped cream," Tookie said.

Sure enough, outlines of two beds quickly formed. Moments later, the pencil-scratching noise rang out. A drawing of Tookie appeared on the white comforter. The likeness was a bit goofier than she looked in real life, her mouth exaggeratedly big, her ears sticking out twenty degrees more than they truly did, but the comforter did draw one of Tookie's eyes darker than the other. For a brief moment, Tookie took in the eyes of the girls in the room and longed for a set of matching irises.

Kamalini's comforter now depicted a caricature of her too. But Kamalini seemed almost saddened by the image, touching her Headbangor and sinking to the mattress.

"Don't you like it?" Tookie asked, peering at her.

"Well, I . . ." Kamalini shook her head. "I love it. Really. It is just, I am nervous about being here. I didn't really try as hard as all the girls from my country did. I was showering and this thing"— she pointed to her SMIZE—"just popped out. So here I am."

"You don't think you deserve to be here?" Tookie could hardly believe Kamalini was saying such a thing—with her big, soulful eyes and her flawless brown skin, she was one of the most beautiful girls here.

Kamalini shrugged. "My parents were so happy, though. But they are worried about my addiction to . . ."

"The drugs?" Shiraz jumped in.

"No, not drugs," Kamalini said.

"The whiskey?" Shiraz guessed again. "I no judge you, I just want to help!"

"No . . . not alcohol either. Worse. This." She held up her Headbangor. "They didn't want me to bring it. I smuggled it in."

Shiraz squinted. "You addicted to the music?"

Kamalini nodded. "My father made it for me—he is dean of my country's most prestigious university and an inventor. My mother is a Chakrawood actress *and* director—a rarity. I started using it after something . . . happened." She lowered her eyes. "It eases the pain. Helps me forget. It's hard for me to be without it. I get withdrawal symptoms." She sighed. "My father even made this one waterproof so I can wear it while swimming and in the shower. I had it on when that SMIZE contraption came out of the showerhead. The girls at school say that I think I'm the most beautiful girl in Chakra and that my parents purchased the SMIZE on the black market, but it's the farthest thing from the truth."

"Can I listen?" Tookie asked hesitantly, almost certain Kamalini would say no.

Kamalini looked into Tookie's eyes and then nodded and placed the Headbangor on Tookie's head. Tookie felt a rush as the music hit her brainwaves. The most crystal-clear jangling tune, with sitars, a high-pitched singer, a tabla drum, and a shehnai flute, filled her ears. She stood, paced around the room, and listened to the words.

"The song is about a forbidden love, right?" she asked.

Kamalini's eyes lit up. "Yes! It is my mom singing. Another rarity. She acts, she directs her own films, *and* she sings her own songs. Most of our actresses lip-sync. My mom's latest song is a hit in Chakra and will be the music for the big dance number in her next movie. But wait a second . . . you know my language?"

"Every language, she knows!" Shiraz called matter-of-factly from across the room as she traced the lines of her face on her comforter. "Magical, Tookie is."

Yeah, right, Tookie thought.

"Ha, did someone say magical?" a voice rang through the room. "That sounds like my cue!"

Zarpessa stood in the doorway, a disingenuous smile on her face. "Well! A room for four! I kind of figured we'd each have our own rooms, but I guess I can live with this."

No, Tookie thought. *Please don't make her be our roommate.* But when Tookie looked at the purple door again, Zarpessa's name had appeared.

No one spoke as she pranced across the room and plopped down on Tookie's bed. "Oh goodness," she said, running her hands over the outline of Tookie's face on the comforter. "This reminds me of my face after the THBC makeup attack! *Aauwwwgg . . . ,*" she growled, monsterlike, and then slapped the drawing of Tookie's cheek. "Guru Gunnero, you in there?" Suddenly, the Tookie drawing vanished and a new face formed. Zarpessa's.

"Now, *this* is more like it!" Zarpessa gazed at her caricature, which accentuated her dramatic eyebrows, full lips, and long, bone-straight hair. She grabbed the fabric of the comforter and ran it between two fingers. "Mmm! Twenty-five-hundred thread count. My mother's brother's son's cousin's mentor is the manufacturer of these linens. You all are going to sleep like princesses in these. I've got them on my bed at home. *Don't I, Too-Too?*"

She whipped around and stared at Tookie, challenging her to say something. Tookie stared at the marble floor.

"It is Too*kie,*" Kamalini corrected Zarpessa.

"Whatever," Zarpessa said loftily.

Head hanging, Tookie walked through the room, trying to feel for another bed. Finally, in the darkest corner of the room, she hit an invisible post. When the outline of the bed formed, it was smaller than the others, and the sheets were the teensiest bit scratchy. *This bed's fine,* she told herself. The pencil-lead sounds kicked in, and soon Tookie's image was staring back at her.

"So, what do you think of your room?" ZhenZhen said, walking in. "Incredible, right?

"Listen," she went on. "You can only keep two things from home. The clothes you wore here are in those burlap sacks. Make your choices by tomorrow morning." Then she stepped back into the hall. "And oh! One more thing. We tell time by color, not by number. Look for the clocks around the Land. You'll get the hang of them soon!"

As soon as ZhenZhen departed, four nightstands appeared. Resting on them were soft, elaborate cotton nightgowns and Modelland-monogrammed toiletry bags. A tag on the gown read *Fashioned especially for you, based on the calculations from your THBC measurements session.*

The girls began removing their uniforms. Tookie changed into her nightie. It had an attached cape that hit halfway down her thighs. It fit around the shoulders, waist, and arms instead of gaping and pulling and pinching like all of Myrracle's hand-me-ups. She pushed her feet into the Modelland slipper booties, happy they didn't cramp her toes.

"Only two things from home?" Zarpessa said, pouting. "That sucks."

But for Tookie, it wasn't a hard choice at all. She reached for her burlap sack. Item Number One: *T-Mail Jail,* which she pulled from her cargo pants pocket and stashed in the top drawer of her nightstand. Next to her, she noticed Shiraz stuffing a stiff piece of paper into her own drawer.

Tookie knew what her Item Number Two was to be too. She reached into the smaller pocket of her cargo pants and closed her fingers around the round, dented button. T O OKE. Just touching it made her feel better. She removed it from her pocket and held it in her palm.

"What's that beat-up thing?"

Tookie's head shot up. Zarpessa was staring at her. Tookie quickly closed her fist. *What was I thinking? I can't have this pin in plain sight—not in front of Theophilus's girlfriend!* Tookie knew the button was damaged and not easily recognizable, but she feared Zarpessa would be able to tell what it was. "It's a . . . a . . . ," she stammered.

"Huh? It's a *what*?" Zarpessa made a face.

Frantic, Tookie skidded around the room, looking for something to cover up the pin. Everyone stared at her, even Shiraz and Kamalini. Then Tookie turned to the hallway. *Yes!* She snagged a large, thorny flower with long streamers and pointy tendrils from one of the art pieces and nervously fashioned the flower into an oversized corsage, which she pinned over the button. The brooch was nearly the size of her head and looked as though it might lash out and bite off someone's arm, but it covered up her secret Theophilus treasure.

As soon as Tookie returned to the bedroom, an announcement blared over a hidden loudspeaker. "All Bellas must retire to their beds and rest up for the first day of classes tomorrow. It is now time for the Lumière."

Snap. The overhead bulbs went dark, but faint light from the crescent moon still shone through the window. Tookie fell into her small, scratchy bed. She felt a throb in her lower back, a kind of ache she'd never felt before. The dull pain traveled to her hips. She was so exhausted from the day, the tiniest muscles, even the ones around her eyes, ached.

The room filled with the soft sounds of everyone pulling back covers and slipping under the sheets. "Good night," Shiraz and Kamalini said sweetly. Zarpessa said nothing. Silence filled the room, and Tookie's mind started to wander and drift. Just as she was about to sink into sleep, a light popped on.

"What *that*?" Shiraz sat straight up in bed.

A spotlight shone on Zarpessa's face. Whenever Zarpessa moved, the light moved with her.

"Hide under the overpass!" Zarpessa screamed, clearly half asleep. Tookie stifled a laugh. *Maybe this is some kind of punishment.*

But then Zarpessa rubbed her eyes, seeming to awaken. She suddenly looked ecstatic. "Ohmigod! It's my Lumière!"

"Loo-mee-air?" Shiraz repeated.

Zarpessa tilted her chin toward the light as though it were a sun lamp. "The Lumière is the special light that shines on Bellas at night. It's whatever their most flattering light is—candlelight, sunlight, whatever. And look! Mine is a spotlight! It means I'm going to be a superstar Intoxibella! My pow-pow-powers are right around the corner! I'm going to be a Quadruple7, bigger than Ci~L!"

Suddenly, a warm reddish light snapped on over Kamalini's bed. Kamalini let out an irritated shriek and pulled the covers over her head. "We cannot sleep with lights on!" she wailed. "We need darkness!"

"But Kamalini," Zarpessa said in a patronizing voice. "It's an *honor*. The Lumière is supposed to give you all kinds of restorative gifts throughout the night. Plus, it helps keep your skin fresh and dewy!"

"And so does sleep!" Kamalini protested.

Down the hall, in all the other rooms, other girls were calling out as well: "It's so bright!" "Mine's glow sticks!" "Are we really supposed to sleep with these on us all night?" Tookie waited for her own light to shine, but the space above her bed remained dark. Then she cast her eyes to the right. There was another dark bed in the room: Shiraz's.

Shiraz's bed creaked. She stood up on the mattress and inspected the ceiling. "Is Lumière supposed to happen to every girl here?"

"Every *model*," Zarpessa corrected her.

Shiraz glared at her. "I model. I just as beauty as you. Maybe my light broken."

"It's not a matter of its being *broken* or not." Zarpessa settled onto her pillow like a princess, fanning her hair around her. "It's more about the quality of the girl in the bed. Maybe *some* of you don't belong here. Maybe some of you are here for other reasons. Oh my, I've *sacrificed* so much beauty rest speaking to you all. Good night."

In the dim Lumière light, Tookie could see Shiraz opening her mouth. A small moan escaped it. Shiraz stared across the room to Tookie's dark bed and met her eyes.

The sacrifices.

That's ridiculous. Zarpessa's just trying to scare us. It's just a dumb rumor, Tookie thought. But when she closed her eyes again, she wasn't so sure.

M

Darkness surrounded her. Cold marble pressed on the soles of her bare feet. A draft cut through her bedclothes and made her body shudder in one hard, painful wave.

A faucet dripped close by. Papers rustled. Over her head, she could hear tiny footsteps. Mice? She blinked hard, but her eyes couldn't pull in more light.

Where am I? Was it all a dream? Am I back home in Peppertown?

Tookie spied a small window high over her head. The tips of the M building glowed not far away. She was still here. At Modelland. But she'd sleepwalked. *This* definitely *isn't the D.*

Tookie found a wall and felt her way around. Slowly, she rounded a dark corner and saw a few flickering candles through an opening. She hoped it was a passage that led back to the D. She *had* to get back to her bed. The Modelland staff and security probably didn't like night wanderers.

She approached the door carefully and put her hand on the knob. Suddenly, a sharp sound made her stop. *Whack! Whack!*

More whacks came, followed by whimpers and the muddy sound of breathy, unintelligible words. Heart pounding, Tookie poked her head around the doorframe. Inside was a cinder-block room that resembled a jail cell. A figure was on its knees, rocking back and forth and mumbling "It'smyfaultIt'smyfaultIt'smyfault" over and over and over. The person held a wooden plank in hand, and their back was bruised and bloody. The only item in the room was a picture pinned to the wall. Tookie squinted at it, recognizing the three pillars immediately: the Obscure Obelisks, the bizarre structures that had arisen in LaDorno seemingly overnight.

More chants and deeper moans came from the figure. The deranged person raised the plank once more. "No!" Tookie said silently. Who could *do* such a thing to themselves?

WHACK!

A gash in the figure's back opened and Tookie could see raw flesh. And still Tookie stood paralyzed at the door.

WHACK!

More flesh broke. What were once pinpricks of red now oozed blood from deeper cuts and gashes.

Then the figure reached up to the Obscure Obelisks, its hands flailing, as if the figure was blind and elderly and desperately trying to connect with an unseen face. Hands clawed at the photo, and the figure started to beat its forehead against it. Then came a wail so deep, so guttural, so agonizing . . . "AAAUGHH! SORRY SORRY SO SO SORRY SORRY SORRY!"

Tookie gasped, never having heard such a horrible sound. The figure in the room stiffened at the noise and raised its head. And suddenly, Tookie caught sight of who it was. It was a face she— and all the world—knew very, very well.

Ci~L.

19

CaraCaraCara and the Dormitory Effect

The next morning, when Tookie opened her eyes again, she was lying on her bed in the D, tucked safely underneath her covers. She rubbed her eyes, instantly remembering the night before. What had *that* been about? Had she seriously seen Ci~L hurting herself? *Why?*

Tookie was used to having awful nightmares and even night terrors when she woke up screaming, so she couldn't tell her friends what she'd seen. Not until she knew it was real.

Disoriented, Tookie stumbled into the large, sterile-looking community bathroom. As she did, a dull pain shot through her legs, hips, and stomach. She doubled over, feeling as though she was about to vomit. *Perfect,* she thought. *I'm sick on the first day of school.*

Everyone in the bathroom wore clear shower sandals and aqua bathrobes with yellow arms and lapels that formed an M. The backs of their bathrobes sported immense eyes decorated with SMIZEs. All at once, every single girl in the bathroom doubled over in pain, gripping her stomach and back just as Tookie had. As a bathroom stall door banged open, Tookie caught sight of scrawled graffiti on the wall. Many of the drawings were just of hearts and initials, but several stood out: *Latta Defacake. 7/7 4 Sure.* And *PERSEQUESHON: NEVER FORGET, NEVER RETURN.*

She trudged up to one of the twenty-five sinks cut into a long slab of white and gray marble. Over each sink hung a white-framed rectangular mirror with different-sized holes in it. One hole spat a perfect plume of cold blue water. Another shot out red-tinged hot water. A large hole emitted purplish-tinged water, a perfect combination of hot and cold.

Tookie spotted Piper at a corner sink and walked toward her, trying not to fall over from another sudden stomach spasm. Piper had laid out a series of toiletries, including a toothbrush, toothpaste, a hairbrush, and a comb, in a neat, even line. When she bumped one out of place, she quickly pushed it back into position. She was also playing with a puzzle that had many moving pieces with scrambled parts of a picture. A golden light overhead danced on her delicate skin, enhancing the elegant angles of her chin and shoulders. *Every movement Piper makes could be a beautiful picture,* Tookie thought. *She's posing, even though she doesn't realize it.*

"Where'd you get all that stuff?" Tookie asked.

Piper looked up at her and smiled. "This I brought from home." The tiles formed a picture of Piper's mother on a throne with a stately man standing next to her. Piper tried to hide the puzzle from Tookie, snapping the last tile into its proper place. "The other stuff was on my nightstand. You didn't get a toiletries kit?"

Tookie blinked. "It's back in my room. Do you mind if I borrow some paste?"

"Sure," Piper said. Then she shoved the puzzle at Tookie, making sure to hold it upside down so Tookie couldn't see the picture. "Would you mind messing this up for me first?"

Tookie stared at her. "But you just solved it."

Piper raised one shoulder. "I know. But I'll solve it again. Playing with it keeps me sane."

Puzzles weren't Tookie's thing—it would probably take forever for her to figure this one out. But she'd heard this about people of SansColor: they were geniuses, adept at all subjects, masters of science, mathematics, music, and art.

She took the puzzle and rearranged the pieces for Piper without looking at it. "Who are you rooming with?" she asked.

"Dylan and I are in with that strumpet Chaste." Piper rolled her eyes. "And the Likee sisters—I believe Modelland is counting them as one. They're all sleeping squashed together in one bed."

"Weird," Tookie murmured. She opened her mouth to receive the waterspout. Bright blue water sprang out, hitting her upper lip and her nostrils, sending shivers and cramps up her nearly bare back.

"You look freezing," Piper said. "Didn't a robe appear in your closet this morning?" She pointed to her own.

Tookie lifted her right shoulder and raised her eyebrows. Then she grabbed Piper's toothpaste, doled out a narrow strip on her left index finger, and started rubbing her teeth.

"Does that *do* much?" Piper asked curiously.

"Better than nothing. Plus, I don't have time for a shower."

Piper looked closely at Tookie. "I would recommend you *not* skip bathing today, Tookie. This is the one week where you want to be as spotlessly clean as possible."

Tookie shut her eyes, wincing again with another pain. "Piper, my back and tummy are killing me!" she whispered.

Piper shrugged. "Join the club, Tookie. Every new Bella started menstruating at the exact same time this morning."

"Wait. *What?*"

"You've never heard of menstrual synchrony, or the dormitory effect?" Piper asked. "Menstrual synchrony is a theory that suggests that the menstruation cycles of women who cohabitate— think army barracks, female penitentiaries, convents, and university dormitories—synchronize over time. It usually takes months for the alignment to occur, but here at Modelland, it seems to have happened in twenty-four hours."

"But I've never *gotten* my period before this," Tookie whispered.

"Well, Tookie, looks like you're a woman now," Piper said.

Tookie was about to protest—there was no way she was any more womanly today than she had been the day before—but all of a sudden, she felt that perhaps something in her *had* changed. Those abdominal pains made so much sense, after all. And that certainly made them more bearable—for once, she felt *normal,* like everyone else.

Then, as she glanced down at the sink again, she noticed Piper's toothbrush. It was made of an iridescent pearllike substance, and its bristles were fashioned in the shape of an eye.

Just looking at the toothbrush made a memory strike her hard: *She is uncoordinated, unattractive, and unmemorable. . . . She's not mine, Creamy.*

The words were like daggers in her heart. She was allowed to keep only two personal items but in reality had come to Modelland with heavy *baggage* she couldn't get rid of. Tookie moved her face closer to the mirror. As if knowing why she was doing so, the mirror inched closer to Tookie's searching face, kindly refraining from spouting any frigid or blazing water. Tookie stared deeply into her multicolored eyes, seeking a clue. She silently begged the mirror for some similarities, for any portion of her face to resemble her father. She took her baby fingers and traced the lines of her face, ending with the outline of her round, full lips.

Nothing.

She looked nothing like him.

Hot tears fell from her eyes. She picked up a spare comb from the counter and ran its teeth through her hair. The comb snagged and then broke into two pieces, just like it always did.

$$\text{M}$$

Moments later, Tookie ran out of the D toward Beautification Boulevard. She was now dressed in the official first-year-Bella green Modelland uniform she'd had on the day before when she'd emerged from THBC. Most of the uniform had been easy to put on correctly, and although wearing the leotard over her pants *felt* strange, it certainly was a cool look. But Tookie didn't understand the Sentura at all. It didn't fit the way it had the day before. It kept slipping off her hips.

When she'd gone back to the bedroom from the bathroom, a bottle of perfume was on her nightstand. POUSSER, said a sign on the plunger. When Tookie depressed the atomizer, a fine blood-orange-scented mist had spritzed into the air. Slowly, the mist had assembled into an onionskin-thin sheet of paper. It was her schedule for this semester—or *quadmester,* as it was called in Modelland.

She shuddered from another abdominal cramp, then looked at her schedule again:

Bella Assignments for this first day of the first quadmester of the first year

Uno: CaraCaraCara. Time: Midnight-Blue, Sharp
Dos: Run-a-Way Intensive. Time: Kelly Green, Sharp
Tres: Mastication. Time: Goldenrod, Sharp

Midnight-Blue? Kelly Green and Goldenrod, Sharp? Tookie needed to learn how to tell time all over again.

Tookie stared at the whirling, kaleidoscopic clock on Beautification Boulevard. All around her, girls were rushing past, just as confused as she was about the wacky colored clock.

She tried going right, thinking CaraCaraCara—"FaceFaceFace" in Gowdee'an—might be in that direction, and found herself on a path she'd never traveled before. An enormous, half-finished stadium loomed in the distance. Hulking male models from Bestosterone worked giant construction machines. Some of them welded metal beams together with silver flashlight-like devices that shot red-hot liquid glue. Others struck overtly sexualized poses for a photographer while they worked.

Suddenly, a deep voice rang out behind her. "Are you lost?"

Tookie turned and saw a muscular Bestostero with chiseled features walking toward her, blueprints tucked under his arms. His pecs swelled under his shirt. His skin was smooth and richly colored, and his eyebrows looked naturally arched, which was almost as bad as if he'd been a religious waxer. Tookie had never been a fan of the pretty-boy-arched-eyebrow look. Theophilus's unique features were more her taste.

"My name's Bravo," he said, looking straight at Tookie. "From Bestosterone. Are you a new Bella?"

Tookie opened her mouth but then shut it again. The guy was staring at her so *pointedly*, like she had worms crawling out of her hair.

"We're building this new 7Seven stadium for you," Bravo went on, gesturing to the site. "A couple of years ago, a huge fireball decimated the old stadium. It came out of nowhere, from the other side of the wall. Some people say the spirits over there get pissed at us sometimes and want to burn Modelland down."

Tookie still couldn't say a word. Then two boys appeared behind Bravo, both in fashionable workmen's uniforms. One had pale skin, an angular face, and piercing hazel eyes, and the other was stockier, with dark skin and the fullest lips Tookie had ever seen—even fuller than her own. "What's *that* you're talking to, Bravo?" the angular-faced one said.

The dark-skinned guy he was with snickered and nudged him. "Webb, you need to stop trippin', man," Bravo said.

Tookie bristled and turned away. Webb's insult wasn't anything she wasn't used to. She glanced over her shoulder just once. Pretty-boy Bravo was still watching her. Finally, he returned to his friends, and they retreated toward an immense eye made out of shiny metal. Its iris was constructed from green jade and the lid wore yellow eye shadow like a SMIZE.

Finally, Tookie found the CaraCaraCara building. It was the massive boat she'd seen during orientation. A bridge made of driftwood led from shore to the vessel's door.

"Hey! Tookie!" Dylan stood in front of the building. Piper and Shiraz were standing with her, both bearing the same achy, period-stricken looks the other Bellas had had in the bathroom earlier. "We were lookin' for you, girl! You made it!"

"Barely." Tookie almost considered telling them about the Bestostero and his rude friends, but she decided against it. Why bother?

The girls walked across the bridge into the floating classroom. An immense bust of the BellaDonna leered from the ship's bow. "It's made out of some element that doesn't exist in the periodic table," Piper whispered.

Tookie shivered. She felt like the stony eyes were watching her. Would they ever see the BellaDonna for real, or only bizarre, rocklike representations of her?

They ducked their heads through the entryway and entered a classroom whose ceiling and walls were made entirely of bleached bones in the shape of a giant skeleton. "Hmmm," Piper said, examining the interior. "Dermal corset of flexible, collagenous fibers, hexagonal tesserae . . . oblique and serrated teeth not attached to the cranium. It's a shark!"

There were no seats, but Zarpessa and Chaste were standing

front and center in the middle of circles on the floor with their names printed in the center. Tookie, Piper, Shiraz, and Dylan found circles of their own in the row behind Zarpessa and Chaste. As soon as they stopped, individual spotlights shone straight into their faces. Piper squinted hard.

"Is it Lumière?" Shiraz exclaimed excitedly.

Chaste turned around. "Of course not, little girl. That only happens at night."

Just then, a wooden door on the other side of the boat snapped open. In bounded a tall man wearing an embroidered cape and a red jumpsuit with a vibrant multicolored serape sash around his waist. He had poochy lips, a button nose, bushy eyebrows, and twinkly, saucer-shaped eyes that immediately generated a smile from Tookie and all of the girls in the shark-room. His features flapped and twisted as if they were made of something much more flexible than flesh and bone. But despite all that, Tookie thought he was quite handsome in his own special way.

"Wassup with rubber man?" Dylan whispered to the girls.

"¡Hola! ¡Hola! ¡Hola! I am Guru Pacifico Cruz from the land of Texicoco!" he announced. "At Modelland, we are not fans of last names, so please call me Guru Pacifico. This, my dear Bellas, is CaraCaraCara class! Being a *modela fantástica* is all about mastering how to maneuver your face. And speaking of faces, this course will prepare you for what you will face out in the real world too, if you become Intoxibellas!"

"*If?*" Zarpessa rolled her eyes. "Not if, honey. *When.*"

"*Mi clase,*" Guru Pacifico continued, "is located within a great white shark not for comedy, no. You sit within the belly of the sea beast to remind you of the *real* sharks in the world. They will swim around you if you become Intoxibellas. They will want to rip you to shreds, jealous of your fame and fortune. They will wait for you to bleed and then swallow you whole, leaving nothing to bury but your fancy stilettos!"

Tookie wasn't sure whether to laugh or cry.

"So my class is *muy importante,* Bellas!" The Guru's eyes sparkled. "It will tighten your guts, cement your resistance, and strengthen your core! If you've noticed, we are on a rocky boat. *Metáfora* intended! And . . . your, shall I say . . . cycles have all been *synchronized,* I'm sure you have noticed by now. Crampy, *sí?*"

Groans sounded throughout the room. Tookie pressed on her abdomen.

"This is not a coincidence, Bellas. Usually it takes *muchos meses,* many months for ladies' cycles to, shall I say . . . organize. But here at Modelland, we have accelerated that harmony."

"I knew it!" Piper whispered to Tookie.

"Why do we do this? Well, Bellas, the life of a model is one of great adventure and many challenges. Modelland tolerates no excuses for tardiness or for faulty or missed assignments. Come hell or high *agua,* an Intoxibella must be ready to shine. To model through mayhem and mishaps. To perform! To be the very best! No excuses! So today your training begins. *Hencio,* your *Tía Flo* is happening right now, yes? How well can you project an image that is opposite of how you are feeling or at odds with your surroundings?

"Your goal in CaraCaraCara is not to mirror, but to mask. In other words, make the opposite expression of what you see or feel. You see happy . . ." The Guru made a gleeful expression, his rubbery lips extending well past his cheeks. "You make sad." He distorted his face into a sappy appearance, his eyes drooping dramatically and his chin sinking, literally, into his neck. "If you are tickled, do not laugh. Frown! Mastering this will get you one step closer to being an Intoxibella.

"But fail, and you may be relegated to spending your life as, heaven forbid, an *actress*." The Guru said this last word in a low, disgusted whisper. "Actresses are incapable of 'opposite performing.' They must think about sad times in their lives to project sadness on the silver screen. Nonsense! We mustn't let that pitiful fate happen to you. Oh, and also, Bellas? You will see that *mi clase* is the best in all of Modelland." His face contorted. "So if you like what you see here, put in a good word for me to the Bored, *sí?* They need a bit of comic relief to join their ranks. They are so god-awful serious all the time." The Guru's fingers stretched out from his hand, curved around the girls, and flicked on a light at the back of the shark-room.

"In just a few seconds you will be tested as you have never been. The challenge begins . . . *now!*"

Pacifico untied the serape sash from around his narrow waist, rolled it into a narrow strip, and tied it around his head, martial-arts-bandana style. "Copy me, Bellas! Copy me!"

The girls yanked their Senturas from their waists and tied them around their heads. As they did so, Tookie noticed that the boat was tilting more rapidly from side to side, like it was caught in a storm. She suddenly felt off-kilter.

"Through your crampy pain and sickness from the sea," Pacifico said, "your Senturas will aid you with power to conjure the opposite expression *perfectamente.*"

A shark-bite sound filled the room and then a three-dimensional image of a two-headed vulture picking at a child's eyes appeared before every Bella. Several girls gasped. Piper covered her eyes, saying it looked like a LeGizzârd. A girl named Bo, who sat on the other side of Tookie and seemed devoid of any expression whatsoever, didn't react at all.

"No, no, no!" Pacifico bellowed. "Opposite, opposite, opposite!"

"Look at me!" Zarpessa cried. She was smiling into the eyes of the two-headed vulture as though it was a cute newborn baby.

"*Fantastico,* Bella!" Guru Pacifico patted Zarpessa on the back.

The boat rocked to the right, making Tookie's stomach swim. The two-headed vulture morphed into an enormous yellow feather that was as long as Tookie was tall. It flitted around the class, tickling girls. Giggles erupted throughout the class.

"Bellas!" Pacifico shook his finger. "Use the power of your Senturas to resist the urge to laugh!"

At once, the Senturas came to life. The two strands that hung at the back of each girl's head reared up and swatted the feather as it approached. Shiraz's Sentura swatted at the feather like a boxer hitting a speed bag. Piper's Sentura took calculated jabs at it. Dylan's clawed at the feather like it was a girl in a catfight. Chaste's Sentura shimmied sexily, pulling the feather toward her body. But when the feather approached Tookie, her Sentura remained limp at her head. She couldn't stop giggling, even as the boat lurched angrily to the left.

"Tookie!" Guru Pacifico declared. "You are all wrong! Frown! Pretend that feather feels like the *mujer*-pain inside you!"

Tookie's cheeks burned. All these years, she had never been called on in class, and now that she finally was, it was for something *negative.* Worse than that, her head was spinning. *Why is this boat rocking so wildly? It seemed so calm from the shore.*

The challenges zipped by more quickly. They had to react to a steaming pile of rotting food under their noses, then a picture of an earless baby rabbit abandoned by its mother. Some girls instantly reacted to the photos before remembering they were supposed to do the opposite, but Piper studied the images quickly and smiled when the image was ghastly, looked surprised when the image was serene, and gasped when the image was gentle and sweet. "Good, Piper!" Pacifico praised.

An image appeared of a bunch of boys mooning a busy highway. Then one of a hooded figure that looked like Death approaching. The Bellas changed their expressions from happy to sad, confused to angry, sexy to serious with each different challenge, but Tookie continued to fail miserably, over- or underreacting to the photos, finding it difficult to focus. Her Sentura remained comatose on her head. "Tookie, Tookie, Tookie!" Pacifico cried over and over again, which made Zarpessa twist around and smirk triumphantly at her. The only girl he corrected almost as much was dead-faced Bo, who didn't even freak over a photo of a dead cat giving birth to an octopus on an abandoned road.

Then an image of an acrobat falling off a dizzyingly high tightrope appeared. Almost everyone else reacted with an opposite expression—boredom, apathy—but Tookie's face froze in the worst possible way. The performer reminded her of Chris-Crème-Crobat, her father—or, well, *whoever* he was. The shame of feeling disowned and unwanted washed over her. She couldn't hide it.

The ship lurched to the side once more. Tookie's insides churned, and her lower back contracted in a sharp cramp. She gagged repeatedly and closed her eyes to avoid the next abominable image. But closing her eyes made her seasickness even worse.

Suddenly, she couldn't take it anymore. She twisted to the right, leaned over, and threw up. Some of it landed in Bo's hair, but to her relief, Bo threw up too. Impassively, of course.

"¡Dios mío!" Guru Pacifico cried. "The wretched scourge of the first-run regurgitators! Seen it before, and smelled it much longer!" The images around them disappeared. "Okay, Bellas. Remove your Senturas from your heads. You will do this again and again this quadmester until you get it right. Do not fret about the mess. Remember, sharks love chum. As far as who did well today . . ." He paused on Piper, seemingly wanting to point to her, but then looked away. He pointed to another girl instead. "Definitely Bella Zarpessa!"

Zarpessa smiled devilishly. "Thanks, Guru. But I have a confession to make: my parents trained me for Modelland at a very early age. They got the *best* coaches—Metopian money was no object. I was being coached up until the Day of Discovery! They spent *fifty thousand* on my prep, and . . ."

She trailed off as she caught Tookie's eye. Her face hardened into a scowl. Tookie quickly averted her gaze. She didn't know whether to feel envious of or sorry for Zarpessa. Envious, of course, because Zarpessa had such a vivid imagination with which to escape from her dreadful life, even if it was a new concoction of outrageous fibs every day. But she felt pity as well.

Guru Pacifico clapped. "Now that you have finished your first CaraCaraCara class, I have two gifts for you!"

Everyone froze, waiting.

"I shall let an esteemed special guest tell you the first gift," the Guru said.

He gestured to the walls of the boat. Instantly, they peeled apart, revealing the masthead of the BellaDonna at the front of the ship. The masthead twisted around and stared at them, suddenly alive.

The masthead-BellaDonna parted her sculpted lips, just as her giant statue in the O had. "Yes, No-Sees, I have a surprise for you," her voice rang out. "Something young, maturing girls can only receive here at Modelland. CaraCaraCara was your first class, or shall I say, your first period of the day, but guess what . . . it will also be your last!"

"Huh?" Chaste pulled out her schedule. "It says I have two more classes after this!"

"Ah-ah-ah!" The Guru shook his finger. "Not *that* kind of period, *mami*!"

The BellaDonna continued. "This *cycle* you had this morning will be the last period you will ever have . . . for the rest of your lives!"

There was silence. Turned heads. Questioning looks.

"We want no excuses for you missing class or shoots or shows, so Modelland is ridding you of the pain and suffering of your menstrual cycles and cramps forever," the BellaDonna masthead explained. "You will still have the ability to procreate as you reach adulthood but no more periods. Period."

The Guru beamed at them. "Isn't that *grandissimo*?"

Almost everyone cheered, although Chaste looked strangely forlorn and confused, clamping her mouth shut and biting her bottom lip nervously. And Tookie felt another kind of cramp in her stomach . . . one of loss and regret. *I finally reached womanhood,* she thought. *I finally got something that Myrracle has teased me about so much. And now it's gone.*

The masthead twisted back around to its original position and then went still again. "The second gift?" the Guru said, facing the girls. "Now you can view your pictures of today's session!"

"Pictures?" Dylan clutched her apple cheeks. "But honey, I didn't have my game face on!"

Pacifico smiled craftily, his rubbery lips curling over his teeth. "This was your first Modelland photo shoot, ladies! Go look, go look!"

The Guru pointed to the exit at the far side of the shark. A second boat had appeared where the bridge had once been. As soon as the girls stepped inside the cabin, the boat moved away from the dock and began to float down the long river. Then three-dimensional images of the Bellas during the CaraCaraCara exercise appeared in midair. The images moved and morphed, showing each of their many expressions.

"Ooh!" some girls squealed. "Yuck!" others cried. "Can I erase this one?" Bo murmured stoically. And Chaste batted her eyelashes at herself. "Honey," she said to her image, "if I were a guy, I'd want a piece of you."

"Look at *that* hideous thing," a voice called from the other side of the boat. It was Zarpessa, and she was staring at Tookie's repeating loop. Zarpessa nudged Chaste. "You know those rumors about Scouts choosing civilian girls to come to Modelland to be used as sacrifices, experiments and food? *I* certainly wouldn't want to eat *that*."

Tookie moved to the front of the boat to look at her images. In each, she looked awkward, confused, and just . . . wrong. She looked over at the Guru. His eyes narrowed and he shook his head slowly from side to side. These were the type of photos that would fail her. The type of photos that would get her kicked out of Modelland and sent back to Peppertown. *Forever.*

She closed her eyes and thought about the fate that awaited her in Peppertown. A family who didn't want her . . . a best friend who probably hated her now that she'd abandoned her . . . a life as a Factory Dependent. *I can't go back there. I can't get sent home.*

But then she thought about the sacrifice rumor. Torturing girls in dreadful experiments. Siphoning their blood for ancient ritual. Making an offering to whatever magical beings had founded Modelland in the first place. If *that* was in store for her, she couldn't imagine staying here either.

Cold fear trickled down her neck. Had she come this far . . . only to be a human guinea pig?

20

RUΠ AΠD GUΠ

Tookie stepped into her next class, Run-a-Way Intensive. It took place in a long, narrow building the length of the Sapphire Esplanade Mall and the width of a half-dozen bowling lanes. A curved staircase led up to a vast mezzanine; each tread bore a hologram of an Intoxibella famous for her runway walk. Tookie spied many Intoxibellas she recognized, including Ci~L. Her hologram was extremely faint, though, a ghost slowly disappearing.

She thought about that terrifying vision of Ci~L beating herself. Had it been a dream?

Shiraz immediately skipped over and grabbed Tookie's hand. "Yay! We are in the Run-a-Way class together too! Stand by me!"

As they scuttled into the classroom, Tookie could feel two pairs of familiar eyes BitterBalling her again.

Zarpessa wrinkled her nose at Tookie like she smelled raw sewage. "I see they haven't turned you into Too-Too Barbeque yet." Chaste laughed so hard she snorted.

Tookie gritted her teeth. She was dying to retaliate and whisper something clever about digging through Dumpsters. But then she closed her eyes and thought of Ci~L's advice. *Don't stoop to her level. Don't stoop to her level.*

Dylan and Piper entered the room as well, beaming as they spied Tookie and Shiraz. Besides the four of them and Zarpessa and Chaste, Tookie recognized only two other girls in the room, tear-streaked Desperada. She was crying even harder now, if that was possible.

Then Gunnero Narzz whirled through the door. Everyone bristled. *Ugh, not him,* Tookie thought.

"We meet again, my dear No-Sees," he growled, sweeping his gray eyes over the crowd. "As you know, I am not only the administrator of the terror-filled THBC, I am also the official, the omnipotent, the one and the only Pace Parader, Sauntering Serenader, Gangway Gallavanter, your Run-a-Way Intensive educator. If you thought you came to despise me during your time at Thigh-High Boot Camp, think again, because you have yet to experience me teach the strut in all of my sumptuous, unfettered glory!"

Gunnero stuck his arms in the air to pose in a V and sashayed up and down the runway between the girls. The door burst open again, and he whipped back around and glared at the intruder. It was Persimmon, the BellaDonna's devoted Mannecant.

Gunnero scowled. "What the—"

Persimmon cleared her throat, cutting him off. "By order of the most beloved of the beloved, the chicest of the chic, the definer of all things beautiful, and the esteemed leader of all Bellas, the BellaDonna declares that today's session of Run-a-Way will be co-instructed by the only living Triple7—"

"Per, you're kidding me, right?" Gunnero closed his slate-colored eyes. "*Body* Girl? In *my* class?"

Tookie glanced at Shiraz, thoroughly confused. Shiraz shrugged.

"The Intoxibella known the world over has refused to follow orders since she has returned to Modelland, so she has been ordered to repent by the chicest of the chic," Persimmon said, pointing through the window to the BellaDonna statue. It seemed to be visible from every corner of Modelland. Then Persimmon yelled, "You may enter now!"

The door flung open, and in walked Ci~L. She had on an outfit made of hundreds of copper- and brass-colored handcuffs. There was a frazzled, pained look on her face.

No one seemed to know how to react. Shiraz clapped tentatively, and a few girls joined in. Zarpessa and Chaste scowled.

"I don't want *her* teaching me," Zarpessa said to Chaste. "I'd rather see her tortured some more in the O."

Ci~L stood before the girls, her eyes lifeless. Then she spied Tookie's small group in the corner. Her face slackened and her eyes bulged, and she became a different person altogether. Her hair began to whip around her face, caught up in its own private wind. Taking a deep breath, she began to speak.

"*A colorless girl in a colorless world,*" she said. "*Now stained crimson because of her quest.*"

It's a new poem! Tookie thought. Ci~L's spoken-word poems were famous, recited by girls all over the world—even Tookie had remembered them. Then she noticed Ci~L cut her eyes to Piper.

"I'm stained crimson?" Piper whispered. "Is she talking about my Auntie Dottie?"

"*A microscopic lass below the criterion,*" Ci~L went on. "*Journey aborted, but soul cannot rest.*"

And then Ci~L looked at Shiraz.

"She mean me?" Shiraz squeaked. "What she mean about my soul? I not dead!"

Ci~L continued, now overwrought with emotion:

"*A Rubenesque damsel, surrounded by twigs*
Her lush carcass devoured, insects infest."

Dylan, who stood right next to Tookie, scoffed at Ci~L. "There better not be no bugs infestin' me," she sputtered.

And then, finally, Ci~L shut her eyes and placed her thumb on her breast.

"*Their crony, elected exemplar of excellence,*
Has failed them, whose soul demons now do possess."

The room fell into a befuddled silence. Guru Gunnero seemed to be amused by Ci~L, a sly smile on his lips. Again Tookie thought of the violent moment the night before. The moaning, the chanting. Ci~L mutilating herself. The whacks. The *Sorrysorrysorry!* Ci~L's haunting wail. Ci~L was acting so strange in the classroom now that Tookie began to believe that maybe she *had* truly seen the terror.

Then Shiraz moved toward the window. "Look!"

She was pointing at the BellaDonna statue. It had begun to blink and move its arms. Slowly, it lowered itself and peered into the Run-a-Way classroom window. Then a crackle filled the air. Suddenly, a bouquet of flowers protruded from Ci~L's lips. Everyone screamed except for Gunnero, who looked quite pleased.

Ci~L wrenched the flowers out of her mouth, but a large rosebush popped out next. She struggled to remove the bush, trying unsuccessfully to avoid the thorns. After that popped out a purple orchid plant, then a mess of daisies and dandelions, then a bunch of springy tulips, then ivy. It was a long magician's scarf of flora, all of which Ci~L yanked from her mouth and tossed disdainfully to the floor. She sneezed and greenish petals shot out her nose.

Gunnero sniggered. "Looks like the BellaDonna wants to pretty up that foul mouth of yours, Body Girl," he said, eyeing Ci~L's body up and down with disdain. Tookie wondered why he was calling her that. Even though Ci~L was still very striking, she wasn't quite as thin as she had been months ago when she was the top Intoxibella.

"All right, all right!" Ci~L yelled toward the window at the BellaDonna statue. "I'll stop reciting poems! I'll teach with Gunnero. I'll do whatever you say! Just stop this!"

The statue blinked placidly. Ci~L coughed, reached into her mouth, and yanked out a perfect miniature bonsai tree. She glowered at the BellaDonna statue. "I know what I did, okay? I know I was wrong. I will comply. I will obey. I will do what you ask of me." This seemed to satisfy the BellaDonna, and she straightened up and resumed her position in the O.

Gunnero cleared his throat, still not looking very happy that Ci~L was there. "Well, my little No-Sees," he said, beginning a lecture. "You all possess Senturas, yes? But simply wearing them round your slinky little waists won't do the trick alone. To bring forth the true power of the Sentura, one must retract one's stomach, letting the Sentura's majestic force soak into one's soul." He glared at Ci~L. "Show them, BG."

Dejectedly, Ci~L sucked her stomach in hard and closed her eyes. Her Sentura began to wave in its own wind.

"*MUSIQUE!*" Gunnero cried. The overhead lights dimmed, and bass-heavy music began to boom.

"*MARCHEZ!*" Guru Gunnero yelled even louder. On command, Ci~L began to parade up and down the runway, her legs fluid, her arms in perfect harmony. With lips pursed and hands on hips, Gunnero watched Ci~L walk back and forth. He looked to be mentally walking as well. His hips swayed a bit while his feet remained in place. It seemed to Tookie that the Guru was doing everything in his power to not jump on the runway and push Ci~L out of the way. His lips pursed even harder when Ci~L completed a triple spin.

I guess Gurus can be jealous of Intoxibellas, Tookie thought.

Ci~L disappeared behind a wall in the back of the room. She returned in less than two seconds, now in a stunning dress covered in teddy bears, complete with bear-claw-like platform heels. Everyone, even Chaste, gasped. Zarpessa eyed Ci~L like she hated her and wanted to be her at the same time. *A private fashion show by Ci~L!* Tookie thought. *And she changed outfits so quickly! How?*

Tookie realized this was how Ci~L had been able to do every designer's fashion show one season as the sole model. One hundred seventy-three fashion shows, probably over seven thousand clothing changes. But how? What was going on backstage that got her back out on the runway so fast?

Disappearing once more, Ci~L reappeared in mere seconds in yet another outfit, a floor-length gown made of various types of chains and a tangle of edgy metal necklaces that glowed neon. One half of her hair was sheared in a pixie style; the other half was a long, curly bush. Mirrors on all sides of the room showed her every angle. Flashes from invisible cameras snapped as Ci~L paused and posed at the end of the runway. She did the same quick-change with four more outfits, the girls clapping with glee every time she emerged from the back room. But as she strutted to the end of the runway again, Tookie could see that whenever the clothing rubbed against the skin of her back, Ci~L did the most minute flinch.

The last outfit she donned was a red polka-dotted jumpsuit with an attached hood and polka-dotted boots. A necklace made of cantaloupe-sized rouge-colored pearls draped from her neck to her knees. Then the music ceased. "Enough, you show-off!" Gunnero blared, looking jealous. Ci~L stopped in the middle of the runway. "Well?" Gunnero crossed his arms over his chest. "Tell them the secret."

Ci~L took a breath and faced the Bellas. "What you saw wasn't real."

"*Spiegels cambio!*" Gunnero yelled.

The mirrors on the walls folded in on themselves and transformed into a new kind of mirror that glowed from within. These mirrors played back Ci~L's impromptu fashion show . . . with one critical difference.

Instead of Ci~L gracefully walking down the aisle, as the girls had witnessed, she was now running. Her arms pumped. Her legs leapt. She dashed as if in pursuit of life-sustaining oxygen. The mirrors also transmitted what happened backstage. Instead of a room full of chaos and fashion show dressers, the space was empty. Clothes flew off Ci~L and disintegrated. New clothes appeared, and dozens of tiny hands pulled them over her head and down her body. Everything happened at a rapid pace, like a pit stop at a car race in the city of FiveHundred.

Finally, the replay showed Ci~L exiting the backstage area in the red polka-dotted jumpsuit. Her poses at the end of the runway were lightning fast and merely split seconds long.

"*Fini!*" Gunnero barked, and the mirrors went dark.

All the girls looked dumbstruck.

"So, No-Sees, you idiots all know that fashion shows appear calm, smooth, and orderly when spectators view them," Gunnero explained. "And models appear to be dressed by human 'dressers' who aid and abet them into multiple outfits, one after the other. That's just how everyone sees it—but it's not how it really plays out. Your Senturas hold the power to hypnotize the audience, whether that's in the fashion auditorium or watching a recording in the privacy of their own master bedrooms. It shows them what Modelland wants them to see. This is the most important class you will ever take at Modelland. For a clumsy No-See will never book a *go-see*."

Dylan jabbed Tookie in the ribs. "All the Gurus got some swelled-up heads, don't you think? I ain't never taken so many *important* classes in my life!" Tookie giggled.

Shiraz raised her hand. "Why do you do the lying?"

Gunnero smirked. "My pint-sized Lilliputian, why does a lady never let a man see her bare-faced, sans makeup? It ruins her glamour, her mystery. It makes her *real*. The more people know of our secrets, the less intriguing this place becomes. That's why I'm the head of security, honey. I uphold the laws, the secrets, and the Run-a-Way."

"So how do you do it?" Tookie dared to ask.

Ci~L raised her Sentura. "In order to make your running look like walking, you must have your Sentura somewhere on your body. It's the only way."

Zarpessa took a step forward. "So *I* can be as fabulous as you, just because I'm wearing my Sentura? Out of my way, honey!"

"Not so fast," the Guru said. "It's not simply enough to run at a super speed. The movements have to be super fast, elegant, precise, fluid, swanlike. Just because you may think you're a swan don't mean ya are one, dear."

Still, everyone leaned forward, eager to try. Only Tookie hung back, her stomach swirling like she was still trapped on the CaraCaraCara boat. *How am I going to do this? I can't even run down a hallway without tripping!*

"So, who's going first?" Ci~L asked.

"I will do the walking!" Shiraz cried, busting in front of even Zarpessa and Chaste.

Narzz eyed her wearily. "Just go up and down the runway once. No ducking into the back room to change clothes. Got it?"

"Yes, yes!" Shiraz had already started down the platform. The lights dimmed. She walked frantically, her face tense and tight. But when everyone looked into the mirrors, it showed what was *really* happening: Shiraz was running so fast that she was a blur. Her arms jutted awkwardly. Her hair flew straight back from her face. Every time she reached the end of the runway, she slid to a stop like a baseball player stealing home.

Gunnero clapped his hand over his cement-colored eyes.

"Girl, you looked like a squirrel stuck in the middle of a busy street, trying to avoid being crushed! Hell, if I had a car right now, I would make a point of running your li'l ass over!"

The lights snapped on again, and Shiraz walked dejectedly off the runway. "But I do the running so fast," she said to Tookie.

Tookie just shrugged and squeezed Shiraz's hand. "You'll get better."

Then, as Shiraz peered across the room, her expression changed. "Ci~L been looking at me funny today. Like she the Labrian evil spirit. *Look!*"

Tookie looked up. Ci~L was staring intensely at Shiraz again. Tookie couldn't tell if she was pleased or disgusted. As soon as Ci~L noticed the two of them staring back, she averted her eyes.

Piper leaned toward them. "Ci~L's making me really uneasy. What did we do wrong?"

"Quiet, chattering, you wannabe-model monkeys!" Gunnero roared.

Bo's turn was next. On the runway, she looked like a walking zombie, her arms hanging heavy from their shoulder sockets. In the mirror, she ran with little energy, her face stuck in a dronelike expression.

"Girl, you belong in Model-*bland*," Gunnero joked.

Desperada was supposed to go next, but she was still sobbing too hard. Ci~L looked annoyed. "What are you crying for? Do you want to be here or not?"

Desperada just sniffled and didn't answer.

"Listen, there's no way you can even try this until you stop crying," Ci~L went on.

Chaste went next instead. In the mirrors, she somehow

made running look almost pornographic, shaking everything she shouldn't. On the runway, she rubbed her body all over, gyrating to the beat like a dancer in an exotic nightclub.

"I not old enough to look!" Shiraz yelped, closing her eyes.

Gunnero groaned. "This is Modelland, not Striptown." He waved Chaste off the runway, then looked at Tookie. "Get up here, Crazy Eyes. It's your turn."

Tookie swallowed hard, her heart pounding. Her limbs felt tangled already. Everyone was staring at her, which made her cheeks feel hot. She got up on the runway and set off, trying to conjure up her graceful inner cat. *Tookie De La Lion.* She extended her leg in a long leap. Then another, then another. She raised her head and tried to remain as calm and composed as she could. *I'm doing . . . okay!* Even her Sentura felt like it was working! Her heart lifted, and her soul soared.

Out of the corner of her eye, she noticed Ci~L and the Bellas staring confusedly from the runway platform to the mirror. "Why are her performance and her reflection the same?" a cleft-chinned blonde named Kieran whispered.

Tookie glanced in the mirror. It showed her awkward running movements. She turned away from the mirror and glanced down at her legs. They were running, the quick pace nowhere near an elegant slowed-down runway walk. *What is happening? Is it my Sentura? The thing hates me.* She glanced out into the confused crowd. One face wasn't fazed at all. In fact, she was sporting a clearly devilish smile.

Zarpessa.

All at once, Tookie knew. *She did something to me. Something to mess up my walk.*

Tookie gritted her teeth and charged ahead. It didn't matter. She ran like her life depended on it, losing sight of her position on the Run-a-Way, determined not to let Zarpessa's evil face get the best of her. Tookie ran and ran and ran and ran all the way . . . off the end of the runway. She knew she was no longer on the platform but was determined not to stop, and ran and ran and ran and ran until . . . *Boom!*

She hit the wall.

"She scores!" Zarpessa hooted from the sidelines.

"Get up!" Ci~L yelled.

Tookie struggled to stand and play it off, but it was too late— Gunnero was already shaking his head. "A failure, on so many levels. On the Run-a-Way *and* off! Maybe those crazy eyes are half blind."

Tookie trudged to the sidelines, rubbing her sore forehead. "What happened?" Shiraz asked.

"I think it's Zarpessa," Tookie murmured. "But I don't know what—or how."

By coincidence, Zarpessa was next. Shiraz turned and faced the runway. "Hmph. I hope she fracture spine."

Zarpessa set off, her long legs extended, her arms swinging confidently, her head held high. Not once did an ankle wobble in her high heels. She reached the end of the runway, posed, then ran back, not stopping. And then, in a display of defiance, Zarpessa eyeballed Ci~L, slipped behind the wall, and returned wearing a studded black bat-themed minidress with pronounced winglike shoulder pads. She strutted to the end of the runway, stopped abruptly, and spun four times—one more spin than Ci~L had done. She then disembarked from the platform like a gymnast and smirked haughtily at Guru Gunnero.

"Insolent," Gunnero gazed at Zarpessa with a mix of jealousy and disgust. Ci~L gave a wave of her hand to Zarpessa as if to say *touché*.

The kaleido-clock glowed chartreuse. "Thank *God*. Class is over." Gunnero sighed. "I guess we don't have time for the rest of you today. Now, one of you, although an insipid show-off, may just have a little skill at Run-a-Way. But just one? That's sad and pathetic, my No-Sees. If you girls don't watch out, actresses will take your place on the future runways. And no, they are not famous or magical, but they're already making their ridiculous crimson carpets a runway event in itself." With a miffed eye-roll and a disgusted sigh, he dismissed them.

As Shiraz waved goodbye and slipped out the door, another figure appeared behind Tookie. It was Zarpessa, and there was a wide smirk on her face. "Tough thing about your Run-a-Way collision," she trilled. "I cannot imagine what went wrong." Her eyes flicked to Tookie's waist.

Tookie whipped her head up. "What did you do?"

There was a devilish look on Zarpessa's face. "I'll tell you a little story. I love the yellow dress I wore here, so I kept it as one of my two items. I still feel that being allowed to keep only two items is not very fair at all—I mean, my acupuncturist's grandmother said when *she* was here, they were allowed to keep *five* things. But then I had an idea. Why couldn't I cut up my dress and make *one* item *ten*! So you see, I've now got a yellow skirt, yellow gloves, a yellow beret, a yellow neck scarf, leggings, panties, a bra, two satin bracelets and . . . oh, did I tell you that I found a Sentura under your bed? I'm still so perplexed as to how it got there. I mean, you're *wearing* it, aren't you? Or maybe you have *two*. One magical and one . . . not."

Tookie blinked, slowly understanding what Zarpessa was telling her. She touched the Sentura around her waist. It was the same yellow as Zarpessa's dress, perhaps a touch off from the yellow of the *real* Sentura. "You *didn't*."

Zarpessa leaned her face close. "That's right. I *didn't*. I didn't do a thing. But you know, if you start telling stuff about me to your friends—to *anybody*—it'll be bad for your soul. I'm a true believer in . . . oh, what's it called? Your Chakra friend would know." Then she snapped her fingers. "I know! *Karma!*"

Zarpessa spun around triumphantly and met up with Chaste. Embarrassed and furious, Tookie turned to exit the class and locked eyes with Ci~L. The Intoxibella peered at her, her eyebrows furrowed in a frown. Tookie's stomach clenched. It was the same ominous look she'd given Shiraz and the other girls earlier.

Ci~L turned and marched away. That was when Tookie noticed that some of the red polka-dots on the back of her jumpsuit were richer, wider, and blotchier than the others. All along Ci~L's back, just under her shoulder blades and traveling up and down her spine, something red seeped through the cloth, growing larger and more garish by the second. It took Tookie only seconds to realize what it was.

Blood.

21

JAMMERS, CHOWERS, AND POACHERS

Rubbing her aching forehead, Tookie walked down Beautification Boulevard to her third and last class of the day, Mastication. She touched her Sentura on her hips—the *correct* Sentura, which she'd found exactly where Zarpessa had said it was: under her bed.

She felt a familiar pang in her stomach again, a mixture of pity and envy for Zarpessa. There was anger in that pang too. Tookie couldn't help it. *I know she's got a secret, but why does that girl have to be so nasty?*

Slowly, she realized that the pangs were due to something else too: hunger. It had been over a day since Tookie had eaten anything—an absolutely rarity for her—but she miraculously hadn't been hungry until this very moment. Now her stomach felt like it was caving in on itself, and her throat felt parched from all the running—into walls—in Run-a-Way.

Tookie finally found the site of Mastication class. The building was a giant bowl made up of multicolored bricks, with a ladle-shaped smokestack poking out the top. As she got closer, Tookie could see that the bricks were actually loaves of wheat, white, pumpernickel, and raisin bread. Butter and cream cheese served as grout, beef and chicken kebabs provided additional building support, and the windows seemed effervescent, like they were carbonated. Tookie stuck out her tongue to lick the window.

"Don't do that!"

Tookie turned to see Dylan running toward her.

"I just tried it," Dylan said, out of breath. "I licked a kebab and . . . *zap! Cuh-ray-zee!*"

Tookie looked at the building with disappointment in her eyes. "But I'm starving. I could even eat chocolate."

"Oh yeah," Dylan said sarcastically. "Disgustin', horrendous chocolate. Well, it is in front of you. Right there," Dylan said, pointing to some brownies serving as window trim. "But it just might kill ya."

"Ha, ha, very funny," Tookie said.

"My first class was so friggin' hard. Oh my gosh, Tookie, it's called Tick-Tock Color Clock—it was *supposed* to explain how to use the clocks around here. But not one of us walked out knowin' a friggin' thing. How was your last class?"

"A pain in more ways than one," Tookie said quietly, rubbing her forehead again. She shared what had happened to her in Run-a-Way, including the story of Zarpessa's Sentura switcheroo.

ModelLand

Dylan clenched her jaw. "That girl deserves an ass-whoopin'! No one treats my Tookie like that!"

Tookie blushed. She'd never been *anyone's* Tookie. It felt good. "It's tempting, but I don't think we should stoop to her level," Tookie concluded as they walked toward the building.

Dylan made a face. "What's she got against you anyway?"

Zarpessa's threat swam into her mind. Tookie thought about sharing Zarpessa's secret with Dylan but then just shrugged. "I have no idea."

They walked into the entryway. Suddenly, Tookie's ears filled with the sound of frying bacon. Her nose twitched with the most delicious smell ever, a combination of the juicy fat from soup dumplings, barbeque ribs, sourdough bread, and rich melted butter. Her stomach let out another grumble.

On a door the word *mastication* was spelled in macadamia nuts. Inside was a large, three-tiered room. Bulbous copper receptacles stood on each tier. Copper pipes connected the receptacles and disappeared into smooth concrete walls. The smell of food was everywhere.

A tall, striking, lovely woman with a round face and brilliant blue eyes burst through two swinging doors at the front of the room. Her legs made an upside-down, bowed-out U, as though she'd just jumped off a horse after a long ride. Her arms were extended, as if she were still holding the reins. She wore a tool belt filled with bright, shiny copper knives, ladles, tongs, and spatulas, and a chef's apron that had all kinds of food—cobs of corn, veggie sticks, blue corn tortillas, and prawns still in their shells with the heads attached—stitched into the fabric.

The walking buffet didn't stop there. She wore armbands

made of roasted garlic. Her pants were made of a burlap potato sack. Atop her head sat a hybrid of a chef's hat and a cowboy hat, filled with tiny bags of spices. And her hair consisted of long, tube-like food items—strands of spaghetti, whips of licorice, blades of wheatgrass.

She sat down on the edge of the desk, nibbling on her hair, saying nothing.

More girls spilled into the room. Something whipped past Tookie's ankle. It made a teeny *boing* sound, like a bug on springs. As the rest of the Bellas filed in—including Chaste and Zarpessa again, the Likee sisters, and Kamalini—more of the creatures zoomed through the air. Girls screamed. Kamalini clasped her hands over her Headbangor. Finally, Tookie spied one standing still on a table. It was a small mouselike thing with pointy ears, a long tail, and a slit across its belly.

"Uh, excuse me?" Zarpessa screamed to the Guru, who didn't seem alarmed by the chaos. "This classroom is infested with vermin!"

The Guru chuckled. "Nah, they're just roo jerky." Grabbing a set of chopsticks from the table, she caught a hopping creature as it passed. "You little bugger!" She tossed it into her mouth. "They taste like chicken. If you catch one, I'll let you eat it."

Half the class shuddered, but Tookie salivated at the jerky. She was so starving she'd have eaten anything.

The Guru grabbed another jerky, then hopped off the desk. "G'day! My name is Lauro Brown. Guru Lauro to you." She had an accent from Didgeridoo, a hot land full of beaches and unusual animals with strange names.

"And this is where Mastication happens!" Lauro continued.

"In this class, the only one who will use magic is me. Therefore, those lovely yellow sashes round your waists have got to go."

She walked around the class confiscating all the Senturas, labeling them with each girl's name so they wouldn't get confused. Tookie breathed a sigh of relief. *At least I know Zarpessa won't sabotage my Sentura in this class.*

Then Guru Lauro returned to her desk. "Okay, Bellas, stick out your tongues!"

The girls looked at each other nervously, then obeyed. Lauro walked up to Dylan and grabbed her perfect pink tongue between her fingers. "Ahhh, Dylan. Your favorite food is . . ." She twisted Dylan's tongue up and around, inspecting it closely. "Bou-Big-Tique deep-dish pizza pie!"

Dylan jolted back and put her hands on her hips. "Honey, don't say pizza pie unless you *got* some!"

Lauro turned next to Tookie's tongue. "Your favorite food is an odd one. Whipped cream . . . straight out of the can . . . am I right?"

Tookie nodded. Immediately her mouth began to water.

Next, Lauro appraised the Likees. All four girls stuck out their tongues, and Lauro frowned. "Sugar-free breath mints?"

The Likees nodded eagerly. "They. Are. Our. Favorites!" they said down the line. "We. Suck. One. Each."

Lauro gave them an odd look. "That's no way to live, dearies. You realize your bodies need fuel, correct? You realize you'll still be beautiful if you chew and swallow?"

The Likees wrinkled their noses in unison.

Then she turned to Zarpessa. "Hmmm," Lauro murmured, looking at Zarpessa's tongue. "White-truffle-wagyu-saffron risotto topped with Almas caviar."

"Right! I'm obsessed!" Zarpessa yelped. "Our private chef prepares it when we're not dining out at Le Douley."

"Oh, but wait, sweetie. There's something else I'm seeing."

Zarpessa's face quivered. "What?"

"A blend of . . . discarded foods. Room-temperature, slightly decaying. Puzzling. Very much *dero* food, mate."

"Dero?" Dylan whispered to Tookie.

Tookie hesitated but decided she would translate. "*Dero* means 'homeless' in the Didgeridoo dialect."

Dylan and Tookie looked back at Zarpessa to find that Zarpessa was already glaring at them.

"Madame, how did you know our favorites?" Kamalini asked. Her favorite food was the special vegetarian samosas she used to eat watching her mother on movie sets.

Lauro adjusted her hat. "Because I, mates, am a tongue-reader. I can tell what all of your tastes are at all times. Reading tongues for me is like reading palms. I know what you want, when you want it, when your tummy's happy and"—she pointedly eyed the Likees—"when it's sad. You're all very hungry right now, aren't you?"

Everyone started to murmur. Tookie clutched her belly.

Lauro removed her chef's hat, revealing a crazy, stiff ponytail that looped straight into the sky. She tipped the hat upside down and made a spilling motion. A fine yellow smoke swept out and slithered around the room, snaking into each and every girl's nostrils.

"Oh!" Chaste took a big whiff. "It smells like honey-roasted almonds and oysters steeped in pomegranate juice!"

"*No,* it smells like virgin olive oil bread with only a slight hint of mold, which is okay because it can be sliced off, and a half-eaten pheasant!" Zarpessa swooned before stopping herself.

Dylan's nose twitched. "Bou-Big-Tique pizza pie," she murmured, her eyelids fluttering with pleasure. "Where is it, baby? Where *is* it?"

And when the smoke trail reached Tookie, she smelled delectable whipped cream.

Suddenly, the pipes leading to the large copper kettles began to tremble. Fifteen harnesses dropped from the ceiling, dangling above each vat. Zarpessa leapt to her feet. "There's food in there!"

"All your favorites," Guru Lauro said. "Find your food receptacle and then climb inside the harness!"

Tookie followed her nose to the vat she was sure was hers, climbed into the harness, and dangled over it. And . . . ohhh. What a delicious spread it was! About a hundred cans of different types of whipped cream—heavy cream, light cream, vanilla cream, all spewing their contents into the air. She tried to grab some of the white stream, but her hands didn't quite reach. "Darn it!" she cried in frustration.

Next to her, Dylan groped fruitlessly as well. Chaste let out a breathy whimper. "Why can't we eat?"

"This is cruel and unusual punishment!" Zarpessa cried.

With a wave of the Guru's hand, a round white kitchen timer appeared on the stainless steel table and counted off the seconds with loud, jarring ticks. After about ten seconds, the timer dinged, and each girl's harness lowered closer to her vat—*almost* close enough to touch the bounty. Tookie groped for the whipped cream cans until her arms ached. She was so hungry her head was beginning to spin.

Lauro strolled around the room, dipping a finger into each girl's slop. "Outstanding pizza pie," she told Dylan.

"The perfect blend of acidity and sweetness," she said about Kamalini's samosas. And she plucked one of the Likees' breath mints from their shared vat and slipped it into her pocket. "I'll save this for later. Roo jerky leaves your breath so rancid it makes koalas fall out of the gum trees."

She plucked a can marked *Heavy Creamiest Cream* from Tookie's giant vat and squirted it into her mouth. "Brilliant!" she announced. A glob of whip remained on her lips.

The timer dinged again and the harnesses dropped a few more inches. Tookie's arms swung. Her legs kicked. She . . . could . . . almost . . . get one . . . but then the harness recoiled and she and all the girls sprang all the way back up. Everyone groaned.

"Patience, Bellas," Lauro chanted. "Patience."

Brrrrrt! The kitchen timer bleated so forcefully it vibrated right off the table. Lauro clapped, and instantly the harnesses went all the way down, allowing the girls' heads and hands to reach their food.

Yes! Tookie grabbed some cans, inverting them and squeezing endless streams of whipped cream into her mouth. Then she did it again and again and again, tossing spent cans to the side and reaching for new ones right away. In no time, her face was covered in cream, her brand-new Modelland uniform slopped with goop, and her arms dripped with dissolved froth. As she brought another can to her mouth, it slipped out of her hands and plopped right into her oversized flower brooch.

Tookie glanced down, befuddled. Somehow, the pin had swallowed up the can. But when she reached into the center of the brooch, *voilà!* Her fingers curled around the top of the can once more.

It's a secret food receptacle, she marveled. *A mini refrigerator! Just like I had in my dumbwaiter locker at B3.*

The class continued to gorge with gusto. Dylan closed her eyes and slowly relished every bite of Bou-Big-Tique pie, laughing like a lunatic after each swallow. Chaste slurped the pomegranate juice. Zarpessa stuck her entire face into a brew of fish chunks, clumps of old spaghetti with coagulated carbonara sauce, half-eaten sandwiches, and gooey yellowish rice. The Likees stared nervously at their vat of multicolored sugar-free breath mints. Finally, each girl used a thumb and index finger to pick one up, and placed it under her tongue. Kamalini was the only one who seemed unfazed, eating with calm, measured bites, savoring the experience.

The vats of food tipped over, the contents spilling onto the floor. The Bellas groaned in unison, still unfulfilled. The empty vats rose to the ceiling and hovered there, and the harnesses released, spilling the girls straight into the food slop. Almost everyone, even Tookie, recoiled at the blended ingredients. Only Zarpessa crawled houndlike on all fours, her head down, scraping the floor to retrieve the vile vittles with her tongue and incisors. It was even crazier than the way she'd scuttled around in the Dumpster behind the restaurant in Peppertown.

The vats then crashed to the floor and morphed into elevators, one per girl. Guru Lauro gestured to them. "Even though Tookie already had dessert, you other Bellas haven't! Get in, mates!"

The girls boarded the food-vat carriages. The elevators didn't go up or down, however, but slid across the floor and transported everyone to a nearby building.

The sound of gushing water filled the air. The elevator doors opened, revealing a bank of group showers in a shiny facility of chrome and translucent surfaces. But the liquid spurting from the nozzles was anything but clear. One nozzle spurted rich cassis. Another spouted thick deep-brown liquid. Another showerhead's waterfall was a rich tan hue. The smell tickled Tookie's nostrils. Lovely scents filled the air. Caramel. Boysenberry. And . . .

"Marshmallow!" Dylan swooned, eyeing the fluffy confection streaming from the showerhead. She looked as though she was about to faint.

"I'm showering you with sweet treats, mates!" Guru Lauro encouraged them. "Go for gold!"

The girls rushed to the showers—all except the Likees, who stood on the sidelines, sucking their mints. Chaste checked to make sure the Guru wasn't watching, then knocked down a brunette girl as she gunned for the dark chocolate shower. Tookie ran over to the fallen brunette, scooped her up, and then made a break for the salted caramel stream, cupping her hands under the faucet and burying her face in her palms. Zarpessa stuck her mouth under a maple syrup spray, but her showerhead jammed as it forced out broken bits of pecan pralines. Letting out a frustrated wail, she ripped the fixture from the wall, allowing a solid stream of maple pecan praline sauce to flow directly into her wide-open mouth. Kamalini let about nine heaping tablespoons of pistachio coulis drip onto her tongue, emitted a pleasant squeal, and wiped her chin clean, being extra careful to not let her Headbangor get soaked.

Dylan dove headlong into the marshmallow shower. The liquid covered her hair and face and melted over her uniform, legs, and arms. There was a look on her face as if her actions were involuntary. "It's so good," she kept crying. "Just so good!"

"Last lick, Bella mates!" Lauro bellowed, and moments later, the showers all dried up. Moans and groans filled the room. "I hope you enjoyed the feast as much as I enjoyed feeding you. Now it's time for the lesson on Jammers, Chowers, and Poachers."

She approached the oyster-and-chocolate-covered Chaste, pulled a green stamp from under her chef/cowboy hat, and pressed it on Chaste's wrist. "Hey!" Chaste said. She stared at her new brand. *Gut Chower,* it said in square green letters.

"You ate very slowly, and when you reached your perfect amount, you stopped, never getting overfull," Lauro explained.

"That's the first time anyone has ever told me it's good to *stop* even when something feels really good." Chaste licked a bit of leftover chocolate off her thumb.

Lauro glared at her.

Then Guru Lauro circled the room. Kamalini also got a *Gut Chower* stamp for eating steadily and continuously and for eating the side of Vitamin C–loaded spiced cauliflower that had come with her samosas. Then Lauro approached the Likees. When the four girls stuck out their hands, their stamps glowed red and said *Gut Poacher.*

"We need to talk, ladies," Lauro said quietly. "You're restricting nutrients your Bella belly needs. And feeling awful about nutrients you *do* get."

The Likees stiffened. "That's. Not. True. Guru."

The Guru gave them a warm look. "When you want help, I hope you give me a bell."

When Guru Lauro approached Zarpessa, only half of the stamp

would materialize in the Guru's hands—the word *Gut*. "Okay, Zarpessa, I must admit, with all *roo* respect, your munching habits are doing my head in. For now, one thing's for sure: you have a gut. So here ya go, mate." And she stamped Zarpessa plain and simple *Gut*.

Then she approached Tookie. A red stamp marred Tookie's hand: *Gut Jammer.*

"You eat with the voraciousness of a preggers Tasmanian devil during her first trimester," Lauro explained. "However, your stomach is telling me that it's never full. Is this true?"

Tookie nodded. *This woman really can read my stomach's mind.*

"All the tummy stuffing in the world won't fill out your fragile frame, mate. Not anytime soon, anyway. When you reach your twenties, your rear may begin to plump up, and then you'll be cryin' a different tune. Until then—and even *after* then—be happy with what the looking glass tells ya. It ain't half bad, kid."

Ain't half bad, Tookie thought. It was as though Lauro had told her she was the most beautiful girl in the world.

Finally, Lauro walked over to Dylan, who was still licking residual marshmallow off the webby spaces between her fingers. She red-stamped her hand *Gut Jammer* too. "You're also a shoveler."

"Just today I am," Dylan said quickly. "I haven't guzzled like that in I don't know how long—really. And anyway, can you blame me? I was starved!"

Lauro gave her an I-know-better look. "I'm also picking up that food has an emotional effect on you."

Dylan froze. "No it doesn't."

The Guru held Dylan's gaze. Dylan lowered her eyes.

Then Lauro tucked the stamps back into her hat and faced

the class. "For the few of you who will make it all the way to Intoxibella status, there are few things that will challenge you more
than food. What to have, when to have it, how to have it, whether
to have it. Starvation and oversatiation are not acceptable, mates.
Models are known for restricting their food or going on binges,
but that's not what we're going for here. And besides . . ." Guru
Lauro trailed off, making a face. "Those lolli-headed leading ladies
restrict as well. *Worse* than models, in my roo opinion. But here,
moderation is what we're going for. One of the things I'll be teaching you here is how to find your *balance*. All your future meals will
be designed by me. How you eat is important to your success. I
hate to sound like I'm up myself, but this is the most important
class you'll be taking at Modelland."

"Yeah, yeah, our last Guru said that too," Chaste said, rolling
her eyes.

The girl named Bibiana from Terra BossaNova raised her
hand. "What do you mean, future meals designed for us? I'm so
full, I feel like I don't need to eat for a week."

A smile stretched across the Guru's lips. She tipped her chef/
cowboy hat again, and the same yellow smoke swirled. "Here's
a little present from you to me. The gift of renewed appetite!
You're now so hungry, you could eat the ass out of a low-flying
duck!"

The dessert showers retracted into the floors, revealing an entryway into an enormous room filled with modular tables lying
within cutouts in the floor. The wall to the left contained floor-
to-ceiling windows, the BellaDonna statue clearly visible through
the glass. The wall to the right was made of hundreds of tiny
glass doors, each with a mouthwatering dish of food inside it.

The doors were separated into color-coded sections and labeled with the three designations that Lauro had given the girls in the shower room: Gut Chower, Gut Jammer, Gut Poacher. The wall in front of the girls boasted the name of the establishment in large letters: EATZ.

"I get it," Tookie said. "*M* is Modelland, *O* is Opera, *D* is Dorms, and *E* is—"

"Eatz," Zarpessa interrupted sarcastically. "*Wow.* You're so brilliant."

Dylan narrowed her eyes.

"There has to be an *L*," Tookie said, ignoring Zarpessa.

"Yeah, stands for L'idiot," Zarpessa mumbled under her breath. "Like *you.*"

"How about Lame-o," Dylan spat back, unable to hold it in any longer. "Like you."

Zarpessa's eyes blazed. "Lardass!"

Chaste snickered.

Dylan whipped around to face Chaste. "Loose Lucy!"

"Loudmouth!" Zarpessa retorted, a little bit of spit spewing from her mouth.

"Leech lizard!"

"Lay off! Lay off!" Tookie interrupted, inserting herself between the two of them.

Dylan turned away, but she was smiling wide, having gotten in the last *L* insult. Chaste and Zarpessa shot Tookie and Dylan looks that seemed to say *Just you wait, hags. You've done it now.*

An upperclassBella approached the Eatz wall and spoke into a large pair of lips. "AmberJoi of AngelCity, cream of wheatgrass soup and a side of wheat toast with butter." With a brief chime, a door opened and a steaming bowl shot out. In it was the most hideous-looking grass-green soup Tookie had ever seen.

"This is the E, Bellas," Lauro announced. "Your cafeteria. And I am its executive chef. Enjoy, ladies. Dine! Appreciate! But please—try to find *balance*."

"We're supposed to dine *now*?" Zarpessa looked nervously from the upperclassBellas to the rotting food all over her uniform. "We look certifiable!"

"I know, mate," Lauro replied. A roo jerky materialized in front of her again, and she chased after it, pinning it with her chopsticks and popping it in her mouth. "But no Bella's first day is complete without a stinky, sloppy, slimy trip to the E. Just another part of earning your keep here at Modelland. *Bon appétit!*"

Everyone collected their Senturas from a bin and hurried to the wall of goodies. Only Dylan remained where she was, her bottom lip trembling slightly, still covered in marshmallow, her Sentura held limply in her sticky hand.

Tookie touched her arm. "You okay?"

Dylan flinched, then tried a smile. "Loved her Didgeri-whatever accent. She was nice, huh?"

"Yeah." Something about Dylan seemed . . . deflated. Tookie wanted to ask what it was, but she was afraid of upsetting her. So she pulled Dylan toward the Eatz wall, trying to ignore the scornful looks from the upperclassBellas. "All of the girls in our class look *cuh-ray-zee,* so why the heck are them Bellas only starin' at *us*? I mean, they actin' like our genes are contagious or somethin'," Tookie joked, trying to imitate Dylan in an effort to cheer her up.

Just then, a loud, collective coo erupted from the other Bellas.

The girls nearest the windows rushed to look outside. The rest of the Bellas in the room followed the stampede.

"Sexified succulence!" someone cried.

"I'm going to hyper-hyper-hyperventilate!" moaned a girl wearing large sunglasses.

"I called firsties!" exclaimed Chaste. "And lasties! And tops and bottoms!"

Tookie and Dylan drifted toward the window. Kamalini stood behind them, trying to peer out too. But there wasn't an inch of space, and no one seemed to want to move aside to give them room. Finally, Dylan pulled over three chairs and stood on one. Tookie and Kamalini jumped onto the others. Outside the window, three strapping young men walked the length of the building. They held a girder of steel over their heads. A photographer snapped their picture again and again.

Tookie squinted hard at the rippling muscles and chiseled face of one of the guys. He was staring, mesmerized, at a building to the left of the E. She knew him. It was the boy who'd wanted to help her with directions earlier that day.

"Anyone know who *he* is?" a girl screeched, pointing to him.

I do, Tookie wanted to say.

"His name is Bravo!" responded another student. "The other two are Webb and Alexander!"

The girls began frantically tapping the glass.

Webb and Alexander noticed the girls and smiled, waved, and licked their lips. Bravo shifted his gaze from the building to the girls, but just smiled politely to the group and then looked away. That just stirred up the girls even more. They slammed their knuckles against the glass.

Bravo tossed the steel girder into the air for a series of action pictures. He caught it once. The photographer snapped the camera. The girls inhaled. He caught it a second time. The girls exhaled. *Show-off,* Tookie thought.

He tossed it a third time and the girder slipped out of his fingers and came hurtling down, sharp edge first, snagging the skin on his forearm. The girls cried out in unison.

Then it happened. Something no one in all of Modelland could have predicted. The bleeding Bravo looked up at the window and focused on only one face.

A whipped-cream-caked, punch-bowl-headed girl with one green eye and one brown eye, to be exact.

22

Fused Flashback Females

Bravo's gaze remained fixed on Tookie. Tookie stood back, utterly confused as to why he was looking at her and *only* her.

The girls around her, including Dylan and Kamalini, seemed just as perplexed. Zarpessa let out a horselike snort. "Come on, everyone, don't you get it? He's staring at *her* because he's never seen someone with such an enormous head."

Bravo reached up and made a wiping gesture across his nose. On instinct, Tookie touched her nose too. To her horror, a trail of creamy pea-green slime appeared on her fingers. She'd been staring out the window with a giant whipped-cream booger on her face. She didn't know whether to run to find a tissue or a bush to hide behind.

"Can someone explain why you are pressing your nasty hands against our windows?"

The girls turned to see Persimmon standing in the doorway. "Get in a single-file line," she demanded. *"Now!"* The Bellas ran to obey.

"Where are we going?" Chaste called out as Persimmon spun around and marched into a dark, narrow hallway. In the distance was a bright flickering light. "I was just about to flash my *breast-osteros.*"

"You need to get that filthy mouth of yours cleaned up," Persimmon said in a disgusted voice.

The fluttering light at the end of the hallway expanded into an immense glowing circle. A Mannecant stood at a reception desk shaped like the letters *H, O,* and *A.* The letters moved around in a disorganized jumble, probably making it hard to set anything on the surface. There was a great round room behind the desk, its walls covered in a furry-looking fabric and its ceiling gently pulsing up and down, as if breathing.

"I know where we are!" Zarpessa boasted. "The OoAh!"

A breathy voice from high above whispered "Oooo-ahhhh!" with great satisfaction. The letters of the desk moved to spell *OOAH.* The smell of blood oranges wafted through the air.

"This is the place where seasoned Bellas go to have their aching joints soothed after their intense 7Seven Tournament training," Zarpessa told them self-importantly while staring at herself in the mirror behind the reception desk. "It's also where instructors and visiting Intoxibellas go to be primed and primped. We have one of these attached to my bedroom at home, you know. But it'll be so much more fun to experience this with all of you!"

Tookie and Dylan both rolled their eyes. *Yeah, right,* Tookie mouthed.

Six blank-eyed Mannecants appeared from invisible doors, towels in their hands. Persimmon turned to the Bellas. "You will break up into groups of three girls. Each group will be led by its own Mannecant. And the rules are . . . well . . . enjoy yourselves. That's it." She seemed very pained to issue such a command.

A Mannecant waved an ornate hand mirror over the group. Instantly, light in one of six colors fell onto the girls. Three Bellas glowed burgundy, making them a group; Zarpessa, Chaste, and Bibiana were color-coded fire-engine-red. Tookie, Dylan, and Kamalini, the last girls in line, glowed canary-yellow.

The Mannecants' plastic bodies shimmered with the colors that matched their group. A yellow-glowing Mannecant approached Tookie, Dylan, and Kamalini. "Follow, please follow," she said in a barely perceptible monotone.

The yellow Mannecant walked them briskly down one of the many paths that split off from the round room. The other groups of girls went down different hallways. Tookie let her hand drag along the soft white wall. "Cashmere," she whispered. Creamy had had a suit made in the stuff a few years ago. Of course, only a month or so later, she'd discarded it, deeming it past its prime. Thinking of Creamy, Tookie got a pang. *What is she doing right now? Does she miss me at all?*

"What kinda place has cashmere on its walls?" Dylan whispered.

Kamalini nodded. "I know. It's ridiculous. Shameful, even."

The Mannecant led Tookie, Dylan, and Kamalini into an expansive rectangular room with a metal floor and walls. Rows and rows of polished stone slabs filled the room, dozens of Bellas lying atop them. Tookie recognized some of the girls from Mastication, but there were others there she had never seen. All the girls were completely nude except for Tookie, Kamalini, and Dylan.

"The OoAh will remove your soiled clothing, shoes, and underwear," the yellow Mannecant informed them.

Dylan stopped short, looking warily at the other girls in the room. "Is there a private area I can use to change? I don't want all these chicks lookin' at my booty."

"I too feel quite uncomfortable with the idea of getting disrobed while so many look on," Kamalini seconded.

Tookie didn't want to get naked around all these people either.

"Lie down on the last three slabs there," the Mannecant instructed flatly, pointing.

The girls hesitantly obeyed. Dozens of hands came up from under the slabs and removed their clothes. The hands were just like those that had dressed Tookie in the THBC bubble and Ci~L at Run-a-Way. Tookie covered her private parts with her own hands. Kamalini did the same. Tookie felt cold, vulnerable, and certain everyone was staring at her, so she fixed her gaze on the ceiling instead. Someone had written something on the tiles in black pen. GEENA HAS TWO SECRETS. ONE: SHE HATES Ci~L. TWO: IT RHYMES WITH DESTROY.

Next a strong cushion of air pushed the girls above the stone slabs so that they hovered over their tables. Warm water spewed down from openings above them. Water rushed *up* at them as well, seemingly gushing from the surface of the stone. The water changed from soapy to dingy to soapy to clear, finally becoming a citrusy orangish spray. Tookie closed her eyes, trying to relax and not fret about her exposed, awkward body.

"Ooh," Dylan said beside her.

"Ahh," Kamalini said, and they all giggled.

The yellow Mannecant gave the girls what looked like green strapless terry-cloth minidresses with asymmetrical hems. The little towel frocks read *Oooo* on the front and *Ahhh* on the back. "Put these on, please. We will care for your Bella uniforms and return them to you cleaned and pressed."

The girls put on the towel dresses, and then the Mannecant led them on a tour of the OoAh.

The place was a labyrinth of narrow hallways decorated with silks, fine chenilles, and more cashmere walls. Lanterns glowed from every alcove, incandescent butterflies providing the light. The scent of blood oranges hung heavily in the air, and the girls felt soft sand underfoot. Down some hallways, they saw elaborate makeup stations and steaming baths. In one, an upperclassBella sat in a pedicure chair and commanded, "Environment: tropical island with pink sand and turquoise waves!" Suddenly, the fabric on the walls melted away, revealing an idyllic island setting, complete with a shining sun, warm breezes, rose-colored sand, and an ocean so blue it looked a swimming pool.

Tookie, Dylan, and Kamalini gasped. "That is a special feature of the OoAh," the Mannecant told them. "One can change her surroundings to whatever she likes. Try it."

"Please, Madame. Environment: home," Kamalini asked politely.

The walls started to reflect an immense room.

"Oops, never mind, Madame," Kamalini said hurriedly. The room immediately turned back to its spa atmosphere.

Tookie bravely stepped forward next. "Environment: inside a whipped cream factory! With beach waves crashing outside the window!"

In an instant, the room transformed into an enormous space with walls and floors made of cream. Machines surrounding the area churned out endless types and flavors—light and heavy, caramel and coffee. There was a five-stories-tall picture window with a perfect view of the sea's surf-worthy waves.

Tookie smiled shakily. She wished Lizzie could see this. "Exodus," she whispered. "Exodus . . ."

"All right now," the yellow Mannecant said, grabbing Tookie's arm and moving down another hall. "We must keep going."

They walked down a long corridor full of treatment rooms. Bellas murmured with pleasure, but when Tookie looked in one room, a Bella was lying on her stomach with an enormous boulder crushing her spine. "The latest in hot stone treatments, years before civilians will hear about it," the Mannecant explained.

In another treatment room, a Mannecant was peeling a layer of skin off a Bella's face. The skin came off in a perfect mask, pigment, pores, and all, and when the Mannecant pressed it up against a plastic-molded head, the mask opened its eyes and smiled. "Facial slough," the yellow Mannecant guiding the girls said. And in yet another room, a Bella stepped inside a giant clamshell. The clam's valves snapped shut rapidly, trapping the Bella inside.

"Let me guess," Dylan said. "Body wrap?"

"Body *snap*," the Mannecant said. "But close enough."

They walked into the next room, a giant space that had a large circle painted in the middle of the floor. Three women dressed in ornately patterned flowing muumuus sat very close together in the corner. Their hair was fused into one huge beehive.

Dylan whispered, "I wonder if their actual heads are connected."

Their eyes were closed, and their beehive hairdo turned

in slow, meditative circles. They seemed unaware of anything around them.

"Flashback Females," the Mannecant whispered reverently. "They have the ability to take a person to a time in her life that has already happened. You cannot *change* the past—only witness it. Most Bellas find it very therapeutic. You can take your friends with you into your flashback, and they will see and hear everything that happened also. But if one of you wants to do it, your whole group must follow. The doors seal once someone has stepped into the circle, trapping everyone inside. No exceptions."

Dylan looked excitedly at the others. "Should we do it?"

Tookie shifted from one foot to the other. She couldn't think of a single thing she wanted to relive.

"I'm not lettin' you chicken out, girl!" Dylan exclaimed, looking at Tookie. "If you don't go, Kamalini and I can't do it. You wanna do it too, right, Kamalini?"

Kamalini pulled in her bottom lip.

"C'mon, Kamalini. You in?" Dylan pressed.

"Well, okay," Kamalini said hesitantly. "But . . . but . . . if you can see the flashback I want to see, I have to prepare you. I am . . . ashamed of my house. Please understand."

Dylan chuckled. "Who are we to judge if your family's hittin' a rough patch? I live in a store! Now, what about you, Tookie?"

"Okay," she said, instantly regretting it.

"Which of you would like to go first?" the Mannecant asked.

"I guess I will," Kamalini volunteered. "So I can get it over with quickly."

She walked farther into the room. One of the Flashback Females stood, approached Kamalini, and led her to the circle. As soon as Kamalini crossed its yellow boundaries, the iron and concrete doors in the room banged shut, making Tookie flinch.

Kamalini stood very still. She nodded as if answering questions, though the Flashback Female hadn't said a word. *"It is so,"* the Female said.

It felt like Tookie's feet were melting into the ground. The sinking feeling crept up to her knees, her hips, her waist, her torso, her shoulders, then her neck. For a moment, all of her senses were muffled, but then they snapped into precise clarity. She blinked slowly and opened her eyes.

Tookie, Dylan, and Kamalini now stood at a window overlooking an immense patchwork of dilapidated shacks. Smoke rose from many of the shanties. Beautiful cocoa-, maple-, and copper-skinned children dressed in bright fabrics ran about. A younger Kamalini, sans Headbangor, climbed out the very window at which the girls were standing and dropped to the ground. She ran toward the middle of the shantytown and stopped at a group of about two dozen people of varying ages. Their clothes might have been tattered and drab, but as soon as they saw Kamalini, their smiles were brighter than the most luxurious silks.

"Kamalini, where are we?" Tookie whispered.

"We are standing in my bedroom. But before you look, brace yourselves."

Everyone turned and gasped. A gigantic four-poster bed stood in the corner, surrounded by jeweled chandeliers and ornate crystal lamps. Plush velvet and bright leather furniture filled the rest of the space. The ceiling was adorned with intricately carved wood and white marble. Cashmere covered the walls.

"You lived *here?*" Dylan's eyes goggled. "What in the heck is there to be *ashamed* of? Are you *cuh-ray-zee?*"

"I enjoyed and appreciated living here, but I felt tormented too." Kamalini pointed to the window. "Right outside are so many people with so much less! And that big group of people the young me is greeting right now? They are the Pande family."

Dylan stared at all the people young Kamalini was with. "Whoa, I thought me havin' four sisses and bros was a big fam, but people in Chakra got bigger ones than mine."

"They are extended family as well," Kamalini explained. "Aunts . . . cousins . . . great-grandparents. But their living conditions were so unfortunate. I used to sneak them unused items. Clothes, schoolbooks, healthy food, and vitamins. I secretly convinced one of the grips on my mother's films to run plumbing and electricity lines from our house to their tiny home too. My family has so much; it felt like a sin to not share."

The young Kamalini in the flashback approached the Pande family and grabbed the hands of a sweet-faced child. "That is Maya, my favorite," Kamalini said to Tookie. "She is eight years old."

"Guess what!" young Kamalini cried to the family. "I actually secured parts for all of you in my mother's next film! And I do not mean a few rupees' worth of background work, I mean bona fide *speaking* parts—real paychecks!"

The family looked gratefully at one another. Some began to sob, but it was happy sobbing, their eyes alight with joy.

"But the scene does not shoot here in Chakra," Kamalini went on. "It is the scene that leads up to the grand dance number, and it shoots in Cappuccina and Très Jolie!"

Their surroundings abruptly shifted to the famous main canal in Cappuccina. Movie cameras focused on the Pande family, who recited their lines with the greatest of ease and grace. Then the scene whooshed again, this time to a film location in Très Jolie, in the shadow of the metropolis's famous sculptural tower. Young Kamalini burst onto set.

"Bonjour, Ma!" she called out. "I will be your assistant director today. Where should the Pande family stand in this scene?"

Kamalini's mother, a tall, striking Chakra woman with huge soulful eyes, a curvy body, and vermillion in her hair, turned and smiled. "*Beti,* did I tell you how proud of you I am?" her mother said to young Kamalini, rubbing her daughter's head. "We are shooting the big thunderstorm scene today. Make sure they have the appropriate props."

Kamalini guided the Pande family to the base of a backdrop depicting a brilliant blue sky. As everyone took their places, Kamalini's mother yelled, "Action!"

The rain machine sprayed the set with water. The cameras began to roll. The thunder sound effect boomed. The Pandes performed well even with faux rain drenching them. Young Kamalini grinned with pride.

"*Beti,* get ready to cue the dancers," Kamalini's mother shouted to her. Just as Maya, the youngest Pande, was about to say the last line of the scene, another earsplitting sound thundered above. The heavy sky-blue backdrop tipped and plummeted to the ground.

Everyone screamed and scattered, but for some it was too late. Thick white dust poured all around like smoke. Tookie waved her hand in front of her face, trying to see. Suddenly, a keening cry rang out. Maya crawled out from under the rubble, blood streaming down her forehead. "*Maaa! Pappaa! Nani!*"

Tookie's heart stopped. She had a sinking feeling about what had just happened. Next to her, present-day Kamalini let out a tortured whimper. "No," she cried. *"No!"* She ran to the rubble and tried to move the bricks away to rescue the other family members, but her fingers just swished through the scene, useless.

Suddenly, the Flashback Female's calm voice rang out through the room. *"It's time to go now."*

The film set receded, and the girls were in the OoAh again. Kamalini crumpled to the floor in tears. "They all perished that day, because of me. This"—she pointed to her Headbangor—"helps me block it out, but I will never forgive myself. Maya became an orphan. She moved in with us, but a week later, she ran away. We searched all of Chakra but could not find her. I do not know if she is dead or alive. I should have never tried to help them."

"It wasn't your fault," Tookie said gently. "You tried to give them a better life!"

Before Kamalini could respond, the Flashback Females approached a shell-shocked Dylan and took her to the center of the circle. Dylan also nodded as if answering questions that weren't spoken. In a flash, they were all in an immense park within the Bou-Big-Tique Nation. Instead of endless posters and signs advertising sales, there were inspirational messages like SMILES ARE THE BEST CURRENCY and KEEP BOU-BIG-TIQUE BEAUTIFUL: SAVE OUR PARK!

A man and a sweet-looking girl about six years old stood next to a jungle gym. The little blond girl had Dylan's sweet, feisty face.

"My God, there's my daddy," Dylan murmured, staring at him. She stepped up to her dad and tried to touch his hair. Her hand swirled through his head, like it was paint being smeared in the air. But that didn't deter her; she leaned in close, her head partly glopping into his.

Dylan's dad picked up six-year-old Dylan and placed her on a slide. He pushed her on the swing set and helped her up onto the monkey bars. But it all seemed too much for him; winded, he kneeled down to his daughter. "Dylan, my baby, Daddy's little girl . . . Daddy's gonna have to go somewhere far away very, very soon."

"On a trip?" young Dylan asked. "Can I come?"

"'Fraid not." There were tears in her father's eyes. "And before I go, I just wanna make sure I say somethin' to you that I want you to remember always. . . ." He cleared his throat. "Dylan, baby, Daddy wants you to know that you are *beautiful*. These other little skinny thangs in the Nation, don't ever let 'em get you down. Don't change nothin' 'bout you, boo. Not one thang. Cuz every-thang about you's perfect."

Suddenly, Dylan's father started to cough. He seemed un-able to catch his breath. His face became bright red and then he dropped to the ground. "Daddy?" little Dylan cried, hovering over him. "Daddy? What's wrong?"

Her father looked at her with glassy eyes. His mouth opened and closed, but he couldn't speak. In seconds, a Bou-Big-Tique ambulance roared up, and EMTs jumped out and loaded Dylan's father onto a stretcher. "Daddy!" young Dylan cried again and again.

A few moments later, the girls returned to the OoAh. Dylan lay on the floor, sobbing.

The yellow Mannecant turned to Tookie expectantly. "Are you ready?"

Tookie shook her head and started toward Dylan. Without seeing her move her mouth or emit a sound, Tookie heard one of the Flashback Females say, *"Let her be, Tookie. The pain is part of the healing."*

Tookie licked her lips, suddenly feeling terrified. She wasn't ready to face the past if it was going to hurt her as much as it had her friends. "Um, I want to skip my turn."

The Mannecant frowned. "But it's a rewarding bonding experience, and it will help you grow as a Bella. And if you refuse, I'll have to mark your time in OoAh as incomplete. OoAh is a class as well, you see."

Tookie let out a huge sigh. Failing something as simple and supposedly relaxing as OoAh wasn't an option. Setting aside all her anxieties, she stepped into the circle.

The Flashback Females walked toward her, mouths shut, but Tookie could hear them speaking, loud and clear. *"Breathe deeply,"* they said. *"Stand very still in the circle to come face to face with your demons. It is from here that we can lead you back to a time that has already happened."*

Tookie glanced over her shoulder at Kamalini and Dylan. Their eyes seemed to silently speak to her too. *It's okay, Tookie. It's okay.*

She turned back to the Females. She didn't even have to speak her request, just think it. *Please just show me something good from my life. Anything. Even if it's something I can't remember.*

"It is so," one the Females answered, shutting her eyes.

There was a whoosh of light. Tookie felt like her brain was being turned upside down and inside out. But it wasn't painful at all—instead, it felt like her head was being relieved of pressure, like a teakettle whistling out steam.

When she opened her eyes, she was in her house in Peppertown. Only, it looked . . . newer. Not as ramshackle. And her bedroom was spotless. Sheer curtains embroidered with yellow ducks flanked the sparkling windows. A stuffed giraffe stood proudly in the corner. A small bed was in the middle of the room, covered with a thick yellow comforter with white tassels along the edge. Plush barriers ran down the sides of the bed, a protective measure to prevent a sleeper from rolling onto the floor.

Mrs. De La Crème entered the bedroom. A man who certainly must have been Mr. De La Crème was holding her hand, though Tookie couldn't see his face. Tookie's jaw dropped. She couldn't recall ever seeing her parents display physical affection. This was before her father's accident, so his body was cut and toned. Creamy was still as wrinkled as she was today, but she looked *softer,* happier. She carried an adorable toddler dressed in bright yellow onesie pajamas. *The Myrracle?* But then she heard her mother murmuring, "There there, Tookie. There there."

Tookie was transfixed. She'd never seen baby photos of herself. *But where's Bellissima?* she wondered. Then she realized . . . the doll didn't exist yet.

Tookie stared at her two-year-old self. She was actually . . . strangely . . . *cute.* Not yet the hideously disproportionate, frustratingly awkward teenager she'd grown to be.

Mr. De La Crème gently touched his baby daughter's head, her hair a mix of textures that seemed deliberate, not random and haphazard. "Six teeth already, dumplin'? You're jumping the gun! You're gonna need one of these soon." He handed her a toddler-sized toothbrush. Young Tookie grabbed the toothbrush and bit on it. Mr. De La Crème turned to his wife and smiled. "Look at her. She's strong, just like her daddy. And she looks just like me, doesn't she?"

"You wish." Mrs. De La Crème playfully smacked him on his muscular arm. "My Tookie is the spitting image of her mommy."

Tookie couldn't believe it. *"My Tookie"? "Mommy"? When did Creamy allow herself to be called Mommy? And when did she stop?*

Mrs. De La Crème laid little Tookie down on her bed. "Time to give that up now, dumplin'," Mr. De La Crème said, taking away the toothbrush. "There'll be plenty of days ahead when I'll have to force you to brush your teeth. Right now, just enjoy being the beautiful baby girl that you are." Her toothbrush. In her father's hand again. But he was holding it with love, not as a weapon.

Then both parents gave baby Tookie a gentle kiss on her forehead.

Tears fell from Tookie's eyes onto her green terry-cloth OoAh dress. Dylan and Kamalini looked at her curiously. "I never knew they loved me," she said, her heart banging fast. "They were going to send me away. They didn't want me anymore." *What changed between then and now? Was it Myrracle? His eye accident? Or . . . something else?*

The memory rolled on. "Sleepy, huh, dumplin'? I know. . . . I see you fighting it," Mr. De La Crème said as he kissed little Tookie's toes. "Just close those eyes and dream those dreams that will all come true one day. Go on now. Go to sleep, dumplin'. Just dream. . . . Just go, for all of us."

Present-day Tookie squeezed her eyes shut. *"It's time to leave now,"* the Flashback Females said.

With that, the flashback disappeared and young Tookie and her tender and loving parents were gone.

ModelLand

Tookie uncapped a pink pen and began to write in Gowdee'an. . . .

Dear Lizzie,

    I wonder if you know where I am right now. If you saw them choose me to come to this special place. I wonder if you think I'm a deserter, a two-faced liar, a selfish egomaniac who ditched our friendship at the very first opportunity. I hope not.

    If you do know where I am, I hope you're looking up at the mountain, wondering what I'm doing right now, not hating me with all your heart. Because I want to tell you everything, Lizzie. I miss our talks. I miss how we laugh. I miss knowing where you are and where you aren't.

    I've got new friendSSSS here, but wait a sec, Lizzie, don't be jealous. You'd love them. They're like us: a little odd, a bit quirky, and definitely real. Their imperfections are what make them shine with the most scintillating, effervescent inner glow you have ever seen. Things have changed in other ways too: I have transformed from the Bangle, Bauble, and Bead Forgetta-Girl into Modelland's Stare-at-Her girl. Everyone either thinks I'm a freak or that I'm here as an experiment—remember those sacrifice rumors, Lizzie? I'm still not sure if they're true.

Maybe they are after me. Now I'm starting to sound like you.... ☺

The latest person to join in on the glarefest is Bravo, a male model attending our brother school, Bestosterone. Everyone else acts as if he's the incarnation of some long-forgotten god, but all I can do when I see him is turn away. He embarrassed me, Lizzie-reaching toward his nose to indicate that I should wipe away some vile olive-tinted whipped-cream snot...in front of everyone. And instead of turning away in disgust, they all stared at me. I was a Rememba-Girl...but in all the wrong ways.

But before Bravo so rudely pointed out the liquid blemish dripping from my nostril, I'd gotten the compliment of my life. A teacher—they're called Gurus here—told me I "ain't half bad." Which to me sounded like a symphony. A warm blanket on a Shivera day. The same kind of affirmation you used to give me, something I miss like cuh-ray-zee.

Lizzie, there are many things I lack here at Modelland. One is the exceptional beauty that the majority of my peers in this paradise have. Another is the gift of Lumière, a special glowing night-light that enhances its recipient's natural beauty. I also lack a family back at home that misses me and counts down the days until they can see me again.

But tonight, you know what? I don't care.

Because tonight, I "ain't half bad."

And I'm praying that wherever you are, you "ain't half bad" too.

I miss you, Hot Queen.

Good night, Lizzie.

Tookie FG?

PS: I hope you're staying far away from sharp rocks.

23

The Diabolical Divide

While Tookie lay fast asleep in her Lumière-less bed in the D, a plan was in action at the base of the Modelland mountain. . . .

An enormous sign swayed crookedly in the breeze. WARNING: ENTER AND YOU MAY PERISH PAINFULLY. Beyond it was a jungle of tangled barbed plants, boulders, and rotting steel. Every few moments, an eerie hoot, screech, or scream was emitted somewhere from in the darkness. Moans. Grumbles. The sound of nails scraping down a piece of glass. Pops of metal underfoot. An insane high-pitched laugh.

Slowly, a ragtag crowd crunched past the sign and lined up against a large rock. Jessamine, a beautiful teenage girl from the

most prestigious section of LaDorno, and her mother, Meena.
Lynne, a woman in her late forties holding a limp advertisement
cut from a newspaper in her trembling hand. After them, none
other than the hairy Abigail Goode, her T-DOD head injury having healed, and her even hairier mother, who was appropriately
named Harriet. The Goode women carried duffels that sported
hairy sewn-on patches promoting their pro-hair causes.

Jessamine covered her mouth in a failed attempt to stifle a
laugh. "Oh wow! I love what they've done with their hair!" she
said in a voice loud enough for the Goode women to hear.

A twitching hunchbacked man strode up, pulling a leather
hood over his head to obscure his scaly skin, beady eyes, and
uniformly pointed teeth. His kind was unfamiliar to the group,
but a certain porcelain-skinned girl named Piper would know
them quite well. She'd lived with the daily terror of scores of them
threatening to penetrate her homeland's grand protective dome,
after all.

All the women nervously stepped back. "What's he doing
here?" Jessamine whispered to her mother. "Everyone knows men
don't usually go on these things, unless they're die-hard and desperate Bestosterone wannabes, like those dumb architects were."

"Shhh," Meena whispered.

Watches were checked. Canteens were uncapped to make
sure an appropriate level of water remained for the first part of the
trip. Hiking-booted toes tapped. Sweaty brows dripped. Temples
pounded in agony. Veins throbbed and bulged. Everyone knew
what the others were thinking: would this be a mistake, as it had
been for everyone before them who'd made the attempt? For
they were victims of the Pilgrim Plague, about to embark on the

treacherous trek up the Diabolical Divide to Modelland. And they had chosen this clear black night to begin the most important journey of their lives. It would take several months.

There would be no turning back.

A final figure emerged from the darkness—their guide, a professional trespasser, or Raider, named Macy Kamata. He wore a large pack crammed with survival gear, the straps cutting into his shoulders. Even though he was as overburdened as a pack mule, Kamata still looked strong and robust. He had weathered, sunburned skin, a thick crew cut, and hooded eyes that constantly darted back and forth. He opened one of the breast pockets on his jumpsuit and retrieved a plastic bag containing several dozen pills. He poured the entire bag into his mouth and swallowed all the pills with no water.

He motioned for the group to line up in front of him. "Time for antibiotics, venom blockers, and miasma inhibitors!" he said, placing a plastic bag of pills in each Pilgrim's hand. "Swallow them if you want to survive the bites and other deadly forces that lurk on the Divide. If you refuse, you're asking for certain death the moment we pass the first junction." The entire group gulped down the pills.

Kamata stuck a needle into his rock-hard butt, injecting a thick, murky liquid. "A booster," he explained. Again, the Pilgrims lined up as they were told. Jessamine recoiled from the acidic burn of the needle plunging deep into her backside.

"You're experienced on the mountain, correct?" Lynne asked. "Your ad said you were, and—"

"I am the best damn Raider money can motivate," Kamata answered gruffly. "But you understand the not-so-fine print, right?

I make no guarantees for your safety, your comfort, your success, your lives. I point, you go. Everyone understand?"

All the Pilgrims nodded. "Okay then. Time to reward the Raider." Kamata extended his palm.

Everyone handed over thick wads of cash. When it was Lynne's turn, she stared tearfully at the money in her hand. "This is my entire life savings. Please promise me that you'll deliver us to Modelland safely."

Behind her, Jessamine snorted. "What is her ancient ass going for, anyway?"

"Shhhh," her mother said, pushing a hand over her daughter's mouth.

"All right," Kamata said, brushing his hands together. "Are we ready?"

The group gave a resounding "YES!" Satisfied, Kamata pulled a flashlight out of his pocket and beamed it toward the Diabolical Divide.

"Wait!" a voice screeched behind them. Two figures dressed in camouflage combat suits bounded up the ridge. Giant transparent packs full of flares, eating utensils, sleeping bags, axes, a fold-up tent, and lanterns swung from their backs. They both wore night-vision goggles.

"Don't leave without us!" the taller of the two cried. "We're on your list! We signed up yesterday." She rifled around in the pocket of her camo pants and pulled out a stack of crisp bills.

The guide instantly smiled and snatched it from her. "So let's see here." He pulled out his registration list. "You must be . . ."

"Mrs. De La Crème," the tall figure interrupted, patting her wrinkly tanned skin. "But you can call me Creamy. And this is my daughter Myrracle. Honey, stop dancing. *Please.*" Myrracle stopped her frantic movements and pulled in her bottom lip.

Kamata nodded. "And what's that?" He motioned to something Mrs. De La Crème had pressed to her chest.

"Her name is Bellissima," Creamy said with annoyance.

"A doll going up the Divide?" Kamata blinked. "Well, that's a first."

He hitched his backpack higher on his shoulders and opened one of its many compartments. "Take these," he said, handing them the packs of pills. He then gave Creamy and Myrracle shots in their derrières. Creamy turned Bellissima over and exposed her hard plastic rear end. "Give her a shot too!"

Kamata studied Creamy. "Whatever you say, lady." He had to push hard to get the needle to penetrate Bellissima's fanny. "I hope you're ready for what lies ahead."

"Ready? I just let you shoot my Myrracle and Bellissima with God knows what! We've never been more ready in our lives! Someone up there has made a grave mistake, and she's going to pay dearly for what she's done." There was such an intense look in her eyes that everyone took a small step away from her.

"Okay then," the guide said. He turned to the Pilgrims. "Off we go."

ModelLand

Tookie selected a purple pen and began a letter in Très Jolie. . . .

Dear Creamy,

You probably can't believe it, but I've been in Modelland for three whole months. I'd like to think you're proud of me, but I know you're not—your hopes and dreams have been pinned on The Myrracle, not me. I know you think she deserves to be here instead, and maybe she does. But I've got a secret: I like it here. In fact, I love it here. And I love my new friendSSSS. You might even say I'm doing okay. In each Run-a-Way, CaraCaraCara, and Mastication class, I get it together just a little bit more. I'm not running into walls anymore, Creamy. I sleep with my Sentura on every night so that Zarpessa (someone who may actually be more evil than you) can't steal it from me. And in GustGape, a class on how to keep our eyes open even in extreme winds, I managed to hold out even in a hurricane. I guess I had some practice from that time you made me go to Shivera and stand in line for five hours for that brand-new, inhumane chinchilla jacket for Myrracle.

Creamy, I want to go for it here. Am I crazy? Am I crazy to think I should try to do my best? If I were still down in Peppertown, crammed in that tiny room with Myrracle, retrieving baby gherkins out of a jar for you and generally being an all-around Forgetta-Girl, I would probably think I was insane. But now I wanna go for it 100 percent. I'm kind of embarrassed to admit that out loud, though, so instead I'll just keep whispering it to myself. And writing it to you.

I know a secret about you: I know you once loved me. I know you once held me in your arms and looked at me like I was a "Myrracle." That hurts, Creamy. What happened? How did you go from love to wanting to send me away to be a Factory Dependent? Even if I became an Intoxibella—which of course won't happen—would you feel different about me?

I wish I could say I miss you, but I don't. I miss the old you. The one I don't even remember. But not the you I know now.

Your daughter,
Tookie
A Bella at Modelland

24

W.O.W.

Our most unusual tale picks up at the start of the next Modelland quadmester, three months and four days into the Bellas' first year at the unusual, untouchable, and never uneventful fantastical land at the top of the mountain. . . .

Tookie stood in front of the mirror in the bathroom of the D, brushing her tongue with her toothbrush. As she rinsed her mouth, her thoughts turned dark. *She's not mine, Creamy.* Every morning when she brushed her teeth at Modelland, her mind would inevitably return to that dismal memory of her father, but it was happening later in the tooth-brushing process each day.

Just minutes later, Tookie, Dylan, Shiraz, and Piper walked

toward the E. They neared the new stadium, now almost completed.

A group of sweaty Bestosteros were picking up construction debris.

"Hey, what's up. It's Tookie, right?"

It was Bravo. For a moment, Tookie just blinked. *He's not talking to me. But he* did *just say my name.* He was coming toward them, carrying a thick tree limb over his shoulder like it was a toothpick. The other girls' mouths dropped open.

"Uh, hi . . . and *bye,*" Tookie said, remembering how Bravo had oh-so-rudely pointed out the snot hanging from her nose after her first Mastication class. She hadn't seen him much since— and she certainly hadn't been looking for him. "Good luck with your manly-man stuff," she added flippantly. "And don't forget to pout your perfect lips and contract your rippling muscles for the cameras."

Dylan shot Tookie an *are you cuh-ray-zee* look and nudged her in the ribs.

"I'm more than just a model or a manly-man," Bravo said. Then he laughed uncomfortably, shaking loose bark and dust from the tree limb. Some landed in Tookie's hair and on her face. *Great,* Tookie thought. *Now he's covering me in splinters. Is it this boy's mission in life to torment me?*

"Oops, sorry." Bravo stepped closer to Tookie. "The Bella-Donna wanted us to clear away some of these dead trees for a better view of the new stadium. Didn't mean to get you, there."

Tookie noticed his irises were a familiar salted-caramel color. *Try not to swoon,* she told herself. *You're not into pretty boys, remember? Especially ones who are training to become male models.*

Then Bravo lightly patted Tookie's hair clean of dust and gingerly plucked a piece of a small shard of wood stuck to her bottom lip. His thumb touched both of her lips, then entered her mouth just a bit. He removed the last traces of chipped wood, but his thumb lingered between her lips and made slight contact with her tongue. Tookie wanted to bite down hard on his hand to teach him a lesson to not touch her like that, but instead she closed her lips on his thumb, locking it inside her mouth, her body betraying her. She smelled him, a mixture of tree bark, sweat, and blood orange, and felt the heat of his sweating body sail toward her. Her knees wobbled, her heart started to flutter, and she felt a warmth gush through her core.

One corner of Bravo's mouth curled into a crooked smile. "Um . . . do I taste good?"

Tookie realized what she was doing and released his thumb. She didn't even *know* this guy. What had gotten into her? She glanced at her friends. To her horror, they were trying to contain their laughter. They all had their thumbs in their mouths, playfully mocking her.

Tookie turned back to Bravo. "Hi," she said awkwardly, as if she hadn't been speaking with him the last few minutes.

"Hi," he said back, breaking into the lopsided smile again. The hairs on the backs of Tookie's thighs stood up.

"Um . . . we have to run," she said, but her feet were planted in place.

And then, suddenly, three figures tumbled out from behind the stadium—Bravo's Bestostero friends Webb, Alexander, and and a guy named O'Neil.

"Well, lookie here!" Webb shouted in a nasty, oily voice.

Alexander made slurping kissing noises. O'Neil thrust his hips forward lewdly like a humping dog. The three of them laughed, their handsome faces twisted and callous.

Tookie stepped away. She could feel their mocking, disparaging stares all over her. "See you, uh, not later, Bravo," she muttered.

"Tookie, wait."

But Tookie didn't turn around. "Come on," she hissed to her friends. "Let's get out of here."

"Pretty boy kooky over Tookie, and want her nookie," Shiraz said sexily to Tookie as they jogged away.

"You sound like Chaste," Tookie reprimanded, not laughing back. Deep down, she felt . . . flushed. Overwhelmed. Confused. *His thumb entering my mouth. Yum—I mean yuck! Was that all just a joke?*

Or something more?

М

After a meal in the E, the other girls took a bathroom break, and Tookie wandered out to Beautification Boulevard and studied her new schedule. Then she felt a hand tap her shoulder. Certain it was Bravo again, she spun around. But it was Bibiana, her hair wet from her morning shower. She peered at Tookie. "Do you understand these clocks at all? They are making me go in circles like I'm doing some crazy samba number!"

Tookie blinked at the girl for a moment. She was still caught off guard when someone actually approached her as though she wasn't invisible. Especially someone as gorgeous as this girl, who was even lovelier than Myrracle.

Tookie turned and looked at the kaleido-clock. The hand was

just past orange. "My schedule says my next class, W.O.W., is at five past vermillion," Bibiana said. "Five past vermillion? What does that mean?"

Tookie still struggled with telling time at Modelland. But for once, she wasn't alone—*none* of the new Bellas could make heads or tails of the colorful Modelland clocks. For the first time in Modelland history, the entire class had had to partake in an impromptu remedial lesson on the workings of the kaleido-clock timekeepers. Taught by head-hand Guru Applaussez, the lesson was meant to last an hour, but the girls had struggled so badly that it dragged on for five and a half. Even after the class *and* a private tutoring session from Piper, Tookie felt just as clueless about the timekeepers as the day she had arrived at Modelland.

"Five past vermillion? I don't have a clue," Tookie admitted.

Tookie was going to W.O.W., War of Words, too, so they walked there together. Soon the girls stood below the gigantic windowless rose-gold metal ball that was labeled THE WAR OF WORDS MAGNETOSPHERE.

The shiny sphere hovered thirty feet above the ground, with no visible means of support.

"How do we get in there?" Tookie asked.

"Let's wait for a guinea pig to show us," Bibiana suggested.

"Hopefully that won't take long," said Piper, coming up behind them. She had fashioned the umbrella she'd been given as soon as they'd landed in Modelland into a unique couture-like hat. It shaded her entire face. Yet again, simply by the way she stood, shoulders rolled back, chin up, her eyes mysterious yet intense, she could've been an unusual Intoxibella in a high-fashion advertisement.

The girls watched as Bo, the emotionless Bella, walked directly beneath the ball and stood there. Within a few seconds, she was swiftly propelled upward, into the ball.

"*Beleza!*" Bibiana cried excitedly. "Let's try that!"

Tookie, Bibiana, and Piper walked up to the ball. After a minute Tookie felt a pull as if a giant magnet was dragging her upward. The other girls were yanked up as well. The magnetic attraction made their bodies go limp. Tookie felt like a marionette.

When they were mere inches from the bottom of the magnetosphere, a circle slid open and sucked them inside a perfectly round room that was the same rose-gold color as the exterior. Girls were standing nervously on a stage that followed the contour of the sphere. Tookie spotted Shiraz and Dylan and grinned. She also noticed the four Likee sisters, as well as Zarpessa.

Over the past weeks, Zarpessa's wrath toward Tookie had only gotten worse. One night, Zarpessa had used her Sentura to make Tookie's hand-drawn image on her bedspread attempt to strangle her. No one but Zarpessa had been in the room at the time, so Tookie had no proof of what had occurred. Tookie had had to punch her own image in the face, knocking her bed sketch out cold.

Don't make eye contact with her, Tookie said to herself now. It kind of reminded her of what Creamy had said about Wingtip.

Tookie wondered what Creamy was doing right now. It felt like she'd been at Modelland for so long. Myrracle must be preparing for next year's T-DOD already. And Creamy had probably renovated the kitchen nineteen times.

Two metal podiums stood at the center of the circular stage. There was a table in the middle that held small metal tags stamped with plus and minus signs. On one side of the sphere's curved wall was an immense green-lit plus sign; a red minus sign illuminated the other.

Around the room, necklaces, rings, buckles, and other metal objects were stuck to the walls. A set of miniature railroad tracks adhered to the shiny surface too. When Tookie got closer, she realized they were orthodontic braces.

Tookie's mouth fell open as she stared at the bizarre wall. Suddenly, she felt a tugging sensation in one of her back right molars. Something dislodged from her tooth and shot out of her mouth before she could stop it. *Clank!* A piece of metal slammed against the wall.

"Oh. Wow. Cool. Beans!" the Likee sisters exclaimed in their odd one-word-per-girl speech. "Her. Tooth. Filling's. Stuck!"

Tookie curled her tongue toward her back tooth. Sure enough, her filling was gone.

"Could. Be. Gold. Amalgam?" the Likees said, staring up at the filling. "Hard. Deciphering. From. Here."

"Looks like the Fraud Quad has their eyes on your filling," Piper murmured to Tookie under her breath. She, Tookie, Dylan, and Shiraz had begun to notice that the Likee sisters liked to claim things that weren't theirs as their own, hence their new nickname.

Other girls began to lose pieces of metal from their bodies. A gold anklet whipped off Chaste's ankle. Bibiana lost a pair of stud earrings.

Tookie felt a pull at her chest. *Oh no,* she thought. The wall wanted her pin! *The* pin! The ceiling yanked the T O OKE button from underneath her garden brooch. It sailed upward and clicked onto the ceiling.

Tookie broke her rule of refraining from eye contact and snuck a peek at Zarpessa, who was lifting her chin up to the ceiling at just that moment. Simultaneously, Tookie felt another tug on her chest. Her plant brooch shot upward too, landing precisely on top of the button. *Whew.* The odd tendriled sprout was beginning to become a bit of a life-saver.

Then Chaste turned to Zarpessa. "Yesterday, in the E, I heard some older Bellas say that someone named MattJoe Von Megalo teaches this class. *Vonnn Mehhhgahhhhlo.*" She stretched the name out like taffy. "I'm calling firsties, so all you chicks better let go my Megalo."

At that moment, the circle entrance opened up in the floor once more. A troll of a man entered. He was balding on the left side of his head, and he walked like a seal scoots when on land.

Chaste leaned around HerLikee to get a good look. "Oh mega-HELL no!" she yelled.

The troll-man was dressed impeccably. He wore an expensive-looking suit complete with a man-couture ascot and freshly shined chestnut-brown boots. He ignored Chaste's remark and looked cagily around the room. "Everyone is here. Yep, yep. Very good, very good." His voice was nasal and high-pitched. He could barely make eye contact with the girls.

"Hello, dear Bellas, my name is MattJoe Von Megalo," he continued. "Yep, yep. Guru MattJoe." He bowed and rocked on his heels. "I will be your humble general as we engage in W.O.W.— a War of Words."

He proceeded to scoot-walk toward Chaste, stumbling over his own feet. Tookie smiled slightly. He reminded her of herself. "You will learn how to use words to convince, to charm, to soothe, and to strike and DESTROY the arguments of anyone standing in your way! And I don't mean the way *thespian dames* do, ladies, just reciting lines from cue cards and crying on command. I mean doing so with Modelland CONVICTION!" The Guru delivered his little speech without looking at any of them, but that last bit was spoken with a torrent of emotion.

"Sorry, sorry." MattJoe ducked his head meekly. "I'm usually not aggressive. I must have learned it from my friend at Bestosterone, Bravo. Yep, yep." He laughed like an out-of-breath hyena.

"He has friends at Bestosterone?" Chaste whispered to She-Likee. "Yeah, right."

Bravo? An unwanted excited shiver rippled through Tookie. Bravo was coming up all sorts of ways that day. She thought again about his thumb in her mouth, trying to make sense of what had happened. Was there something she should have done differently? Acted seductive, like Chaste? Snide, like Zarpessa? Even confident and sassy, like Dylan? Instead she'd just stood there, sucking and sucking like a baby.

MattJoe deployed a small mirror and a miniature ruler, measured the space between his eyebrows and the width of his lips, jotted something in a small notebook, then quickly returned the items to his pocket. "Now, where was I? The class. Yep, yep. This is War of Words. In your previous lives, you may have called it *debate*. Today I will begin by observing your natural skills, and from there, I will mold your use of language so that you are, um . . . skilled artisans. Bellas, this is, um . . . the most important class you'll ever take at Modelland. Why? Well, as Intoxibellas, you must master the art of speaking about the products you are hired to represent, yep, yep. You must clearly convey your love and use of them, whether you adore the item or actually detest it. The job of an Intoxibella is not necessarily to love the products you sell, but to make your public become enamored with them."

Tookie immediately thought of chocolate. She couldn't imagine having to eat it and then smile and lie about loving it. Just thinking about it made a bit of throw-up creep into the back of her throat.

"So let's have a little fun first, shall we?" Guru MattJoe said, his nose twitching like he was about to sneeze. "It's always nice to start off with a fun and frivolous topic. Anyone have any ideas? Anything at all."

No one volunteered.

"Nothing's off limits, yep, yep," Guru MattJoe said.

"If he says *yep, yep* one more time, I'm gonna scream," Dylan whispered in Tookie's ear.

"I have an idea!" Chaste's hand shot up. "How about we debate free swing versus firm sling?"

A few girls giggled. MattJoe scratched his bald spot, confused. Flakes of dandruff fell on his shoulders. "Do you wish to debate the merits of different types of hammocks?"

"Kind of." Chaste seductively twirled a piece of hair around her finger. "Hammocks . . . for honkers."

The giggles persisted. MattJoe remained just as perplexed. *Bra versus no bra,* Tookie wanted to yell out, to spare him the embarrassment.

But Chaste just kept going. "You know. Bazookas? Cha-chas? Chesticles?"

"Okay, then you go over there." Guru MattJoe pointed Chaste to the side of the room with the green plus sign. "You're free swing."

"And . . . you." He pointed to Shiraz as if his finger were a pistol. "You're firm sling."

Shiraz hurried to the minus side of the room. "I ready!"

MattJoe hobbled onto his stool. "You see the metal tags on the table. Chaste, please apply a plus sign to your forehead, and Shiraz, a minus sign."

"I think that plus sign would be more appropriate on Dylan's buttocks," Zarpessa trilled, eyeing Dylan.

Dylan's mouth fell open, but Tookie reached over and squeezed her hand. Since their arrival at Modelland, Zarpessa had been making all kinds of jabs like that at all four of them. *The girl is a bully strategist,* Tookie thought. *She knows to not just attack the enemy, but to hit those the enemy cares about too.*

"Each girl gets one statement, no rebuttal, yep, yep," the Guru said. "Ready?"

Shiraz and Chaste nodded.

The Senturas on Chaste's and Shiraz's waists slid off and bound their wrists to each other like fabric handcuffs. Neither looked happy with this new development.

"Free swing versus firm sling. Proceed!" MattJoe said.

"To bra or not to bra. That is the question," Chaste started.

A resounding clap of electricity echoed through the sphere, and Chaste's and Shiraz's foreheads were magnetically drawn toward each other. The girls tried to fight the force, but it was no use. In seconds, their faces were mere inches apart. Shiraz shot a frantic look at Guru MattJoe.

"Stay in the moment, ladies," he said. "Focus on your opponent, yep, yep. Opposing sides can both attract and repel, depending on their position. From the force that seems to be pulling you toward each other now, you are truly on conflicting sides of this matter. With magnets, remember: opposites attract. Positive, go! Now!"

Chaste inhaled deeply, exhaled slowly, and began. "The melon fruit is one to be supremely relished. A sweet treat one should enjoy in its pure rawness, without a fork to spear its tender flesh or a napkin to sop up the luscious juice that drips from our chins. Honeydews, cantaloupes, casabas, crenshaws, muskmelons, and watermelons. Best appreciated without the interference of objects created by man's hands, mm, mm!"

MattJoe's face was very red. He turned to Shiraz. "Er, okay. Your turn."

"Ah, um . . ." Shiraz cleared her throat, seeming a little knocked off her game. Then she launched into a song. *"The boobies high and tight on me."* Everyone laughed. *"My knobbies pert and firm, agree? But forever young they will not be. No bra, they'll sag with grav-i-tee!"*

The entire class launched into thunderous applause. Zarpessa even lifted her hands to start clapping, but she lowered them quickly.

Silence fell over the room.

"Chaste offered a passionate argument," MattJoe said. "She used food as a metaphor for . . . for . . . um . . . yep, yep. But she may have skewed to a more testosterone-laden audience. Shiraz, on the other hand, had a lyrical presentation that used both humor and logic, which appealed to her target audience. Thusly, I declare the winner to be . . ."

Suddenly, the circle opened up in the floor. Two figures rose through it. The first figure was Persimmon. She held on to a second figure, who was bound and gagged. Tookie gasped.

Ci~L.

The fallen Triple7 had a muzzle over her mouth. Her normally caramel-colored skin was pale, and she wore a baggy gray jumpsuit with a metal zipper up the front. On the back of the jumpsuit, the words *UGLY ROOM* were scrawled in large black letters.

Persimmon stood at attention. "By order of the most beloved of the beloved, the most esteemed of the worthy, the definer of all things beautiful, and the leader of all of those lucky enough to be led, Ci~L is delivered to the War of Words Magnetosphere."

Ci~L turned her head away in shame. Tookie felt a lump in her throat. What had Ci~L *done*?

"She comes here because keeping her at Modelland has not been enough," Persimmon recited. "She has continued to spout her insolent, disrespectful, heinous messages and vile verbiage that has denigrated all we stand for. And so, as an attempt to truly get through to her so that she understands the hideousness of her actions, we must step things up a notch. Today, Ci~L is return-ing to her roots to be . . ." Persimmon paused dramatically. ". . . a first-year Bella. A *No-See*."

Everyone gasped, including Zarpessa and Chaste. Even Matt-Joe looked uncomfortable.

Persimmon poked Ci~L's shoulder. "The BellaDonna com-mands you to remove the ugly suit."

Ci~L swallowed hard. Slowly, she unzipped the jumpsuit. It dropped to the floor in a dingy pile. Everyone gasped again. Underneath the jumpsuit was a green Modelland Bella uniform.

But it was too small.

Bursting at the seams.

"Now I know what Guru Gunnero means when he calls her *Body Girl*," Zarpessa hooted.

Persimmon gazed at the Bellas. "Today, Ci~L is on the same

level as all of you—*beneath* you, actually, as you are in your second quadmester and she is in her first. The BellaDonna has commanded that she return to her Bella ways of yesteryear, when she complied with the rules of authority. After this course, she will return to the Ugly Room for more shock treatments."

"Persimmon, is all this really necessary?" Guru MattJoe asked, looking pityingly at Ci~L. "To do this to a girl who was so far ahead of everyone in my class not too long ago? To make her suffer so?"

Then he spied a BellaDonna bust across the sphere and straightened up. "Of course, I assume the esteemed Madame BellaDonna has her reasons for doing this. . . ." It was as though the BellaDonna was in the room with them. Maybe she was.

"Ci~L poses a risk to herself and to all of us," Persimmon said. "She *must* be reformed by any means necessary." The Mannecant stepped up to Ci~L and removed the muzzle. Little droplets of blood oozed from the corners of Ci~L's mouth.

Zarpessa snickered. "Wow, the famed Intoxibella is slumming it with the No-Sees."

Tookie whipped around, filled with rage. "Yeah, well, you're no stranger to slumming it yourself!" she snapped before she could stop herself.

Zarpessa's eyes blazed. *Uh-oh,* Tookie thought. *You've done it now. And anyway, Ci~L is crazy! Why did you even defend her? At least, I think she's crazy.*

"Listen, you crazy-eyed, watermelon-headed freak who's only here for a Modelland sacrificial science project—"

"Stop!" MattJoe intervened. "Save the passion for the War of Words!"

Persimmon spoke. "Make sure Ci~L is assigned the argument

that will aid her best in reform. The one that will please the Bella-Donna most." The circle in the floor opened once more, and Persimmon disappeared.

MattJoe faced the girls and cleared his throat. "Sorry for the interruption, Bellas. Let's continue where we left off. Okay then, I guess the next debaters have chosen themselves! You there"—he pointed at Tookie—"and you"—he pointed at Zarpessa.

"Oh, I can't wait," Zarpessa growled, strutting up to the podium confidently, her shoulders thrown back and her head high.

Tookie froze, petrified. She couldn't debate Zarpessa. There was no way. She peeked over at Ci~L, who was no longer staring at the floor but directly at Dylan in the same spooky, hypnotized way she'd gazed at Shiraz during the very first Run-a-Way class. She started moving her mouth, chanting inaudibly. Her body rocked steadily.

"She's practically frothing at the mouth," Zarpessa whispered from the podium, eyeing Ci~L.

"All right," MattJoe said. He looked at his roster. "Tookie versus Zarpessa. But let's add another ingredient—partners!"

He extended his arm again, looking down it like he was aiming a rifle. At first he set his sights on Chaste, but then he decided to continue hunting. He spun around and brightened at Ci~L.

"Bang!" he yelled. "Ci~L. Join Zarpessa."

Ci~L just stared at him catatonically.

MattJoe looked nervously around the room. "Ci~L, *she's* probably watching you," he said in a whisper, clearly meaning the BellaDonna. "You used to ace this course in your sleep. Just get it done."

Ci~L snapped out of her trance and walked to the podium.

Then Guru MattJoe turned to Dylan. "And, um, the recently

attacked should have a chance to have her say as well against her, uh, oppressor. Dylan, please join Tookie."

Dylan reluctantly climbed up the steps. She gave Tookie's hand a nervous squeeze.

MattJoe pointed at Ci~L and Zarpessa. "The topic for this last debate is going to be unusual physicality versus defined beauty. You two will argue that atypical features are superior to conventional beauty."

"Are you sure?" Ci~L looked skeptical. "That's exactly the opposite of what you know *she* wants." Ci~L peered at the Bella-Donna bust across the room.

The Guru ignored her, turning next to Tookie and Dylan. "And your team will argue for narrowly defined beauty and that anything else is absolutely worthless. Like the kind of defining we do here at Modelland."

This should be easy, Tookie thought. All she has to do was concentrate on Myrracle's perfect face and speak from her soul.

The girls placed the respective negative and positive tags on their foreheads. Instantly, Tookie shot across the podium and landed forehead to forehead with Ci~L. Dylan was locked to Zarpessa. Their Senturas released from their waists and bound them together as one. Tookie had never been this close to anyone in her life, not even Lizzie. The extreme proximity was beyond uncomfortable.

"War of Words starts . . . *now!*" MattJoe proclaimed.

Zarpessa jumped right in. "Funny-looking people like you two girls and your mini and pasty friends over there"—she paused, indicating Shiraz and Piper—"deserve to feel attractive too, even when you are nowhere near even *average*-looking and have everyone at Modelland beyond flummoxed as to why you Unfortunate-Lookings—ULs, for short—are even here. But let me leave you with something positive: you UL's are beautiful too, even if it's just way deep down within the depths of your insides. And I mean mining-for-*coal* deep."

Chaste guffawed in the audience. Tookie's stomach did its familiar lurch. MattJoe ducked his head, ran his hand over his bald spot, then quickly measured his features once more. "You have a sharp tongue, Miss Zarpessa," he murmured. "Perhaps it cuts *too* sharply," he added under his breath, his voice cracking.

He turned to Ci~L. "You're next."

Ci~L shut her eyes. For a long moment, she didn't say anything. Tookie could feel Dylan breathing shallowly beside her.

Then Ci~L's hair started to blow wildly around her face. She opened her mouth to speak: "Yes, lustrous is your hair," she began. "Agreed, bewitching is your stare."

It's a poem! Tookie realized. But she was also confused. Ci~L was looking at Zarpessa, not at Tookie and Dylan.

Ci~L continued:

"Perhaps perfection is your snout.
Queen bees have stung your handsome pout.
What lies within your cantankerous head:
Infected hard pus in ol' blackheads.
Strength be with you, 'pessa, as you fade
whilst the UL's dance upon your grave."

When she was finished, Tookie felt the urge to cry and clap at the same time. Unfortunately, her bound wrists prevented her from applauding. Zarpessa's eyes narrowed, but then she lowered her gaze and swallowed hard. It looked as though Ci~L had actually *gotten* to her.

MattJoe paused from measuring the squareness of his chin and looked at Tookie and Dylan. "You're on, Bellas."

Tookie's mind raced, and her heart started to beat faster. She gazed at Ci~L in her uncomfortably small uniform. It was clever and generous the way Ci~L had defended Tookie and her friends, but Tookie had a strong gut feeling it was just a consolation prize, a pat on the back before they were inevitably booted out of here or turned into Mannecants. This might be the only time Tookie would be able to tell Ci~L her feelings. And so she took a deep breath, stared into Ci~L's green eyes, and began to speak in her own special way: in letter form, as though she were writing in her *T-Mail Jail*.

"Dear Ci~L," she said. "When you chose me on The Day of Discovery, you were my savior. When your hand touched mine and not my sister's, it was surreal. Suddenly, I wanted something so badly that I never knew I really desired. You're amazing. You've accomplished so much. You stand up for what you believe is right. But I lie awake at night thinking about you. Sometimes I'm confused, sometimes I'm proud of you, and often, I think you are deeply troubled, perhaps even mentally ill. But mostly, I tend to think the latter.

"Zarpessa says she has no idea why my friends and I are here at Modelland. It's not like I have a clue either. I know people here see a midget and a whale and a ghost and a freak of nature. My friends know it too. Maybe our presence at Modelland is just a big joke. Or something else. A sacrifice." She paused, glancing up at the room. Her friends visibly shuddered. Zarpessa grinned.

"Maybe this whole place is only in my dreams and none of you really exist. Still, I'm happy here. I've never felt better. But there's a harsh truth I have to face up to: ideal beauty is the only accepted and celebrated kind. Take my sister, Myrracle. Whenever she walks into a room *anywhere,* people lose all self-control, laser focused on making sure she's taken care of, made comfortable, kept happy. And they don't even know her." Tookie paused for a moment. "So that is proof within itself that the definition of beauty is universally narrow. While my sister is worshipped, I am ignored, forgotten, the quintessential Forgetta-Girl. We all have a place in life, and for the majority of mine, that's all I've been. And I think that's all I'll ever be.

"Ci~L, Thank you for standing up for me earlier. But please allow me to accept my fate. Your crusade is useless, pointless. Perhaps it's what is driving you insane.

"From one Unfortunate-Looking girl to one unquestionably ravishing one, Tookie De La Crème."

Beside her, Dylan gasped. In the audience, Shiraz and Piper held each other, tears in their eyes. The Sentura bindings on their wrists released. Zarpessa, who looked overjoyed, opened her mouth to speak, but Ci~L cleared her throat and spoke over her, venom lacing her voice.

"They have lobotomized you!" she cried, staring straight at Tookie. "We've all been brainwashed to think that beauty is this"—she pointed to her own face—"or *that*"—she pointed to Chaste—"or *that* or *that* or *that!*" She pointed in turn to Bibiana, MeLikee, and Zarpessa.

"When in fact, if we reprogram our brainwashed-with-extra-strength-bleach minds, it can be *that!*"—she jabbed her finger at Shiraz—"and *that*"—she motioned to Piper—"and *this*!" She grabbed hold of Tookie's face. "And—"

"*Fat!*" Dylan screamed.

The class froze. Zarpessa let out a snicker.

"What?" Tookie and Ci~L said at the same time.

"Y'all listen to me right now!" Dylan yelled, trembling. "There may be different types of girls in this room from different countries all over this damn different world. But y'all have ONE thing in common! And I refuse to stand here and state the obvious!" She gestured to her body. "Y'all can debate 'unique features' this and 'atypical looks' that all damn day long, but what in the hell is unique about *me*? A waist as wide as this damn sphere is round, legs as thick as tree trunks, a butt as big as the Bou-Big-Tique Nation! Oh, ladies, do not waste any more of my precious time with your nonsense word war. Because none of it, not a smidgeon, not a drop, not a damn thing pertains to *me*!"

Ci~L looked enraged. "Dylan, beauty is what we believe it to be. If you would just look in the damn mirror, girl, you'd appreciate—"

"That's where you're dead wrong, Ci~L!" Dylan's lips were quivering uncontrollably. "You may be right about one thing, that beauty is what we believe it to be, but that's from the neck up! And you know it!"

Ci~L shook her head. "Oh, so, you're going to give up that easily, coward? You're just as bad as *they* are! You have to *defend* your body! *To the death, if you have to!*"

"Shut up, Ci~L! Just shut. The hell. UP!"

Dylan ripped the plus sign off of her head and ran to the circle outline in the floor. She frantically jumped up and down on it until it finally glided open, sucking her out of the classroom's sphere.

"Dylan!" Tookie, Piper, and Shiraz yelled.

But Dylan was gone.

Guru MattJoe pressed a palm over his eyes. "Tookie, your partner has committed acts of insolent yelling, unsavory language, and departing class before being dismissed. But that being said, your arguments, well, they were the most eloquent speeches I've heard in quite some time. Your words cut so close, got to the root of what we all feel—well, *many* of us feel, anyway. Yep, yep." He paused to nervously clear his throat. "Well done, my dear. Tookie, you have won your first War of Words."

Tookie barely heard Guru MattJoe congratulating her. The circle had opened again. "Dylan?" she cried, rushing toward it. But it was Persimmon. She stalked right up to Guru MattJoe.

"You let her spout her sickening poems without doing anything about it?" she hissed at the Guru. "How dare you! While we work overtime to reform Ci~L, your lackadaisical attitude has regressed her reprogramming by a fortnight! You know *who* you will have to answer to for this."

Guru MattJoe turned away, looking guilty but satisfied. Persimmon re-dressed Ci~L in the gray Ugly Room jumpsuit and replaced the muzzle on her face.

"Class is allowed to, um, depart!" MattJoe announced. "I'll see you soon, but now I have to go make a, uh, a special deposit, yep, yep."

"Ew," Chaste snickered. "I can only imagine what kind of *deposit* he's talking about."

MattJoe ignored her and pressed a button under his stool. All the jewels and other metal paraphernalia stuck to the wall crashed to the floor. The Likee sisters rushed to the sparkling pieces, pocketing items Tookie had a feeling weren't theirs. Tookie grabbed her T O OKE button and flower brooch before the Likees could steal those too, then followed Shiraz and Piper to the center of the circle and out of the Magnetosphere. Once they were on the ground, they spotted Dylan in the distance, running into the plaid cube balanced on one of its points. They darted off after her.

They entered the cube through a door just above the balance point. Dylan was climbing a stepladder up ahead. "Dylan!" Shiraz screamed. "Why you run? We want talk to you!"

But Dylan didn't answer. The girls scrambled up the ladder after her and entered a hallway that smelled strangely of wet fur. As the girls careened down the increasingly narrow hall, a loud hissing sound reverberated off the walls.

"Dylan! Are you in here?" Tookie yelled.

The noisy hiss ended in a piercing screech. The girls ground to a halt. "What was that?" Piper looked at the others with terrified eyes.

"Do you think it was . . . *Dylan*?" Tookie whispered.

The screeching escalated, growing into a full chorus of growls and hisses. All of a sudden, Shiraz's eyes widened. "I know where we are!"

At that, words lit up on the corridor's wall. They looked like they'd been written with ragged claws. Tookie read them silently, her heart sinking to her feet.

"Catwalk Corridor!" Shiraz screamed.

And that was when the first set of claws ripped into Tookie's flesh.

25

Oпе Bee-yoтcнɴɴ

Tookie grabbed hold of her ankle and felt a warm flow of blood trickling to her foot. She wiped her hand on the pants leg of her uniform. She could hear the hisses and vicious animal noises growing closer. Something furry and blurry moved in the darkness. And then, suddenly, a shining claw reached out again and struck her mouth. *Rip!*

"Ow!" Tookie whispered. The familiar trickle of blood dripped down her chin. Joining the trickle was a tickle at the back of Tookie's nose and throat. "Achoooo!"

"Bless you," came a high-pitched female voice with an accent from the slums of the famed country of TooLip. "And hallo, big noggin'. Aren't yoo an oogly one!"

"Hey there, bigfoot." Something soft and furry brushed up against her leg.

Tookie tensed. "Who's there?"

Her throat itched something terrible. Hives broke out on her skin. As her eyes adjusted to the dim hallway light, she saw hundreds of eyes staring back at her.

"Cats!" Piper screamed.

Two striped animals with amber eyes slinked out of the shadows, stalking Tookie, Shiraz, and Piper. Their fuchsia-painted claws extended like switchblades. In even dimmer light, the larger of the two stopped to lick its paws and rear end.

"Whatchoo lookin' at, nosey?" a voice scoffed. "Can't I bathe in peace without your ugly butt staring at my beauty and my booty?"

Dozens of felines crept out of the shadows, their tails puffed, their backs arched, their eyes flashing green, amber, and yellow. They hissed and spat in unison.

Tookie's eyes felt like they were on fire. She was having a monster of an allergic reaction.

The cat's fuchsia claws extended more, and it prepared to pounce on Tookie. Tookie turned to run, but a massive gate slid from the ceiling and slammed down in front of her, the spikes at the bottom piercing the floor. She was trapped.

Then she spied a fluffy, long-haired white cat lounging lazily on a high shelf. Its sapphire eyes widened. As Tookie peered more closely, a strange realization came over her. This was no ordinary feline. Its face looked *human*. To Tookie's astonishment, the cat stared straight at her and spoke.

"Can you do a Persian a favor?" it said. "Before my hair gets any more tangled and ends up looking like your heinous and confused bird's nest of a head, can you comb mine, please? I haven't seen my hairdresser in weeks."

Tookie's hand instinctively reached up to her own hair, but stopped midway to her head. She felt ashamed that a cat, even one with a human face, could make her so insecure. Not only did the Persian have a human face, Tookie realized, but she looked oddly familiar. A lot like the Intoxibella Anka, who was a favorite at Cappuccina fashion week. At least, Tookie thought, it wasn't Anka's overcaffeinated, high-strung best friend Fiona, who drove everyone crazy.

Tookie sneezed again, and then turned and saw that Piper had been backed against a wall by a gang of hairless sphynxes. "Blank girl needs some color!" they chanted in unison. "Take one of these. . . ." The skinniest of the cats extended its paw to Piper, revealing a round pill that glowed green. "It will make your skin toasty and rich-colored."

"And you won't sleep for days!" a mangy tabby cat added.

Wow, Tookie thought. The tabby looked like hyperactive Fiona from Icylann.

A Siamese with oddly human lips, large blue eyes, and a conniving smile, which looked a lot like an Intoxibella Tookie had seen in Wrinkle Redux ads, was no competition for Shiraz's blazing speed. "I've coughed up fur balls bigger than you!" the Siamese spat at Shiraz as the girl dodged a paw with ease.

"You look like Intoxibella Phara!" Shiraz exclaimed, noticing the cat's human resemblance to the model whose famous crescent-moon-shaped eyes sold countless tubes of mascara.

"The repugnant, moronic, miniature midget is correct!" the

Siamese jeered, the hair on her back standing on end. "Phara, the Princess of Verbal Barbarisms, *Modelland* magazine calls me."

"So wait, you actually *are* the Intoxibella?" Tookie asked. *"How?"*

The cats didn't answer—they'd all noticed something at the end of the hallway. The Catwalk Corridor sign suddenly burned brighter, revealing the arrival of two more girls: Zarpessa and Chaste.

Dozens of cats circled their ankles. A calico zeroed in on Zarpessa, murmuring, "I want this pretty one right here!" Then, to everyone's horror, it squatted and urinated on Zarpessa's feet, marking its territory. "This one is Mine. Mine! MINE!"

Zarpessa screeched and ran away, frantically shaking her feet. All the cats laughed.

Tookie sneezed several times. Then she felt a tap on her leg. "Hey, you." It was the scrawny hairless sphynx. "Want one?" She offered Tookie a pill. "Like me, they're hypoallergenic, and no side effects, except for a little fun. . . ."

Tookie shook her head. A shiny-furred Abyssinian that looked exactly like the Intoxibella Daisy-Ellen from FiveHundred bit her leg. "Ow!"

"That ankle was tasty," Daisy-Ellen cooed, batting her eyeliner-rimmed eyes. "Tasty like sweet cream. I want me some more!"

"Sweet cream?" a black cat that sounded just like the Intoxibella Donyelle exclaimed. "Gimme some of that!"

"Get your own leg!" Daisy-Ellen screeched.

"No, I want this one!" Donyelle yowled, extending her claws.

"Me-owch!" Daisy-Ellen screamed, and pounced on Donyelle.

The felines landed on top of Tookie's head. Tookie felt their claws dig into her mouth and she screamed in pain again. She gazed across the room at Piper. "We have to find a way out of here! Has anyone seen Dylan?"

Piper ran over and grabbed Tookie's hand. They raced down the corridor. "Come on!" Paws swiped at them from all sides.

When they reached the end of the corridor, Shiraz, Zarpessa, and Chaste stood in the way, staring at something obscured in shadows. They all looked horrified.

"What is it?" Tookie asked, clutching Shiraz's shoulder.

"Not sure," Shiraz mumbled, her voice quavering. "But look!"

She pointed at an audience of cats facing the same direction. Loud, wailing purrs came from deep within their throats, echoing through the hallway. Slowly, they all began to make yowling noises at the obscured shadow. They bent down on their front legs and arched their backs, then buried their heads under their paws, as if they were praying to whatever lay before them in the darkness.

Suddenly, a light illuminated the mysterious being. It was an oversized lion's face. Its eyes were golden and its mouth was practically as large as the wall.

The girls held their breath. The cats remained silent and still. The lion-face's expression changed from ferocious to enraged. Tookie sucked in her breath even more. The face looked remarkably like the BellaDonna.

"I am utterly ashamed of each and every one of you pathetic, paltry pussycats," it roared in the BellaDonna's voice. "You Intoxibellas have been in this incarcerated purgatory for an exponential amount of time and *still* behave like the savage animals I've turned you into!"

The cats bowed their heads in shame. The BellaDonna lion exhaled and fire spewed from its nostrils, singing the whiskers of the front row of cats. The smell of wet and burned fur mixed with the stench of kitty litter.

The BellaDonna lion continued. "The Catwalk Corridor was created as a correctional facility for you to reverse your abominable behavior—to be *domesticated*. This is a jail to teach you to stop being such catty wenches. Because in the land of Intoxibellas, whether down below in society or up here at our beloved Modelland: There. Is. Room. For. Only. One. Bee-yotchhh." She made the last word sound like an extended, pissed-off meow.

"And you, my despicable dears, are looking right at her," the lion boomed. "I am ashamed that you malicious models cannot utter one single positive phrase to those you come upon. You will remain confined to the corridors until you change your evil ways! And not a day before that redeeming day will I release the curse that has been put upon you. Return to your pens, *now!*"

The cats ran toward the lion-face and jumped into its golden eye sockets. As the Daisy-Ellen-faced Abyssinian jumped through one of the openings, she yelled, "Watch out, De La Crème. This kitty-cat got a taste of your sweetness and wants more of your cream!"

After all the cats vanished, the lion opened its mouth even wider and extended its tongue out like a cushy red carpet. Its jagged teeth dripped saliva, and its hot breath blew through the girls' hair.

Shiraz looked around. "What we do now, Tookie?"

"Oh, screw it," Tookie blurted out. She walked up to the tongue, stepped on it, and walked toward the teeth. "I guess we follow the taste-bud road. Anything to get to Dylan. C'mon, guys. . . ."

Piper, Shiraz, and even Zarpessa and Chaste tentatively followed Tookie past the teeth into the throat of the lion . . . and emerged in the hallway of the D.

"What in the hell was *that*?" Tookie whispered. And when she turned around, Catwalk Corridor and the BellaDonna lion-face were gone.

26

THE PORCELAIN PACT

The girls walked into Dylan's room and found ILikee, MeLikee, SheLikee and HerLikee all in one bed. The quadruplets wrinkled their noses in unison.

"Yuck!" SheLikee exclaimed.

"Horror," MeLikee said.

"Movie," HerLikee said.

"Approaching!" ILikee finished.

Then they added, "You. Are. Disturbing. Naptime."

"Where's Dylan?" demanded Tookie.

The Likee sisters smirked.

"She's. In. The. Bathroom."

Tookie, Piper, and Shiraz sprinted down the dorm corridor. They heard a groan echo through the tiled space.

"Dylan?" Tookie called.

The groan was coming from the toilet stalls. Knees touched the cold marble floor at the last stall nearest the wall. Tookie opened the door. Dylan was crouched over the toilet moaning. Her hair hung down, obscuring her face. The tips of her hair were dripping wet. The floor was splattered with bile and bits of expelled half-digested food.

Tookie hesitated, then kneeled down to Dylan's level. Dylan turned to face Tookie, revealing bloodshot eyes and a bleeding nose. Along with the ends of her hair, the front of her uniform was soaked. Tookie hoped it was mostly from tears, but she knew better. "Dylan?" Tookie said softly. "You okay?"

Dylan looked at Tookie and then her body involuntarily heaved, her head returning to the toilet. "It . . . came back . . . ," she sputtered when she was finished.

"What did?" Piper rubbed Dylan's back.

"I had it under control for three years. But what you were sayin', Tookie, and what Ci~L . . . It brought it all back."

Tookie shut her eyes.

Dylan's hunching shoulders drooped even lower. "I'm usually good now with the way I am, but that magnet forced me to stare at Zarpessa. And, well, I wanted to have what she has."

Tookie, Shiraz, and Piper encircled Dylan and hugged her tightly. "And n-n-nobody looks like me here, a-a-and—"

"Nobody tiny here like me either, Dylan," Shiraz said softly.

"And the last I looked," Piper said, "I was playing solo for the Albinism Modelland World Cup."

"Dyl, we all have our . . . stuff," Tookie said quietly.

Dylan looked up, tears still in her eyes "Yeah, but that's the obvious stuff. It's not true vulnerability. True friendship is about bein' *really* vulnerable. About sittin' around a toilet and, uh . . . I don't know . . . lettin' loose."

"Okay, well, um . . ." Piper looked at her hands and rubbed their pale skin. "I mean, I don't like . . . well, actually I *hate* that I am . . . what I am. I pretend to detest my mom because of her political views, but the truth? I hate my mom because she married my father, a person with albinism. If she had just picked someone normal, I might not be this way. I wouldn't have had to live in that damn dome. I wouldn't be a pale freak who has to worry about my skin burning or being eaten by LeGizzârds."

"But Piper," Dylan protested, looking at her like she was crazy. "You're the smartest girl I've ever met. Your people are like geniuses."

"My *people*?" Piper objected. "I don't want anyone seeing my whole group when they look at me. I want them to see *me*." She reached into her pocket. "I kind of can't believe I'm showing you all this. It's one of the two items I kept from home."

She passed a photograph to Tookie. It was a girl wearing bronze-colored foundation. Her eyes were deep brown. Her lashes were caked with heavy black mascara, and her eyebrows were filled in with dark eye pencil. On her head was thick chestnut-brown hair.

"It's me," Piper said. "In foundation and a wig. Colored contacts. I hold on to these pictures. I look *normal* in them."

"Oh, Piper," Dylan said.

Piper gently touched Tookie's cheek. "I've always wanted skin like you have. Still do. But I'm trapped in this skin forever."

Suddenly, Tookie remembered Piper's puzzle of her mom and dad—the one she had tried to hide. Tookie leaned over and wiped Piper's face with a tissue. Tears were streaming—quite beautifully, in a strange way—from her rose-colored eyes.

Shiraz stood up. "I small. Not normal small, but very, very small." Then she raised her arm high into the air. "Tall, my parents were. Both of them. Papa and I, we best friends. He called me his runt. Peanut. Dwarf. Preemie. Affectionate, he said it was. But for Shiraz, the words hurt. They did not feel good like the affection words. To keep up with his long leg, I had to run fast, fast, fast. And we do everything together! Travel for singing show on road. We famous in my country. Shih-Pappa, we were called. We dance and sing, for audiences big! Bring home country's best candles, for sick mommy! But I not good enough." She lowered her eyes. "In the end, I not good enough at all."

"Why would you say that?" Tookie asked.

"Because he leave me," Shiraz said. "At school in Canne Del Abra, here at the Modelland, to be first, I always try. When you go first, you can never be left behind. Every day of the life, Shiraz has been that way. Every day of the life since Papa left me. After Mommy died from sick, Papa die too. But not from sick. Die from broke heart. Which mean he no love his Shiraz Shiraz. Only Mommy. I just his runt, his midget, his dwarf, his preemie for road show."

Tears flowed from everyone's eyes now.

Shiraz pulled a square of paper from her pocket. It was a small leaflet for Shiraz and her father's act. In the photo Mr. Shiraz stood with pride, holding his petite daughter on his left shoulder. But there was a gouged-out hole where his face should have been.

Shiraz sighed. "Papa leave me. So I cutting him out of my life, leave him too."

"And yet you keep the picture with you," Piper said.

Shiraz blinked, then looked away.

Dylan turned to Tookie. "Your turn, okay?"

Tookie closed her eyes and thought of what she could tell her friends. She stood and left the bathroom. Within moments she returned holding her *T-Mail Jail*. The book had always been something she'd wanted people to see, but now that she was actually going to show it to someone, she felt horribly uncomfortable.

"I write letters to people in this book," she said, settling down next to the girls and opening the book. "Letters I never intend to send. My innermost feelings. And I wrote this one a long time ago to someone I hated."

Tookie turned to a blank page. She brought the book within an inch of her cut mouth and breathed a flow of hot air. Words instantly appeared. This was her most secret of entries. The one she didn't like to reread. Quietly, she began:

Dear Tookie,

Do you know how much I detest you? How the very sight of you makes me want to stab you through the heart? Why do you rise each day? What is the point of you even existing? Of breathing this earth's precious air, which rots each time you exhale?

Do you know how much I hate you? How the very thought of you continuing to inhabit this world makes me ill? Why are you even writing this right now? What is

the point of you even lingering any longer?
Of using up ink and killing trees to record
thoughts that no one will ever care to see?

I hope you go to sleep tonight and
don't wake up. Oh, how beautiful the world
will be tomorrow, with you dead. Oh, I
can't wait. . . .

Please hurry up and end it.
Just go . . . for all of us.

Regretfully yours,
FG
Tookie De La Crème

The girls didn't say a word.

"I feel so guilty!" Dylan said, breaking the silence. Piper and Shiraz reached in to Tookie and hugged her tightly.

Dylan held onto the paper roll mounted on the wall to support herself. "I've had issues with my body my entire life, but I never, *ever* wanted to be dead."

"Me neither," Shiraz said.

Piper sighed. "And here I am, since the very day I entered Ci~L's pouch, envious of you because of your skin. Don't you realize how special you are? How *amazing*?"

A rush of emotion overcame Tookie. First she felt numb, then she wanted to run, then her body went limp and sank into Piper's arms. It was the most wonderful thing anyone had ever said to her. But as she hugged all three girls, she got a twisting pang deep in her heart for Lizzie. She missed Lizzie so much.

The girls remained in a tight group hug on the cold floor of the bathroom. Then Dylan sat up. "You know, I think our group needs a name."

"What you mean?" Shiraz raised an eyebrow.

"You know, like a show of solidarity," Dylan explained.

Piper thought for a moment. "The Vulnerable Four. Or maybe The V4?"

"How 'bout Krapper Sisters?" Dylan joked, looking at the soiled toilet and disgusting floor they all were sitting on.

"What about the ULs?" Tookie suggested.

Dylan frowned. "That's what Zarpessa calls us . . . Unfortunate-Lookin's."

"So what? We can take the power back. Have it mean something else. Like . . . *Unique-Lookings*."

"I kinda like it," Dylan said slowly, "but I hate that *U* and *L* are a big part of *U-G-L-Y*."

"Good point," Tookie said. "What about . . . the Unicas?" She pronounced it "you-KNEE-kuz."

"Seems fitting." Piper's eyes gleamed. "I like it!"

"Me too!" Shiraz said.

"Well, hot damn, we stinkers got a name!" Dylan shouted with glee. "And yeah, y'all, we *do* stink. Badly!"

"I will attest to our present collective foul odor," Piper said, trying to sound clinical. "But what needs immediate attention is our dear Unica sister, Ms. De La Crème." She pointed to Tookie's face. "That waterfall of blood flowing from your lips needs a stitch or two . . . or twenty."

"Those mean cats slice you good," Shiraz lamented.

Tookie touched her lips again. Blood was still trickling from her Catwalk Corridor wounds.

"I'll take her to the Fashion Emergency Department Store—the FEDS," Piper offered. "This sun-sensitive, pigment-free, pale-faced inhabitant of Modelland *and* newly ordained Unica, who has had *many* burns healed there, knows the way."

"Watch out for that corridor catty thingamajigga!" Dylan yelled out. "Y'never know where it might pop up!"

"I'd have no problem running into it again," Tookie said, laughing. "As long as I could watch that cat pee on Zarpessa one more time!"

27

Z

The cool air outside was a welcome change from the stuffiness of the bathroom and the kitty-litter stench of the Catwalk Corridor. The pastel yellow flowers on the Beautification Boulevard pathway to her classes now seemed to Tookie an even more brilliant saffron and electric lemon. Perhaps, she thought, the world had become a brighter place now that she'd revealed the scariest skeleton in her closet.

Piper hurried Tookie along. "Come on. Thirty-three point four seconds is all it takes."

"All it takes to *what*?" asked a friendly, bouncy voice behind them, followed by a familiar giggle.

Tookie and Piper turned to see a couture-clad ZhenZhen running in their direction. Her outfit was made entirely of autumn-colored leaves. Today her hair was almost all black, save for one streak of Ci~L–like auburn at the front. Her eyes widened at Tookie's lip. "Owie. Catwalk Corridor, right?"

Tookie nodded.

ZhenZhen clucked her tongue. "You have to learn how to strut even under their scrutiny. Those catty divas have to learn how to behave."

"So they're trapped as cats because they're wicked mean on the outside, right?" Tookie asked.

ZhenZhen nodded. "When they stop yelling insults, being lazy, showing up late, ingesting narcotics, they get turned back into people."

"So is that what the newspapers mean when they say an In-toxibella is taking an 'extended vacation'?" Tookie asked. She read stories like that in the *Peppertown Press* all the time.

ZhenZhen laughed. "Sure. But the Catwalk Corridor hardly ever works permanently with the types who are sent there. Once trouble, always trouble. You just have to stay away from them." She glanced at Tookie's lip again and winced. "That looks *awful*."

"It probably looks worse than it feels," Tookie lied. In truth, her lip felt like it was about to fall off.

"You need to get to the Fashion Emergency Department Store before that gets infected," ZhenZhen said.

"En route now," Piper said.

Tookie had noticed a large duffel bag slung over ZhenZhen's shoulder. "Are you going somewhere?"

ZhenZhen nodded. "My Go-See-Go. I'll be gone for a month. It's part of our final exam." She twisted her mouth nervously. "We meet with clients and stuff. We even get to stay in our own apartments. And all day, we 'go see' if we're really capable of book-ing jobs. It's a test to see if we can make it in the real world. Some girls drop out at this point—they get into drugs, they get caught up with the wrong guys, all kinds of stuff. But I'm gonna try my best. The Go-See-Go weighs heavily in the final selection of the 7Sevens—and that's approaching at the end of the quadmester!"

"So when you do this Go-See-Go, you're gonna be *you*, right?" Tookie said. "Not Ci~L? Because if you knew the real Ci~L, I don't think you'd be so fixated on her."

"Tookie's right," Piper said. "Ci~L's recent behavior borders on spooky."

ZhenZhen waved her hand dismissively. "Spooky's the new edgy. Whatever my girl Ci~L does is good for me." Then she leaned closer. "Tell me exactly what she is doing to freak you out. It'll probably work well for me at Go-See-Go!"

"ZhenZhen!" an upperclassBella called from a few yards away. "C'mon!"

"I'm coming, I'm coming," ZhenZhen answered. She looked at Tookie and Piper once more. "I'm so glad I'm leaving, to tell you the truth. I was going stir-crazy here. I almost took the emergency ZipZap to LaDorno!"

Tookie and Piper exchanged a confused glance. *Huh?*

"I'm just kidding. Only an idiot would use that thing. So many girls died using that emergency exit trying to get to La-Dorno during the big stadium fire," ZhenZhen explained, notic-ing their looks. "I think it's somewhere near the stadium. It's super dangerous."

"Why?" Piper asked.

ZhenZhen leaned closer. "Well, it's only a rumor, but they say this ZipZap is . . . *different.* That there's a fork in the zipper that you can't control. Sometimes going left takes you to LaDorno, but sometimes it takes you straight into the Diabolical Divide. Rumor has it that those girls who used it during the fire went straight to the Divide and that's where they died." She shut her eyes tight. "I bet that's why they closed it off and hid it." Then she shrugged and glanced at Piper. "You never answered me. What takes thirty-three point four seconds?"

"Burning my skin in the sun," Piper admitted. "Multiply that by twelve if I have an umbrella. That's why I know the way to the Fashion Emergency Department Store so well. I should buy real estate there—it's practically my second home. They put a super-long-lasting sun shield called BurnBattler on my skin, eyes, and hair. All I have to do is return every three days for a new application."

"Wow, I wish they could fix expando-hair," Tookie swooned.

"Oh, the girl who tells me to love and accept *my* natural self and the hair that grows from *my* scalp now wants a super-long-lasting mop fix of her own!" ZhenZhen smirked playfully. "So I'm supposed to Run-a-Way walk your walk, but what about you?"

Another group of excited yet nervous final-year girls rounded the corner. They were dressed not in uniforms but in expertly styled individual outfits, all with a Mother Nature theme. A few of them looked like they were a hair away from being Intoxibellas. Tookie worried for ZhenZhen, who was beautiful but not as polished as her classmates. "ZhenZhen!" the tallest girl in the bunch yelled. "The shuttle's leaving now!"

"Okay, okay, okay." ZhenZhen gave Piper and Tookie tight hugs and ran off toward the group of upperclassBellas. Tookie's eyes followed her. She had never met anyone who smiled and giggled nearly all the time. *ZhenZhen could be an honorary member of the Unicas,* she thought. Then she caught herself. *Of course, ZhenZhen is far too stunning to be a member of our wacky crew.*

ᛗ

Tookie and Piper took a ZipZap behind the CaraCaraCara boat and entered the Fashion Emergency Department Store courtyard. The atrium was open to the sky, like a riad in the alchemy-and-spice land of Medina, and there was a pool in its center filled with a mysterious greenish substance. Various IV-like tubes were submerged in the liquid; the tubes trailed upward to the atrium's second level, their destination unseen.

Around the perimeter of the atrium were uniquely shaped doors marked WIG-A-WEAVELESS HAIR LENGTHENING AND THICKENING RESEARCH DEPARTMENT, DEGREE OF FACIAL SYMMETRY DETERMINATION DIVISION, and INTENSITY OF DESIRE FOR INTOXIBELLA-NESS CALIBRATION. Piper led Tookie toward a set of double doors marked THE DRAMA TRAUMA CENTER. "This is the FEDS intensive care unit," she explained.

As soon as they approached the entrance, the stark white doors turned to a bloody, gory red. Then they flung open, revealing a large, noisy, crazed room filled with Bellas suffering from various degrees of odd and unspeakable injuries.

Doctors' offices always made Tookie uncomfortable. They reminded her of her endless medical visits when she was younger. In addition to submitting Tookie to endless forehead-growth-pattern testing, Creamy was determined to figure out what disease her daughter had that gave her dirty and snotty eyes and a frame that refused to gain weight. Even though Tookie had been poked and prodded by hundreds of needles, the painful tests were always inconclusive.

Tookie and Piper approached the check-in counter. A woman who looked about one hundred and fifty years old sat behind the desk. She wore an elaborate sage-green cape made of multiple types of pistols, knives, nooses, and razors, with a hat shaped like a pair of angry scissors. Upon closer inspection, Tookie realized that the blades of the scissors were really *blades*. Sharp serrated knives. *Comforting,* Tookie thought. "Uh, excuse me, ma'am," she began.

The old woman's eyes bulged. "'Ma'am'? You called me ma'am? Ohhhh noooo . . . you should never call me that. My name is Purse Drestookill. Remember that, because from the looks of those enormous feet of yours, I'm sure you're quite a clumsy one, am I right?"

Tookie opened her mouth, but no words came out. *At Modelland, I guess nurses are called purses,* she realized. *You shoulda seen that coming, Tookie!*

Purse Drestookill sighed and shuffled some papers behind the desk. "The Corridor Kitties have tetanus on their claws. Pretty soon you'll be spasming, so you'll be called shortly." Then Purse Drestookill put her head down on the desk and aimed her scissor/knife hat toward Tookie. "Place your arm in my head device, please."

Tookie backed away. "Uh . . . excuse me?"

The woman frowned. "You heard me, little Miss Forehead the Size of the South Seas! Do it!"

Tookie looked to Piper for help, but Piper just motioned for Tookie to do as she was told. Swallowing hard, Tookie slowly placed her hand through, then her wrist, continuing until her bicep was right between the blades. They came crashing together toward her arm, and just before Tookie was about to scream, a sticker band marked *Clawed by Catwalk Corridor* slapped onto her wrist.

"I put a rush on you, Five-Head," the woman said in a no-nonsense voice. "Wouldn't want those bubble lips of yours to get gangrene and *really* have to be amputated. Next!" she said to the injured girl behind Tookie.

"You should hear some of the ghastly insults she hurls at me," Piper whispered as they walked toward the waiting area. "Every three days, she thinks up something new—Red-eyed Peas, Frosty the SnowBella, Al-*Bella*-bino . . ."

They fell into seats. Tookie was next to a soaking-wet girl gasping for breath. The girl's uniform was five sizes too small, hitting her midcalf. It reminded Tookie of Ci~L's too-small uniform in War of Words.

"Do you mind if I ask what you're here for?" Tookie whispered to her.

The girl flashed Tookie the diagnosis sticker on her arm. *Flooding Pants.*

"I washed my uniform in super-hot water today," she explained. "They told us only to wash it in cold, but it was so stinky from Run-a-Way Intensive 201, I had to. When I took it out of the wash, it was tiny-tiny. My D mates told me to turn it in for a new one, but I was late for History of Modelland class, so I just threw this on. All of a sudden, I was submerged in water. I felt like I was going to drown. Now I can't get the uniform off, and the floods have been happening like clockwork. I can't swim, and I can only hold my breath for—"

Suddenly, water rose from the girl's feet as if she was in her own private fish tank. The water swelled higher and higher until it completely covered her head. The girl flailed about, eyes bulging, panic-stricken. Purse Drestookill ran over, yanked a razor from her arsenal of weapons, and punctured the bag. The water spilled out onto the waiting room floor. The girl collapsed on her side, gasping for air like a hooked trout. Purses scooped her up and swept her through the Drama Trauma Center doors.

Tookie turned to Piper. "Okay, that was weird."

"Oh, that was nothing," Piper whispered. "Take a look around."

Tookie surveyed the rest of the chaotic waiting room. Across the aisle was a girl with blackened eyes and foul-smelling dark puffs of exhaust coming out of her sockets. *Smoky Eyes,* her armband read.

A loud wail filled the waiting area. Tookie turned and noticed Desperada, the girl who hadn't stopped bawling since she'd arrived at Modelland, collapsed in a corner. Not far from Desperada was Zarpessa, sitting in a chair, poking at bleeding gashes all over her hands.

Tookie smirked. *The cats did a lovely job on her!*

Just then, as if she could sense Tookie was thinking about her, Zarpessa looked up. She shot Piper and Tookie a resentful look, as if they were the ones who'd scratched her skin raw.

Desperada's wail filled the waiting room again. Purse Drestookill placed a pair of rusted silver bullets in her ears to drown out the noise. Since no one else was paying any attention to Desperada, Tookie stood and limped over. Desperada didn't even seem to notice her approach, wailing and sobbing so hard she could barely catch her breath.

"Did you get scratched by the cats?" Tookie whispered. "Are

your cuts really deep? They said infection sets in fast. You can go in front of me if you want." Even though Tookie barely knew Desperada—no one did, as she spent all her time crying—she hated the thought of Desperada being in pain.

Desperada glanced into Tookie's eyes for a beat. "I don't have any cuts. I—I'm sick. My stomach . . ." She let out a long, deep, guttural groan.

Suddenly, the doors that led to the Drama Trauma Center burst open. A woman with oatmeal-colored hair done up in dramatic coils emerged. Even amid all the chaos, she wore a soft, placid smile on her face and seemed to . . . *glide* across the room. Tookie looked down at the woman's feet and realized why: she was on roller skates.

Tookie watched the woman zig and zag through different girls in the waiting room. "I want some of those so I can get to class on time!"

"Not what you think," Piper murmured. "Not what you think at all . . ."

Zarpessa rose to her feet and ran toward the rolling woman. "Oh, Nurse—I mean *Purse*! I really need to go first! This crying girl's racket is really killing me!" She gestured toward Desperada.

The roller-skating woman looked at Zarpessa. "I am a *doctor*, not a purse."

"Of course!" Zarpessa put on her fakest of fake smiles. "I'm sorry, Doctor, of course, Doctor. But you only handle the small stuff, right? Like knitting up cut knees and putting patches on bumps and scrapes. The big stuff is for a man's mind. Open-heart surgery, brain trauma, that kind of thing."

"It sounds like brain trauma might be something I should

check *you* for," the doctor shot back. She gave Zarpessa an icy stare and rolled away.

The woman whizzed past Zarpessa to get a closer look at Desperada. Her uniform was a cloak covered in stiff white bristles like the one Creamy used on her face twice a day in the shower. Her thick stockings resembled an elastic version of the material Tookie had used to deep-clean the pots at B3 when she was on cafeteria duty. Her hair was a rather floppy, odd material . . . a mop, perhaps? Tookie then got the pun right away. The bristle-brush jacket, the grime-removing stockings, the literal mop head . . . *scrubs.*

"I'm Dr. Erica," the woman said, taking Desperada's hands. Dr. Erica frowned at Desperada, then pulled a piece of sandpaper out of her breast pocket. It danced and wiggled in her hands as if alive. After she pressed the sprightly sandpaper to Desperada's forehead, it wrapped itself around and around her head like a strip of gauze.

The doctor inspected the paper closely and sighed. "Just as I thought. Temperature is standard, blood pressure is perfect, gastric and skin acidity suggests electrostatic normalcy, but texture of epidermis indicates elevated hormonal activity."

She can tell all that from sandpaper? Tookie thought, amazed.

"Does that mean I'm dying?" Desperada bleated.

The doctor frowned again. "Not any faster than the standards of beauty, missy. But you are suffering from BW. Boy Withdrawal. There's a guy, right?"

Desperada froze midwail.

"Bingo!" Dr. Erica turned to exit the waiting room.

"Wait!" Desperada yelled. "Okay, my *stomach* doesn't hurt— my *heart* does! I miss my boyfriend so much I think it might stop!

Please write me a note so I can go down the mountain to see him! I don't know what he's doing while I'm gone! What if he's messing with another girl?"

Dr. Erica clucked her tongue. "Little missy, or little miss-*him*, no Bella is ever allowed to go home of her own accord. You can't leave the property just because of some silly guy. What a mistake that always is, whether you're at Modelland or not. Talk about crippling yourself . . ."

"But my heart is *killing* me! I have to see him, just for a second. I swear, I'll be back so fast and—"

"Even if I could, I wouldn't allow you to do it," the doctor interrupted.

Desperada clapped her mouth shut. Her eyes turned from bloodshot red to a cold iron-gray. "Fine, then," she said stubbornly. "I'll just leave!"

The doctor smirked. "Just leave, you say? At Modelland, Bellas pay a pricey toll for hopping the fence. You do *not* want to do that." Dr. Erica pointed to the exit doors. "Suck it up, girl. And don't come back here unless you're being strangled by a choker necklace!"

Desperada trudged out of the room. Dr. Erica rolled her eyes. "These parents, they've got to be careful with how they name their kids." She sucked her teeth. "Desperada? What did they expect the poor girl to grow up to be?"

Then all eyes whipped to the door through which Desperada had just exited. A new patient had strolled in. He had glowing skin, a sharp jawline, and deep-set eyes. Tookie's heart did a flip.

Bravo.

There was a fresh gash on his neck.

All the girls in the waiting area let out sympathetic moans. Piper nudged Tookie. "There's thumb boy!"

"Shhh." Tookie just looked away, mortified.

Bravo approached Purse Drestookill's desk. Even she looked smitten, perking up and pushing out her chest . . . of knives. "Just here to get my stitches removed," he said. "Don't fuss over me." Then he walked over to an oversized chair in a corner, picked up an old copy of *Modelland* magazine with Ci~L on the cover, and sat. Alone.

"Next!" Dr. Erica called. She glanced at Tookie. "Looks like that's you."

Zarpessa let out a little whine. "But I have—"

"Faces before hands, missy," the doctor interrupted.

"Good luck," Piper whispered, shooting Tookie a *be brave* smile.

The doctor led Tookie through the double doors and directed her to a white bed in the corner. Tookie sat down on it and immediately sank into the mattress.

The pillow rubbed against her mouth and she winced. Her lip was hurting so badly now, tears brimmed in her eyes.

"You're in agony, aren't you?" the doctor said.

Tookie nodded.

"You hide pain well," Dr. Erica went on. "Something tells me you've been doing that for a long time." She placed her hands on each side of Tookie's head and stared into her eyes. "On a pain scale of one to ten, I see you're at about a seven and a half. Here's a bit of Zed Med for the agony while I fix you up. I have to warn you, though. The Zed Meds mess with you. They have a Z effect."

"A Z effect like getting some Z's?" Tookie asked. "Like falling asleep?"

"Not exactly," the doctor murmured.

Two strands of the doctor's mop hair started to lengthen. They snaked through the air and entered Tookie's nostrils. Tookie's pain slowly started to subside.

"Where'd you get your skates?" she asked woozily as the doctor inspected her wounds.

"These?" Dr. Erica glanced at her feet. "I got them at birth."

"Huh?"

The doctor lifted up her pants leg and revealed that the skates were actually attached to her body, the same color and texture as skin.

"All doctors here at Modelland have them," Dr. Erica stated matter-of-factly.

"It seems like there are a lot of . . . um . . . different-looking Gurus around here," Tookie said softly, thinking of Guru Applaussez and its hand-head and Guru Pacifico with his rubber face.

"That's because hundreds of years ago, Modelland took us all in," the doctor explained, her hands moving quickly over Tookie's sliced ankle and then her lips. "Anyone born . . . different. We would be locked up and tested on without this place. If it weren't for Modelland, my kind and others like me would be freaks. Like her . . . ," she said, referring to Purse Drestookill, who passed by in the corridor outside. "All I'll say is . . . that's, uh . . . not a hat."

"Whoa," Tookie whispered.

"It was a blessing for my kind, because the powers that be at Modelland recognized that skates for feet would be put to good use in emergency medical situations," the doctor continued. "They figured we could get from one patient to the next with speed and ease. So they trained us all and . . . here I am. They take good care of us." She smiled and pointed to a picture of a girl in the corner. "My daughter, Camina Marche, she's about your age. She's just like her mama. Got roller skates for feet too. She wouldn't have a chance in life without this place. She's in medical school right now."

"Where?" Tookie asked. A person with roller-skate feet would be big news in places like Metopia and beyond. She was surprised she hadn't read a news article about it.

"Modelland isn't just what you see when you go from class to class," the doctor explained. "There is a whole underground world here. Parts of it are still a mystery to even me, and I was born here."

"But what about Bellas?" Tookie asked. "Modelland has such strict rules for Bellas to enter. They have to look a certain way. Perfect . . ."

The doctor gazed at Tookie curiously. "*Do* they? I have a confession to make, missy: when I first saw you, I thought you were an injured new Guru, not a Bella. Especially with how you helped that sad, desperate girl. Plus, with your protuberance of a forehead and wild dual eye color and poufy hair, kind of like mine . . . well, you know. But word has traveled about the four, uh . . . interesting-looking new Bellas this year, so I quickly realized my assumption was wrong when I saw you were with Piper."

"Okay, okay, *I'm* not really sure why I'm here either," Tookie admitted. "But seriously. The rules for Bellas, they're so different from the rules for Gurus . . . and that doesn't seem fair. It's *not* fair. Why is there such a double standard?"

"I don't know." Dr. Erica shrugged. "I know it's wrapped up

in some old Modelland history, though. I wish I could help you. But your guess is as good as mine. And that's all that doctors do, anyway. Make educated guesses. Get yourself educated, missy, and you'll find the answers you're looking for."

With that, the doctor announced, "Bleeding's stopped. But before I stitch you up, I want to give you some stronger Zed Med. Lips have lots of nerve endings . . . pleasure and pain ones."

The doctor's tickly mop-hair strands entered Tookie's nose again, a bit deeper this time, and she could feel them reaching her throat and numbing her skin. "I'll tend to some others while this sets in," she said. "Oh, and I know you heard me talking about how children grow up a certain way depending on what their parents name them. Dig deep to see if your name is something to follow or fight against. *Tookie.* The last syllable sounds like *key.* Maybe you're searching for something, and you have the power to unlock it or set it free. I tell Camina Marche to think about her name all the time.

"Okay, missy, I'll be back in a few."

She whipped back the curtain to reveal a long line of beds.

Tookie woozily turned her head to the left as two roller-skate-footed doctors and four purses flopped four new patients onto a single bed. It was the Likee sisters, and they were bucking and kicking violently. Bizarrely, their teeth were enormous, and their blue, green, pink, and purple hair had grown long and morphed into long, flowing Mohawks.

"The Likees practically live in here," one of the doctors restraining the girls said to Dr. Erica. "None of them can stop hoarding fashion that's *not theirs.*"

Tookie caught a peek at HerLikee's arm band. *Clothes Horse.*

Dr. Erica sighed. "Take them to the Intensive Couture Unit and let them hold some hay and straw handbags. That should calm them down."

The Likees were taken away, making whinnying noises. Just seeing them reminded Tookie of something, and she turned to Dr. Erica. "Do you think you could replace a missing filling while I'm here?" She poked her tongue into the spot in her mouth where her filling used to be. She had a feeling the Likees—the Fraud Quad— had pilfered it after War of Words class.

Dr. Erica nodded, then left. After a few minutes she brought a new patient back from the waiting room. Tookie's eyes widened. It was Bravo. Her heart started to speed up. *It's just the Zed Meds,* she told herself. *It's not because* he's *here.*

Bravo stopped at the edge of an empty bed. "Doctor, I really don't need to lie down, I'm just getting my stitches taken out."

Dr. Erica placed her hands on her hips. "The last Bestostero whose stitches I removed fainted right into my arms. Just lie down and relax. Look at it like a mini vacation from building the stadium."

Then she disappeared.

Bravo glanced in Tookie's direction, raising his eyebrows in surprise. He looked like he was going to say something, but then Zarpessa materialized at Bravo's bedside. "No need to wait alone," she said in a silky voice. "I'll keep you company until the doctor removes those manly stitches of yours. You poor, poor baby!" She reached out to touch Bravo's neck.

More injured girls limped over to Bravo's bed. "Must take lots of muscles to pose with those big tools," one uttered in a deep voice.

Ignoring them, Bravo walked over to Tookie and sat down on the edge of her bed. Tookie stared straight ahead, not knowing what to do.

"What's he doing sitting with *her*?" a snarky voice hissed.

"Is that her forehead's normal size or is it swollen?" another voice cackled.

Bravo cleared his throat, and Tookie snuck a woozy peek at him. "Hey," he said.

She pushed through her numbness and daze and mustered a sloppy smile. "Hey."

"What happened to you, Tookie?" Bravo asked. "Just this morning, those lips of yours looked good."

Tookie stiffened, still not sure if she was the butt of a joke or something else. All at once, the strong medicine's numbing effects kicked in. Tookie's tongue felt like it had been strangled by an enormous boa constrictor. Her mouth went bone dry, and she longed for water.

Bravo was still waiting for her answer. "Zats," Tookie admitted, shakily pointing to her sliced lip. Then she shut her eyes. She'd meant *cats*, but her anesthetized lip had other ideas.

But Bravo seemed to understand. He smiled teasingly. "Zats, huh? So that *Zat*walk *Zor*ridor actually exists? Is it really scary?"

"Zarry, zarry zarry," Tookie said, turning beet-red. She had wanted to say *Very, very scary*. "Do you have a Zorridor at Zeszosterone?" Maybe *this* was the Z effect, she realized. The Zed Meds Z'd up your speech.

"Are you kidding?" Bravo grinned. "We're not magical like you Bellas. We're mere mortals. But . . . there have been a few Intoxibell*o*s in history who have had it, that magic thing. We B boys hope, but it's one in a million. If it happens for me, that's cool. But I'm really here for the architecture of this place. That's my real love. One day, I hope to—"

"Architecture?" Zarpessa interrupted from the other bed. "Why, that's my first love too! I'm just here to study the unique Modelland buildings. I could care less about becoming an Intoxi-bella."

But Bravo didn't even glance at Zarpessa. His eyes seemed to be firmly planted on Tookie. That was when her stomach decided to growl disgustingly. She flushed red again.

Bravo smiled. "You hungry, huh? Or should I say *zungry*?"

Tookie nodded, which made her feel dizzy.

"I'm hungry too," Bravo said. "Can that lip handle some food?"

Tookie touched her tongue to lip. Her lips were so numb, she felt nothing. She continued to run her tongue over the exterior of her mouth, attempting to feel anything. "Uh-huh, I think so," she said, though it came out "Zuh-huh, I zink zho."

Bravo stood up from Tookie's bed and exited the room. He returned with packaged snacks labeled *Modelland Munchies by Guru Lauro*. "I love this stuff," he whispered. "Tastes like what you want it to taste like, loaded with the vitamins you need at the moment, melts so smoothly on the tongue. We male mortals can't get this good stuff on our side of the mountain. They load us up on protein only. If it's not a piece of meat, an egg, or some powder, we don't eat it. Lucky girl you are."

Tookie smiled sloppily, ripped off the top of one package, and tried to bite the treat. It landed on her cheek.

"Lemme help you with that," Bravo suggested. He took the Munchie from Tookie and held it to her lips. She opened her mouth to take a bite, and as she was wrapping her lips around the sweetness, a thick pool of her bloody saliva dribbled onto Bravo's hand.

"Yuck!" Zarpessa screeched from her bed. "Too-Too just mouth-pee-peed all over you!"

"Too-*kee*," Bravo corrected her a little sharply. "Her name is Tookie. You two haven't met yet?" The drool was still on his hand. He hadn't wiped it away.

Zarpessa shrugged nonchalantly. "I kinda know her. She's my D mate. Honestly, most of the time I just call her Unfortunate-Looking. Modelland will enjoy sacrificing her. They can make pea and lentil soup with her eyeballs." She winked at him, expecting him to laugh, but Bravo only appeared uncomfortable.

"That sucks that those cat-girl mutants scratched your lip up like that." Bravo reached forward to touch her lip. "It probably hurts, huh? Nothing worse than a cut on your lip when you kiss."

Heat rose to Tookie's cheeks. First thumbsucking . . . now cut-lip kissing?

"*Puh*-leeze," a voice butted in. Zarpessa tilted her long, slender legs so that they touched Bravo's. "Like Chaste would say, there are plenty of other ways to get busy even with a cut lip, right, Too-Too?"

Tookie blinked at her, now feeling both woozy and embarrassed. After a few awkward seconds passed, Zarpessa leaned back and crossed her arms over her chest. "You've never done it, have you, Tookie?"

Tookie lowered her head. Bravo shifted nervously. "Uh, I think you should leave her alone. . . ."

"You've never kissed anyone, have you?" Zarpessa needled, her eyes growing wider and brighter.

Tookie desperately wanted to prove her wrong. Her cheeks blazed with shame. A knot lodged in her throat.

"Tookie is as pure as Shivera snow!" Zarpessa crowed. "Awww, that's so cute!"

Bravo whipped around and glared at her, his muscles tensed, his eyes blazing. "Look, I told you to leave her alone," he said in a biting voice. "Why can't your bitchy little brain understand that?"

The room went silent. Every girl's eyes widened. Zarpessa's jaw dropped, and redness crept up her swanlike neck and into her cheeks. "Purse Erica?" she screamed. "This bed hurts my back," she snapped. "I'll wait in the waiting room till it's my turn!"

Before she flounced away, she gave Tookie a dark, sadistic glare. *I can't wait till they burn you alive,* she mouthed.

Tookie's stomach made a loud growling noise again.

"Wow," Bravo said. "You still *zungry,* huh?"

He broke off another piece of the Munchie and fed Tookie. Tookie didn't drool this time, but she tasted fresh blood, probably from chomping down on her numb tongue and cheeks.

"Zoo zry," Tookie said to Bravo, trying to say *too dry.* "Zit zeeds . . ." *It needs.* She reached into her flower brooch and pulled out the can of whipped cream that had dropped in during her first class with Guru Lauro. She sprayed a dollop of cream onto the Munchie in Bravo's hand.

Bravo stared at the last bite of the cream-covered Munchie, then at Tookie's flower. "You carry around random stuff on your chest?"

Tookie hesitated. If Bravo didn't think she was freaky already, this would probably push him over the edge. "ZI'm zalways zungry."

"Good for you," Bravo whispered, kindly not pointing out

how strangely Tookie was talking. "Some of the girls around here are afraid to eat, especially around us guys. It drives me nuts. Open up."

Tookie opened her mouth for Bravo to feed her his cream-topped Modelland Munchie bite. She closed her eyes to fully appreciate the surge of flavor hitting her tongue.

Then Bravo leaned down. "What other kind of stuff does that hold in it, anyway?"

Tookie shrugged.

With a devious look in his eye, Bravo leapt off the bed and grabbed a jar of gauze. He held it up to the brooch, and the flower sucked it up. "Whoa!" he said.

Tookie giggled and pointed to a pair of discarded shoes in the corner. Snickering, Bravo grabbed them and held them up to the brooch. The flower gobbled the shoes up like a Venus flytrap hungry for insects. But the brooch didn't get any bigger from its new cargo.

The two of them went around the room stuffing more things into the brooch—a pillow, a box of magical sandpaper, a pair of crutches. Tookie was giggling so hard her stomach muscles hurt. *I'm having fun,* she thought. *With a guy. A guy every Bella wants the attention of.* It didn't seem real.

"Tookie?" Dr. Erica called, peeking around a curtain. "You're numb enough now. Time for me to work my Modelland magic on those precious lips of yours. We'll be rolling you into the operating room—or as we say here at Modelland, the OR-U-OK. My own special Lumière lighting and tools are in there for special cases. Time to say goodbye, Bravo."

Bravo rose from Tookie's bed. "Zoodbye, Zookie," he said

softly, curling his lips into a lopsided smile. He was looking at her so fondly, like he didn't want her to leave. When they arrived in the OR-U-OK, he retreated toward the door. Tookie gazed at his hands. They were so lovely. Strong. And his nails were chipped. Perfectly imperfect.

"Zoodbye," Tookie finally answered. As he slipped behind the curtain once more, she peered up at Dr. Erica. *I must have just hallucinated all that.* Surely Bravo hadn't just come and sat with her. *Fed* her. Let her *drool* all over him.

But Dr. Erica smiled kindly. As if reading Tookie's mind, she said, "Yes, Tookie. He was really here. And I think he likes you."

Tookie's head spun. *He likes me? There's no way. Absolutely no way . . .*

Dr. Erica wheeled Tookie under a column of bright lights. "Okay now, relax, missy," she said. "Close your eyes . . . count down from ten to one."

"Zen . . . ," Tookie slurred.

Something touched her lip, startling her. She opened her eyes and tried to focus on the doctor. "Keep your eyes closed, Tookie," Dr. Erica said softly. "This lip procedure's not pretty . . . but you are."

Tookie wanted to react—*Pretty?*—but the lights and the Zed Meds were making her sleepy. Dutifully, she shut her eyes. "Zine," she struggled to say. She *knew* she was hallucinating now. No one had ever called her pretty.

"Zeight . . . Zeven . . ."

She had just gotten used to *ain't half bad.*

"Zix . . . Zive . . ."

She closed her eyes and thought of Bravo leaning over her. It was a million times better than Theophilus leaning over her long ago, asking Tookie if she was okay. Today, she and Bravo had had a whole *conversation*. *And he'd* fed *her!* A Forgetta-Girl, fawned over by such a gorgeous specimen . . . was it possible?

"Zour . . ."

Could she actually *like* him? The guy who was more striking than most girls at Modelland, and one hundred times better-looking than Tookie herself? Could she like a naturally-arched-eyebrowed pretty boy?

"Zhree . . . Zwo . . ."

But his nails were chipped, so he wasn't perfect. Maybe she could like him. Maybe a myriad of things were changing for Tookie De La Crème—and maybe it was time to change with them.

28

†HE †HREE DECREES

". . . One," Tookie said aloud.

When Tookie opened her eyes, she saw a rainbow of colors on the hazy glass ceiling. *How beautiful,* she thought. *But I don't remember a glass ceiling in the OR-U-OK.* She brought her hand to her lips. They were smooth, as if she had never been attacked by the vicious cats of the Corridor. Then she sat up. There was no trace of Dr. Erica, or of Purse Drestookill, Zarpessa, or Bravo. She wasn't in the Fashion Emergency Department Store anymore. She was lying not on a hospital bed, but on a long glass table that had clear glass chairs neatly tucked around it. A floor-to-ceiling window looked out onto the M plaza.

Ugh! I sleepwalked again! Where the heck am I?

The walls were made of glass. On two long tables against the window sat all kinds of optical devices: spectacles of every sort, monocles, jeweler's loupes, microscopes, viewfinders, magnifying glasses, and even a large prism, which cast a giant rainbow onto the floor. She reached out to touch a pair of ancient-looking glasses that had a pair of cloudy blue eyes drawn onto the lenses. As Tookie stared at them, the spectacles reared up on their earpieces and glared back at her. Slowly, the cloudy film over the eyes vanished, revealing two hazel irises.

She crawled onto her hands and knees and looked down. The golden plaza was sixty or seventy stories below her and it was nearly dark outside. She could barely make out some Bellas using the pliable gold surface as a mirror, fluffing their uniforms and hair.

I'm in the M building! she thought, starting to panic. All the Bellas knew that this place was strictly off-limits. Being found here would surely mean consequences Tookie feared to even imagine.

She jumped up from the table, feeling a rush of light-headedness. *The Zed Med,* she thought. *There's still some left in my body.*

Tookie cracked open the glass door just a bit. The hallway walls were also made of glass panels, which went from clear to cloudy, then back to clear. If Tookie was very careful, she could stay out of sight.

Tookie saw Guru Applaussez having coffee with Guru Lauro Brown. Lauro had her feet propped up on a glass table with a glass mug of coffee in her hand. Guru Applaussez had a crystal coffee cup in each of its three hands. The largest cup was in its hand-head, its pinkie extended. When Applaussez suddenly turned in Tookie's direction, she ducked and the glass wall went opaque. *Whew, that was close!* Tookie thought.

Cautiously, she raised her head and peered through the wall across the hall, spying a large set of risers in the shape of a tic-tac-toe board. There were thrones in each square. The throne in the center square looked like it was made of pure diamond and crystal—and Gunnero Narzz was in it.

Tookie's heart dropped to her knees. The blood rushed from her brain.

Gunnero Narzz. Sitting in the diamond throne. Staring. Right. At. Tookie. With those terrifying gray eyes.

A sly smile blossomed on the Guru's face. He brought something to his lips. *A whistle? A weapon? I'm going back to Peppertown,* Tookie thought. *This is it.*

Gunnero smeared the mysterious item over his lips. A stripe of red appeared. *Lipstick!* Next, the Guru blew a kiss straight at Tookie. He ran his manicured fingers through unbound locks of flowing blond hair and started to apply mascara to his lashes.

And then it dawned on Tookie: the Guru couldn't see her. He was admiring his own reflection in a two-way mirror!

Angry voices floated from the end of the hall. Heart racing, Tookie tiptoed along opaque walls before they became clear again. Up ahead, Tookie spotted an EMERGENCY EXIT TO THE M sign with an arrow pointing to the left. Her way out! But she would have to pass the angry voices to get there.

Slowly, she slinked closer to the exit sign. The muffled voices grew louder and angrier. *Four more glass doors. Three more.* She rounded the corner and approached a massive set of double doors. To Tookie's surprise—and horror—they were slightly ajar. Persimmon stood guard outside, hands folded across her hard, flesh-colored plastic body. But she was facing the doors, not the hallway. Eavesdropping.

A voice floated out from behind the door, and footsteps paced angrily. "So tell me how you did it? Huh? What did you do? Did you use a shovel? Your bare hands?"

It was the *BellaDonna*! *In the flesh!*

Tookie could hear sobbing. Someone was in big trouble with the BellaDonna. And the BellaDonna seemed to be enjoying the show.

"Oh, so now you're all sad and weak, but to the whole world you act like some damn martyr! You talk such rubbish about abolishing everything this place stands for, spewing trash about undoing the very place that *made* you! You scheming, conniving hypocrite! You phony, worthless wench! The mere sight of you makes me want to vomit!"

"If I'm so bad, so vile, so disgusting, why have me return here?"

Tookie's eyes widened. It was . . . *Ci~L*!

The BellaDonna let out a shriek. "Don't you dare open your traitor lips to me unless I have granted you permission to speak! Do you know what it took for me to clean up that mess you made? I have been the BellaDonna of this school for ten years, and I thought I had seen it ALL! But what you did . . . what you thought acceptable to do with those girls' bodies . . . it scares even me."

Tookie blinked hard. "Girls' bodies"? What did Ci~L *do*?

The exit sign blazed in the distance. Tookie knew she should run for it as fast as she could, but she inched toward the Bella-Donna's office door instead, closer to Persimmon.

Ci~L's sobs escalated. The BellaDonna's voice lowered. "Yes, dear. You frightened ME. And no one can scare me—at least, that's what I thought. And now you've dug up some new trash. What are you planning to do with that round one, that wee one, and that wan one? They were funny here at first—amusing, even, kind of like hideous-looking masked mascots. But I'm over them. Abolish them now."

Tookie's eyes widened. She knew immediately that the Bella-Donna was referring to Dylan, Shiraz, and Piper. *But she didn't mention me?* Tookie wondered, both guilty and relieved that the BellaDonna had left her out.

"Uh~uh. I want to keep them around," Ci~L said boldly, her voice gaining strength. "And you have no choice but to let me."

The BellaDonna scoffed. "Why in hell would I do that?"

"Well, contrary to what you—the most *un*loved of the be-loved, the *cliquiest* of the chic, the definer of all things *stereotypical,* and the *extreme* leader of all of Bellas *un*lucky to be led—think, *knowledge* is power. And the knowledge I have will make you do whatever the hell I want. Because if you don't, I will tell everyone your little secret."

"And what secret is that?" the BellaDonna asked, in a voice that was nervously subdued.

"You made one grave mistake," Ci~L said. "And I don't mean torturing me for a half a friggin' year. Or making me redo War of Words in my first-year uniform. Or demanding I answer calls at the Modelland agency, where I've had to tell clients 'Ci~L is not available to model for you because she's an ingrate.' Or forcing me to clean the floors of the Ugly Room with my tongue. Or gagging me like a horse while you pry my eyes open and make me watch old Modelland propaganda films for seven hours at a time while you drip saline in my eyes so they don't dry out. Or denying me food for three days in a row to slim my 'thick hips.' Or making me feel so crazy and deranged that I have to freeze my face into a half-pleasant expression to hide the agonizing pain my body is truly suffering from every day!"

Ci~L stopped and gasped for breath. "No, woman, you made the mistake of insisting I work in the admissions department. Where I have full access to the new Bellas' admissions records. Do you want to know what I saw? What I was shocked to see?"

The BellaDonna was silent.

"Before we go there," Ci~L continued. "Let's go over the three most important rules that each BellaDonna must abide by."

The BellaDonna gasped. "That's highly confidential! How do you know those rules?"

"I *read* them when I was enslaved in your admissions room, you idiot. So let's go over those rules. I'll let you go first, out of respect."

"I will NOT play your little game," the BellaDonna growled.

"Fine, then I'll list them for you, in case you've forgotten," Ci~L said. "One: You must set a world-changing definition of beauty and stick to it for five years. Two: All Gurus must have a combination of a defect and a power. And last but not least, three: Do not tamper with the predetermined admissions list!"

Predetermined? Tookie thought. She'd never heard that. Girls everywhere trained and practiced and walked, hoped and dreamed! Nations made their fortunes promoting their local

T-DODs; companies reaped massive profits selling beautification methods for hopeful competitors, pushing the message that the dream was alive for all! Desperate girls lost their lives every year to the Pilgrim Plague, certain that Modelland got it wrong! She thought of the protest signs in the square: IT'S ALL A SHAM! A PHONY EXAM!

Were they . . . right?

"You tampered with the official list of new Bella candidates," Ci~L said. "You scratched out one worthy candidate. And you know the consequences. You'll be forced out. You'll live a life of immense physical pain and suffering. The Ugly Room would be just the beginning."

There was a long pause. Tookie waited, her heart pounding hard.

"Ci~L, what do you want?" the BellaDonna demanded.

"You're not abolishing those girls. I want them."

"Why?" The BellaDonna's voice was laced with something that almost sounded like fear.

Ci~L laughed devilishly, almost evilly. "You know why. They're my experiments."

"If you don't let me, what I did to those girls' bodies just might have to happen again. This time, I'll be successful—let the death march begin! C'mon, BellyDonna. You're up for a little sacrifice, aren't you?"

The BellaDonna sucked her teeth. Tookie bit down hard on her tongue to keep from crying out. *Experiment? Bodies? Sacrifice?*

There was another long pause. Then the BellaDonna uttered one word in a tiny voice Tookie hadn't thought the woman possessed. "Okay."

"Good girl," Ci~L said, like she was speaking to a dog that had just sat at his master's command. "You hold up your end of the bargain and I won't say a word about *your* little experiment either. How you replaced a worthy candidate with . . .

"Tookie De La Crème."

29

FLUTE CREEPERS

"Tookie De La Crème," Myrracle's voice floated from the back of the line of Pilgrims, "and *Intoxibella*. They don't really go together like ballet and tap shoes, do they, Creamy?"

"Of course they don't," Creamy snapped, stepping gracefully over a rocky outcropping.

The Pilgrims had been hiking for months. Bruised and battered, hungry and dirty, the Pilgrims trudged to an overlook and collapsed against the rocks.

Suddenly, ominous winds blew in. The Pilgrims raised the makeshift weapons they'd fashioned from random metal items they'd discovered on the mountain and sharpened: Abigail held up a piece of metal siding; Harriet, a rusty belt buckle; Lynne, what looked like a piece of a twisted car bumper. By now, they knew that as soon as these winds kicked up, horrible creatures known as Tumble Terrors blew in with them.

But they'd learned the hard way. Abigail Goode's legs had been deeply gashed by the unseen critters. One of the pug-sized creatures had extracted a three-inch chunk from Abigail's mother's shaggy buttocks. Lynne, the Pilgrim who had passed her Modelland prime but was still intent on reaching the peak, had lost the middle finger on her left hand when she'd batted at something crawling up her thigh. Lynne had wailed not in physical pain, but for the middle finger she'd planned to use to flip off one particular person once she was crowned an Intoxibella at Modelland.

Only Creamy and Myrracle remained calm. Creamy had packed her own special concoction made from insect repellent, paint remover, and turpentine to spray on Myrracle's and her own limbs. The brew protected them from harm somehow, allowing them to be calm spectators of the vicious action the storms brought on. But they didn't let anyone else see the potion—let alone *use* it.

Now, Lynne chanted a rhythmic phrase each time she stabbed at one of the Tumble Terrors. "Intoxibella Larcenina! Intoxibella Larcenina!" Before losing her middle finger and a bit of her sanity, Lynne had confessed to the group that Larcenina was the name of the Intoxibella with whom her husband was having a torrid affair, and for whom he had abandoned Lynne. Larcenina was the reason Lynne had embarked on this unauthorized trip to Modelland.

"Shut up already!" Creamy yelled. "I've told you a thousand times. Larcenina won't be an Intoxibella any longer, once everyone finds out she's mating with a civilian!"

"I know!" Lynne answered. "And when I make it to Modelland and become an Intoxibella, he won't be able to resist me and he'll leave her."

Creamy chuckled. "Hate to break it to you, wrinkle-face, they won't pick you with that finger missing."

Lynne's mouth fell open. "Who are *you* calling wrinkle-face?"

Meanwhile, the twisted, rabid, hunchbacked figure the Pilgrims had named Hunchy expertly speared a Tumble Terror and hurled it to the ground. Then he took off his boot, revealing razor-sharp claws, lifted his foot, and sliced the creature's human torso. It yelped in a deep, human-sounding voice.

Hunchy reached into the fresh gap in the torso, sifted through various organs that were still operating, and pulled out the pancreas. He then placed the entire bloody organ in his mouth.

An unsatisfied look illuminated his face and he quickly spat the pancreas out, wiping his tongue of any trace remnants. The sweetbreads he desired, the reason for his trek, were so close, yet so far, within a certain pale-skinned Unica who resided in Modelland. . . .

Macy Kamata slid his backpack straps over his shoulders and glared at his group. "Okay. Today marks our passage through the first level of the barrier."

"Are you friggling shticking me?" yelled Jessamine. "Only the FIRST friggling level?" She looked like she was going to burst a blood vessel. Jessamine was the prickliest of the Pilgrims, and she clearly gave Myrracle a serious run for her money in the beauty category, with her thick cocoa-brown hair, warm sepia skin, and bright tiger-striped eyes.

"Get ready, Pilgrims," Kamata said. "This is the part where you all will crap your pants."

The group shifted nervously.

"Now assemble the camp for the night," Kamata said. "We attack zone two tomorrow. Hurry now . . . packs and food in the middle. Sleeping bags in a circle."

"Excluding my daughter and me," Creamy interjected. "We'll sleep in our blow-up tent, as usual."

Lynne rolled her eyes.

Myrracle and Creamy climbed inside the tent they'd brought from home. Myrracle handed Creamy some of her freeze-dried mango rations. "You have to eat, Creamy."

Creamy wrinkled her nose. "You know me. I can't eat that. Old food, dehydrated, then wrapped airtight to allow it to fester and get even older? No thanks. I'll eat more of those tree saplings along the way. I'll be fine, Myrracle dear."

Just then, an eerie song floated into the cozy white tent. Myrracle unzipped two inches of the tent's zipper and peered outside. The Pilgrims lay in a circle, their backs to the heap of backpacks piled in the center. Their eyes were closed. Long silver plants that resembled musical instruments had wrapped themselves around the heads of the snoring Pilgrims and were starting to enter their mouths. All the while, the strange stalks emitted a spooky, haunting melody.

"Flute Creepers," Mrs. De La Crème whispered.

Kamata had told them that the Flute Creepers snuck up on sleeping victims, anesthetized them with Flute Sleeper venom, and then crawled into their windpipes. They digested their victims slowly over a period of weeks, working from the bodies' deepest interiors to their exteriors, all while the victims remained alive but paralyzed, feeling every bit of the pain. The key to preventing

Flute Creeper death was for someone to stay awake throughout the night and keep watch. That was Kamata's job. He'd failed miserably.

"Do we let them die, Creamy?" Myrracle said calmly, peering at the knocked-out Pilgrims. The Flute Creepers were now about one-third of the way inside most of the Pilgrims' throats.

"There's strength in numbers, Myrracle, dear. We need them for later," Creamy said, walking up to the group. "The *mountain* needs them for later," she added under her breath.

Mrs. De La Crème picked up one of the shank spears and hoisted it over her shoulder like a javelin. She tossed it and it struck its target, a Creeper that was halfway up Kamata's arm.

The spear split the silver creeper in half, and Creamy reached in to grab the slithering creature's pulsing metallic red heart. "Eww!" Myrracle cried. "What are you doing?"

"The heart of the creeper has the antivenom. The victim has to eat it to live." Creamy opened Kamata's mouth and moved his jaw up and down. "Ugh! Disgusting! Chew already!" she said.

Kamata's mouth began to move on its own. Each time he bit into the creeper heart, silver and red blood squirted over his shirt onto his pants. And then Creamy went around and saved all of the Pilgrims.

Myrracle gaped. "Creamy, how do you know how to do that?"

Mrs. De La Crème looked off into the wild expanse around her, then stared cunningly at her daughter. "Personal research, Myrracle, dear. Personal research."

30

D-Head and Dread

Tookie ran out of the M building faster than she'd ever run in her life. The journey was a blur: she had been on the seventy-seventh floor and she knew she hadn't taken the elevator, but she only remembered charging down a few flights of stairs. And she couldn't recall dodging Mannecants or Gurus or snaking her way to the ground-floor exit. But she had made it out of the building without being detected.

She ran across the gold-tinted surface of the plaza. The floor bubbled, creating for the first time not question marks, as it had when Tookie had arrived at Modelland, but three-dimensional Tookies. She ignored them. The last thing she wanted to do at that moment was primp.

As she neared the D, her brain replayed the same questions over and over. *Did the BellaDonna really choose me over someone else? Is Myrracle the person I replaced? Or is it a girl in another town across the world . . . a girl who is worse off than even I was?*

Shiraz had been right all along. *Zarpessa* had been right all along. The four Unicas had been blithely sailing along at Modelland, attending their classes, becoming more and more relaxed, and all this time, Ci~L and the BellaDonna were plotting to . . . *do* things to them. To abolish them. To experiment on them. To do *gruesome* things. For the rumors always dealt with heinous tortures of the mind and the body. Acts so torturous the victims begged to be killed and put out of their misery. And when death came, it was not a reprieve, but eternal damnation.

Suddenly, something else occurred to Tookie: The bodies the BellaDonna had mentioned to Ci~L in the M. The horrible thing Ci~L had done. What if that had something to do with the experiments, torture, and sacrifice too? What if Ci~L had taken the torture too far, had done something even Modelland didn't stand for?

The BellaDonna said Ci~L scared even her! *Oh God! Ci~L is the most twisted, diabolical person here. . . .*

Tookie headed straight for the path that led her to the D. The face-shaped hedge rustled, its expression turning from a sensitive smile to a disappointed frown as soon as it laid its ivy eyes on her. *Even the bush wants to hurt me,* she thought, barreling onward. And then, *slam!* Tookie made contact with something hard and solid.

"Whoa there, Creamy," Bravo said, his eyes scanning her from head to toe.

Tookie gasped. "*What* did you just call me?"

Bravo's smile faltered. "Creamy. Because of the whipped cream you keep in that flower thing. Among *other* things now." His eyebrows rose.

Tookie raised her chin a notch higher. "If you know what's good for you, you won't ever call me Creamy again!"

"Sorry!" He held up his palms in surrender. "Would D-Head be more appropriate? The shape of your head reminds me of the D."

"Ex*cuse* me?" His insults were getting worse, sounding eerily similar to things Zarpessa would say.

"No, Tookie. I mean D-Head in a *good* way!" Bravo backpedaled. "It's my favorite building here! I love uncommon beauty, and the D is a perfect example." He looked her up and down. "It's a curious collection of peculiar things. Apart, they would be less than ordinary, but together, they're special. You remember me telling you I'm really into architecture, right? I'd love to show you all my favorite buildings at Modelland someday. If you're interested, that is."

Tookie lowered her eyes. Then she cleared her throat, remembering the task at hand. She had to get to her friends and tell them what she'd heard. They had to form a plan.

"Are you okay?" Bravo asked.

Tookie couldn't tell Bravo what she'd just found out. She'd violated all kinds of rules, spying on the BellaDonna, being in the M building. "I'm fine."

"Your lips look perfect," Bravo said, eyeing Dr. Erica's handiwork. "No swelling, nothing. They look ripe for your first kiss."

If Tookie could have crawled under a rock and died right then, she would have. She'd forgotten about how Zarpessa had teased out her secret, taunting her for having never been kissed, making her look even more like the awkward, inexperienced, funny-looking girl she was. And yet, when she peeked up at

Bravo, he was smiling at her expectantly, hopefully. Almost like he wanted to give Tookie her first kiss *himself*.

A gust of wind kicked up, blowing around stray leaves from the bushes. A leaf landed on Tookie's bottom lip. Smiling, Bravo reached out to brush it away. His thumb touched both of her lips, then entered her mouth a bit. He removed the last traces of leaf, but his thumb lingered between her lips just like before.

Tookie's heart pounded. Her knees wobbled, her heart started to flutter, and she felt a warm gush through her core. *Try not to suck on his thumb again!*

"You have such pretty eyes," Bravo whispered. "They're a mixture of chocolate and mint."

Tookie made a face. "Yuck. I hate chocolate."

"*You* might hate it, but *I* love it," Bravo whispered.

Blood crept to Tookie's cheeks. *Seriously?* "Look, Bravo." She began to turn away. "I really want to hate you. I mean, you're not my type. If you and I entered a Peppertown beauty pageant, you'd win every category. And I . . . well . . . it's kinda obvious."

"But you *don't* hate me, right?" Bravo asked, almost sounding worried.

Tookie swallowed hard. "No." She couldn't believe she was having such a candid, honest conversation with a guy—especially *this* guy. In some ways, she wished Creamy could see her now. She wished everyone at B3 could see her too. Even though they never did.

"Good," Bravo said. He touched the side of Tookie's face as if she were clay and he were a sculptor. Her pulled gently on a frizzy portion of her hair and smiled. His hand then moved to the back of her neck.

"Hi," Tookie said awkwardly to Bravo, as if she were just seeing him for the first time.

"Hi," he said back, breaking into the lopsided smile again. He moved closer. The hairs on the back of Tookie's neck stood up. *Is this going to be it? My first kiss? Am I ready? Is this actually happening?*

But then Ci~L's horrifying words popped into her head again. "I have to go," she said, turning away.

"Wait up! I—" Bravo cried, but Tookie pushed past him before he could finish his sentence. She felt his eyes on her as she darted farther down the hedge, but she didn't turn back.

ᛗ

Tookie ran into the D, sliding on the slick floor of her dorm room. Shiraz, Dylan, and Piper were there, in a cheerleader-type pyramid. They were yelling random things at Kamalini, who was ignoring them.

"What are you guys doing?" Tookie was so out of breath she was barely able to get the words out of her mouth.

"We've been doin' all kinds of hijinks for the last half hour and she still hasn't looked up," Dylan answered, pointing to Kamalini.

"She's so lost in the Headbangor!" Shiraz said, waving her Sentura in the air. "We make the bet to see how long it take for her to see us!"

Dylan nodded. "The girl who loses must give your bestie, Zar-*Opressa,* a shove the next time she spews evil. Wanna play?"

"Actually, guys, I need . . ." Still out of breath, Tookie walked to her corner of the room and sat down on her as-yet-unmaterialized bed. She motioned for the girls to join her. While the bed was appearing, Tookie formulated what she wanted to say.

And then it all spilled out of her in a flustered, emotional jumble—the Zed Meds, finding herself in the M building, Gunnero and the lipstick, Persimmon listening at the door, and the awful conversation between the BellaDonna and Ci~L. "We're not supposed to be Bellas here." Tookie finished. "I think . . . I mean, I *know* the sacrifice rumors are true."

The three girls stared at her as though Tookie had sprouted another head. "Wait, *what* you hear Ci~L say, again?" Shiraz said. Tookie looked at her friend's worried face and for a moment felt like this whole mess was her fault. She wanted to hug Shiraz tightly. To tell her it would all be okay. But Tookie knew they were far from okay.

Then she glanced at Kamalini, but she was still listening to her Headbangor with her eyes closed. "Ci~L said that she wants to experiment on you. And she sounded like a . . . a *demon* when she said it," she whispered. "And the BellaDonna wants to do the same to me."

Everyone gasped. "Are you sure they meant experiment on us in . . . *that* way?" Piper asked. "Human sacrifices that lead to our agonizing deaths?"

Tookie took a deep breath. She hated telling her friends about this. But they had to know. "Yes. I'm sure. I think Ci~L's done this before. See, I have an, uh . . . a minor sleepwalking problem I've been struggling with since I could walk. And the first night here, I sleepwalked and I saw Ci~L. It was . . . *weird.* She was chanting in some dark red basement here, and . . . she was . . . she was *beating* herself to a pulp. She kept saying *I'm sorry, I'm sorry, I'm sorry.* And today, the BellaDonna kept referring to this *awful* thing Ci~L did to dead bodies. I think the things I saw are connected. I think she was apologizing to the people she tortured . . . and killed. But she's ready to do it again!"

Dylan blinked hard. "Wait. This happened the first night we were here? Why are you *just* tellin' us now? You *know* how Ci~L's been starin' and scarin' us! *You're* the one who made up this whole Unicas thing. Helloooo . . . Unica . . . UNITY . . . And you were right there, Tookie, when Ci~L went all demonic in War of Words and brought back my *own* demons."

"I'm sorry, Dylan. I didn't know if I was hallucinating or if I really saw Ci~L doing that stuff. I should have told you sooner. I just—it sounded crazy. And I didn't want you guys to think I was crazy. I wanted you to accept me! I wanted you as friends!"

Dylan sighed and shook her head. An agonizing half-minute ticked by, Tookie's heart pounding hard. *What if Dylan is really pissed with me? What if she never speaks to me again? I can't lose her—not now.*

Finally, Dylan's face softened. "I understand, Tookie. I don't know what I woulda done with that information either."

Dylan hugged her knees. "I'm really scared, y'all. I don't wanna die. I'm still so young. We all are. I'm tryin' to do somethin' with my life to help my momma, my sisters, and my brothers. Y'all know I got four of each. And none of 'em have ever been outside the Nation."

"I no want to do the dying either!" Shiraz cried. "I am Shiraz Shiraz! I want bring happiness and light to Canne Del Abra!"

"Well, *I* certainly don't want to die," Piper murmured. "I've never felt so alive. It feels so good to not start every day in fear of the LeGizzârds taking my life."

Piper grabbed Dylan's hand. Dylan reached for Shiraz's, and

then Shiraz grasped Tookie's. Everyone was shaking. Then Tookie steadied herself, took a deep breath, and said, "Unicas, there is only one thing to do. .

"We have to escape."

There was a long pause. Piper nodded. "I'm in."

"I will do the escaping too," Shiraz said.

"I'll do anythang not to get tortured," Dylan said. "Even if it means goin' back to work in customer service."

"All good plans, especially ones involving crime, start with assigning roles. Giving people with certain talents particular duties and then designing the operation around what they all do best," Piper said.

"Then, Piper, you should be our researcher and technology expert," Tookie said.

"I got a big mouth," Dylan volunteered.

"Yes you do!" Shiraz teased, opening her mouth wide.

"I can distract people," Dylan said, popping Shiraz playfully on the mouth.

"Good, we'll need that," Tookie said.

"I speedy," Shiraz declared. "I be messenger. The outlook!"

"The lookout? Absolutely," Piper said. Then she looked at Tookie. "What about you?"

Tookie felt her friends' eyes on her. All at once, she felt as lost as she'd been at B3. *What am I good at? SPLDing? Having no one notice me?* "Uh . . . the linguist?" she volunteered.

"I know!" Shiraz yelled. "You be our leader!"

"Huh?" Tookie swallowed. "I'm not really leader material, guys."

"Who says?" Dylan stood up and placed both hands on her

shapely hips and said, "*Who* got our scaredy butts out of THBC without us goin' through the Home doors like all those other girls? *Who* commanded we hightail our punk booties onto the BellaDonna's lion tongue in Catwalk Corridor? Who thinks Tookie should be the Head Bella in Charge? A show of hands!"

Dylan raised a balled fist in the air like she was inciting a revolt. Shiraz and Piper did the same.

"It's unanimous, Tookie. You're the official leader of the Unicas' escape plan!" Piper said.

Tookie shut her eyes. Her mind flashed back to the Corridor and to the THBC. *Was that leading? Have I been leading them without even knowing it?* Pride began to flow through her body like liquid gold. *I can do this. I can lead them. I will get all of us out of here.*

Not that she had the slightest clue where to begin.

31

DESPAIRING DESPERATION

One week passed. Then another. And yet Tookie still could not think of a plan that would get her and the other Unicas away from Modelland safely. But Modelland went on. And *plenty* was happening: the entire school was planning for the 7Seven Tournament, in which the upperclassBellas would compete to see which seven graduated and went on to become Intoxibellas. Girls began to trickle back from their Go-See-Gos, and nearly everyone in the D caught 7Seven fever, debating who they thought would be chosen as Intoxibellas.

"Oh please, I'm positive Chrisby's gonna make it. That girl's ThirtyNever power is gonna be more like *TwentyNever,*" Bibiana shouted, and Zarpessa countered, "Whatever! Gishella can multiply herself by eight. That's a record. Ci~L could only do seven!" The Likee sisters replied in their one-word-per-girl speech, "Zhen"—"Zhen"—"will"—"fail." Tookie and her cronies wanted to defend their friend and other favorites, but they had something more pressing on their minds.

Staying alive.

Any day could be the first day of the experiments. The sacrifice. The torture. Every day in GustGape class, as a blast of arctic air or a tempestuous sandstorm flew at them, Tookie felt the BellaDonna statue's eyes on her. In War of Words, as they debated merino versus mohair, cotton versus cashmere, retouched versus raw photos, and real versus faux fur, Ci~L, shackled in her shrunken Modelland uniform, stared sadly at Piper, Dylan, and Shiraz. Guru MattJoe had to call Modelland security to physically subdue Ci~L three times, always telling her to save the fighting for War of Words.

There were brighter moments for Tookie with Bravo. Through the CaraCaraCara classroom's portholes, he had seen her get hideously seasick, and had stood outside waving at her, being her stomach-calming horizon. And he'd left a can of whipped cream with a note that said *Zello and Zood Zorning, Zookie* on the doorstep of the D every day for two weeks. But even those endearing gestures couldn't pull Tookie out of her fear. Every time she rounded a corner, every time she heard a creak in the night, every time she felt a hand on her shoulder, she was sure it was Ci~L, coming to haul her off for her sacrificial torture.

Tookie could not recall ever having lost her appetite before. But every evening at the E, she sat at dinner with the Unicas in silence, staring at full plates of some of her favorite foods since she had been upgraded to Gut Chower. Braised short ribs with apple-cider-vinegar barbeque sauce. *Haricots verts* sautéed in garlic olive oil. Soup dumplings filled with melted fat. Pecan pie topped with the creamiest of whipped cream. And yet she couldn't eat a bite. All of it went cold and coagulated, never touching her lips.

None of the other Unicas could eat either. They would stare blankly at the bustling E around them. All the happy girls in their colorful Modelland uniforms, talking about the day's classes, upcoming photo shoots, the boys of Bestosterone. Girls who *belonged* there, girls who were on the predetermined list. Tookie glanced at her friends; by the looks on their faces, they were thinking the exact same thing. *This is really all a dream. And soon we'll be living a nightmare.*

Ж

The Bestosteros had almost finished building the 7Seven stadium, and Tookie's class of green-clad Bellas were given a tour by Zhen-Zhen. The young girls marveled at the stadium's size, ogling the gilded seats, gaping at the obstacle course on the enormous center stage. ZhenZhen tried to act confident as she explained how the obstacle course functioned, but her face looked as if she might wet her uniform pants. While she babbled on nervously, Tookie had an epiphany.

"Maybe we can escape through the emergency ZipZap to Metopia!" Tookie whispered to the Unicas.

Piper flinched. "The one ZhenZhen told us was dangerous, with a fifty-fifty chance of survival?"

Dylan narrowed her eyes. "Tookie, have you lost your damn

373

mind? ZhenZhen said that all those Bellas died in that thang during that big stadium fire! It spat them out in Diabolical Divide hell
instead of LaDorno!"

"Shhh, keep your voices down," Tookie whispered, checking
to see if any Bellas were eavesdropping. "Maybe it would spit us
out in the *right* place," she urged. "Maybe we should take that
chance."

"But they hide the ZipZap, no?" Shiraz asked.

"True," Tookie said, pulling in her bottom lip. "But we know
it's here in this stadium somewhere. We just have to find it."

"Instead of lookin' for this crazy dangerous ZipZap thingy,
why don't we just jump over the damn wall?" Dylan whispered.

Shiraz's eyes lit up. "That good idea! I am good climber. I
can scurry over wall with rope, then I throw rope over for you to
climb too!"

"But what about the Divide?" Tookie whispered, growing im-
patient. "Whether we take the emergency ZipZap or scale the wall,
we still have to face the DD."

Dylan shrugged. "I don't know about y'all, but I'd rather know
exactly where I'm goin' instead of some twisted Zappy thang sur-
prisin' me."

Everyone exchanged long looks. "The wall it is," Tookie said.

Later that night, before bedtime, they scouted the surrounding Modelland walls to find an area that wasn't patrolled by Guru
Gunnero and his guards. Finally, Piper identified the perfect hidden spot. "No one will see us here," she whispered. To remember
the exact location, she wedged a strand of her white-blond hair
between two cracked bricks.

Later, Tookie lay in bed in the D, staring at the ceiling in
her darkened room. According to the still-somewhat-confusing

kaleido-clock on the wall, she'd been lying awake for four and a half hours.

Countless terrifying images flashed through her head. Jagged and exotic murder weapons being thrust by a woman's hand. Pieces of body parts flying through the air in slow motion. Ci~L coughing out a malicious laugh as blood squirted from her eyes. Shiraz's, Dylan's, and Piper's rotting dead bodies, their glassy eyes staring up at Tookie . . .

SCREEEEEECH!

Tookie jolted up.

SCREEEEEECH!

It was some sort of horrible alarm. Tookie covered her ears and winced.

Shiraz bolted upright too. "Ugh! So loud!"

Zarpessa woke next. Doors throughout the D crashed open. Searchlights blazed outside the window. Only Kamalini lay blissfully in her bed, Headbangor on full blast. Tookie ran over to her and shook her awake, nearly jostling her out of bed.

Girls emerged groggily from their rooms and staggered toward the back exit. The night air felt cool and crisp. Tookie immediately shivered, wishing she'd brought her robe.

Bestostero security guards ran to and fro. A dark-haired person in a Modelland nightgown streaked past the face-shaped hedges, the cape of the nightgown flowing behind her in the wind. The largest hedge sprouted arms out of its ears and attempted to grab the figure as it ran past, but it was too late. The renegade headed for the wall surrounding the school, its musical instruments, canvases, and various odd parts casting bizarre shadows on the ground. Tookie caught sight of her face.

It was Desperada.

Desperada ran toward the wall. When she was a few feet away, she turned back and spoke to the crowd of gawking girls. Her eyes were puffy and red-rimmed. "My life is not worth living without him! You all can have this Intoxibella nonsense. I am intoxicated by his *love*. I need to be with him!"

She then backed up slowly. When she reached the wall, she turned around and began to scale it nimbly, climbing on the objects jutting out like a narrow staircase.

Oh my God, Tookie thought. She and the Unicas had just been talking about escaping over the wall at dinner, and Desperada was actually *doing* it!

"Excuse me!" a voice called from the back of the group. Suddenly, Ci~L pushed to the front. She was dressed in a Modelland nightgown. The sheerness of the fabric exposed the welts on her back for all the Bellas to see. Tookie shuddered. Shiraz, Dylan, and Piper took terrified steps away from her.

But Ci~L was only interested in Desperada. "What are you doing?" she screamed to the girl on the wall. "Get down!"

Gunnero Narzz pushed through the girls and eyed Ci~L. "Oh, it's *you*," he said, a sinister grin widening across his face. "We let you out of the Ugly Room for good behavior and *this* is what you concentrate your efforts on? You should let the desperate Desperada throw her life away for a lad! It would be some vintage entertainment for our nosy eyewitnesses here. C'mon, Body Girl, you know you want front-row seats to this old-fashioned show." He motioned to the audience of openmouthed girls.

"Body Girl!" Shiraz whispered. "Now we know what that mean!"

"*Dead* body girl," Piper said, remembering the terrifying story Tookie had told them. The four Unicas shuddered

Desperada climbed higher. Ci~L leapt up to try to grab her ankles but missed. The moonlight danced upon Ci~L's hand, and Tookie saw claws on the tips of Ci~L's fingers, not nails. When Desperada was almost at the top of the wall, she swiveled around and stared at the crowd of Bellas. "All of you who have left your boyfriends back at home are idiots! Do you know what they're doing with other girls? Other girls who are jealous and wish they were *you*?"

"Desperada, you're acting like a damn fool!" Ci~L exploded. "If you go, you'll regret it! What happens to you will be permanent."

Desperada softened for a moment, looking torn. Sensing that her words were sinking in, Ci~L climbed a few feet up the wall toward her. But that just prompted Desperada to climb even higher, to the very top of the wall.

"What the hell is wrong with you?" Ci~L warned. "Once you cross that wall, you'll—"

"—get exactly what young girls want!" Gunnero interrupted triumphantly. "To mature faster than nature intends! How fashionably late you'll be. Climb, girl! Climb!"

Desperada stared at Ci~L, then Gunnero, confused. So was Tookie.

Ci~L glared at Gunnero. "Shut up! You're just miserable about the way your life turned out, so now you're trying to ruin everyone else's!"

Gunnero smirked at her. "And you're happy with the way *yours* turned out?"

Ci~L turned to Desperada. "Well? What are you going to do?"

Desperada was already eyeing the blackness on the other side of the wall. "I have to do this. . . ."

"Then do it!" Gunnero urged. The scar on his face stood out in the moonlight. "Run-a-Way Intensive to your man, honey!"

Desperada's face went from panicked to calm. She looked at all the girls' faces and then jumped down to the other side of the wall. Everyone screamed, waiting for some awful explosion or monstrous roar. Ci~L just stared at the wall blankly.

Then . . . dead silence.

Zarpessa wrinkled her nose. "Is that it? What a letdown! I thought whoever crossed would—"

A thick lightning bolt struck the wall, making everyone jump back. It sent an immense fountain of color into the air, and the barrier became transparent. Suddenly Desperada was visible on the other side, lying still on the ground.

"Is she dead?" Zarpessa chirped a little too excitedly.

Desperada's body jolted, and she struggled to stand. Slowly, she rose to her feet, facing away from the crowd, her hair blowing in the howling wind. She brought her hands to her face.

Tookie looked around at her friends. "She seeming okay," Shiraz said.

Gunnero snorted. "Be patient, little midget, the show has just begun. Desperada, turn to your adoring public!"

Desperada slowly turned to face the wall of girls. There was a chorus of screams. Tookie looked at the girl on the other side of the wall.

Desperada's body was unchanged. But dark brown spots covered her cheeks and forehead. Wrinkled jowls drooped on either side of her jaws, and deep lines ran from both sides of her nose to the sides of her mouth. Her skin was pale and crumpled, like a cotton shirt that had been rolled up into a ball. The outer corners of her eyes had branches upon branches of crow's-feet leading off to her temples. Her hair had turned gray, thin, and brittle, exposing parts of her scalp.

"Oh my God," Tookie whispered. Desperada's face looked as though it belonged to someone of almost seventy, not a girl of fifteen.

Lightning struck again, and the wall reflected Desperada's image back to her. She let out a bloodcurdling scream. "I'm sorry!" she said, pawing at the wall. "Let me back in! He won't want me like this!"

Gunnero smiled and blew her a kiss.

"Wow, it *is* true," Zarpessa said gleefully, completely without sympathy. "You age fifty years if you cross without permission." She turned to the Unicas. "Oh, look, everybody! These four have crossed the aging barrier too! No, wait. They're still young, but just *naturally* disgustingly ugly!"

Tookie turned around and glowered at Zarpessa, fuming with rage. She had never met anyone so foul and black-hearted in her life.

"This would be an opportune time to cash in on our Kamalini Headbangor bet," Piper whispered. "Unfortunately, none of us won, so . . ."

"I'll do it!" Tookie said furiously.

Instinctively, Tookie turned and *accidentally* tripped, shoving Zarpessa hard. Zarpessa stumbled back and fell to the ground, but sprang back up almost as quickly as a blow-up punching bag. When she saw that Tookie was the culprit, her lips spread into a smile.

"Oh, I see, you big-headed Unfortunate-Looking punk," Zarpessa said so calmly it rocked Tookie to her core. "So, now you're ready, huh? Let's go at it, then!" Zarpessa raised her fists. Tookie tried to summon every ounce of courage that hopefully lived somewhere deep inside her scrawny body.

"I'm ready for you, Zar-*Opressa*." Tookie raised her fists as well. But they shook ever so slightly.

Dylan moved and stood between them. "Guys, don't! Not now!"

"Aw, how cute," Zarpessa said nastily. "Miss Parade Balloon comes to Miss Watermelon Head's defense." Then, shrugging, she stalked off to stand next to Chaste. "Oh, it's *really* on now, big-head!" she yelled at Tookie over her shoulder.

A gondola-type roller coaster car appeared on Desperada's side of the wall. "Take this senior ex-Modelland citizen down to her brace-faced teenage fellow!" Gunnero commanded. A large crane picked Desperada up by the collar of her uniform and placed her in the seat of the contraption. A U-shaped bar lowered in front of her, securing her in. Then the car zoomed away. "Here's hoping your boyfriend is into discarded Modelland cougars!" Gunnero teased.

Thunder rumbled. Lightning struck the wall again, sending shock waves of electricity through it, reversing the transparency. And then a second rumble, far deeper in tone than thunder, shook the entire wall and the ground beneath them. Girls flew right and left as a wave traveled across the solid ground beneath their feet.

Gunnero smiled, then pointed into the distance at the O. The BellaDonna statue glowed, its arms outstretched, vibrating violently. Ci~L just stood there with a foreboding look in her eyes as everything started to crash to the ground around her. Tookie somehow knew that Ci~L, in tandem with the BellaDonna, was responsible for the devastating tremor. Debris was falling everywhere. Everywhere but *on* Ci~L.

The Bellas all screamed and ran wildly, looking for places to duck and cover. Tookie and the Unicas found shelter under a large wooden table. They huddled there for what felt like forever as potted plants, tree limbs, chunks from the D, even dead birds that had apparently been struck midair, came crashing to the ground. The earthquake lasted three long minutes, until finally, the shaking abruptly stopped. The area looked ravaged and war-torn. Face bushes were uprooted. Statues lay in pieces on the path. The liquid gold in the M plaza was a sooty black. When Tookie looked over at the distant BellaDonna statue, it was no longer there. But immense footprints, each the size of a car, tracked through the once-golden plaza, straight to the M building.

Gunnero turned to address the girls. "The sun's about to come up and show off those dun-colored faces of yours. Make sure you slap on lots of concealer to cover up those dark half-moons under your eyes, witnesses."

Everyone trudged back to the D except Tookie, Shiraz, Dylan, and Piper. They stood at the wall, staring blankly at the spot where Desperada had climbed over. In the distance, Ci~L stared at them staring at the wall.

"We can't leave this way," Tookie whispered, turning to eye Ci~L. "We have to find another way out."

Shortly after they returned to the D, Tookie selected a green pen from her journal and began to write in Oktooberfestian. . . .

Ci~L,

I really don't understand you. One minute you're beating yourself, the next you're rocking and chanting, then you turn into a blackmailing devil with the BellaDonna, and just now you faked concern for Desperada. I've wondered if you are mentally disturbed, but now you've truly confirmed just how sick you really are.

I was once told by a supportive Triple7 Intoxibella who seems to have just up and disappeared that people who hurt others are hurting even more themselves. You must have been talking about yourself. Is that what the sacrifices are about? Are you a broken, barren soul, feeding on suffering to maintain your flawless existence?

Your maverick ways, your renegade fight . . . it's a booby trap, a gimmick, an illusion, so you can strike your victims while they're distracted by your unpoetic gibberish.

I've already been the victim of evil here at Modelland, you know that. In fact, I LIVE with it, literally, and she is bathed in a glowing Lumière as I write you. But THAT evil, as hurtful as it is, I kind of understand. THAT evil is living a lie and grabbing on to the handlebars of dear life to maintain her fantasy for an existence. While yours just seems selfish, pure evil for evil's sake.

I thought you were an inspiration, Ci~L— most of the world thinks so. So you've broken my heart in more ways than one. But the Unicas will beat you at your own game. We are getting out of here; we won't be more of your victims.

"Where the hell is Ci~L?" they all ask. When I get away from this place, the first thing I'm going to do is tell the world what a phony, evil, sick bitch you are.

Tookie

32

THERE IS NO, HAS NEVER BEEN, AND NEVER WILL BE

The morning sun had come quickly. The rays of light cut through the fog that hung low over the mountain's post-earthquake debris. Huge tree roots had been yanked out of the ground. Broken bricks from the D were strewn everywhere. As Tookie exited the D, the feeling in the air was funereal, as if they'd all attended a burial ceremony for someone who had died much too young. Even though everyone hadn't witnessed the incident, the plaza was still atwitter with rumors and speculation.

"I hear it's the BellaDonna's doing," Bibiana whispered as a clump of girls walked to class.

"I think she enjoys tormenting us," Chaste added. "Every time a Bella ages, I bet she gets a huge shivery thrill up her stony spine."

"There is something malicious surrounding Modelland!" said Kamalini.

"Maybe bad curse!" Shiraz said.

"Yeah, that's why the mountain is so deadly," Bibiana suggested. "I bet that's why no one who tries to get to Modelland survives. What if demonic dead Bellas live there?"

The group of girls approached the area of the wall where Desperada had made her leap. The air there had a solemn feel to it, the temperature at least five degrees cooler than anywhere else in Modelland. Already, girls had placed bouquets of flowers and trinkets at the base of the wall to honor Desperada's memory. A handmade sign read DESPERADA, FOREVER YOUNG TO US. Piper lit a candle.

As they stood before the wall, Tookie noticed something. She brought her hand to her mouth. *"Look!"*

The wall had reconfigured itself to create a collage of Desperada before jumping and after. The image of her before she crossed the divide was made of smooth, lineless, polished stone. But the image of her after she'd crossed was constructed with weathered and cracked wood.

"Is like a warning to the rest of us," Shiraz said morosely.

"Sickening." Piper turned away from the distressing art. "I wonder how long it will be on the wall."

Dylan looked up and down the barrier. "I wonder how many others have jumped and if the change hurts."

"How are we going to get out of here now?" Tookie whispered to herself.

Suddenly, four tones sounded, and the outline of Guru Gunnero's face appeared as a hologram. "This is a recorded announcement from Modelland security," Gunnero's face said. "Attention, all new Bellas: report to the M building immediately. Enter through the north ZipZap."

Tookie and her friends froze and exchanged worried glances. *The M building.* Where she'd heard they were all going to be experimented on and sacrificed. *Why of all places are we being summoned there?*

Whatever it was, Tookie knew it wouldn't be good.

Ϻ

Two columns of expressionless Mannecants guided the Bellas through the M building's doors and past a guard station heavily manned by Modelland security. Tookie looked at the hulking brutes standing guard and wondered how she had managed to sneak past them the day before. The whole ordeal was just a blur now.

Gunnero met the anxious girls in an annex and led them down the glass hallways of the M building. Mirrored doors opened into a cramped rectangular meeting room. The walls were made of alternating slats of mirrors and patterned glass. At the front and back of the room were items Tookie remembered from her last visit: long tables holding all kinds of optical devices from jeweler's loupes to microscopes, monocles to viewfinders, magnifying glasses to antique eyeglasses to prisms.

Her eyes settled on the wall in front of her. All kinds of shapes drifted past. One section of glass looked like a rooster crowing. Another section looked like a harp. Another looked like an eye. But then one eye became two. Slowly, the eyes opened slightly into slits. They looked just like the eyes of the BellaDonna statue. And they seemed to be looking directly at Tookie.

The slatted wall in the front of the room opened. Persimmon entered and walked to the podium. A hush fell over the crowd.

Persimmon began her usual speech. "May I present to you the most beloved of the beloved, the chicest of the chic, the definer of all things beautiful, and the esteemed leader of all Bellas lucky to be led . . ."

There was a loud sigh. Tookie glanced over and saw Guru Gunnero standing in the corner, his arms crossed over his chest. As Persimmon said the words, he moved his lips silently, mocking Persimmon, or perhaps the BellaDonna. Tookie wasn't sure.

"I present to you the BellaDonna of Modelland," Persimmon finished.

The eyes in the wall protruded until they were three-dimensional. They blinked once, then twice. But instead of being full of rage, these BellaDonna eyes were downturned and filled with tears.

Then the eyes grew lips for top and bottom eyelids and began to sing in a quavering but mellifluous voice:

"Modelland was once her home . . . home . . . home,
But foolish lust we don't condone . . . done . . . done.
Now a cursed and cracked gemstone . . . stone . . . stone,
Modelland is not her home."

"Sing with me!" the BellaDonna shouted. She launched into the chorus again.

Girls began to sing in uncertain voices. "Louder!" the Bella-Donna screeched. Everyone belted out the lyrics. They sang through the chorus six more times, their voices rising with each line. Gunnero rolled his eyes and kept his lips firmly shut.

The BellaDonna abruptly stopped singing and cleared her throat. Rustling could be heard throughout the room. And then she spoke.

"My heart, which you probably believe to be a bottomless pit, bleeds torrents for the loss of one of our own," she said solemnly. "Be damned, the shortsightedness of her lost soul, the young Bella's sanity wrapped up in the meager charms of some civilian boy down the mountain. I hope it's a nightmare that has haunted all of your dreams so you do not make the same imbecilic mistake."

Suddenly, the room went dark. Nervous murmurs rippled through the crowd.

Dylan shrieked. "Someone's breathin' in my ear!"

Tookie felt Dylan collapse on her shoulder. She nudged her and Dylan came to. Then Tookie felt someone else's breath in her ear. "Who *is* that?" she cried.

Simultaneously, girls all around the room were calling out in the same panic. It seemed like phantom breaths were everywhere. And then the familiar voice returned.

"Leaving for a man! Leaving for a man! Leaving for a MAN?" the BellaDonna whined. The room trembled.

The next time the BellaDonna spoke, she sounded like she was poised on the ceiling. "Desperation," her voice continued, "clouds your minds, robs you of clear thoughts, makes you think that a man is the answer. He. Is. Not. In the civilian world, women are more valued for giving birth to babies than for giving birth to their dreams. Not here. Not now. Not ever.

"In the civilian world, it is acceptable for a woman to settle, to subvert, to dilute and diminish her dreams if it's to help, or to be with, a man. That's somehow noble. Not here. Not now. Not *ever*."

"But Madame BellaDonna." Even in the darkness, the voice was instantly recognizable. Zarpessa's voice continued. "I don't think it's wrong to live for a man. Their intelligence is far greater than ours, and it is our duty to submit and love and—"

"How dare you speak when I am speaking, and such nonsense on top of that!" the BellaDonna roared. "Where on earth did you manage to come up with that rubbish? So you would derail your life to be with a man, you would risk your *face,* your Modelland Intoxibella future, for that nonsense you call . . . *love?*"

The room fell silent for a moment. Then, startlingly, small halting breaths rang through the darkness. Was the most beloved of the beloved . . . *crying?*

"Love," the BellaDonna repeated, "is an excuse to be stupid. When we come to Modelland, we say goodbye to love. We commit to succeeding at any cost. We relinquish our ties to our families, our friends. We sacrifice our souls to be one of the 7Seven. There is no, has never been, and never will be room for love at Modelland. *Ever.*"

Is it really a mandate that we give those things up? Tookie thought. It seemed so . . . cold. Heartless. *What kind of place is this?*

"But what about my family?" a girl's voice rang out.

"What about my best friend, Gingi?" another voice asked.

"What about my momma, my sisters, my brothers?" sobbed Dylan.

"Papa," sniffed Shiraz.

Tookie thought of the only person she'd left behind whom she dearly, truly loved. "Lizzie," she whispered.

And then Tookie heard the sound of loud sobs from someone she didn't believe had the capacity to shed tears: Zarpessa. The BellaDonna's banishment of love had shaken even her.

Tookie reached out in the darkness and felt for her friends' hands.

"Tookie," Shiraz hissed next to her. "I able to *see*."

"What?" Tookie asked, startled. It was so black in here Tookie couldn't see her hand in front of her face.

"Because of low light in Canne Del Abra. I almost seeing the BellaDonna!"

Suddenly, Shiraz cried out. There was a loud *thump*. "You will not see what you are not supposed to see, little runner girl!" the BellaDonna's voice resonated. Her voice was so close and loud, Tookie clapped her hands over her ears. The BellaDonna was right *next* to them! "Keep your eyes shut tight from now on, you hear me?"

"Y-yes," Shiraz whimpered.

Then the BellaDonna leaned in closer to Shiraz. So close that Tookie could hear her inhaling and exhaling. Her breath smelled sour, a little like Mr. De La Crème's after he'd drank his weight in TaterMash. "You think you can run away, elfin girl?" the Bella-Donna whispered in Shiraz's ear. "With those stunted legs of yours?"

Shiraz sucked in her breath. Tookie could feel the BellaDonna moving to Dylan next. "You're full of attitude, fleshy one, but not even *your* sass can save you."

Dylan gasped.

"A mind like yours is a terrible thing to waste," the Bella-Donna said into Piper's ear next. "I'll make sure she sautées it and eats every last drop."

All the Unicas made tiny whimpers. *Ci~L is coming for them any minute,* Tookie thought. *This is the BellaDonna's warning!*

Finally, the BellaDonna sidled over to Tookie. She planted her feet right in front of Tookie, and even though it was pitch-dark, Tookie could feel the BellaDonna's eyes on her, glaring, boring into her, *hating* her. Tookie cowered, hunching her shoulders to make herself smaller. She was sure the BellaDonna could hear her heart rocketing in her chest.

Without a sound, the BellaDonna vanished, but her words filled Tookie's body, weighing her down. Tookie held on to her friends tightly. They had to get out of this place.

Now.

33

The Mutant Music Monster

Back on the mountain, the Pilgrims had crossed into the second level of the barrier. The trek had begun to take a toll on their bodies in more ways than just the many injuries from the mountain's terrors. Dark circles surrounded their eyes. Clumps of dirt clung to their hair, and their ashy skin was covered in bug-bite welts the size of silver dollars. They'd all lost quite a bit of weight, their clothes now hanging off their bodies, the bones of their spines jutting out from under their shirts. They walked stiffly, their muscles having broken down long ago. Occasionally, one of them stumbled and fell. It was taking longer and longer for them to stand up again.

Creamy made an announcement to the crowd.

"After the many near tragedies at the hands of our drowsy, irresponsible leader, I am now assuming control of this group."

Kamata's head shot up from his crouching position. "Irresponsible? Lady, you do *not* know the Divide like *I* do and—"

"*Who* is ready for a change?" Creamy shouted, cutting him off. The entire group tentatively raised their hands.

"Mr. Kamata, you're outnumbered. So you either march along with us or turn back to Metopia. Your choice," Creamy declared.

Kamata looked at the ground and sheepishly whispered, "I'll stay. I wanna see it finally."

"You've never even laid *eyes* on Modelland from the Divide? Not even from a distance?" Jessamine asked, scowling.

"Um, no. This would be a first."

"I knew you were a friggling phony loser the moment I met your pathetic wannabe-ridge-raiding ass!" Jessamine spat.

"Okay then, packs on and let's go!" Creamy ordered the group in an authoritative voice, swinging her pack onto her back. Bellissima sat strapped to the top of Creamy's backpack for the best view of the Divide.

Lynne glanced over her shoulder. "Quick! Let's hurry up before you-know-who comes back!"

But it was too late. Hunchy's arms suddenly split open the bush. He stepped through, wiping his mouth of what appeared to be blood. Lynne shuddered.

The group continued their climb up the steep slope that would lead them to Modelland. Zone two was nothing like zone one. The air smelled of rotten eggs. And as they walked across the charred landscape, they came upon evidence of past Pilgrims: an old white sneaker, bitten in half. What looked like human bones, some eaten away by time, others relatively fresh. A leather jacket that seemed full. No one dared to check if there was a body inside.

"What in friggling hell happened here?" Jessamine yelled.

"They're dead," Myrracle replied innocently. Oblivious to the danger around her, she was still prancing as she walked. "They can't hear you."

"I know that, you dumb whirling-dervish dancing fool!" Jessamine's eyes blazed. "I don't think I've ever met such an idiotic dimwit as you in my entire fourteen years!"

Myrracle just shrugged, but Creamy stiffened. She shot Jessamine a dagger-sharp expression, then spun away toward Kamata. They began to speak quietly, out of earshot of the rest of the group.

After a moment, Kamata cleared his throat. "Listen, everybody . . . if I may, Mrs. De La Crème . . . ," Kamata said sheepishly.

"I prefer *Mizz* De La Crème," Creamy said. "Sounds so much fresher."

Kamata nodded. "From what I remember, there's a watering hole not far from here. Fresh water. Good for drinking and bathing. I know we could all use some sips and some suds?"

Everyone in the group cheered their approval. Kamata led the group down an embankment, past claw marks around a burned-out campfire, soiled Pilgrim socks and underwear, and a human jawbone. Finally, they arrived at a pristine lake.

The group let out a collective, relieved *ooh*.

"Like my beautiful black-bottomed pool at the home where I used to live with my husband before *she* . . ." Lynne's voice cracked, and she fought back tears. She then removed her clothes and stayed in the shallow part of the pond near its edges, her injured hand held high. Hunchy paced, excitedly or perhaps nervously, around the edge, as if he had never seen water.

Myrracle started to strip down too, but Creamy held her back. "Let them go first, Myrracle, dear. They've suffered more than we have."

She nudged Kamata, shooting him a reminding look. Kamata cleared his throat uncomfortably. "Uh, the legend of this pond is that the center is reserved for only the purest beauty," he said, though he didn't seem quite sure of his words. Still, Mrs. De La Crème gave him a satisfied nod.

"Well, we all know who that is!" Jessamine crowed. She swam fast toward the center of the pond, her quick fluttering feet kicking Abigail and Harriet in the face. "The man said 'purest,' not ugliest or hairiest!" she yelled, stopping to tread water. "Nothing pure about a friggling gorilla-monkey suit!" she yelled as she resumed swimming to the middle of the pond.

"Can I go in now, Creamy?" Myrracle pleaded.

"Not yet." Creamy stared at Jessamine as she frolicked at the center of the pond. "Lights out, shining star," she murmured ominously.

As if on cue, the pond began to bubble. Jessamine whooped. "It's a hot tub too!"

A wave of bubbles swept across the pond. Things began to rise to the surface. *Skulls*. Thousands of them. They bobbed on the water, forming a perfect circle around Jessamine.

Abigail and Harriet scampered to shore. Hunchy climbed a dead tree. But Jessamine was trapped in the middle of the pond by the skulls. Meena grabbed a tree branch and extended it toward her daughter. "Come with me, Jessamine. Come!"

Then something rose from the water, taking Jessamine's mother's breath away. A muck-covered creature, as tall as a giraffe. Its body was made of dozens and dozens of human arms, and its head was a mash of ancient musical instruments contorted into an evil, hungry-looking array of sharpened, sideways-turned cymbals for teeth, hollow eyes made of tuba bells, and a steaming nose made of organ pipes.

"Pond monster!" Jessamine screamed. She tried to paddle away, but the monster scooped her up and took a large bite out of her torso, carefully avoiding her arms.

"No!" Jessamine's mother wailed. She tried to fight the monster off from the shore with the stick, but it was like fighting a dragon with a toothpick—useless.

The monster tossed Jessamine's head and thrashing legs into its cymbal-toothed mouth. Then it set its sights on her mother. Hunchy howled wildly at the sky.

Meena spun around and ran, but the pull of the water was too great. The pond monster caught her after only two steps. With its empty hand, it grabbed her. It ate everything but her arms, just as it had done with her daughter.

The monster carefully placed mother's and daughter's arms on its head and they suddenly came to life, skillfully playing a haunting melody on the monster's various instruments. Everyone screamed. And when *that* was done, the pond monster stomped its foot, sent a tidal wave to the shore, and eyed the group, spotting its next prey.

Myrracle.

In seconds, the creature was out of the water and zipping toward Myrracle, who cowered behind Creamy. If Creamy was frightened of the music beast, she did not let on. She stared viciously at the creature, then spat out a five-word warning. "Touch. Myrracle. And. You. Die."

The monster blinked. After a moment, it took three large steps backward. It then walked dejectedly into the pond and disappeared into the drink. Everyone stared at Creamy, astonished. Who *was* this woman?

"Well now," Creamy said, as if she had just taken a refreshing shower. "The clock is ticking and we have someplace to be. Shall we continue?"

34

The Madwoman of the Modelland

Tookie's head fell hard onto her pillow before her bed had fully materialized. Her body was racked with exhaustion, but the heavy burden of impending death robbed her of the ability to fall asleep.

Four days had passed since Desperada had scaled the wall and the Unicas' plans had been foiled. That day, after Guru Lauro's class, in careful whispers, the girls had seriously considered scaling the wall and succumbing to aging; old-looking is better than dead, they reasoned. But then Piper had questioned whether fifty years of physical aging also shortened their life spans. Which wasn't any better an option than staying where they were.

Tookie stared into the darkness, wide awake. With her finger, she traced a single word onto the sheets:

How?

It was the question she had written on a scrap of paper to Dylan, then Shiraz, then Piper, in Run-a-Way class. While dodging Guru Gunnero's gaze, Piper had tirelessly drawn fifteen different diagrams of the Modelland grounds, but they all led to dead ends.

How will they choose to torture us? Burning? Drowning? Boiling? Stoning? Strangling? Sawing? Scalping?

How can I get my friends out of here?

The moonlight on the ceiling intensified and the stars in the Modelland sky had come out to play. As they had every night since the girls had been there, Kamalini's and Zarpessa's Lumières shone magically on their faces. The luminescence displayed their exquisite features and dewy skin.

A scream echoed through the room, making all of Tookie's nerves snap. Was it Ci~L attacking Shiraz? Tookie bolted upright.

Across the room, Zarpessa sat up in bed. "Get off me!"

Shiraz sat up too, staring curiously at Zarpessa. "What her problem?"

"Is she having a nightmare?" asked Tookie.

"Get it off of me! They'll find me! I CAN'T have them FIND me!" Zarpessa ranted. Her eyes were wide open and they darted around the room. Her head and body twisted in opposite directions from each other. Her feet were taking her to parts of the room where her eyes weren't looking. Her arms flapped. The Lumière darted right in step with her like a police helicopter's searchlight looking for a perpetrator.

"Stay away from me, lady! You disgust me!" Zarpessa shouted, waving her arms at the searchlight. "I'm not hiding you anymore, so don't follow me, or they'll find you!"

Tookie blinked hard. What was Zarpessa dreaming about?

Zarpessa jumped in the air and swatted at her Lumière. "Stop it, you hear me?"

Then she turned and her crazed eyes locked on Tookie's mismatched ones. She stomped up to Tookie and yanked hard on her nightgown. "I saw this dress first, damn it! And I WILL wear it on The Day of Discovery!"

The dress. The yellow dress she fought over with Lizzie. Was Zarpessa dreaming about *that*?

Zarpessa tramped up next to Shiraz. "If you had let Poppi handle everything, we wouldn't be in this mess!"

Poppi handle everything? Tookie's skin prickled. Was *Poppi* Zarpessa's father?

Zarpessa's body began contorting again and bouncing around the room. Tookie felt a sudden temptation to rush over to Zarpessa, wrap her in her arms, and soothe her, like she had done with Desperada. The feeling quickly abated.

Nope, I just can't.

Zarpessa ran out of the room and down the hallway. Her Lumière stalked her hungrily around the corner, as if it were an anaconda in the rain forest that hadn't eaten in two months.

Tookie and Shiraz ran into the hall, leaving Kamalini sleeping peacefully, comforted by her Headbangor. Other girls were now awake and in the hallway, including Dylan and Piper.

"Now I presenting Zarpessa Zarionneaux as . . . the Madwoman of the Modelland!" Shiraz blurted out, running down the hall after her, erupting into giggles.

"Well, I guess we found out what the double *L*'s in *Modelland* stand for," Dylan joked to Bibiana. "*L-L* for . . . *Loony Lumière!*"

Zarpessa had moved to the kitchenette, zeroing in on the bank of refrigerator drawers that housed various Modelland Munchies. "The Lumière can't follow me in here. And neither can that stupid lady. C'mon, Poppi! Protect us from her. Get out of the light! It can't find us in here!"

But Zarpessa's snakelike Lumière illuminated her face even in the UnCommon room. The light, which still seemed to be coming from her bed, was bending perfectly around every corner and coming down hard on Zarpessa.

Zarpessa squeezed into the refrigerator, ripping open a package of Munchies. "I'm so hungry, Poppi! It's six p.m.! Time for Dumpster-dive dinner! I'm starving!"

"Starving?" Chaste, who had emerged out of her room, asked. "What's she talking about? That girl eats. She doesn't have the Likee sisters' problem."

The Likees, who were standing beside her, stiffened. "We. Have. No. Problem!"

"And that girl wouldn't Dumpster-dive if her life depended on it," Chaste went on. "Her family's, like, billionaires or something! They could probably buy and sell all of Modelland!"

"You're her friend. Help her!" Dylan shrieked. Zarpessa's eyes were now rolling into the back of her head.

"Oh hell no," Chaste replied, stepping back five full paces. "I don't do crazy."

The door flung open and Dr. Erica speed-skated into the room. "What's going on here?" she demanded.

Shiraz raised her hand. "Girl wake up, scream like nutcase about Lumière and T-DOD dress, go more wacko, came here, binge on Munchie."

Slam. Behind them, Zarpessa shut herself inside the

refrigerator. Muffled shrieks could be heard from inside. Dr. Erica tapped lightly on the fridge door. "What's her name again?" she asked the group.

"Who? The *cuh-ray-zee* monster? Zar-*Opressa*," Dylan huffed.

Tookie started to snicker, then clapped her mouth shut. Despite how evil Zarpessa was toward her, she felt sort of bad for what was happening. This was a full-fledged *breakdown*.

"I've seen this many times at Modelland before, missy," Dr. Erica said. "Too much Bella pressure . . . experiencing terrifying things like THBC, witnessing a girl aging fifty years before your eyes, can cause a drop in serum glucose—"

"Aughhhhh!" Zarpessa wailed. "The refrigerator light! My Lumière followed me in here!"

Dr. Erica peered at the girls. "Does anyone know what she means? Perhaps one of you knows her from home. Did something terrible happen to her?"

Piper turned to Tookie. "*You* know her from home, don't you?"

Everyone looked at Tookie, including Dr. Erica. "Tookie!" the doctor said gratefully. "Is there anything you know about this girl?"

Tookie felt a lump the size of a grapefruit in her throat. If there was any time to expose Zarpessa's secret, this was it. But she could just feel the anticipation in the room. The delicious, perverse glee of the other girls, who were just waiting for a scandal. There might be others besides Tookie and her friends who wanted Zarpessa to fail. Jealous girls. Envious girls. Girls who were not performing half as well as Zarpessa in class. Telling all Tookie knew, right now, would ruin Zarpessa.

Ci~L's words rang out in Tookie's head: *The girl who is sucking your blood is hurting way more than you.* Tookie knew Ci~L was right. She should have compassion and understanding even for an enemy. Being the bigger person was what leaders did. Yes, Ci~L was crazy. Yes, she wanted to torture and kill Tookie and her friends. But in the end, exposing Zarpessa's lies wasn't something a leader would do.

All eyes were still on Tookie, waiting for her answer. Even Zarpessa had gone silent in the fridge, as if she suddenly had her wits about her and sensed what was coming next. Tookie lowered her eyes and shrugged. "I know nothing about her," she said in a low voice. "Nothing at all."

35

Deco

The morning sun blazed brightly, but to Tookie, it felt as if the sky were covered with angry storm clouds. "She wasn't in her bed this morning," Tookie said to her friends as they gathered in the UnCommon room.

"She's probably still in the FEDS," Dylan whispered. "Givin' a Zar-Opressa Madwoman of Modelland performance. I bet they put her mean butt in some wild-animal restraints. What I wouldn't give for a CaraCaraCara picture of that!"

Piper, who was watching them from the windowsill, the filtered light backlighting her face, sighed. "She did appear to be a danger to herself and others."

After Tookie had denied knowing anything about Zarpessa's past, the rest of the evening had gone by in a blur. Dr. Erica had finally managed to wrench the refrigerator open and drag Zarpessa out. The girl had been kicking and screaming about peanut butter, her eyes wild, still tangled in a dream. It had taken several security guards to carry her out the door.

The girls turned to the sound of rapping on the front window. Bravo was standing in the bushes.

"Hello, my favorite Bella!" he called to Tookie, his voice muffled through the glass.

Dylan grabbed Tookie's wrist and squeezed. Shiraz swooned. Even Piper looked flustered and flushed. Bravo was looking more dapper than ever, dressed in spit-polished boots, a uniform similar to Bestosterone everyday-wear but made of finer material, and a capelike coat with padded shoulders and six pockets running up the front.

Tookie opened the window so he could climb in. Dylan caught her arm. "Girl, you know we're not allowed to have boys in the D," she whispered in Tookie's ear. "Especially not fine, sexy tenders like Bravo!"

Tookie shrugged and whispered. "He'll only be here for a minute. And we're leaving this place soon, anyway. What does it matter if I get in trouble?"

"Pardon me, ladies," Bravo said, dusting off his pants, "but would you mind if I stole your friend Tookie for a few minutes?"

Dylan stepped back, now smiling. "Well, I suppose not. But take good care of her, ya hear?"

And then all three of Tookie's friends disappeared from the bedroom, giggling. Shiraz hooted.

"Hi," Tookie said, her insides turning boiling hot.

"Hi," Bravo replied.

"You're following me, aren't you?" Tookie said, realizing there was a touch of flirtation to her voice. She didn't even know she knew *how* to flirt. "I saw you outside the CaraCaraCara boat again. Three times in one week, huh? But you do help me to not be so seasick."

"Really? Well, uhhhh . . . yeah, if you want me to be completely honest, I am following you. And I'm glad you're not seasick anymore." Bravo's lopsided grin snaked its way up the side of his face and right into Tookie's heart. "Oh, I hurt my hand during a photo shoot on the roof, and I came here today cuz I needed to have my thumb sucked."

"That wasn't nice," Tookie said, blushing.

"Oh no . . . it was." Bravo was the one to swoon this time. "It really was."

They were silent for a moment. Then Tookie swallowed. "So why are you stalking me? I mean, we've had a few nice conversations, but what do you *really* know about me?"

"Well, let me see." Bravo paused as if he was trying to recall a list. "You hate chocolate with a vengeance. You're always hungry. You appreciate things that aren't conventional."

"Correct. And how do you know that?"

"The friends you keep. That unusual flower you wear. It holds tasty things. But it's hiding something too, isn't it? I saw a piece of it when you were getting patched up at the FEDS. So what's under there?" he asked, trying to move the brooch aside.

Tookie swatted his hand away, afraid for him to see the T O OKE pin. "That's none of your business."

"Well, it's right over my heart," Bravo said, completely earnestly.

Tookie's jaw dropped. "YOUR heart? Since when has my body become yours?" Then she laughed. "And come on! That is such a line." But in truth, she loved that he'd just said that. It made her heart beat at warp speed.

Bravo smiled sincerely. "You're a good girl, Tookie, and I respect you. I guess it's just wishful thinking, the wanting-your-heart thing. . . ."

Tookie blinked at him. All of a sudden, she felt the urge to laugh—or maybe cry. She remembered what she looked like, and all the insults that had been hurled at her by her family, Zarpessa, Gunnero. And here was this faultless specimen of malehood, a guy prettier than Myrracle, wanting to spend time with her. She just couldn't understand it.

"Are you kidding me?" she blurted out. "You want *me*. Seriously."

Bravo didn't break his gaze. "These other girls here, they chase after me like I can solve all their problems. It's always been that way for me, not just here, and it sucks. I open my mouth to say hi and women damn near pass out or wanna marry me, and I'm not even old enough to get into a club in LaDorno."

"Oh, the trials and tribulations of the exquisite male. I'm so sorry for your pain."

"I know, I sound ridiculous. Like a conceited egomaniac."

"*You* said it. *I* didn't."

"But I'm serious, Tookie," Bravo went on. "You're . . . different. You could care less about my outer shell, this thing I had absolutely nothing to do with creating." Then he shifted his weight. "I wanna tell you a story."

"A story?"

"Yeah, about somebody I know. Will you listen?"

"Of course. Who doesn't love a good story?"

"Man oh man, where do I start?" He shoved his hands deep into his coat pockets, exhaled deeply, and then said, "Okay, here goes. More than anything, a little boy named Deco wanted to be an architect. When he was six years old, other kids were drawing two-dimensional houses and stick figures, but Deco was building three-dimensional cities with discarded pieces of junk. But no one paid much attention to Deco's beautiful work because there was something that was more striking than his creations: his *face*.

"No matter where he went, people would stop in their tracks when they saw him."

Sounds like Myrracle, Tookie thought.

"Two years later, the conductor of the prestigious Philhar-monic Orchestra spotted Deco and his parents at a music street festival. The composer convinced Deco's parents to allow him to compose a whole symphony dedicated to Deco's face."

"Really?" Tookie interrupted. "That's just plain weird."

"I know. But just listen, okay?" Bravo pleaded. Tookie nodded.

"On opening day," Bravo continued, "Deco stood on the con-cert hall stage as the musicians stared at him. But he wasn't mis-erable. 'Cause from where he stood, he had a perfect view of the entire hall. The swaying walls, the building's undulating curves. He was transfixed by the scale and scope of the place and how, if given the chance, he would design it differently. He resketched and redesigned the space, all within the confines of his eight-years-young head."

Tookie pictured the young boy and softly smiled at the

thought of him getting whatever pleasure he could from such an odd circumstance.

"When Deco reached his teen years, the attention he received from the opposite sex was startling. One young lady actually fainted when she saw him on the first day of school. Deco wasn't interested. He concentrated on his architectural career instead. He tried to sell his ideas to multiple architectural firms. They were always impressed with his skills, but his face stole the show and the conversations soon turned to the beauty of his visage, not his designs.

"So what happens to a child whose true gift is ignored, forgotten, looked over? What becomes of a boy people don't listen to, only stare at?"

"I don't know," Tookie answered. "What happens to him?"

"That was a rhetorical question, Tookie." Bravo smiled. "Deco had been approached countless times to attend Bestosterone, but the very idea turned his stomach. One day he overheard a conversation between his heroes, two leading architects. The men spoke in hushed tones about the rumored gravity-defying, stupendous architecture and design of Modelland, and about how they were going to Pilgrim up the mountain to view it for themselves. Just one week later, Deco read a headline on the front page of his local newspaper about two missing architects. All that was found of them in the Diabolical Divide were their bloody, torn clothes and an architectural drafting kit. The media was stumped that two grown male architects had attempted to Pilgrim, a Modelland first. They speculated that the men had caught the first cases of the Pilgrim Plague for men. But only Deco knew the real reason for their fatal excursion."

"This is so intense," Tookie whispered.

"From that day forward, Deco became obsessed with the reason why his two favorite architects would risk their lives to see Modelland's structures with their own eyes. Their obsession, even in their deaths, became Deco's. But he wasn't willing to risk his life for a viewing. His safe way up the mountain . . . ?

"Bestosterone," Bravo and Tookie said at the same time.

Bravo exhaled deeply, like a huge weight had lifted off his chest. Tookie touched his arm. "Hi, Deco."

"Hi, Tookie," Bravo replied. His eyes were glassy, and Tookie wondered if he was holding back tears. "Thanks for listening." Then he leaned toward her. "You have a hair that's about to go in your eye. Let me get it."

Tookie remained very still. He licked his thumb and then brought it to her eyebrow, slowly smoothing the unruly hairs down as he smiled into her mismatched eyes.

Tookie stared deeply into his caramel ones, and her knees felt like they would buckle. She sensed a gentle burning inside her stomach, and her hips felt like they were being tickled, even though Bravo's hands were nowhere near them.

Bravo put his hand on the side of Tookie's face. The warmth from it felt like sweet tea pouring into her mouth. He whispered straight into her ear, his lips brushing against her earlobe.

"I really like this, Tookie. It feels . . . right. I know I have to get out of here before you get in trouble, but . . . I don't want to leave."

His words felt like maple syrup coursing through her veins. "And I don't want you to," she replied. "You make me feel . . ." A single tear fell from her brown eye. ". . . like . . . like a . . . Rememba-Girl."

"Really? A remember girl? What's that?"

"What I have always wanted to be. Someone . . . beautiful."

"You *are* beautiful. On the inside *and* the outside."

Tookie wrinkled her nose and shook her head.

"You really are, Tookie. Beautiful. In a special, unique way. You're so different, and you deserve someone who will treat you like the unique princess you are. And that's me. Tookie, I don't want *anybody else* to have you. I guess you can say I'm selfish. I want you all to myself. Your first time should be special and tender. And it should be with me."

"That's awfully bold of you!" Tookie pulled away from him. "I'm just getting to know you! You're claiming my first time already?"

"Yes, Tookie. Your first time. Your first . . . kiss."

"Ohhhhh . . . sorry."

Tookie's cheeks flushed. Her mind spun. *He wants to be my first! ME? The expando-mode six-headed Forgetta-Girl? Is he sight-impaired? But he's looking right at me. CLOSE UP! Oh God, I promised myself to Theophilus. Have you no loyalty, Tookie?*

Then Tookie calmed down. "You can be my first."

Bravo ducked his head. "I feel like a charity case."

"No, no, no . . . I didn't mean it like that. How's this: I *want* you to be my first."

"Really?"

"Really."

"And what about the being-my-girlfriend part? Being my, ummm . . . my lady."

Tookie couldn't believe her ears. "Yes to that part too."

"For real?"

"For real, Bravo."

They fell silent for a moment. Tookie ducked her head. "I can't believe I'm about to say this, but I can't wait to lose my . . . lip virginity to you."

He smiled his luscious crooked smile. "Have you ever thought about what your first kiss might be like?"

Tookie's heart stopped. *Only a million times,* she was tempted to say. "I guess so," she said instead, trying to sound nonchalant. "But I've always wondered—will people *know,* afterwards? Will they be able to tell that I've *done it*?"

"Well, maybe not." Bravo smiled. "But *you'll* know."

"And . . . will it . . . *feel* weird?"

"I hope it will feel amazing," Bravo said. "And I know the perfect place our first kiss can happen."

Our first kiss. That sounded so good. "Where?" Tookie whispered.

"I'll sweep you away, where no one at Modelland can see us," Bravo said. "We'll go on a magical ride down a secret ZipZap that we hid under the new 7Seven stadium and land in the most beautiful fountain in LaDorno."

Tookie tried her hardest to keep her face tempered and nonreactive, but inside, her stomach twisted. Bravo knew where the emergency exit to LaDorno was hidden?

"I can make it happen after ManAttack tomorrow."

"Wait." Tookie frowned. "A ManAttack? When?"

Bravo looked caught. "Bestosteros aren't supposed to tell any Bellas about the ManAttack challenge before it happens, but you're my lady now, so I don't think there's any harm. It's happening tomorrow. It's a big challenge. For us, it's to measure Bestostero Intoxibello potential.

"Only a few of us every five years or so have Intoxibello powers," Bravo said. "The ManAttack is an early indication in determining which of us boys just might have the magic touch. It's ridiculous, if you ask me, but if participating allows me to build more Modelland buildings *and* to be around you every day, sign me up!" Then he moved closer. "You're one of the competitors, Tookie. But all Bellas and Bestosteros are going to watch."

Tookie's heart pounded harder and harder. *You're one of the competitors. All Bellas watch. A secret ZipZap. Through the 7Seven stadium . . .*

This was the Unicas' chance—maybe their *only* chance.

Tookie cleared her throat. "Um, Bravo. Can you show me where that secret ZipZap is?"

He blinked innocently. "Before we go tomorrow? Why?"

Tookie swallowed hard. She couldn't look him in the eyes and blatantly lie, so she stared at his chipped nails instead. "I, um . . . I'd love to see the thing that will, um . . . lead us to our first kiss." The words came out in a messy jumble. Tookie was almost certain Bravo could smell the guilt wafting off her skin.

But he smiled brightly. "Of course, Tookie. I'll show you the ZipZap tonight." He gave her a warm smile, which just made her feel worse.

Too much worse. She couldn't do this to him. "Uh, Bravo?" she said, peeking at his eyes. "There's something I have to tell you." She had to tell Bravo the truth, even if he wouldn't like it. He'd just poured his heart out to her; he deserved honesty in return.

"What is it?" Bravo asked gently.

Tookie breathed in. "It's about me and my friends. We're—"

"What in the hell is a Bestostero doing in here?" a voice boomed through the door, interrupting them. Suddenly, Ci~L appeared.

The Unicas tumbled in after her. Ci~L's eyes were on Bravo, and her face was bright red. *"Get out!"* she screamed at him. Then she glared at Tookie. "Do you know what happens to girls like you who break the rules? Do you know how much I want to *kill* you right now?"

Ci~L raised her arms in the air and fabric covered in fire shot from her fingertips. Everyone screamed. Ci~L advanced toward Tookie and Bravo, her shape shifting and twisting with the power of Chameeleoné. Her face morphed from a mixture of Gunnero's and Applaussez's to a gory combination of Chaste's and Zarpessa's. It then shifted to a mishmash of Dylan's, Piper's, Shiraz's, and Tookie's faces, her skin melting, her tendons popping, her eyes blazing bloody red. Steam puffed from her nostrils. She bared sharpened teeth and extended her hands toward them, her razor-blade claws extended.

The girls backed into a corner. They held on to one another for dear life. Shiraz started praying in Labrian. Dylan began reciting all of her brothers' and sisters' names, saying "Goodbye, I love you" after each name, and then she fainted. Piper closed her eyes and leaned her head back as if she had accepted her fate and just wanted whatever pain was approaching to be over quickly.

This is it, Tookie thought. *She's going to kill us all now!*

"Ci~L!" a voice screamed behind them. Persimmon stood in the doorway, her mouth in a tight line. "What in BellaDonna's name are you doing?" She grabbed the Intoxibella's arm and dragged her out of the room. As she was being pulled away, Ci~L glanced over her shoulder at the girls. When she shook her finger at them, her nails were still long and pointy talons. "I should just burn you alive," she hissed.

Over my dead body, Tookie thought.

36

All Hail Queen Creamy

"Are we there yet, Creamy?"

"Not yet, Myrracle," Mrs. De La Crème answered wearily. "Just lie back and relax, okay?"

"It's hard to relax when I *stink* so bad."

"I know."

The De La Crème women *did* smell; all the Pilgrims smelled like a Peppertown sewer on its foulest of days. The body odor had gotten worse because of the intense physical labor they had all endured recently. Creamy had created her own mountain monarchy after the group had elevated her to the position of *secret weapon* to get them to Modelland. And Creamy, never known to let an opportunity wither, had leveraged that status to be *elevated*, quite literally: she had ordered the Pilgrims to fashion a *double sedan chair* from scraps found on the Divide. Which they did. To carry the De La Crèmes up the mountain. Which they were doing. It was a small price to pay for Creamy's brave confrontation with the pond monster, after all.

"Remind me *why* are we hauling Queeny and Dope-ical?" Lynne complained while trudging up a steep incline, the post from the thronelike chair digging into her shoulder.

"Break requested, Creamy!" Kamata yelled.

Creamy jutted her mud-caked chin in the air. "Request . . . approved."

As they lowered the women to the ground, Creamy gazed up the mountain. The peak still seemed so far away.

But ahead of them, the scenery changed radically. A lush garden of flowers no one in the group could identify greeted them. The aroma of the buds was almost overpowering—strong citrus that stung their nostrils and a sweet aroma of honey that made their eyes water. Myrracle twirled around the floral bushes and deeply inhaled their scent.

"Yum, Creamy. They all smell so good. I wanna pick *boo-tays* of them!" she trilled, kicking her leg up, smacking it into her ear.

"Bou*quets*, sweetie. You want to pick *bouquets*," Creamy said tiredly.

Suddenly, a haunting, keening sound snaked around the group.

Lynne froze. "It sounds like a woman moaning in pain!"

"Look there!" Abigail said. She pointed her hairy arm toward a small, well-tended cemetery made up of six old polished-marble tombstones with elaborate engravings.

Creamy marched up to the headstones and stared at the markers: MUSE MELODIA, MUSE PRANCIA, MUSE CHROMIA, MUSE DRAMATIA, MUSE FABRICIA, and MUSE CHITECTIA.

"Wow . . . who were they?" Lynne whispered, leaning closer to touch one of the stones.

At her touch, the headstone glowed a golden yellow. The burial ground began to pulse. Kamata pulled his shank spear from his knapsack and crouched into a defensive position. Then came the sound of hundreds of pitter-pattering feet.

"Defensive mode!" Creamy ordered.

Harriet, Lynne, and Hunchy jumped in front of Myrracle and Creamy as if guarding treasure.

The tombstones began to emit angry sparks. A primal scream rang out. But it wasn't coming from the tombstones. It was Abigail. She was looking up the mountain, toward Modelland.

"I have taken your crap for too long!" Abigail screamed. "But I have had it up to *here*! I should have known you wouldn't help me change the world. To spread the word about how beautiful a hairy body can be. And now I . . . have . . . had . . . *enough!*"

Harriet ran over to Abigail and tried to soothe her, but Abigail scuttled toward the rocks and picked up something shiny and metal. It looked like a dagger. "What are you doing, baby?" her mother asked.

From the look in Abigail's eyes, it was clear she couldn't hear her mother. Her mind had gone elsewhere. Abigail yanked at her soiled clothing, pulling everything off. She stood before the Pilgrims stark naked. She gripped the shiny dagger.

"Abby, baby," Harriet pleaded. "Please don't hurt yourself. We can change the world. Get them to accept our kind."

Abigail brought the knife to her chest. "Noooo!" Harriet screamed. But instead of impaling her body with the weapon, Abigail began to scrape her body with it. A tuft of her thick underarm hair tumbled to the ground. With lightning speed, Abigail shaved her sideburns, her arms, her most private of parts, and then her legs. She finished by removing all the knee-length black hair from her head. Every trace of her hair, eyebrows included, was gone and lay in clumps at her feet.

"*Why?*" Harriet wailed. She could barely stand; Lynne held her upright.

"Mom, I am giving it all, minus the portions deemed inappropriate, to Hair for PitterPatter," Abigail said calmly.

Now that she was completely without hair, the group could see the Abigail who had been hiding all along.

"*Preee-teee . . . ,*" Hunchy slobbered, ogling Abigail.

The organ eater was wrong, though. Abigail was not simply pretty. She was out-of-this-world, breathtakingly beautiful—absolutely, undeniably, soul-stirringly stunning. Kamata smiled at her for the first time since the journey had begun. Creamy's expression, however, was the polar opposite of those of the rest of the crew. With Jessamine out of the way, Myrracle had become the most stunning girl in the group. But now, with countless flicks of a makeshift razor, that was no longer the case. Creamy shot Abigail a jealous look of death.

As the group continued to stare, the air filled with the sound of feet flitting toward them, and in the distance, the source of the noise appeared. It was a spiderlike creature three times the size of a Peppertown city bus. But instead of eight legs, this creature had thousands. And the legs looked . . . *human.* They stuck out of the creature's body like the spikes of a porcupine. When the monster

reared up, it revealed a soft, fleshy underbelly. There was an immense leech's sucker in the middle. Tiny but numerous sharp,
toenail-shaped teeth rimmed the opening.

"Oh my," Creamy said, showing a hint of fear for the very first
time. "It's some sort of Leg Leech."

Abigail screamed.

"We should run!" Harriet screamed.

Hunchy howled.

Strangely, Lynne heckled the monster. "I should have dragged
my cheating husband up here! He is a leg man, after all. He would
love you! And the leggy ones always want to take your husband!"

The Leg Leech glared at the group. Then it extended two of
the legs on its body so that they stuck out farther than the multi-
tudes of others, and clicked them together.

"What's it doing?" Kamata whimpered, standing behind
Creamy for protection.

"It's snapping its leg-fingers!" cried Myrracle, and she started
snapping in the same rhythm the creature was. The creature
seemed almost delighted with Myrracle. It turned to the others,
and they all started snapping too. Finally, the creature looked at
Lynne, who wasn't snapping. It waited.

"Huh?" Lynne looked confused.

"Hurry up!" shouted Myrracle. "Snap your fingers like me,
Lynne!"

Lynne began snapping with her right hand to the rhythm of
the Leg Leech's head-bopping beat. The creature seemed pleased,
and motioned for Myrracle and Lynne to join in with both hands.
Myrracle complied, snapping double time while doing her signature high kicks. But Lynne just could not double-snap to perfection, given that she had lost her left hand's middle finger weeks

before. Harriet stopped snapping and walked over to Lynne to help her out.

The creature contorted, then reared back and exposed its toenail-sucker mouth. A forked tendril extended from the center. Two sharp, toenail-clipper blades on the end of the fork made scissoring actions, slicing both Harriet and Lynne at their hips.

"*Oh my God!*" Abigail screamed. "*Do something, Creamy!*"

"I'm your leader, not a magician, dear," Creamy said dryly.

The Leg Leech burped out a pile of Harriet's hair and threw the two women's legs onto its body. They instantly attached, still kicking wildly. Then the creature balanced itself on a group of ten legs. It began to waltz to a place in front of the surviving Pilgrims.

"*I* know how to save us, Creamy!" Myrracle yelled. "*Dancing!*"

Creamy looked at her, relieved. "Do your thing, Myrracle, baby. Dance in your spirit *and* in your body."

Myrracle gazed up at her mother, touched that for the first time Creamy supported her dancing. She proudly ran in front of the Leg Leech and began a rousing back-and-forth dance routine with Bellissima in her arms.

Slowly and joyfully, the Leg Leech retreated, backing away like a thousand ballerinas in unison. If anyone had been standing just a bit closer, they would have noticed that swaying along with Myrracle and Bellissima was one of the ancient tombstones. The one marked MUSE PRANCIA, to be exact.

Just then, a ring of fire encircled the cemetery, Myrracle, and Bellissima.

"Oh my Lord!" Creamy began to run in hysterical circles. "My babies! Somebody get my babies!"

The circle of flames burst high into the air and amassed into a huge fireball, freeing Myrracle and Bellissima. The fireball then flew straight toward Kamata and Abigail. Kamata grabbed Abigail's hand in panic and started to run.

Creamy shouted, "Run that way, Kamata!" Kamata looked disoriented and ran straight into the flames, just as Creamy had instructed. In seconds, nothing of Kamata and Abigail was left. Not even ash.

"Ah, the beauty balance is restored," Creamy said under her breath.

Myrracle stood in shock. "Oh my God. Oh my God. Oh my God."

Creamy walked over and slapped Myrracle hard across both cheeks. "We did not come all this way for you to lose your damn mind! Look at Bellissima! She is handling this so much better than you! Pull it together and let's go!"

"Okay, Creamy," Myrracle whimpered. But as her mother turned her back, Myrracle took her shank and sliced Bellissima's plastic flesh down her hard back.

As Creamy, Myrracle, Bellissima, and Hunchy, the last four surviving Pilgrims, traipsed through the field, Myrracle began to stare at something in the distance. "Ooh . . . look at the pretty lights!"

A terrified scowl appeared on Creamy's face. "Those aren't lights, idiot! Those are more fireballs!"

Four fireballs raged toward the group—one for each of them, even Bellissima. Myrracle and Creamy ran one way and Hunchy ran the other. The fireballs landed, throwing massive sparks everywhere. And then . . . silence.

After a few minutes, Hunchy opened his eyes. He wiggled his toes. Moved his fingers. He was still alive.

He called out, waiting for Creamy's answer. But none came.

Hunchy jumped up from the mud and shook himself off. All that running and dodging had worked up his appetite. He followed the sweet scent not of blood orange, but of the pancreas and thymus glands that lived within one particular platinum-headed Unica, and he resumed his trek to Modelland.

Alone.

37

MANATTACK AND HEARTACHE

Late that night, Tookie and the other Unicas huddled in a circle just outside the D.

"So . . . you're sure that's where the emergency ZipZap is?" Dylan looked uncertain.

There was something about Dylan's voice that bothered Tookie. "For the tenth time, Dylan, yes. Bravo took me there to see it. I don't know how many times I have to repeat myself. I saw the ZipZap with my own eyes. And it's not far from the OrbArena, where ManAttack is happening tomorrow."

"And you're competing?" Piper asked.

"Correct, Piper," Tookie replied.

"Then you leave with pretty boy after AttackMan without Unicas?" Shiraz sighed.

"No. I can't do that," Tookie said sharply, feeling a rush of nausea as soon as she spoke. As much as she'd tried to tamp the feelings down, it was undeniable: she was in love. A love so deep, she never thought it could happen to her. But in order to survive, she would have to leave Bravo and Modelland forever.

She sighed and looked at the Unicas. She didn't want to be in this life-love-or-death situation. And yet she was. "We're going to take that ZipZap," Tookie told the Unicas. "But we need to create a distraction tomorrow so we can get to it without getting caught. You guys have seen the OrbArena, right?"

"Yes, in first-day tour," Shiraz said. "It that crazy egg building with open steel and expose wire."

"Right," Tookie said. "Maybe Piper can scout it out while ManAttack is going on. The exposed wires will make it easier for you to follow the trail to the main lighting switchboard. You need to find the on/off switch and create a blackout."

Piper squinted. "A blackout?"

This response rankled Tookie too. *"Duh,"* she snapped. Piper sounded like a parrot. "I thought you were the *intelligent* one."

Piper recoiled. She exchanged a look with Shiraz and Dylan. Then she fiddled with the puzzle game in her hands and said, "What if I don't find the switchboard?"

"You will," Dylan assured her.

"You is being princess of SansColor!" Shiraz whooped.

Piper narrowed her eyes at her; she seemed annoyed too. "There's no such thing."

"This is Modelland, Piper," Dylan said. "Anything's possible here."

Even a Forgetta-Girl being adored by the most wondrous, lovely Rememba-Boy in the world, Tookie thought.

"Tookie?" Piper said. "Did you hear what I said?"

Tookie turned to Piper and blinked. "Huh?"

Piper's top lip curled over her teeth. *"Duh,"* she mimicked. "I was saying that Dylan needs to be ready for a fainting spell in case we need a diversion. Isn't that right?"

"Uh, yeah." Tookie straightened up. "And that's when you'll find the switch, Piper. And Shiraz, you'll be our natural night-vision so we can find our way out."

Then Shiraz peered at Tookie. "I no like this. This plan all goosey-loosey."

"Look, I'm doing my best here." Tookie gritted her teeth. "You all elected me leader, so I'm *leading*! If you wanted someone else to lead, you shouldn't have picked me!"

"It looks like someone's abusin' their power, Gunnero—I mean BellaDonna. Oops, I mean Tookie," Dylan muttered, rolling her eyes at Tookie so hard that only the whites showed.

"I'll pretend I didn't hear that, Zarpessa—I mean Chaste. Oops, I mean Dylan," Tookie retorted.

"I no like Unicas fighting!" Shiraz took Dylan's and Tookie's hands and made them touch.

"Shiraz, we don't have time for this," Tookie said yanking her hand away from Dylan's. "Do you wanna *die* or do you wanna *live*?"

"Live, I want!"

"Then we have to be *sharp*!"

Shiraz wrapped an arm around Tookie's shoulder. "You tense, no? Because of Bravo?"

Tookie snuck a peek at Shiraz, surprised that she had guessed her secret so easily. Instead of saying anything, Tookie let out a stifled sob.

Dylan's face softened. She wrapped an arm around Tookie too. "Maybe he can come with us."

This just made another rush of emotion swell in Tookie's heart. She hated that she was leaving Bravo behind. She hated that she'd finally found something amazing, Bravo and Modelland, and had to give it up. But Tookie slowly shook her head and held back the tears she knew would render her a weak leader. "No, this is it, girls. Bravo's in heaven here, surrounded by Modelland architecture," she said. "He's living his dream. What we need to be focusing on for ourselves is not living a dream, but just *living*. Pure survival. We have to get out of this place before we are killed. It's as simple as that."

$$\text{M}$$

The next morning, Tookie stood at the bathroom mirror, holding her toothbrush in her hand. Something seemed . . . *different* that morning. No longer did the sight of her toothbrush make her feel a pang of rejection. In fact, when she looked in the mirror, she thought she saw a miracle. A *real* miracle. One that had nothing to do with *The Myrracle* from back home.

Her body no longer resembled a Peppertown twig. There were slight curves at the base of her hips, the same hips that had tickled when Bravo had smoothed down her eyebrows with his dampened thumb. *Am I hallucinating?* she wondered. *Creamy said that the only thing that would develop on me would be a larger forehead as my hairline receded from age. Is this mirror warped?*

Tookie ran her small hands up and down the mirror. The surface was as smooth as the first day she had arrived at Modelland. *Yes, I am definitely hallucinating.*

Crazier still, Tookie could swear that she was—well, she hated to even think the word about herself. The word Dr. Erica had used to describe her. *Prett—*.

Guru Gunnero's voice blared through the air: *"All you pure-and-prude Bellas, it's time to lose it! Your ManAttack virginity, I mean! Report to the OrbArena at once! And don't forget to bring protection! Elbow and knee pads, that is!"* He snickered lewdly.

Every girl in the D seemed surprised except Dylan, Shiraz, Piper, and Tookie.

"Try to kick some Bestosterone prissy-boy ass," Dylan whispered behind Tookie.

"Yes, Tookie," Piper added with a smirk. "We'd appreciate departing this fantastic land with a victory under the Unicas' Sentura belts."

"I'll try," Tookie whispered.

Suddenly, she felt a presence behind her. When she turned, she saw Ci~L standing in the middle of the bathroom, glaring at her. All the red, blue, and purple water spouting out of the holes in the mirrors came to an abrupt stop, as if even the liquid were terrified of Ci~L's presence.

"Uh . . . ," Tookie said, taking two steps backward and hitting the sink behind her. Ci~L stalked up to Tookie and grabbed her wrist. "I'm here to collect you. You're one of the contestants for ManAttack today."

Ci~L yanked Tookie out of the bathroom and walked her down Beautification Boulevard. Banners for the 7Seven Tournament, which would take place the next day, fluttered in the wind. With each step, Tookie considered the could-have-beens and if-onlys that would have meant a different experience at this magical place. *I could have been free of all this dread and doom if only I'd been born looking like . . . like Myrracle.*

"Don't worry," Ci~L said in a cackling voice. "The torture won't last that long. It'll all be over in a flash."

Tookie's mouth fell open. Was the sacrifice going to happen *now*?

Ci~L turned to Tookie as they walked. "After ManAttack is over, you and your little friends better come straight to me."

Tookie froze. There was no way in hell she was meeting Ci~L.

Ci~L leaned closer. "And if you don't find me, *I'll find you.*"

Luckily, they had reached the OrbArena. A Mannecant stepped out from a doorway. "In here," she said, pushing Tookie up a staircase and into a smaller room through a door marked BELLA PREP ZONE. The OrbArena loomed around her, a lattice of metal. Powerful spotlights ran along the outer frame, bouncing beams of artificial light off the structure and illuminating a long wooden plank that traversed the orb. Hundreds of seats were attached to the metal struts on the frame. The seats were empty now. Tookie wondered when the Unicas would arrive. As soon as they did, Piper would scout out the place for the switchboard. She'd report back to Shiraz, who would tell Dylan, and then Dylan would faint. When Piper turned the lights out, Tookie would know to meet them at the southwest corner of the OrbArena, and Shiraz's night vision would guide them to the 7Seven stadium, where the ZipZap was.

"Strip," the Mannecant said.

Tookie stared at her. "Ex*cuse* me?"

"Didn't you know?" The Mannecant's thin lips curved into a smirk. "The ManAttack is performed in one's *underwear*." She pointed at the table; there was a stiff bra-and-panties set marked *Tookie* that was made with complicated strips of fabric.

"How do I put this on?" Tookie asked helplessly.

"Figure it out," the Mannecant said in a cold voice. "The other contestants will be here shortly."

"Who else is competing?" Tookie asked, but the Mannecant had already marched away. Seconds later, two figures stepped through the door. Tookie's heart dropped.

Chaste and Zarpessa.

Zarpessa looked fresh and polished, nothing like the ragged, wild girl who'd been caught in her very own personal Loony Lumière nightmare many nights before. This was the first time Tookie had seen her since the episode. She wondered if Zarpessa had spent the whole time in the FEDS.

Zarpessa glanced over at Tookie, but her face didn't register irritation or malice. Neither a nasty look nor a wicked comment came. *Wow, she's been reformed,* Tookie thought.

"Are you . . . okay?" Tookie asked, walking over to her. She would never have had the courage to do that in Metopia—nor would she have wanted to. But a lot had changed since she'd been at Modelland. "About the other night, I mean. We all do strange things at night sometimes. I sleepwalk, in fact. So I can under-stand what you're going through."

In a flash, Zarpessa's face turned from meek to malicious. She moved so close to Tookie that their noses almost touched. "You understand? You understand *nothing*! You have no idea what it's like to be *me*. You can't, because you and your useless friends have never been on top. And stop being all sweet, pretending like you aren't thrilled about what happened to me that night. When Dr. Erica took me away, did you tell *anyone* about my family?"

Tookie blinked hard. "I didn't say a word! I swear!"

"Yeah, *right*." Zarpessa's eyes narrowed. "If you ever try to say you *understand* me again, I will cut your tongue out. Because your freak-a-zoid, Unfortunate-Looking, water-headed-baby self can't, and you *never* will!"

And then Zarpessa spun away, shoulders squared, her hands repeatedly opening and closing into fists. Chaste followed, shooting Tookie a nasty look. *You weren't so crazy about Zarpessa the other night,* Tookie wished she could remind Chaste, remembering how the girl had taken a big step away from Zarpessa in the throes of her breakdown.

Zarpessa and Chaste stepped through the door to the Orb-Arena and out onto the wooden plank, testing how it felt. Chaste started bouncing up and down on the plank, higher than possible in regular gravity. A giant scoreboard loomed in the sphere. Tookie spotted her name immediately—she would compete last. And then, to her horror, she spotted her competitor.

MANATTACK	
MODELLAND	BESTOSTERONE
CHASTE VS. ALEXANDER	
ZARPESSA VS. WEBB	
TOOKIE VS. BRAVO	

"No," Tookie whispered. *Anyone* but Bravo.

Within minutes, the seats filled with excited Bellas and enthusiastic Bestosteros, as well as a sprinkling of Gurus. Tookie spotted Guru Pacifico, his eyebrows looking as if they were having a conversation with the ebony-skinned Bestostero on his right, while his mouth seemed to converse with the hazel-eyed Bella behind him. Guru Applaussez's hand-head waved in the air like a beauty queen on a parade float.

The girls disappeared back into the Prep Zone and put on their undergarments. Chaste and Zarpessa fit into theirs nicely, but Tookie just looked ashy and sticklike. *Shoot, I'm going to have to escape in this lingerie!* Tookie thought. She hated the idea of leaving through the ZipZap in just her skivvies.

After they'd changed, Zarpessa, Chaste, and Tookie stepped out of the Prep Zone and were assaulted by the roar of rowdy crowd noise. Bellas had taken off their Senturas and were using them as flags. And everyone, of course, was staring at the six scantily clad girls and boys, for the Bestosteros had donned couture briefs made of strips of material like those of the girls' costumes. The briefs exposed slits of their buttocks, and left bare all of their rippling muscles. Tookie peeked at Bravo. He looked so amazing and gorgeous she felt the urge to throw up.

"Welcome, pretty ladies and even prettier gentlemen, *bienvenue* to ManAttack!" Gunnero Narzz's voice boomed from the sky. The crowd yelled and stomped their feet. Gunnero lowered into the OrbArena standing on top of a hovering podium shaped like the male and female gender symbols. "It's been a while since the two sexes got to have a mix-up like tonight. I'm sure everyone's hormones are raging more than mine!"

Just then, Tookie spotted a flash of white hair between the steel beams. *Piper!* She was looking for the switch! She glanced at Bravo again, standing across the plank with Alexander and Webb. Her eyes filled with tears.

Narzz continued. "As it has been played for eons, there are four phases to ManAttack. First, the Touch. Oh yes—contact, people . . . between man and woman. Second, Wardrobe. But if you want, you can stay half nude. Fun for the crowd, oh yes indeed, but point deductions for the players. Third, Maquillage. Makeup, that is. Foundation for the girls, Mandation for the boys. Can someone get me some? My color is Ivory Sands Number Three. Oh, and watch out for those pesky explosives, lads and lasses! And fourth and finally, the Snaps. The Photo Finish. Yes, we take pictures here 'cause they last longer!"

"Bravo, I want to have your babies! We can start trying right there on that plank, right now!" a Bella behind Applaussez shouted from the crowd.

A couple of Bestosteros whistled lasciviously. Tookie noticed Bravo trying to catch her eye down the plank, but she pointedly looked away. She'd thought she could avoid him today, escape without having to have a conversation. It would be easier that way, after all. Cleaner. Fewer tears. Less desire to stay. But now she had to *battle* him. *Maybe Piper will find the switch before I have to go through with it,* she thought. *Maybe we'll get out of here before I have to face him.*

"One more thing," Gunnero said, still balancing primly on the masculine- and feminine-symbol plank. "Please, boys and girls: no strikes to the face or to the boys' 'neither-nether' regions. Pain of that kind is *not* beauty. Now, on with the show! Up first! Chaste from Modelland and Alexander from Bestosterone! The rest of the competitors, return to your Prep Zones!"

The crowd roared again, and Tookie and Zarpessa walked back into the girls' zone. A buzzer sounded and Chaste walked a few paces more out onto the plank on the Bella side. Alexander moved onto the plank from the Bestostero side. Chaste stood seductively and stared at her opponent, giving him a full dose of her sexual power. Her Sentura motioned seductively, looking like a beckoning finger.

"Look at you, girl, knowing the ropes!" Gunnero said. "Methinks somebody took part in the new Civilian-Modelland Man-Attack Summer Program in Beignet!"

Chaste posed sexily, hands in her hair, one toe pointed. She was truly a sight to behold. Tookie saw Alexander's knees buckle just slightly.

"Be warned, Alexander! Chaste is randy hard-up candy!" Gunnero announced in falsetto. "Listen up! First theme: Fitness Battle. Yoga versus karate. You both have opened new businesses next door to each other. WHO refuses to go bankrupt? Get ready for the Touch. . . ."

Suddenly, there was a knock on the Bella Prep Zone door. Zarpessa turned and answered it. "Oh!" she chirped, a welcoming grin on her face. "Well, *hello* there! I don't think you're supposed to be in here, but . . ."

Tookie's heart flipped.

It was Bravo.

Bravo pushed past Zarpessa, barely noticing her. "Tookie! Isn't this incredible?" He grabbed her hands. "They put us together. I'm excited *and* nervous."

Bravo turned to her. "Uh, Zarpessa, right? Would you mind going out in the hall so I can speak with Tookie in private?"

Zarpessa looked like she was about to laugh. "Really? *Why?*" Bravo stared at her until a look of disbelief crossed her face. "You *can't* be serious." She jutted a thumb at Tookie. *"Her?"*

"Yeah, *her*," Bravo said, clenching his jaw. "And she has a name that I know you know."

Zarpessa pushed through the door and slammed it hard.

Bravo's hand caressed Tookie's shoulder, and he began to sink his fingers into her back muscles. Tookie let out a breath; his touch had made that tickling in her hips return. "What's the matter, pretty girl? Pre-competish jitters?" Now his hands massaged Tookie's scalp, his hands tangling in her curly, wavy, straight, frizzy hair. "Understandable. Gunnero loves to just throw new Bellas out there and watch them struggle. Let me tell you how this game really works so you won't be too surprised. That center plank?" He pointed at it. "That is your friend. Stay on it. You fall off while we're playing, you lose ten points. See?"

He gestured out the window. A piercing buzzer sounded, and Chaste and Alexander ran at top speed toward each other. When Chaste was five feet in front of the boy, she grabbed Alexander and gave him a big, wet, sloppy kiss on the lips and then pushed him off the plank. Alexander tumbled toward the ground but seemed to land on an invisible trampoline, suddenly bouncing back into the air.

"Antigravity," Bravo explained. "Much better than circus nets." He pointed at Chaste. "Wow, she may be loose, but her game is tight. We're just supposed to run at each other at full speed and just touch hands or something, minimum. By the way, that's *not* how I'm going to kiss you."

Tookie's stomach churned like a blender on high. "Bravo," she said in a tiny voice. "I really need to tell you something."

But Bravo didn't appear to hear her, explaining more of the challenge. "Next, clothes come shooting out of those three holes in the struts." He pointed to places on the struts above the plank, to the left and right and center. "We have to assemble a high-fashion—and on-theme, don't forget—outfit from what's thrown at us. You have to think really fast. Chaste and Alex will be trying to pick an outfit that matches their yoga/martial arts theme."

As Alexander struggled to get back up onto the plank, the three holes on the struts began firing clothes at Chaste. A black-diamond-studded belt with black tassels streamed out of the hole to the right, and ruched leotards came out of the one to the left; raw-silk karate parachute pants came from the hole up above, the matching jacket from the left; stretch pants and even yoga mats flew out of all the holes.

It quickly became clear that Chaste had picked the part of karate instructor since she was putting on the white jacket and pants and was holding on to the black-diamond-studded belt. As Alexander struggled to his feet, Chaste hurled a mass of yoga clothing into his face. He had no choice but to assemble the feminine pieces into an outfit.

"Chaste scores a point in my book!" Gunnero commented. "Picking kick-ass over stretch-ass!"

"Bravo," Tookie pleaded. "I need to—"

"Hold up, hold up." Bravo tenderly squeezed her hand. "Now it's time for the Make-Up phase. You don't need much. Just a little cream-flavored gloss, maybe, so I can taste it when we kiss. . . ." Then he pointed. "You have to be careful of those Makeup Bombs, though. They're actually called Maki Balls. Look!"

Sure enough, red and blue balls appeared out of thin air. The red ones whizzed around Chaste's face. She did two fast backward cartwheels to catch two. She rubbed a red one, and shimmering pink powder appeared on her fingertips. Chaste spread it over her cheeks. She threw a blue one at Alexander. Oil and flesh-colored ooze and black soot exploded onto his chest.

"Way to give a guy blue balls, honey!" Gunnero crowed.

"Those red Maki Balls have makeup inside them for Bellas—blush, eye stuff, and lipstick. The blue ones are for us and are filled with stuff called Mandation. Our Maki Balls also have body oil, and charcoal for smoky eyes," Bravo explained. "Just rub your fingers on the various parts and dab it on. Applying makeup is mandatory—you get points taken off if you don't. The more skillful the job, the better."

Chaste smeared black eye shadow over just one eye and a jagged line of bright red lipstick to one side of her mouth. The red ball beeped faster and faster the longer Chaste held it.

"Once you touch them, they're activated, and after a short while, *kaboom!* They explode!" Bravo explained. "So throw them away as fast as you can—your opponent gets ten points if one explodes on you."

Bravo gently turned her around to face him. He slowly put his hand to his mouth, licked his thumb, and gently rubbed Tookie's eyebrow with it. Tookie's body tickled all the way from her hips to her ankles. He then wrapped his strong arms around her and pulled her in tight. The side of her face was pressed against his bare chest and she could feel his heart pumping in sync with hers.

Tookie's eyes fluttered closed. She loved having him caress her. She knew she would never have a stunning young man like this cradle her with such tenderness ever again. She wanted to hold on to this, on to *him*, until the very last drop was left. Three drops left . . . two . . .

But she couldn't do this. She couldn't lead Bravo on. Tookie looked around the arena. She didn't see Piper's pale hair anywhere. Hadn't she found the switch yet? What was taking her so long?

She pulled away and stared into Bravo's eyes. "Bravo, about what happens after ManAttack—"

Bravo's mouth was close to Tookie's ear. "The next part is the most important part. See that Gyro up there along the strut? After we're dressed and made up, it starts jerking all around us and starts a countdown from *Z* to *A*. When it reaches *A*, it snaps a photo of us. If Chaste manages to be the focal point of the photo, she gets more points. If Alexander overshadows her, he gets more. The important thing to remember is that Modelland is competing against Bestosterone, but we're also competing against our own team members to be number one. Kinda like gymnastics in the world games."

Two camera flashes turned the OrbArena bright white. Three-dimensional images of Chaste and Alexander flashed above the plank in the middle of the OrbArena. A sports siren sounded, indicating the end of the round and also the beginning of Tookie's momentary deafness.

"Bold-faced Chaste. Black-eye and bloody-lip maquillage, to boot. I guess the girl knows her way around Cosme-*dics*," Gunnero trilled over the loudspeaker.

A charge of electricity sparkled through the scoreboard, which promptly displayed the score.

Modelland: Chaste, 85 points. Bestosterone: Alexander, 30 points.

"Yes!" Chaste screamed. She took a huge bounding leap off the plank and made a soft landing in a group of Bestosteros sitting in a line of seats along the struts.

Gunnero then called Zarpessa's name. "Okay Miss Zarpesta, let's see what you're made of! Your theme? Lady spider and her insect of prey! Can our sexy arachnid catch her fly, or will you get caught in *his* web of leather and lace?"

Bravo turned back to Tookie. "I know it's a lot to absorb, but it's actually a fun game," Bravo said. "Do I need to take you through it again?"

Tookie stared at him. Suddenly, she felt full of rage. "No, I *don't* want you to take me through it again. I've been *trying* to tell you something for the last fifteen minutes, and you haven't heard me at all!"

Bravo blinked at her. "What is it?"

He was staring at her so patiently, without a clue of what was coming next. It felt like there was a huge rock on Tookie's chest, preventing her from taking a full breath. "I'm escaping from Modelland. Today."

His eyes bulged. *"What?"*

"I've been trying to tell you! My friends and I—we have to. We're going through the hidden ZipZap soon—maybe in just minutes. This is goodbye."

Bravo's eyes darted back and forth, trying to make sense of Tookie's news. "You're leaving through *our* ZipZap? The one you asked me to show you? The one *I* wanted to take you through *tonight*?"

"That's right."

". . . With*out* me?"

"Yes." She turned away, not wanting to look at him.

"Why?" Bravo asked.

In the arena, Gunnero crowed at the Wardrobe battle. "Nice use of fishnets, Webb! Way to trap that itsy-bitsy spider!"

Tookie lowered her eyes. She couldn't tell him the truth. "Because I *have* to, okay? I can't stay here. It's something I can't explain."

Slowly, Bravo's eyes grew cold. "You weren't going to tell me about this, were you? If we weren't paired up today. If I hadn't come to see you just now. You were just going to . . . go! Through *our* ZipZap! You *used* me!"

Tookie's heart felt like it was being squeezed in a vise. The crushed tone of Bravo's voice made her want to wilt to the floor. But she tried to stay strong. "I didn't use you."

"Yeah, you did! After I poured my heart out to you! After I told you a story I *never* told anybody before!"

"I'm sorry," Tookie said, trying to shove all her tumultuous feelings aside.

Then Bravo crossed his arms over his chest. "Well, Tookie, I'll tell you a little secret, too. You and me, kissing? It was nothing but a bet with my boys."

Her head whipped up. *"What?"*

"That's right." There was no joy in Bravo's smile. "I made a bet with Webb and Alex that I could get a funny-looking girl to fall in love with me. The pretty ones . . . they're easy. But the weird-looking ones . . . they're the ultimate challenge."

Tookie took a huge step back. It felt like he'd reached into her body and pulled out both her lungs. *You can't be serious,* she wanted to say. But maybe . . . he *could.* Look at her. She was a circus freak. Nothing like the gorgeous creatures who populated this school. All her fears, all her instincts, had proven to be true. She *was* nothing but a joke.

"So I guess we're not so different, you and I," Bravo said in a stoic, iron-cold voice. The voice of someone who didn't care—who had *never* cared. "We're both heartless. A perfectly imperfect match."

"*Get out!*" Tookie screamed.

"Peace." He spun around and stormed away.

Tookie was so stunned and shaken she could barely move. *I almost let him in. I should have* known *better! Look at him! Why in the hell would you think he would ever want a fugly freak-a-zoid Forgetta-Girl like you?*

Thunderous cheers rumbled from the OrbArena. The Gyro reared back to life and jerked around the duo, gearing up to take its photo of Webb and Zarpessa, who was dressed in a black cat-suit with dangling strips that looked like spider legs, complete with a webby mesh mask on her face. The crowd began to recite the alphabet backward. . . .

"*Z . . . Y . . . X . . .*"

Zarpessa eyed the jerking Gyro as she flitted around Webb. She jumped up to avoid a blue Maki Ball that scurried along the plank. Meanwhile, Tookie held on to the wall, realizing she was on the brink of breaking down to a place so deep and dangerous she wasn't sure she could return. *A fugly Forgetta-Girl. That's all I'll ever be.*

"*. . . M . . . L . . . K . . .*"

But then, suddenly, an inner light flicked on inside Tookie. She let go of the wall and mustered the strength to stand tall. *Hold it together,* she told herself. She was the leader of the Unicas. They needed her to be strong to get them out of Modelland.

"...*G*...*F*...*E*..."

I'm tired of feeling powerless, Tookie thought. Powerless against her mother's favoritism of Myrracle. Powerless against her father's decision to throw her away. Powerless against Zarpessa and her wrath. But now, she *could* have the power. She could change her future. She wouldn't let Bravo's verbal blows make her crumble.

"...*D*...*C*..."

Tookie peered back out into the arena. With the speed of a black widow going in for the kill, Zarpessa leapt into the air, tightened her Sentura around her waist, and fell at Webb's feet.

"...*B*..."

Zarpessa gazed up at the moving Gyro. Her body went artistically angular. She wrapped her many fishnets around Webb as if her web was strangling him to death.

SNAP! The image was displayed above Zarpessa and Webb.

"Isn't she lovely?" Gunnero cooed. "A deer-widow caught in Webb-lights! She may be a brat, but our Zar also may be a star."

The scoreboard delivered its verdict:

Modelland: Zarpessa, 92 points. Bestosterone: Webb, 25 points.

"Oooo, ninety-two," Gunnero announced. "Sorry, Chaste, but our little tarantu-*pessa* got you beat. Up next . . . Crazy Eyes—I mean Tookie from Modelland! And . . ."

Tookie eyed Bravo on the other side of the OrbArena. All of a sudden, her trembling hands went still. Her heart thudded, full of blood and adrenaline. *You're powerFUL,* she told herself. *And you're going to let Bravo and all those other Bestosterone brats see that. You're going to Kick. His. Ass!*

". . . beauteous Bravo from Bestosterone!" Gunnero finished.

Tookie lurched out onto the plank like a tiger sprung from its cage. Bravo stepped out on his side. His hunched posture made him look self-conscious in his couture ManAttack underwear.

"Tookie and Bravo?" Gunnero crowed. "The Beast and the Beauty, right? Theme? Queen versus Court. Court wants to overthrow Queen and steal her crown and jewels. Bravo, you can steal my family jewels any day. . . ."

The piercing buzzer sounded. Tookie and Bravo ran down the plank toward each other at top speed. Bravo stretched out his hand. Ten feet away . . . six feet . . . three feet . . . and then . . . *Contact!* Tookie's arm hooked Bravo across the neck, throwing him off the plank headfirst. The crowd gasped. Bravo's head was an inch from the ground, and then he was yanked back up by the antigravity pull of the OrbArena.

"Crazy Eyes may not just *look* crazy . . . ," Gunnero trilled.

The crowd let out a mix of cheers and boos—but Bravo was obviously the favorite. As the antigravity pushed Bravo back to the plank, he shot Tookie a look of surrender. But Tookie glared at him, years of pain and rage bubbling up inside of her. No way was she was backing down. Not after she found out she was nothing but a *bet*.

"Phase two . . . Wardrobe!" Gunnero crowed.

A crown whipped toward Tookie, hitting her square in the face. The force knocked her backward. Then a queen's dress with a Jeremy Jurk label pelted her leg. Next came a ruby-encrusted bracelet that was as long as her entire arm. She struggled to put the bracelet on.

"Stop!" Tookie moaned, kicking and thrashing at the clothing and crown. A blazer embellished with an armor breastplate punched Tookie in the stomach. She floated awkwardly away from the plank. Bravo grabbed her waist and pulled her back onto the plank.

Gunnero snickered. "Bella girls, that fire you smell? It's your representative from Modelland, and she's being barbequed . . . going down in flames. Me? I'll have a hot dog. Plain, without the bun, please . . ."

Tookie squirmed away from Bravo's aid. When she turned around again, Bravo wore the blazer of armor with no shirt and a royal soldier's helmet made of wool. He looked so handsome her insides did a flip. But reality kicked back in quickly—*the bet.* She puckered her lips.

"What are you doing?" Bravo whispered.

"Giving you your first smacker from me," she teased. "Oh, come on, Bravo, baby, close your eyes!"

He did. Tookie brought her ruby-braceleted arm behind her, clenched her fist, and hit Bravo in the face.

"Ooh, baby, does it feel good?" she yelled, a crazed look in her eyes.

A penalty horn sounded.

"Minus five points before Maquillage?" Gunnero tsked. "That's one bitter queen!"

"Kick her in the head, Bravo!" Webb yelled from the audience. "That should be an easy target to hit!"

Bravo stood and gaped at Tookie. Blood dripped from his nose. "I'm not a punching bag, Tookie!"

"And *I* am *not* a joke!" Tookie screamed.

The blue and red explosive Maki Balls appeared. In frustration, Bravo kicked them to the ends of the plank, away from him and Tookie. But they bounced right back up.

"Kicking the Maki Balls? Ouch! Ten points off Bravo!" Gunnero admonished.

"Tookie, you have to get dressed!" Bravo urged. "Put something on!" He gestured to the floating clothes around her head.

"Why the heck are you helping me?" Tookie snapped. "I don't need your pity. I'm nothing but a bet to you!" She grabbed one of the Maki Balls and rubbed it. Lip gloss spilled out, and she smeared it on her lips. "My first kiss, Bravo—my *real* first kiss? Know what it's going to be?"

He paused, waiting.

"It's going to be under a perfect sunset, near a garden of golden flowers spreading as far as the eye can see," Tookie said, making it up as she went along. "The lucky guy who will get to pucker with my suckers will be wearing a . . . tuxedo. And . . . and he's going to sing to me a song he wrote, and he'll . . . dance to it. It needs to make me laugh and make me cry."

Bravo blinked. "Are you for real?"

"Hell yeah, I'm for real! Then he will open up his shirt like a superhero," she went on. "On his chest will be written *Tookie, you are the most amazing girl I have ever laid eyes on. And I can't decide which I love more, your green or your brown eye.* Then he'll have to touch my face gently with both hands." Her eyes spilled newer, fresher tears. "And he'll kiss my forehead, both of my cheeks, and then my nose. Then he'll spray whipped cream straight into my mouth and then his. And then he'll part his mouth just a little and press his lips against mine. And for me, it will feel like the kiss will never end. Because it won't. It will go on forever. And it will be *amazing!*"

Tookie's chest was heaving. Between sobs, she was having difficulty catching her breath.

Bravo just stared. Suddenly, the photo Gyro came to life, bucking and weaving around them. The countdown began.

"Z . . . Y . . . X . . ."

Bravo moved closer to Tookie. "I want you to win. Mess me up really bad, okay? I don't care how hard you go at me. Throw a Maki Ball at me."

"Don't take any more pity on me!" Tookie roared.

"But I *haven't*," Bravo said. "I've never pitied you."

"You're a big fat devious *liar*!" Furious, Tookie plopped the queenly couture crown on her head but held on to it. *I should throw it at him.* She held it in her hand, debating what to do.

". . . S . . . R . . . P . . ."

Bravo sank to his knees. "You realize, Tookie, that even if you throw that crown at me, you'll still lose. But there is one way you can win."

"What?"

"Maki Balls. Two of them."

". . . N . . . M . . ."

"Activate them," he urged. "Then I'll take them both and hold on to them."

Tookie stared curiously at him. "You'll lose fifty points."

"And you'll get them."

". . . I . . ."

She placed her hands on her hips. "Why are you doing this, Bravo? Feeling guilty?"

". . . H . . ."

"A little bit," Bravo said. "You . . . you deserve better than me, Tookie."

". . . G . . ."

Tookie stared at him, a whole new kind of rage boiling inside her. "I deserve better? Damn right I deserve better! And there *is* better than you, Bravo—believe it or not. Theophilus Lovelaces!"

The crowd fell silent. But suddenly, from the wings, Zarpessa let out a shriek. "Theophilus? *My* Theophilus?"

Bravo blinked hard at Tookie. "Who's Theophilus? D-do you have some other dude at home?"

"He's not tall and not a pouting Bestostero pretty boy like you. Girls everywhere don't scream out that they want his babies. But he's *better* than you, Bravo. Smarter than you."

"Is *that* why you're leaving?" Bravo whispered. "Because you wanna be with *him*?"

Tookie turned away. If Bravo wanted to think that, then let him.

Bravo shook his head in disbelief. "I can't believe you, girl. And just so you know, there was *never* a bet. I just said that because I was pissed at you—because you used me and I wanted to hurt you back. But now I think there *should* have been."

Tookie blinked at him. Could he be telling the truth?

". . . F . . ."

Bravo's salted-caramel eyes looked so sincere. His lips were still moving, but Tookie couldn't hear a word over the roar of the crowd. She tried to emblazon him in her memory. A person who could seem so genuine but totally fool you. Just like Ci~L had.

"Tookie," Bravo said, "just pick up the damn Maki Balls and get this over with."

Without a word, she picked up a red Maki Ball, her touch activating it. Tingly jolts of electricity tickled her palms. Instead of blush or lipstick, though, streaks of yellow liquid appeared on her fingers. *That's weird . . . is it the body oil Bravo was talking about?*

But that was supposed to be in the blue *Maki Balls.* The liquid began to solidify and then buzzed in her hands. Was it about to explode?

She stared at the peculiar half-liquid/half-solid substance. The buzzing turned into convulsions, and then, gradually, the substance formed into a cellophane-thin sheet. The object was now rising and falling as if it was alive. Tookie's mouth dropped open. *Is this . . . ?*

"A SMIZE!" Gunnero called. "Hot damn, we haven't had one of those little babies appear in our Maki Balls for quite some time! It's a lucky charm, Crazy Eyes! Cover those loony peepers of yours and put your spectators' eyes out of their misery!"

Slowly, Tookie put the SMIZE on her face. The moment it touched her skin, she felt a jolt in her heart. Her head cleared and filled with an incredible pulsing energy. *So this is what a SMIZE feels like,* she thought, feeling stronger and more powerful than ever before. She felt beyond special—as if a switch had been turned on, illuminating her from the inside and dimming everyone else.

Her senses were on fire. Each breath Bravo took reached her ears. Her taste buds were flooded with every delectable whipped cream she'd ever tasted. Neon colors dazzled her eyes, and the air smelled like lime and crushed mint, island coconut and rosemary and buttercream frosting.

Tookie felt—no, she *was*—intoxicating. Waves of words flowed into her brain.

Magnifique. Omorfos. Vacker. Schön. Mei-li. Mooie. Guapa. Sundar. Maganda. Chachowww. Belle. Hundreds of words coming from the SMIZE that all meant the same majestic, wonderful, marvelous, magnificent, mind-blowing thing.

Beautiful.

As she turned to Bravo, his jaw dropped.

"Oh. My. God," he said, staring at her, transfixed. When Tookie looked into the crowd, everyone else was gawking at her too. Even Webb, Alexander, and O'Neil. Even Zarpessa, who, like the other Bellas, paled in comparison to Tookie's ravishing glow. Even Gunnero looked spellbound as he whispered "Whoa . . . Super Modelland Eyes . . ." into the microphone.

Then Bravo stood, took the second red Maki Ball from Tookie's hands, and placed it on his chest. The Maki Ball rose and fell with his fast breath.

"... E ..."

Tookie watched him. The Ball's beeps quickened.

"... D ..."

She stood over Bravo. In the few remaining seconds, she placed her hand near her mouth, stuck out her tongue, and licked her thumb ever so slowly. Then she leaned down, glared into Bravo's eyes, and wiped each of his eyebrows with it. It felt good. *Vengeful.*

With three big leaps, she was back near her end of the plank.

Kaboom! The Maki Ball exploded, spraying its contents all over Bravo, covering him in bright, garish color.

"... C ... B ..."

In what seemed like the millisecond that Tookie had remaining, she ran back to Bravo and stood over him, and remembering her CaraCaraCara lessons, she made her face express the exact opposite of what she was feeling.

She smiled.

Bravo turned his face *away* from the camera.

SNAP!

The Gyro's image floated above the OrbArena.

For Modelland: Tookie, 106 points. For Bestosterone: Bravo, 19 points.

"Is that thing broken?" Gunnero cried. "It beauty-is-pains me to say this, but you all have just witnessed the greatest turnaround in ManAttack history! Tookie from Modelland has scored 106 points, Run-a-Way-ing past her competitors! Tookie is . . . ugh, it hurts . . . our, uh . . . new champion."

"I won?" Tookie asked incredulously. "Are you serious? I won?"

Suddenly, a high-pitched scream rang from the crowd. "She fainted! Oh my God, that big girl fainted!"

Dylan!

And then the OrbArena went dark.

Pitch-black.

It was time.

38

LEFT, RIGHT, LEFT

It sounded like the whole OrbArena was screaming. There were clangs, then shouts, then a blaring fire alarm. Tookie blinked in the darkness. She couldn't see a thing.

A voice yelled in her ear. "Is me! Shiraz. Come. I see perfect!"

Shiraz grabbed Tookie and led her off the plank, back through the Prep Zone, and down to the ground. As she hit the earth, she felt the SMIZE flutter away from her face. She tried to grab for it, but the rice-paper-thin talisman had disappeared into the darkness. "Where are the others?" she whispered.

"Here!" two voices said in unison. It was Dylan and Piper.

Inside, panicking ManAttack spectators pushed and

screamed. Shiraz muscled through an unnoticed door and the girls stumbled through it. Tookie looked back at the OrbArena. The rumbling of trapped spectators practically shook the steel struts. "We created this chaos," she cried. "We can't just leave them in there!"

"We gotta get outta here now," Dylan said. "We made an opportunity. Now we gotta take it!"

"Not only did I find out where the switch was," Piper said as she panted, out of breath, "I found the emergency ZipZap too. It's exactly where you said it was. C'mon!"

They ran to the stadium. Now completed, it was massive. Its elaborate architecture cast eye-patterned reflections on the ground. The girls scampered up a path cordoned off by a metal banner, across which scrolled blinking words that read NO ENTRY UNTIL THE 7SEVEN TOURNAMENT! Making sure no one saw them, Tookie and her friends scooted around the blockade. Before she went into the stadium, Tookie turned back, exhaled, and took one final look at Modelland. *Goodbye, Kamalini. Goodbye, Guru Lauro. Goodbye, Dr. Erica. Goodbye, Bravo. . . .*

"It's time, Tookie," Piper urged.

Tookie ducked under the banner. Instantly, Piper rushed down four flights of stairs into the depths of the stadium, the girls right behind her. A giant pile of stones lay in front of them. Following Piper's lead, they began lifting the rocks until a horizontal ZipZap flush with the ground appeared under the rubble. It had jagged, pointed, rusty teeth and a zipper pull that flamed crimson, as if warning not to touch it. Taking a deep breath, Tookie yanked it open. "Ouch!" It was hot to the touch. A whirlpool of thick, hot air and reddish liquid whipped inside.

"Is blood?" Shiraz wondered aloud, holding tightly to Dylan's hand. Muted screams streamed out from the deep.

"Let's go," Tookie said. And then, after a slight hesitation, she fell straight backward and disappeared into the hole.

$$\text{M}$$

The girls' bodies twisted around the curves of the ZipZap. It was pitch-black inside the tunnel; terrifying growling and wailing sounds echoed off its walls. The tunnel's surface was hot, burning through the girls' clothing and singeing Tookie's bare legs. Everyone yelped in pain.

Suddenly, the path leveled off. Tookie saw a fork straight ahead.

"Left or right? Left or right?" Tookie screamed. "I think we should go left!"

"No! Right!" Shiraz answered.

"Left!" Piper said.

"No, right!" Dylan said.

Tookie leaned to the right. The girls did the same. They whipped through a new tube. Gradually, a pinprick of light appeared at the end of the tunnel. Where would they end up? In LaDorno, or in the Diabolical Divide? Tookie's heart thumped.

The light grew closer and closer. Dylan screamed. As they reached the end, they picked up speed, their bodies whipping against the tube. And then, suddenly . . .

Thump!

The girls fell into a pool of thick red mud. The air smelled charred and rotten. There were no telltale signs of LaDorno anywhere. No buildings, no streets, no cars. Tookie looked into the air and saw four fireballs shooting straight toward them.

"We're in the Divide!" she screamed. "Get back in the ZipZap!"

They all tried to stand, but the mud sucked them downward. Tookie rose and then fell face-first in the mud. It stung her eyes.

"I got you!" Tookie yelled. From somewhere deep within, she found the strength to rise. She then reached down and, one at a time, pulled Piper, Dylan, and Shiraz free.

"Hurry up!" Tookie screamed over the sound of crackling flames. "Back in the ZipZap!"

Just before the four fireballs were about to consume them, the girls jumped back into the ZipZap. Tookie took the left fork and the girls continued to slide, until . . . *splash!*

Tookie's nose burned with the scent and taste of chlorine. Blue-gray buildings rose around her. The moon hung high in the sky overhead. A few lonely cars whipped around a traffic circle. Beyond it was the mist-covered mountain of Modelland.

She looked down and saw water lapping at her neck. She looked to the side and saw a statue of Mayor Devin Rump standing beside her.

They were in a fountain in LaDorno.

"We made it!" Dylan yelped. She splashed over to Tookie and gave her a huge hug. "And you were right. We shoulda gone left!"

Piper waded over and hugged Tookie, and then Shiraz did too.

"Now what?" Dylan said, tucking a clump of wet blond hair behind her ear.

Once they broke free, they looked around at one another, suddenly realizing something.

"I guess we go our separate ways." Piper pointed out what they were all thinking. "I'll find my way back to SansColor. And . . . to Mother, the *queen*." She made a face.

"Back to Canne Del Abra," Shiraz said morosely. "Will again deliver good news to the people, but no to me."

"I'll hop a train or somethin' to Bou-Big-Tique, I guess," Dylan murmured. "Back to the customer service desk. Back to life confined in a store." Her jaw trembled slightly. She gazed up at the mountain.

"What do *I* do now?" Tookie said aloud, not expecting an answer.

Suddenly, Dylan's face fell. She stared at something in the sky. "Tookie . . ." Her voice shook. *"Run!"*

To Tookie's horror, she saw Ci~L's familiar pouch, in flying mode. It swooped ominously above them, dropping lower and lower with each rotation. She was coming after them!

The girls screamed and clambered out of the fountain, running down an alley, ducking under fire escapes and around garbage containers, and climbing over fences, Ci~L's pouch in pursuit.

They skidded to a stop at an open manhole cover. They scooted down the ladder and ran through a labyrinth of dark, steaming tunnels. "Where we go now?" Shiraz yelled.

"We're heading north by northeast," Piper advised. "Head up the next ladder we find!"

Fifty steps later, they found a ladder leading up through an open manhole. Tookie scrambled up and out once more, emerging in the deserted town square. She looked around at the marble ground and the giant clock in the center. *This is where Metopia's T-DOD is held,* she realized. It looked so empty and desolate, devoid of people, walkers, souvenir sellers. The clock tower loomed in the corner, and various fountains spewed water on all sides. Immense billboards of Intoxibellas Evanjalinda and Bev Jo decorated the sides of buildings.

As Tookie spun around, she noticed a telltale question-mark-shaped crack in the pavement and felt a clenching in her stomach. This was the exact point where Ci~L had selected her for Modelland. Right here, on the edge of the square, Ci~L had appeared out of the top of the car, extending her hand to Tookie. Over Myrracle. Over *everyone*.

She gazed up at the mist-covered mountain once more, a pang of regret and nostalgia mixing inside of her. So much had happened, she felt like an entirely different person. And yet she was in the exact same place she'd started.

A strange scratching sound emerged from behind a nearby trash can. Shiraz grabbed Tookie's arm. "What that?"

"I don't know," Tookie whispered. "Shhh."

The scratching noises intensified. Something breathed raspily in and out, in and out. A dog? A cat?

"What if it's Ci~L?" Piper whispered.

Tookie stepped back, her heart thudding hard. But before she could turn around and make yet another escape, something larger than a cat climbed out of the trash can. A burr-riddled, dread-locked redhead dressed in a hospital gown, a series of fresh cuts and burns on her arms.

Tookie's jaw dropped. "Oh my God," she whispered.

Lizzie.

Lizzie's eyes locked with Tookie's and she let out a joyful yet mournful yelp. The two girls ran for each other, crashing together hard. After a long embrace, Lizzie stuck her hands out to her sides, palms up. Tookie did the same. Both girls pointed to the sky, then made a motion as if checking their underarms for a scent, then did a deep curtsy. *"What's up, Hot Queen?"* they cried together. Lizzie stared at Tookie's arm, which was still adorned with the long ruby bracelet from ManAttack. "You really *are* a queen today, girl!" she whooped.

"You have no idea, Lizzie." Tookie had *felt* like a queen with the SMIZE. It had fallen off after ManAttack. *I wonder where it went.* Maybe one of the crazed Bellas back in the OrbArena had found and pocketed it. Maybe the Likees. . . .

The Unicas watched them, cocking their heads, trying to make sense of the reunion.

Then Tookie grabbed Lizzie's hands. "Is it really *you*, Lizzie? I was sure you'd be *gone* by now!"

"Oh no." Lizzie shook her head. "I've been waiting for you, Tookie. Right here, all day, every day. Well, I hide in the daytime, of course—they *see* me, during the day, they keep looking for me—but every night, I'm right here in that trash can. I saw you get chosen. Your face was huge for the world to see on the big screen on T-DOD!" Then Lizzie trembled a bit, looked down at her feet and said, "I always told you that you were special. . . ."

"I'm sorry," Tookie said. Her worst fear had come true—Lizzie *had* seen her take the Scout's hand. She remembered how Lizzie had stood in her driveway the morning of T-DOD. How she'd let out that scream, thinking Tookie had abandoned her. "I wanted to escape with you, Lizzie. But they threw me into the car—I was stuck!" Tears fell from her eyes. All this time, she'd feared that Lizzie hated her for leaving.

"I understand," Lizzie said. "I mean, at first I was confused. And hurt. And angry. But it's *you*, Tookie. I know you wouldn't do that to me. I knew you'd come back."

Tookie put both hands to Lizzie's face. "I *did* come back, Lizzie." Guilt shot through her body. Yes, she was back. But the reason for her trip was not to be with Lizzie, but to dodge danger and death. Still, Tookie continued, because the look in Lizzie's eyes felt like home. "And . . . and I'm ready. For Exodus. *Really* ready. Let's go. Right now."

Lizzie gazed into Tookie's eyes and nodded, her eyes filled with sad joy. "Really?"

"Really." Tookie turned and grinned at Shiraz, Dylan, and Piper. "This is Lizzie, guys. My very best friend from Peppertown."

When she turned back to Lizzie, Lizzie's expression had changed from bright and lucid to something tortured and crazed. She stared at the sky, her eyes stricken with fear. "They're coming for me!" she shrieked.

Tookie and the other Unicas gazed at the sky too. Ci~L's pouch whizzed past her own billboard, which now read WHERE THE HELL IS Ci~L, DAMN IT!? WE *NEED* HER!

Lizzie started to shiver and convulse, her eyes locked on Ci~L. Then, turning, she broke out into a run down the city streets.

"Lizzie!" Tookie screamed, chasing after her. The Unicas followed. "Lizzie! Where are you going? Come back!" She pounded down the LaDorno streets, passing spas, high-end hotels, jewelers, exclusive nightclubs, all kinds of things she used to dream about as a simple girl in Peppertown. But she barely noticed them right now, the storefronts streaking past. "Lizzie!" she screamed again, catching a glimpse of Lizzie's bright red hair rounding a corner. She looked over her shoulder to tell Shiraz, Piper, and Dylan to hurry up. But they were gone.

Her stomach twisted. *Nooooo!*

Tookie walked in circles on the sidewalk, wondering which way to go. Just then, a huffing, puffing bus from Peppertown—

the only one that trekked into LaDorno—pulled up beside her. Vigorous knocks pounded on the windows. Tookie looked up and her heart lifted. Shiraz, Dylan, and Piper were inside.

Get in now! Piper mouthed through the window.

Tookie peered up the steps. The freckled driver grinned down at her. "Come on the board!" he said in broken English, with an accent that sounded just like Shiraz's. "Your little Labrian friend, all my Canne Del Abra so proud of her. She tell me your plight! I help you get away from crazy flying lady!"

Tookie climbed aboard and gazed at Shiraz, who shrugged and shot the driver her best CaraCaraCara expression, which made him break into a googly *I'll do anything you want* smile. It seemed they *had* learned something valuable at Modelland after all.

"Where's your friend?" Piper asked.

Tookie looked around desperately. She couldn't even form the words that she'd lost Lizzie again. It couldn't be happening.

"Oh my God!" Dylan gazed through the side window. "There she is!"

"Who? Lizzie?" Tookie asked, brightening.

"No!" Dylan screamed. Tookie followed Dylan's gaze. Ci~L soared through the sky. But then, suddenly, Ci~Ls appeared on either side of the bus as well, keeping pace with the speeding vehicle. *She's using her power of Multiplicity,* Tookie thought. *Now there are THREE Ci~Ls trying to kill us!*

"Down that alley," Piper commanded the driver. He turned a corner fast, losing the two Ci~Ls that flanked the bus. At the opening on the other end of the alley, Tookie could see the Obscure Obelisks towering in the sky, all lit up by the moon. She was surprised Mayor Rump hadn't taken them down yet.

"There's Ci~L!" Dylan screamed. "She's—all of her are—landin'!"

Tookie whipped around and saw the three Ci~Ls skid to a stop on the bricks behind them, their pouches retracting into their arms. As soon as the three Ci~Ls noticed the bus, a determined look settled over their identical faces, and they sprinted after it again.

"Faster!" Shiraz ordered the bus driver.

"You gots it." The Labrian man sped down the alley toward the Obelisks, hydroplaning on the slick street. The bus then hit a pothole, sending the girls flying out of their seats. When Tookie scrambled up again, one of the Ci~Ls was right alongside the bus, staring through the window at them!

Everyone screamed. Dylan looked like she might faint. "Have the mercy!" Shiraz wailed.

Then Tookie looked out the front windshield. Ahead of them stood Lizzie. Frozen. Staring at the oncoming bus. "Don't run!" Tookie screamed at her through the glass. "Lizzie, stay right there!"

Lizzie blinked, then stared at something on the ground. It glinted in the moonlight. She bent down to pick it up. Tookie stared at the shiny sharp metal object in Lizzie's hand. Lizzie then raised it and brought it down hard onto her inner wrist. "Noooo!" Tookie wailed.

The bus sped fast through the alley. A lone shopkeeper locked up his store, then headed into the alleyway right in front of the bus. The driver slammed on the brakes, and the bus lurched to the left. Everyone screamed and shot forward. Tookie's head hit the windshield, and she immediately felt a jab of white-hot pain.

And then everything went black.

39

Breathless Sister-Friends

Searing pain pulsed at Tookie's scalp. The cold ground chilled her bones. After a moment, she opened her eyes. The night stars and round moon glowed overhead. The Obscure Obelisks towered off to the left, three giant spikes in the sky.

Where was she? The last thing she remembered was Lizzie picking up a piece of sharp metal and—

Tookie shot up. The bus lay on its side next to the Obscure Obelisks, its windshield smashed, its tires flattened, its front end crumpled. The driver was nowhere to be seen.

"Dylan? Shiraz? Piper?" Tookie called quietly, her heart hammering. *Please make them be okay,* she silently willed.

"Over here," Dylan's voice meekly responded. "All of us."

"Are you hurt?" Tookie scrambled toward them.

"No," Piper said weakly. Shiraz murmured that she was all right too.

Tookie peered into the darkness. One friend left to find. "Lizzie?" she cried.

Nothing.

Tookie leapt to her feet. "Lizzie?" she called louder. "*Lizzie?*" Again, nothing. Tears began to spill down her cheeks. *No. No!* The image of Lizzie slamming the sharp metal into her wrist swam through her mind. She had failed Lizzie again.

And then everything just came to a head. Everything Tookie had been through—people walking over her like she was trash during every SPLD; the daily fear that the Unicas were going to be mutilated and murdered; Zarpessa's nasty secrets and cruel spirit; Tookie's toothbrush bulging in her father's pocket on its way to prove she wasn't his; Gunnero's mean taunts; feeling unlovable, then loved, then humiliated by Bravo; every second, every minute of her existence suddenly erupted like lava from a long-dormant volcano.

"*How could I have lost you again?*" Tookie wailed loudly, her voice echoing into the night. "*Why do I keep letting you down? I'm so sorry. I'm so sorry! I'm so sorry!*"

The sobs made her buck and shudder. Her wails were so intense they reverberated off the mountain in stereo. Finally, Tookie stopped, held her breath, and looked around. Even though she'd quit crying, the wails kept coming.

"*I'm so sorry. I'm so sorry. I'm so sorry. . . .*"

Tookie spun around in the direction of the noise. Was that

someone *else* sobbing? A figure kneeled at the base of the Obscure Obelisks. And then . . . *thwack*. A twisted reed struck in the moonlight, landing on the figure's back. Blood rose through the figure's thin shirt. *Thwack. Thwack.* "Oh my God," Tookie whispered.

Ci~L.

Before Tookie's eyes, Ci~L—and only one Ci~L this time, not three—started to claw at herself. Tears mixed with blood streamed down her face. "I'm sorry!" she wailed, her voice raw. "I'm *sorry!*" She tore at her shirt to get down to her bare flesh. Huge new welts rose on her skin. Older ones were still an angry keloided red. The blood dripped down her back, pooling on the ground.

Tookie gasped.

Ci~L raised her head and spied Tookie. Her eyes widened. Her mouth became tense and hard. Her nostrils flared. She stood and advanced toward Tookie with her bloody hands outstretched, her expression unhinged and twisted, her hair snarled around her face. Tookie backed away, her heart fluttering madly in her chest.

But instead of running away again, Tookie mustered up all her courage and stood firm. It didn't make sense to keep running. Ci~L would just find them again and again and again.

"Take me," she said softly to the advancing Ci~L. "Experiment on me instead of my friends. Torture me, sacrifice me, kill me. Let them live."

Ci~L halted in her tracks and stared at her. After a moment, she started to tremble. She covered her face with her hands and turned away. *"I'msorryI'msorryI'msorry . . . ,"* she began to moan once more.

Tookie frowned. "What's happening to you?" she demanded. "Why are you crying?" She certainly hadn't expected this from

Ci~L. Rage, yes. Fury, certainly. Painful death at her hands, absolutely. But not desperate sobs.

"It—it's my . . . my fault," Ci~L blubbered into the concrete. "It's m-my fault. M-my . . . f-f-f-ault!" She could hardly get the words out through her choking sobs.

Tookie blinked at her. *The sacrifices.* Clearly Ci~L was racked with guilt over what she'd done to earlier sacrificial girls, perhaps to become a Triple7.

Then Ci~L turned to Dylan, Piper, and Shiraz. "*With all my powers, I should have been able to save you!*" she screamed.

The girls looked at each other, confused. "Save them?" Tookie repeated in a whisper.

"I don't think she is meaning Unicas," Shiraz said.

Ci~L took in huge gulps of air, whirling around to face the Obelisks. "I miss you s-s-so much!" Then she collapsed onto the base of the Obelisks, her forehead against the tallest pillar. "Every day I told you that you were good enough, special enough, *beautiful* enough, that you deserved to be at Modelland. All I wanted was for you to know how amazing you were, how perfect you were just as you were. I should have shut the hell up when I noticed your night sweats, your headaches, your bulging veins. It's my fault you got sick and caught the . . ."

"Who is she talking to?" Piper murmured. "She needs to be hospitalized."

Then Ci~L rose once more, and turned to the mountain. "*You killed them!*" she yelled to the mountain, her whole body shaking. "*Bloody murderer!*"

She turned back to the Obelisks. "I searched for you," she moaned. "I searched and searched. I couldn't find you. But I kept searching. And then I found you, underneath. I dug and dug and dug till my hands bled, and there you were . . ." Ci~L smiled dazedly, as though in a dream. ". . . all three of you. I don't know how long you were buried, but you still looked so beautiful to me. And we were together again. But you didn't wake up. You wouldn't open your eyes!"

Then Ci~L whirled again and pulled on Tookie's arm. Tookie reared back, afraid, but Ci~L's face was crumpled and extremely vulnerable. "Help me, Tookie," Ci~L whispered. "Help me open their eyes. Help me wake them up."

Tookie stared at the Intoxibella. All at once, everything she'd assumed about Ci~L flipped upside down. She still wasn't sure what was tormenting the Intoxibella, but one thing was certain: Ci~L was not guilty of murder. The guilt she felt right now was over something far more abstract, something more like bereavement and failure.

When Tookie didn't move, Ci~L groaned and fingered the reed on the ground, preparing it for her back once more. Moving quickly, Tookie reached out and grabbed her wrist. "Ci~L! Stop it!"

Ci~L paused and stared at her through cloudy, dazed eyes.

"Please, Ci~L!" Tookie sank to her knees in front of her. "Give me the reed. You can't do this to yourself. Not anymore."

Ci~L clutched the reed hard. "I deserve this! I need to pay for what I've done!" Her eyes darted to Dylan, Piper, and Shiraz. "I need to pay for not saving you!"

"Ci~L, look at me," Tookie commanded. "You're not talking about *them,* are you?" she asked tentatively, gesturing to her friends. "You're talking about someone else, right? Someone who died in the Diabolical Divide?"

Ci~L shut her eyes tightly, as though reliving some terrible, debilitating pain all over again. "My sister-friends from home— Hendal, Woodlyn, and Katherine. When I became a Triple7 Intoxibella, the first thing I did after that tournament was tele-portal back home so I could celebrate with the three of them. I told them they were worthy, that Modelland's rules were ridiculous and that they deserved to be there more than I did. Hendal was so beautiful, so voluptuous, with bright lavender eyes. Woodlyn's hair and skin were pale and luminescent like a full moon, and Katherine was so tiny and had the cutest freckles and the most luxurious curly brown hair."

Tookie flinched. She looked over her shoulder at Dylan, Shiraz, and Piper. Their mouths hung open in shock.

Tookie turned back to Ci~L. "So what happened that got you in so much trouble with the BellaDonna?"

Ci~L shut her eyes. "Because of my SixxSensa power, I feel things intensely. I was living in an amazing penthouse in LaDorno, and my sister-friends would visit me every day after I finished with photo shoots, Run-a-Ways, posing for my picture on Metopian money, being the guest of honor at parties thrown by royalty, worldwide televised poetry slams, and autograph signings. My life was an insane dream overnight, but I would always, every day, run back to them. But when a week passed and there was no sign of them, I knew something was wrong, and I knew exactly where to go. To the Divide. The creatures there are like things you wouldn't even see in your worst nightmares, and there were moments I wasn't sure I'd get through it alive. But I found my sister-friends, one by one. Two were buried and . . . I . . . I dug up their bodies with my bare hands. I was planning to trot their bodies through

LaDorno in my own personal parade to show the world—it was time people understood that Modelland's narrow beauty ideals are flawed and in need of a change. But Gunnero got wind of my plan and went on a search for me. Luckily, I heard about his pursuit before he caught me, so I quickly created this monument in my sister-friends' honor and buried them here." She pointed to the Obelisks. "I couldn't parade their bodies through the town square, but this was the next best thing I could do. Then I gave myself up to him."

Dylan backed up from the three pillars. "Wait. There are dead *bodies* under here?"

"Body Girl . . . ," Shiraz whispered.

Ci~L nodded and fought back another sob. "That's why the BellaDonna has been punishing me."

Piper rocked on her heels. "Why didn't LaDorno just demolish the three Obelisks when they first went up?"

Ci~L wiped her bloody hands on her shirt. "Most people in LaDorno thought the Obelisks were some kind of mystical sign, and in the six months after I put them there, tourism increased tenfold, so the mayor allowed them to stay. The BellaDonna demanded they be taken down, but she has no jurisdiction over Metopia. So she takes her frustration out on me." Suddenly, Ci~L's face twisted with pain, and she gripped her stomach and raised the reed to beat herself once more.

Tookie caught her arm again. "Don't. *Please*. What happened is *not* your fault. You can't literally beat yourself up over this. You were chosen to be an Intoxibella—a Triple7, Ci~L. And you've used your fame to spread your message all over the world, and everyone loves you. Your friends . . . yes, they're dead, gone forever. But they still live inside of you. And now, inside of Piper and

Shiraz and Dylan. Maybe it's time to let them go. Let their souls rest. So that *you* can rest."

Ci~L shook her head. "But Tookie, I feel like my soul is dead. I feel so lost. Like I've gone insane."

"With all due respect, Ci~L, I must agree with your last statement," Piper murmured.

"Me too," Shiraz said. "You cry lots, but how we know you still won't do the tortures to us? The killings?"

Ci~L flinched. "Hold up. *Kill* you?"

"First there is the experimenting," Shiraz clarified. "And then the killings."

Ci~L blinked hard. "*Killing?* Are you serious? Do you realize how I rebelled to get you three to Modelland? The rules I broke? On The Day of Discovery, you weren't on the list they gave me. I got rid of that thing and specifically chose you three instead."

"So we really *weren't* on the list," Piper said morosely.

"No, you weren't." Ci~L shrugged. "The only one who was on the list was Tookie. She was the first pickup, and when I saw how unusual-looking she was, I thought maybe this was my chance. I could be a renegade. Pick girls *I* wanted, girls who could make up for Hendal's, Woodlyn's, and Katherine's deaths. It was my experiment. My grand project."

"But why *me*?" Tookie blurted out. "Why did Modelland want *me* on the list? You just said I'm unusual-looking!"

Ci~L raised her hands helplessly. "I'm sorry, Tookie. I don't know."

Shiraz still didn't look convinced. "But you looking at us so strangely in class!" she protested. "You give us evil eye! Like you want to squash us like bug!"

Ci~L winced. "If I've been looking at you like that, I'm sorry.

It's just . . . you remind me so much of *them*. Your spunk, your sassiness, your intelligence. Do you know how refreshing it is to have girls like you at Modelland? It's never been done before! So sometimes I stare at you and can't believe I did it—I can't believe I actually got you to Modelland, and I can't believe I figured out a way to get the BellaDonna to *keep* you there. And then I get flash-backs of my sister-friends and my mind starts doing crazy things. I'm sorry if I scared you—it was a combination of crazy and tough love. But I feel like you're making a huge leap . . . for *all* of us. For girls everywhere. You too, Tookie. Don't think you're excluded from this."

Tookie and the others exchanged uncertain glances. Tookie thought of the terrifying conversation she'd overheard in the BellaDonna's chambers not long ago and realized she'd had it all wrong. They were Ci~L's experiments, all right . . . but not in the way she thought.

"But . . . we're *not* at Modelland anymore," Piper said slowly. She gestured around at the Ladornian skyline. "Obviously."

"And that's why I'm here. To bring your butts back," Ci~L said.

"How did you know we left?" Tookie asked. "How did you know to follow us?"

Ci~L put her hands on her hips and looked down at Tookie. "Girl, I have SixxSensa. One of my Triple7 powers, remember? That look on your face when I was taking you to ManAttack . . . I just *felt* that something was up." Then she checked the kaleido-watch on her wrist. "Oh Lordy. They're gonna notice you're gone soon, and I can just see Gunnero's bitchy little face if he catches us. Then you all *really* won't be able to come back to Modelland. C'mon now. We gots ta go!"

Shiraz shifted her weight. Piper tented her fingers at her breast-bone, thinking. Dylan raked her hands through her long ponytails. And Tookie shivered in her couture underwear from ManAttack.

Go back. Just like that. Back to their Lumière-less D rooms. Back to Zarpessa. Back to Gunnero. Back to Catwalk Corridor and the taunting, loveless BellaDonna and the accusation, always the accusation, that they weren't as good enough as the others. That they didn't deserve to be there. The threat that they could still be sacrificed—maybe not by Ci~L, but by *someone*.

"I can feel what you're thinking," Ci~L said softly. "You haven't had it easy this year. And you probably won't have it easy your whole life. I know you girls have struggled with all your baggage—but hell, we *all* do. You're not wrong if you don't think you belong there. Because, yeah, you don't look anything like those girls at Modelland. I know I might sound crazy, and as you know, I kind of am, but I really believe the four of you have the *power* to kick beauty's *ass* and turn it on its head. Beauty really can mean so much more than what the damn BellaDonna dictates every five years—and I want all the dumbass idiots with their heads in the beauty sand to wake the hell up! But I can't do it alone. I know. I've tried."

The girls glanced at each other again.

"If you go back to Modelland," Ci~L went on, "you'll be sym-bols. I chose you three because I felt you could carry out my mis-sion. And Tookie. Don't you see how much you've changed? You've become this . . . ass-kicker in ManAttack. A winner. A *leader.* We *need* more girls like you at Modelland. *Please* come back with me. *Please.*" Then she shook her head, gazing at them almost lovingly. "Will you do it for *me,* at least? Will you *try?* Because maybe if I know you're up there, trying, maybe I can let this guilt go." She gestured to the Obelisks. "Maybe I can let them rest in peace. And let the wounds on my back heal too."

There was a long silence. Owls hooted in the distance. Leaves on the mountain rustled ominously. The lights from LaDorno twinkled. Tookie considered her friends. By the looks on their faces, she could tell they were thinking about exactly what she was: the positives of Modelland, all the wonderful things they'd experienced there. The amazing architecture and design. The gorgeous fabric flowers and sunsets. ZhenZhen. Kamalini. The D, the E, the classes with Guru Lauro and even Guru Pacifico. The sense of *belonging* somewhere, even if others didn't believe they did. Running *toward* a challenge instead of *away* from it. *No longer being a Forgetta-Girl.*

Slowly, everyone began to smile. Dylan reached out and grabbed Tookie's hand. Tookie reached out and grabbed Shiraz's hand, and Shiraz took Piper's, who held Dylan's, completing the circle. Then Tookie broke the chain and held out her hand to Ci~L. "We'll only go on one condition." She gestured to the reed. "Hand it over."

Ci~L glanced at the reed, looking at it almost like she was about to part with a piece of herself. Then she rolled her shoulders back, stood up straighter, and placed it in Tookie's hands. "Promise me you'll stop this," Tookie said. Ironically, they were the exact words she wanted to say to Lizzie about her sharp objects. She only hoped that someday she could.

"I'll try," Ci~L agreed.

"You promise?" Dylan asked.

"Yeah, Miss Bou-Big-Tique Nation!" Ci~L assured her. "I promise. . . ."

Tookie turned back to the others. She thought about how

helpless she'd felt in the past, like she had no control of her destiny. But now she realized it was all about choices. She had much more control over her future than she ever thought she did. "Then I think there's only one logical choice, isn't there."

"Pouch!" Shiraz bellowed.

"Thank *God*," Ci~L said, rolling her eyes. "Y'all had me sweating bullets there! And ya'll *know* how hard I sweat. Now let's go. Otherwise we'll miss the whole 7Seven Tournament."

With that, fabric flowed from Ci~L's fingers. One of the jeweled tentacles that came from her body gently wiped the tears from her eyes. She glanced at the Obelisks again, then walked over to them and kneeled down. "I love you chicas," she whispered. "And I'll never forget you. *Ever.* But these girls?" She gestured to the Unicas. "They're going to do it for you, okay?" One by one, she kissed the obelisks, starting with the tall ivory one, then the thicker golden one, and finally the smallest, speckled one. And then, with a swish of her pouch and a stretch of her arms, she swept Piper, Dylan, Shiraz, and Tookie up, up, up into the clouds.

To Modelland once more.

40

†he 7Seven †ournamen†

Oh my poor, dear dahling. You thought it was over, didn't you? That the Unicas piled into Miss Used-to-Be-Sweet-Then-Turned-Crazy-and-Now-Is-Sweet-Again Intoxibellas's pouch-let and sailed up, up, up into the sunset, the end. Dahling, you should be ashamed of yourself. There's so much more to this story to tattle-tell you.

And how dare you assume otherwise!

It was quite the shocker that Ci~L was not a murderess sociopath, wasn't it, dahling? Might I suggest the next time you come 'cross another vindictive, vile, venomous creature, you stop, drop, and roll around the idea that maybe the, shall I say, bitch did not spring out of her mother's birth canal that way. I can money-back-guarantee that her sorrowful, sourpuss saga would be quite interesting, but nowhere near as juicy as this one.

But enough about powerful bitches, dahling. Let's move on to bewitching powers.

Of the 7Seven kind.

The Stunning, Statuesque, Strobotronic Stars with Stupefying Stratospheric Struts kind, to be exact. For today, the brand-new 7Sevens will be anointed. Seven girls—and only seven, mind you—will graduate to become Intoxibellas, the pinnacle of a Modelland Bella's existence, dahling. The grand culmination of all of her skills and powers. The chosen seven will join the ranks of the only famous, the most celebrated, and the most admired people in the world. Their whole lives will become the stuff of jealous dreams.

And there are certainly name-calling jealous dreamers among us, dahling, uttering the much more pejorative 7Seven nickname—you know, the one about Stuck-Up, Straggly, Strep-Throated Strumpets with Stenchy Stupid Styes—under their espresso-, cigar-smoke-, and egg-salad-sandwich-scented breaths. (Why is it that bitter bitches have the worst halitosis?) But let's not dwell on their mouthy stench now. I'd rather stick to sweet-smelling topics. So someone please get them some eucalyptus, bergamot, and ylang ylang breath mints, stat.

Now, while The Day of Discovery can be attended by anyone and everyone—even your one-toothed cousin or hog maw–gnawing aunt— the 7Seven Tournament is Invite-Only and is reserved for a chosen few—forty-three thousand three hundred and forty-seven, to be exact, but who's counting? The brand-new obstacle course gleams in the new stadium, ready for the upperclassBella challengers. And there's an extra-special seating section reserved for every living Intoxibella, all of whom are required to return to witness the spectacle. Get your designer *shades (and envy daggers) ready, dahling, because your eyes will ache from all that pulchritude concentrated into one tight space.*

Backstage, powers are tested and finessed—a Multiplicity mess-up where a girl spat into two fountains instead of splitting into two of herself here, a Chameeleoné slip-up where an anxious girl accidentally transformed into an actual chameleon there—and Senturas are knotted and reknotted for good luck. And while the The Day of Discovery selection has fixed predeterminations, like college basketball finals scores, the 7Seven Tournament is free of black market schemes, dahling. All I can say is, may the best Bellas win.

Those who don't must return to society, no powers, no fame, no nothing. A lucky few B-minuses will be selected to become Scouts, choosing future girls at T-DOD, as well as running errands for Modelland as the institution sees fit. But everyone else gets sent thru Gunnero's famed Home doors. Ta-ta.

For Tookie De La Crème, such options don't apply. Our favorite not-so-Forgetta-No-See is just reaching the tallest peak of Modelland and landing outside the gates, thrilled to be back on The Land. Safe. Sound. Happy.

But maybe not for long.

ﻡ

When Ci~L's pouch landed at the Modelland gates, the area was luckily devoid of guards. Putting a finger to her lips, Ci~L rushed Tookie, Shiraz, Piper, and Dylan through the mosaic check-in face, whispering secrets to its pouty tiled lips once more. The face let them pass, whispering "Authentiquated," "Balidated," and "Zertified," and instead of "Entrez" said "Appetizer," but the gates opened all the same.

They raced past the row of BellaDonna statues as fast as they could. In the distance, Tookie heard the sounds of drums beating, people cheering, and a nonspecific frenzied rumble of activity. "Hot damn, we're going to be so late," Ci~L murmured, glancing at her kaleido-watch again. "We'll probably have to stand." She paused to rub her feet. "And I'm not standing, 'cause after three of me running after the four of y'all, my dogs are killing me!"

Shiraz looked nervous. "Please, Ci~L, no say the killings word, 'kay?"

As they burst onto Beautification Boulevard, Tookie and the others gasped. Frantic 7Seven competitors dressed in elaborate, otherworldly couture ensembles and the most glittering, complex jewelry Tookie had ever seen—intricate headpieces that draped over entire faces, necklaces that swung around the wearer's necks like Hula Hoops, a giant tiger's-eye ring that actually winked at Tookie as she passed—ran in circles around them, as if the Unicas and Ci~L were invisible. *They are so obsessed with the 7Seven Tournament, they can't even see how crazy and muddy we all look right now!* Tookie thought. Which was maybe a good thing.

Mannecants rushed to and fro as well, some directing traffic with hefty batons. A long line of Bellas snaked around the outside of the stadium, and a Mannecant doled out wristbands that assigned each Bella to a specific section according to her uniform color. Devin Rump, mayor of Metopia, trundled in with dignitaries from all of Metopia's quadrants. Their wives followed, more weighted down with fashionable wares than they had been on T-DOD the year before. After them came what looked like a hundred slack-jawed civilians of all ages, staring around at Modelland in wonder and awe.

Contest winners, Tookie thought, looking at them. The people who'd won the drawings that took place in every country, who got to attend the most amazing tournament in the world—in the most amazing place in the world. One of the winners raised a camera to her eyes, but a Mannecant grabbed it away. "Mental memories only!" Another winner plucked a perfect fabric flower from the soil and cradled it in his hands. "A souvenir!" he gushed. A second Mannecant snatched it from his hands. "Pluck another and I'll pluck you right out of here."

"It's crazy here at the Modelland," Shiraz bellowed, dancing around in a circle.

"Yeah, yeah, mass hysteria, crazy times twelve, the pinnacle of belovedness, chicness, and bedlam," Ci~L said in a blasé tone. "Let's move it, chicas. We need to get to the stadium before they slam the doors on us. They don't let latecomers in."

But Tookie couldn't help pausing for a moment and staring up at the majestic buildings all around her. She was back. She wasn't going to die. It was a better feeling than having cold whipped cream poured down her throat. If she'd had time to sink to her knees and kiss the Land, she would have.

Ci~L paused a few paces away from the stadium and whipped around. "Oh Lordy." She smacked her hand to her head. "I gotta get you into your dress uniforms—otherwise everyone will know we were up to something." She pointed to Tookie. "Especially you, Miss Muddy-Undies ManAttacker. Okay, pit stop!" She switched directions and headed for the D.

7Seven hopefuls swished by them in a herd. "My Sentura!" one contestant screamed into Tookie's face. "Where is my Sentura? Did you see that skank Emerald with it?" Tookie just shrugged— how would she know?

"I tried out Seduksheeon on a Bestostero this morning, and he told me I smelled like a bitch in heat!" another girl shrieked, staring morosely at the 3-D replication of her that had arisen from the gold walkway. "How am I gonna improve my scent in a few minutes?"

"I'm doomed too!" another girl moaned. "The BellaDonna said I was Edgy and Strange—with a capital *E* and *S*! I should just volunteer to be a Mannecant *now*!"

"Tookie! Guys!" A voice pierced the raucous din. Tookie looked over and saw ZhenZhen pushing through the crowd toward them. She had on a fuschia puffy-sleeved dress that spelled out *Zhen~L* in 3-D. "Ooh, you wouldn't believe what happened to me during Go-See-Go!" She lifted her foot and showed off a glittering tan platform heel with long black shingles. "Maurizio, shoe designer to the Intoxibellas, created a shoe just for *me*! He calls it the *Zhen-letto*! Like them?"

"Love 'em." Tookie grabbed ZhenZhen's hands and glanced at the stadium. "Wow! You're finally competing! Are you excited?"

"Excited—but *scared*!" ZhenZhen giggled nervously. Then she noticed Ci~L beside Tookie. Her straight black hair instantly morphed to mimic Ci~L's lustrous auburn waves. "Ci~L!" she cried. "OhmyGod, I'm freaking out! I keep *trying* to stay myself, but I keep turning into you! Do you think that's okay? I mean, my power is Chameeleoné!"

Ci~L touched ZhenZhen's head, transforming her hair back to its authentic black. "You're using the power wrong, honey. Chameeleoné is the ability to assume different *looks*—not to impersonate another Intoxibella. People want an original—not a knockoff. The *real* you is far more special than the you who tries to be me."

ZhenZhen pressed her hand to her breast. "Do you really think so?"

"ZhenZhen, girl, you are way more beautiful than I could ever be. If I was insecure, I'd be changing into you. Every single day." Ci~L smiled beatifically.

Tookie couldn't help but grin too. There was something so different about Ci~L ever since she'd shared the story about her dead friends—*and* told them goodbye. It was like a huge weight had been lifted from her shoulders.

Then a horn sounded, and ZhenZhen's eyes widened. "Ohmy-GodOhmyGod, that's for *me*! I have to go!" ZhenZhen's hair then began zapping back and forth between black and auburn.

"ZhenZhen!" Ci~L said both sternly and lovingly.

ZhenZhen paused, squeezed her eyes shut tightly, and shook her head hard left to right. Her black long tresses returned and she ran toward her Bella mates.

"Smoke the competition, girl!" Dylan yelled after her.

Finally, they made it to the D. Ci~L shuttled them into their bedrooms and flung open their various closet doors. Inside each closet was a shimmering two-tone green leotard bodice with a deep V-neck and a stiff floor-length skirt with a long slit in the front, exposing their bare legs. There were green thigh-high boots as well. "Dress fast!" Ci~L commanded. "And don't forget your Sentura!"

Once they dressed, Ci~L, now clad in the same outfit as the Unicas, hurried them out onto Beautification Boulevard once more. But eerily, the courtyard was empty. The golden walkway was as smooth as glass. The tree branches rustled quietly in the breeze. The hedge faces frowned disparagingly at Ci~L and her charges. *You're too late,* one mouthed.

"Not if I can help it," Ci~L said through her teeth, yanking Tookie's wrist and pulling her forward. "You four are seeing that ceremony if I have to teleportal your butts inside."

They sprinted toward the stadium but were too late. Two Mannecants had just shut the big iron doors.

"Dammit, dammit, dammit!" Ci~L yelled as she stomped her foot.

Piper suddenly froze. "What was *that*?"

The others, even Ci~L, stopped and stared at her. "What was *what*?" Dylan asked.

"That noise." Piper gestured at the wall. "I heard something on the other side!"

Tookie listened hard, which wasn't easy over the cheers from the stadium. But then she heard a gurgle too. And a snapping twig. Whatever it was sounded close.

"Oh my God!" Piper shrieked. *"Look!"*

Shiraz, Dylan, and Tookie followed her gaze. On the top of the wall was a sooty, skeletal, groping *hand*.

Everyone shrieked and jumped away. Five angry fingers twitched as though stricken with palsy. When its second hand appeared, the girls grabbed one another. The hand's flesh was filthy and bloodied. Each fingernail was long, comma-shaped, and obsidian-black. They looked like the talons of a prehistoric flesh-eating bird.

The top of a muddy head appeared next, followed by two bulbous, demonic, cruddy eyes. Everyone screamed and took another step back.

Two shoulders appeared next on the wall, then an abdomen and legs. As the figure caught sight of them, its eyes widened. A growl emitted from the depths of its belly.

Piper gasped. "It's a *LeGizzârd*! They killed my father! And now one's come for me!" Tears streamed down the face of the normally stoic girl.

"What? That's impossible," Ci~L whispered, placing her hands authoritatively on her hips. But even she took one timid step backward.

The figure hefted its body onto the top of the wall and then dropped down in front of them in a cloud of dust to rest on its haunches. It had a gnarled, hunched back. It licked its lips as if it hadn't eaten for days and considered them an acceptable meal. Thick saliva dripped down its chin. Piper shrank behind Dylan. Tookie squeezed her hand.

The scaly, charred monster turned and stared directly at Tookie. Its sooty eyes narrowed, and hundreds of cracks of dry mud covered its face. Tookie's gaze fell to the monster's hands. There was a filthy, tattered doll tucked under its arm. A doll Tookie knew all too well. This wasn't a LeGizzârd. It was . . .

"C-C-Creamy?" Tookie cried, and promptly passed out.

41

Stone to Bone, and Flesh

"Tookie, get up, damn it!"

The voice sounded foggy and far away. Bright light shone in Tookie's eyes, and she sat up, looked around, and gasped.

She was in her old bedroom in Peppertown. The room was its usual mess, Myrracle's things strewn over every inch of space. Myrracle lay in her bed by the window, giggle-snoring happily.

Tookie ran her hands down her face, her heart pounding fast. Everything she'd endured and experienced, Piper, Shiraz, and Dylan, Bravo and Ci~L and seeing her mother climbing over the wall . . . none of it had been real.

It was all a dream.

She felt a strange mix of loss, devastation and relief—at least she didn't have to face Creamy's wrath in Modelland now. But then tears dotted her eyes, revealing the truth and her disappointment.

"Tookie, get *up*!"

Tookie looked around her bedroom, and before she could respond, her vision went foggy. Giggle-snoring Myrracle started to fade, and once more, Tookie descended into maddening darkness.

"Tookie, I *know* you hear me, damn it!"

She opened her eyes again. And leaning over her was the monster. A giant wall rose up behind it.

"If I have to tell you *one* more time to stand. The hell. Up . . ."

Tookie sat up and stared at the monster with the voice of her mother. A hot ball of fear simmered in the pit of her stomach. She felt suspended between two worlds.

"C-Creamy?" Tookie whispered again to the creature, drawing back.

Shiraz helped Tookie to her feet. "Who is monster, and how you know it?"

"It—it's my mother," Tookie sputtered. The girls gaped at her. Tookie reached out to the cruddy beast. "Are you *real*?"

"Did you fall on your big head just now?" Creamy spat. "Of course I'm real!"

Tookie gazed around dazedly. She felt caught between the Tookie she had been and the Tookie she now was. The M building loomed in the distance. The golden plaza sparkled.

Piper, crouched in a ball, screamed. "Look! Another one!"

Another hand appeared at the top of the wall. An instant later, a second body dropped spastically into Modelland. When it turned, Tookie's heart stopped in her chest. Those perfect aqua-blue, single-colored eyes! *Myrracle!*

"My sister?" Tookie said in disbelief. The words didn't sound quite right coming out of her mouth.

"Your *sister* is part LeGizzârd?" Piper asked, looking at Tookie with the same fearful expression she had once reserved for Ci~L. Dylan grabbed Piper's hand.

Everything seemed like it was happening in both slow and sped-up motion. Tookie felt dizzier and dizzier. Creamy and Myrracle were . . . *here?*

She remembered Creamy pointing to the sky as if she was cursing Tookie when Ci~L had carried her away in her pouch on T-DOD. Then she thought of what she'd overheard in the Bella-Donna's chambers. How the BellaDonna had switched a girl who rightfully belonged at Modelland with Tookie.

And now Tookie's suspicions had proven true. That rightful girl was . . . *Myrracle*. And Creamy was there on a mission.

"Long time, no see," Creamy said to Tookie, taking her in from head to toe. "You look . . . different." She reached back and yanked the hunch off her back. A cruddy backpack fell to the ground. She then forcefully pulled Tookie up. "Take us to the BellaDonna. Now."

"Excuse m-me?"

Her mother's grip on Tookie's arm strengthened. "Are you deaf?" she mocked.

For a moment, Tookie couldn't speak. She couldn't take Creamy to the BellaDonna. If she did, her stay at Modelland would be all over. "Y-you could get in huge tr-trouble, Creamy. Y-you can't be here."

Creamy waved her hand dismissively. Then her eyes brightened as she noticed something behind Tookie. She marched ahead, crossing the golden M plaza. Golden exclamation marks followed her as she made her way to the O. "Myrracle, come!" Creamy shouted, snapping her fingers and shifting Bellissima in her arms.

Myrracle and everyone else trailed behind. Tookie turned and felt a momentary jolt of pleasure at seeing Myrracle looking so wretched while she herself wore Modelland Dress Uniform couture.

Creamy marched right up to the BellaDonna statue and stared at it. "BellaDonna!"

The statue remained still. Creamy stomped her sooty foot. "BellaDonna! I know you hear me!" Creamy roared. Brown spit spewed from her mouth with every syllable.

"Lady, today Madame BellaDonna may be a bit stone-faced and temperamental," Ci~L said in a teasing, confiding voice, leaning close to Creamy. "Especially 'cause today's the 7Seven Tournament."

Creamy rolled her eyes, which, after months of starvation, looked like deep pits far back in her skull. "The 7Seven Tournament? That idiotic pomp and circumstance?" She turned back to the statue. "BELLADONNA!" she roared. "STOP IGNORING ME!"

"Oh my God! Look!" Dylan shrieked. The BellaDonna statue's eyes began to blink. Her hands moved from their alluring pose. She arched her neck way down and gazed upon the filthy woman in the O. Her brow furrowed. The corners of her mouth dipped into a frown. Then she burst into song.

"Silly moppet, foolish wench,
Creatures of abominable stench,
You crosseth mine gold path today,
So welcome to your dear doomsday.
The punishment deserved you
Will—"

Creamy stomped her foot again, interrupting the BellaDonna's song. "Will you stop that ridiculous singing?"

Tookie and the Unicas exchanged shocked looks.

The BellaDonna continued to scowl. Her gaze scanned the others. Her eyes narrowed, especially when she noticed Ci~L. "Of course *you'd* be part of this," she hissed.

"I don't know what *this* is, but it's pretty damn entertaining," Ci~L said.

"Well?" Creamy stared at the statue. "Where the hell are you? You and I need to have a serious talk!"

The BellaDonna paused. More cheers exploded from inside the 7Seven stadium. Drums beat wildly. Tookie waited for Modelland security to approach. She knew the BellaDonna would not conduct a visit with a mere mortal just as the most important tournament of the year was about to begin. Not with her public waiting. Not with grand, important, life-changing decisions to be made. Not with the entire Bored waiting for her.

Amazingly, the giant BellaDonna statue sighed and stretched her arm toward a thick hedge. "All of you, go to the last ZipZap on the left through there! *Now!*"

Tookie gasped. *Seriously?* Then the statue went stiff, the decision made.

Everyone marched off toward the hedges to the ZipZap. "Creamy!" Myrracle cried. "Do we *have* to go inside that jiggedy-jaggedy thing?"

Tookie turned to Ci~L, who lingered outside the hedge with her. "You're coming with us, right?"

"I don't think so, Tookie," Ci~L said, scratching her back. "Your mom and your sister remind me of when I, um . . . when I dug up my . . ."

Then Tookie heard a horn blare behind her. When she turned, she saw a familiar face staring with wonderment at the brand-new stadium. His hair slicked back, his formal Bestosterone uniform tightly fitted to his body, and a little bruise over his left eye, perhaps from where someone smacked him hard during ManAttack.

Bravo.

He turned, as if sensing Tookie watching. When he saw her, his expression was one of utter confusion. The last he knew, she had said she was leaving Modelland.

Everything Bravo had told Tookie just before they fought in ManAttack flooded her brain like a disease. *I made a bet. The weird-looking ones . . . they're the ultimate challenge.* She let out a sniff. But as she was about to turn away, she noticed the look on his face, as if he didn't want her to break eye contact. And then he licked his thumb and pantomimed wiping Tookie's eyebrows.

Tookie's mouth fell open. How dare he do *that*, of all things? She made up her mind that she would never forgive him. *Ever.*

You might as well be dead to me, Bravo.

"We're waiting!" Creamy said from inside the hedge.

Ci~L backed away. "I'm sorry, Tookie, you're on your own with this one. I'm so sorry, but I'm feeling the urge to go find a reed."

But Tookie looked at Ci~L pleadingly. This was all too much: her mother's return, Myrracle, the stress of Bravo . . . "Please, Ci~L? I can't do this alone. And I don't want *you* to be alone right now."

Ci~L wavered for a minute, then nodded.

Tookie walked into the clearing and approached the ZipZap on the end. She glanced over her shoulder and then ducked inside. Creamy followed. In seconds, they had all slid through the long tube and emerged at the end of a dim corridor.

Piper inhaled. "Blood oranges."

"At least *somethin'* smells fresh," Dylan said, eyeing Creamy and Myrracle.

And then they heard them: the calming, soothing undulations of the unseen voices chanting "Ooh" and "Ahh." Tookie glanced at her friends. The BellaDonna had ordered them to the OoAh?

"Guess Madame BellaDonna needed her butt waxed before her big 7Seven speech," Ci~L said, smirking.

They walked into the spa lobby. It was much more humid than when Tookie had been there. Purplish light spilled into the hall. The check-in desk was unoccupied, and a serene tableau was reflected on the walls. A cobblestone street, church towers, a burgeoning butcher shop, a cobbler's shop, and a spinning windmill surrounded them. The sound of church bells reverberated so loudly that Tookie felt they were suddenly trapped in a belfry.

"Quaint," Piper murmured, looking around.

"It like village in Labrian fairy tale!" Shiraz whispered. She reached out to touch a jolly white-bearded man with droplets of sweat on his brow, but her fingers slipped through his transparent image. There was no one else in the room.

487

"BellaDonna?" Creamy called out. "Where are you? This place has you written all over it!"

"It *does*?" Tookie whispered. Ci~L caught her eye and shrugged.

"BellaDonna?" Creamy roared again. "I swear to God, woman, if you don't answer me, I'll—"

"In here," a voice boomed, and everyone jumped.

A gauzy curtain materialized in the corner. Persimmon stepped through it, her hands clasped at her waist. As soon as Creamy saw her, she let out a gasp. "Good Lord, what is *that*?"

"She's naked and has black eye-whities, Creamy," Myrracle said fearfully.

Tookie nudged her. "That's Persimmon. A Mannecant. Myrracle, have some respect."

"More like *Persecution*," Creamy muttered. Persimmon flinched slightly.

Then Persimmon gestured to the curtain. "I will lead you to see the BellaDonna now. But let me run down the rules first. No touching of the BellaDonna. No getting too close. No incessant breathing in her presence."

Piper nudged Tookie. "We're going to actually *see* the Bella-Donna?"

"Like, all up in the *flesh* and everything?" Dylan said, her eyes wide as saucers.

Persimmon listed the last of the rules. "Only speak when spoken to. If in doubt, remain silent."

"Oh, *puh-lease!*" Creamy exploded, pushing past Persimmon and bursting through the curtain.

Everyone followed her inside. Tookie held her breath, unsure of what they were about to see, but it was just an empty room. The walls were blank. There were no cushy chairs, no cashmere walls, no treatment beds. The only thing in the room was a large slate-gray statue of the BellaDonna in the corner.

All at once, as Creamy moved closer, a giant jagged crack appeared on the statue's shoulder. The crack widened, snaking all the way to the BellaDonna's belly button. The rocky exterior rumbled, as if stricken by a tiny self-contained earthquake, and an enormous chunk of the shoulder and torso broke off and smashed into a hundred pieces on the ground.

Everyone jumped back. Myrracle shrieked. Tookie clapped her hand over her mouth.

"Ooh, you broke it," Dylan murmured under her breath to Creamy. "And as we say at the Bou-Big-Tique Nation: you bou-break it, you bou-buy it, baby."

Another chunk fell off the statue. Its right bicep crumbled, then an elbow, then the stone that formed the BellaDonna's sinewy fingers. But there was something *inside* the statue's stony interior, something the crumbling rock was slowly revealing. Five human fingers emerged from their slate shell. A thin rose-gold sleeve, made of the finest silk, appeared next. Then a swanlike neck and a pair of round, pert breasts.

Flesh, bone, a *person* was under there.

And then the person began to move. The fingers on the right hand twitched. The chest heaved in and out. Its feet, which were clad in sharp seven-inch-high stilettos, tapped.

Everyone, even Creamy, stared as more and more pieces from the sculpture tumbled to the ground. Finally, the entire statue had chipped away except for one large piece of stone over the face.

"How dare . . . ," a muffled voice said from behind the stone.

Tookie glanced at the others. It was definitely the BellaDonna's voice. They were actually going to see her. *In the flesh.*

". . . you demand to see . . . ," the BellaDonna went on.

Tookie, her friends, Myrracle, and even Creamy took one step backward, holding their breath. *This is it,* Tookie thought. *Here it comes.*

". . . *me!*" the BellaDonna boomed.

The BellaDonna's stone mask fell to the floor and shattered.

42

LES TROIS COPINES

"Oooh," all the Unicas said at once.

"Boooo . . . ," the BellaDonna answered, like a seductive ghost.

"A humor of sense, she has," murmured Shiraz.

A heavenly glow emanated from the BellaDonna, as though she was not a human but a goddess. Her hair was wild and black and fell past her waist. Her skin was olive, her cheekbones high, her lips defined. And her eyes . . . the darkest coal-black irises Tookie had ever seen. The expression on her face was one of utter poise but also extreme annoyance.

She was beyond striking. Possessing a divine, otherworldly type of beauty.

Shiraz dropped to her knees, and the rest of the girls followed.

"Supernatural!" Piper blurted out reverently.

"Dang, am I seeing things? Did her dress just up and change up on me?" Dylan whispered.

The BellaDonna's dress had quickly morphed from metallic rose-gold ruffles to a kaleidoscopic snakeskin frock with thousands of pleats. The shape-shifting dress finally settled into a dramatic black floor-length gown with sharp spikes around the high-necked collar. Every so often, the spikes writhed and twisted, alive.

Ci~L whispered, "She's a fashion dictator. Her clothes shift, and the world's fashion trends follow. I'll bet my Ci~L–face money that tomorrow, spike-dresses will be all the friggin' rage."

"*Shh!*" Persimmon hissed, giving Ci~L a swift kick in the side with her pointy-toed boot. "Speak only when spoken to! And if you don't have anything worthwhile to say, say nothing!"

The BellaDonna stared—or actually, *squinted*—at Creamy, almost like she couldn't quite see her very well at first. Then her forehead crinkled in a scowl. "This is not happening. This creature has not invaded my chambers on such an important day."

Creamy bristled. "I'm not afraid of you, Rock-Wench."

"You know," Ci~L murmured to Tookie, "I kinda like that mother of yours. She speaks my language."

"You can have her," Tookie murmured. Her heart was pounding wildly. What was the BellaDonna going to do to Creamy? She'd overheard what the BellaDonna did to Ci~L, and was sure that the "Rock-Wench" was capable of worse. "Creamy, maybe we should go," she whispered to her mother.

A bemused smile crept onto the BellaDonna's face. "Creamy?

What's with this *Creamy* nonsense? Is that what you're making your children call you? If I am seeing what I *think* am, you are a far cry from creamy. *Clumpy* is more like it. Or *Craggy*."

"At least my soul isn't rotten," Creamy shot back. Then she turned to the group. "Listen up, everybody, there's a rumor going around that the BellaDonna's soul is as filthy as a truck-stop urinal. Word has it that she traded it away."

"No, I can't say I had any idea." Ci~L moved closer to Creamy, intrigued and amused. "And how did she sell her soul, if I may ask?"

Creamy's eyes gleamed. "Well, she—"

"Silence!" the BellaDonna roared. "I'm supposed to be changing lives right now! Making the grand decisions that keep the world as we know it running smoothly!" Then she snapped her fingers and stared at the bare walls. "Environment, STADIUM!"

With a whoosh, the majestic grandstands of the stadium appeared on the walls. The BellaDonna walked up to them until she was about an inch away, taking in the scene. The stage was a half-moon of pure gold, and the various challenges for the obstacle course were set up and waiting. The 7Seven upperclassBellas stood in a nervous huddle in the wings, many of them holding hands and chanting calming prayers.

The Bored filed in and sat on the tic-tac-toe risers Tookie had seen in the M building. Only the middle square, the BellaDonna's seat, remained empty. The Bored glanced at it with alarm, perhaps worried that she hadn't yet appeared. Gunnero eyed the middle seat as if he wanted to be in it.

The brand-new sparkling seats were filled to capacity with staff, Bestosteros, and civilians. Hovering above were special skyboxes for every living Intoxibella. Tookie spotted Katoocha from last year's ceremony waving to the crowd. Sinndeesi had Bestosteros waiting on her hand and foot. Dalmah, one of the most amazing catwalkers of all time, walked in place regally for the crowd. Then Tookie noticed a skinny Intoxibella popping pills and offering some to the Intoxibella to her left. She looked like she hadn't slept for weeks. *Is that Fiona from Catwalk Corridor?* she wondered. It was! *She must have gotten out for good behavior.* But it appeared she'd be sent back soon.

The Modelland Bellas filled the floor section of the stadium. Zarpessa and Chaste lounged in the back rows, whispering, and Kamalini bopped her head from side to side, listening to her Headbangor. Filing in through the side entrances of the stadium were dozens of acrobats and exotic jungle cats, lending a circus-like atmosphere.

"Can they really not see us?" Piper whispered, tiptoeing over to the seats and waving her hand through Zarpessa's transparent hologram. She stuck out her forefinger and thumb and mimicked crushing Chaste's and Zarpessa's heads. And in an uncharacteristic way, she said, "Take that, bitches! Who's translucent now?"

Dylan sidled up next to Piper, lifted her train, and pulled aside her leotard, baring her butt. She wiggled it at the girls. "This is for you, ladies! Some Bou-Big-Tique booty!"

"Behave!" Persimmon hissed, pulling both girls away. "You are in the presence of the BellaDonna!"

But the BellaDonna was unaware of the Unica Bella hijinks. Her eyes were darting back and forth from the stadium to Creamy.

Creamy tucked Bellissima under her arm, marched over, and yanked Tookie's hand. "Look, BellaDumba, since you have to greet your adoring public, I'll make this short and sweet. She"—Creamy jabbed a finger at Tookie—"doesn't belong here. My Myrracle does."

"What?" Shiraz blurted out from the sidelines. "Tookie do too belong here!"

"Silence!" Persimmon snapped, kicking Shiraz.

The BellaDonna launched herself forward and groped for Tookie's other arm. She missed, but then she grabbed hold. "Excuse me? No mistakes were made on The Day of Discovery."

Tookie glanced nervously at Ci~L, knowing the truth. But Ci~L just shook her head and made a *zip it* motion across her lips.

"You lying stone-faced woman!" Creamy gripped Tookie's wrist hard and pulled. It felt like rope burn. "I know why you did this. You're still bitter after all these years. You're still holding a ridiculous grudge."

With another tug, Tookie went stumbling back to the Bella-Donna. "You're right! My heart has never healed and never will," she said cryptically. "But revenge is so sweet. My bringing Tookie here instead of Myrracle made you catch the Pilgrim Plague—and that tastes so good to me. But yuck, you survived the journey."

Creamy pulled Tookie back so hard, Tookie felt like her insides were going to split open. Suddenly, Creamy's gaze landed on Myrracle, who was watching the 7Seven stadium preshow dance number with amazement. Her toes tapped to the music. Her arms wiggled and her head bobbed. Dust and soot flew off her body like she was a rug that had just been shaken out.

"Myrracle!" Creamy shrieked, and slapped Myrracle across the face.

"Owie, Creamy!"

"Then stop that damn devil dancing! This is our *life*! Our *chance*! And I refuse to let you just prance it away!"

Myrracle fought hard to not cry. Her cheek bore an exact imprint of her mother's hand and ring on it. "But it looks *funner* out there than it is in here with . . . you."

A vessel in Creamy's forehead bulged. "I trekked up this damn mountain and almost died for *you*! Do you even *know* what that was like?"

Myrracle stared, slack-jawed, at her mother. "Of course I know what it was like, Creamy," she said in a voice that sounded lucid—almost intelligent. "I was *there*." And then, before anyone could stop her, she ran out of the room.

"Myrracle!" Creamy screamed. "Come back here now!"

But Myrracle was gone.

Creamy clamped her mouth shut, looking flustered and bewildered. Clearly, this *wasn't* part of the plan. "Well, at least she'll be in the stadium, surrounded by other Bellas, where she belongs!" She whipped around and transferred all her aggression to the five fingers that still held tightly to Tookie's arm, squeezing so hard that Tookie let out a small, pained *eep*. "Now make it official," she said to the BellaDonna. "Or else."

"Or else what?"

"Or else I'll tell them." Creamy's eyes glimmered darkly.

"What are you two *talking* about?" Tookie cried, caught between them. "Tell us *what*? What are you both hiding?"

The BellaDonna snickered. "I have no idea what your mother is talking about, Tookie. But there are two things I *do* know. *Uno:* your mother is evil. *Y dos:* she doesn't really care about you. All she cares about is *herself*. And maybe that bizarre baby doll she's carrying around."

"That shows how blind you *really* are," Creamy snapped. "Bellissima is beautiful, not bizarre!" Then she moved her face close to Tookie's and put her cruddy hand on Tookie's cheek. It was sweet and terrifying at the same time. "As for what I've never told you, Tookie, it's all in the past, dear—the ancient past. And you know *ancient* isn't my thing. Plus, it doesn't concern you."

"Of course it concerns me!" Tookie wriggled her arms. "I'm caught in the middle!"

"Yeah, crazy mama. Let go her!" Shiraz yelled.

Both women stared only at one another. Tookie gazed with disbelief at her mother, nearly unrecognizable with the soot all over her wrinkled face, her normally pristine clothes in tatters, and her hair a filthy rat's nest atop her head. All at once, Tookie realized how little she knew about Creamy. How her own mother was one big mystery to her, except for the clear disdain she had for Tookie. To Creamy, Tookie was a waste of time, deadweight. That was why Creamy was fine with sending her away to become a Factory Dependent. Tookie just didn't matter. She was in the way. And now, she was in Myrracle's way.

Tookie's shock over finding out that the BellaDonna and Creamy knew one another was replaced with rage. Whatever had happened between them, she wanted to know about it. She *deserved* to know. It was time for the truth.

As she stood there in front of her tormenters, Tookie caught sight of the long corridor of the OoAh. A plan began to form in her mind.

"Give her to me, you blind bat!" Creamy screamed, yanking on Tookie's arm. And at that, Tookie moved a smidgen to the left in the direction of the hallway.

"She is property of Modelland now!" the BellaDonna roared, using Tookie as her tug-of-war rope. Tookie shifted toward the hallway a little more.

Back and forth they went, until they were halfway down the hall. Finally, Tookie broke free and sprinted toward the Flashback Females.

"Tookie, where in the hell are you *going*?" Creamy squawked.

Tookie skidded to a stop in the Flashback room. The three Females sat cross-legged on the floor, calm looks on their faces. They hardly seemed surprised as Creamy, the BellaDonna, Persimmon, Ci~L, Myrracle, and the Unicas tumbled in after Tookie.

"Milky, or whatever you call yourself, leave my premises right now!" the BellaDonna roared. "This is a sacred place, and I will not have your filthy mouth, body, mind, and *bizarre* doll dirty it up any more than you all already have!"

Tookie approached the Female closest to her. "I deserve to know what happened between these two," she said aloud. "Can you show us?"

The Female frowned. "But it is not your flashback, Tookie. Only the one who is *part* of the flashback may access it and show others."

Creamy stepped forward, her footsteps making dirty smudges on the gleaming white floor. "Then *I'd* like to access it. We *all* can see."

"Don't you darc!" the BellaDonna roared, reaching for her but missing. Exasperated, she groped toward the wall. "Narzz! I need you! Come now! There's an intruder in my OoAh!"

Behind them, in the projected image of the stadium, Gunnero flinched as though he'd heard the BellaDonna's message loud and clear. The crowd was getting restless. The Bored was on their feet, trying to calm everyone down and determine the cause of the delay. "Where's the BellaDonna?" voices cried. "She's never late like this." Gunnero promptly abandoned his post and vanished.

Creamy moved toward the Flashback circle. "*Well?* Show us!" she commanded the Females.

The room started to dim and the walls began to pulse.

"Don't listen to her!" the BellaDonna screamed. She glared around at Tookie's friends and Ci~L. "All of you, you must leave with me *now!*"

Immediately, Tookie and her friends ran toward the door—the place was in chaos, but still, they knew they couldn't disobey the BellaDonna. Shiraz made it out first. Then Piper. Then Dylan. Tookie was close behind but tripped and fell. And then Creamy jumped into the circle, making more dust rise off her body in a thick black cloud.

Instantly, the heavy metal doors slammed down, sealing Tookie and Ci~L inside with the two deranged women and the Flashback Females. The sounds of the 7Seven festivities were instantly muffled. The room descended into darkness. An eerie reddish mist wafted through the air.

"No!" the BellaDonna wailed, scratching at the heavy iron and concrete doors with her fingernails, trying to lift them. "Persimmon, do something! Get these doors open!"

But Persimmon just shook her head helplessly. "O beloved BellaDonna," she said in a monotone. "There is nothing I can do to lift them until the flashback is over. You know that. You put these doors here."

"Yes!" Creamy hissed triumphantly. "The stone woman is trapped by her own man-made rock!" Then the Flashback Females stepped up to Creamy and leaned their heads close to hers, telepathically interpreting Creamy's wishes.

"*It is so,*" the Females said, lowering their beehived heads.

Creamy turned and faced the others. "Here we go, darlings."

Here we go, Tookie thought nervously. *Am I* really *ready for this?*

All at once, Tookie felt that familiar tingling sensation. A pin-prick of light appeared at the end of a tunnel. More light streamed in, and shapes appeared. The shapes became buildings, and then Tookie was standing in the O, alone. And yet . . . much about her surroundings looked different. A stadium stood off to the side, but it was made of ancient stone. The M building glistened a tad less, but it was still a shimmering behemoth.

"Tookie?"

Turning, Tookie saw Ci~L across the O. "What's going on?" Tookie cried, rushing over to her.

"I—I don't know." Ci~L spun around, taking in their sur-roundings. She ran her hands down her face and took a couple of deep breaths. "*When* is this, I wonder?"

"Shhh," Creamy hissed from close by. Tookie caught sight of her too, standing on the edge of the golden walkway, still caked in filth. The BellaDonna stood next to her, covering her eyes. Persim-mon was at her side, staring straight ahead.

Just then, a stream of girls in yellow uniforms walked off an escalator onto the ground. The escalator was alongside the electro-magnetic sphere that housed War of Words class—except instead of being suspended in the air as it normally was, the structure was on stilts. The girls' uniforms looked similar to ZhenZhen's upperclassBella one, but instead of pants, they had on skirts that stopped at their knees. The flashback followed two of them, one with very dark hair and olive skin, the other with blond hair and beautiful pink cheeks.

"I *still* think my argument that fuller lips and butts are no lon-ger on trend is correct, but yuck, so cruel. I hope I got my point across in rebuttal without hurting anyone's feelings," the olive-skinned girl said. "Pouty, tarty, juicy plump lips . . . don't go well with slender, tender, slimmer, thin hips!" She sang this last part, stretching out her arms as if completing an aria. She was undoubtedly the BellaDonna, but she couldn't have been more than eighteen years old.

"You always manage to win War of Words but never lose friends. That's a gift, Ladonna," the blonde said brightly, reaching over and giving the brunette a friendly hug.

Ladonna? Tookie thought. *Oh my God! Is that the BellaDonna's real name?*

Ladonna playfully smacked the blonde. "Like *you* aren't full of magical gifts, seven of them to be exact, little Miss Future Triple7? Sometimes I wish those magnetowaves would scramble your brain so the rest of us could shine."

Then Ladonna started belting out a song about being free as a bird. "One more War of Words and we're free for a whole month!" she gushed. "Go-See-Go can't come soon enough."

The blonde poked her side, smiling brightly. "That's just because you're jonesin' for that hunka man of yours."

"*Shhh!*" Ladonna whispered, glancing at an enormous Bella-Donna statue across the square. It had the same defined lips and arched eyebrows as Ladonna.

"That's the Queen BellaDonna," Ci~L whispered, as though reading Tookie's thoughts. "Our BellaDonna's mama. I think they're from a long line of royal Intoxibellas or something."

Just then, a third girl ran up to the group. She had silky brown hair, smooth tan skin, and large, alluring tiger-striped eyes. She wasn't in a yellow upperclassBella Modelland uniform like the others, but instead wore a long couture gown. It was flesh-toned and made of the finest lace and tulle. Tookie leaned forward, frowning.

Ladonna's eyes widened, admiring the brunette girl. "Nice *vestido,* girlie!"

"Yep," the new girl said, doing a shimmy and a twirl. "I just came from a fitting with Guru Applaussez. It just needs a few more tweaks. I'm going to wear it for the big day. It's kind of hard to walk in, but easy to turn!" She spun like a top, completing four circles, spotting perfectly.

The blonde clapped gleefully. "You're definitely going to be chosen to be a 7Seven wearing that, Latta."

Latta. The name rang through Tookie's mind like a siren.

"I hope so. Because if they don't pick me, I think I'll literally die, Percy," she replied.

Someone in the room gasped. Tookie turned and saw Persimmon the Mannecant in the corner. Her head shook with sorrow. Was she Percy?

Then Tookie's gaze moved to the brunette girl again. There was something vaguely familiar about her mouth, her eyes, the color and tone of her silky skin, but Tookie was too scared to admit the undeniable truth. Then her gaze returned to the dress and her heart stung once more. It was the dress Creamy had specifically picked out for Myrracle for T-DOD at the Jurk boutique one year ago. Creamy had chosen it, touched it. Even though it was *vintage. Old.*

Tookie's stomach turned over as the weight of what she'd just discovered fully hit her.

Latta was Creamy! Her mother! And Creamy, the BellaDonna, and Persimmon had once been best friends on their way to becoming Intoxibellas at Modelland.

43

PORCELAIN LIVING DOLLS

All at once, they were whipped out of the flashback, back in the Flashback Females' room once more. The BellaDonna and Creamy were staring at one another, their faces two inches apart.

"Ladonna," Creamy hissed.

"Cremalatta Defacake," the BellaDonna answered.

Tookie widened her eyes, hardly believing what she was hearing. *Cremalatta.* And . . . *Defacake?* Disgusting!

She stared at her mother. "Why didn't you tell me any of this? Why didn't you ever tell me you were a B-B-Bella here?"

Creamy just shrugged. "Oh whatever, Tookie. It's one minor detail of my life I just . . . left out. Get over it."

Ci~L sniffed with disdain. "You're telling *Tookie* to just get over it? That's rich, considering it's obviously something *you're* clearly still seething about!"

Tookie's mind continued to spin. "Creamy, is this how you knew so much about Modelland? Is this how you knew Myrracle was going to g-get chosen?" Daughters of Intoxibellas had almost a 100 percent chance of getting into Modelland, after all, higher than the chances of SMIZE finders.

Before her mother could answer, the Flashback Females looked at everyone, communicating without moving their mouths. *"We're going back in, everyone. To a different flashback now. Hold on. . . ."*

There was a whoosh, and the tingly feeling gripped Tookie once more. When the pulling sensation abated, the group had landed backstage at a busy fashion show. Magical disembodied hands flitted around Ladonna and the other Bellas, dressing them in feathery frocks of red, black, and orange. Percy's dress was so elaborate that twice the number of hands swirled around her, getting her dressed. Mannecants fluffed their hair and did final touches on their makeup. It was clear without anyone having to say anything that Percy was the star.

Ladonna peered through a curtain, then gestured for someone to come forward. "It's okay," she whispered. "Drop off the stuff and work next to me. We're safe back here."

A warm-skinned man, handsome in an approachable, non-Bestostero kind of way, rolled in an enormous crate on wheels and began to unload it. His strong back muscles flexed. Magical hands scurried over and began to rummage through the items he'd un-packed. Gracefully and secretly, the man reached for Ladonna's pinkie and quickly spun her around.

Ladonna giggled. "Cremalatta, Percy, this is him. The first and only love of my life."

"Holy hell!" Ci~L blurted out, watching the flashback. "The BellaDonna was dating a *civilian*? You're kidding me!"

"Be quiet!" the present-day BellaDonna shrieked. She stared at the man in the flashback with a devastated look on her face.

Meanwhile, the young Bellas in the memory greeted Ladonna's beau. "She's told us so much about you," Percy said brightly, her whole face a smile. "Anyone who makes Ladonna happy makes *me* happy."

"Ladonna's told me about you too," the man said, bowing kindly to Percy. "She says you have the chance to be a rare Triple7."

Percy ducked her head modestly. "Let's hope so."

Cremalatta just stared darkly at the boyfriend, then pulled Ladonna aside. "I can't let you do this," she hissed to her friend. "It's one thing if you were going after a Bestostero. But *he's* against the rules!"

Ladonna waved her hand. "I am so tired of rules. Every day my mom comes down on me about some old or new rule I'm not following. The pressure is eating me alive. I think those rules are simply to punish us."

"What rules?" Tookie whispered to Ci~L.

"The cardinal rule at Modelland is that a Bella cannot date a civilian." Ci~L rubbed her palms together. "This is priceless. Methinks Mizz BellaDonna will think twice before lambasting me again about going *off message*!"

"One minute to the start of the show!" a fashion assistant in the flashback called from the edge of the curtain. "Percy, you're first! Best Go-See-Go model leads the show! Ladonna, you're second!"

Ladonna turned away from Cremalatta and clutched her beau's hand. She hid their interlocked fingers behind a large clutch purse she had in her other hand. Nervously, she began to hum a lullaby.

"You'll be wonderful, darlin'," the man whispered. He nervously glanced around and then started to dance with her in time with her humming. His movements were utterly graceful, his body one long, sinuous muscle. "And have I ever told you that you have the voice of an angel? It's even more beautiful than that breathtaking face of yours."

"Yes, you tell me that every time I see you," Ladonna swooned. "That's why I love to sing for you." She raised the clutch higher now, hiding their passionate kiss.

Ladonna and Percy skipped away toward the front of the fashion show lineup. As soon as the music began, Percy gracefully ran onto the runway, employing all her Run-a-Way skills. Only Cremalatta remained behind, still getting dressed by the magical moving hands. As the hands stripped her down to her underwear, she fluttered her eyelashes at Ladonna's love. "Hey there," she purred to him. "You know dating Ladonna is wrong, don't you?"

The man looked away, seeming uncomfortable at staring directly at Cremalatta and her overt seminakedness. "Just a bunch of stupid rules," he murmured in a deep voice.

"*I* like breaking rules too." Cremalatta edged closer to him, trapping him against the wall. The magical hands followed her, pulling at her bra straps. In seconds, she would be topless.

"I suppose," the boyfriend said. He hopped up on a low beam that surrounded the backstage area to get away from her. His balance was perfect.

Cremalatta reached out and touched his cheek. He flinched at first, but then she innocently pulled away. "You had an eyelash," she said, holding it on the tip of her finger. Then she blew on it, sending the lash flying. "I made a wish. Want to guess what it was?"

"Ooh, that mother of yours is trouble," Ci~L muttered.

"Damn right she's trouble!" present-day BellaDonna screamed from the sidelines.

The scene whooshed again, and once more everyone was transported to the Modelland grounds—the *old* grounds. They were still caught in the flashback.

Tookie and the others followed young Percy into the D.

A terrible, animal wail rang out. Percy ran toward the sound, and Tookie and the others watching the flashback followed her into the D's bathroom. Percy locked the main bathroom door, ran to the last stall door, and peered under it. There was a pair of knees on the floor. Someone was throwing up.

"I think it's that chicken you chowed in the E, Ladonna," Percy whispered through the door. "You'll feel better soon. Why don't you try singing? That always cures your aches and pains."

The girl on the other side of the stall just groaned again. Then the knees rose from the ground and the girl slumped onto the toilet. Tookie could practically feel her pain—she'd had a similar reaction to her chocolate binge, which was why she couldn't have even the tiniest taste of the stuff anymore. After a moment, there was a large splash in the porcelain. Suddenly, a small, piercing cry rang out. But it wasn't the sickened cry of a young woman wrecked from tainted food. It was the cry of a tiny baby emerging into the world.

Ci~L's eyes widened. "You are *kidding* me."

A booming knock sounded on the bathroom door. "Why is this door locked?" an angry voice yelled. "Ladonna? Are you in there? It's the Queen BellaDonna. Your *mother*. Open up!"

Both figures in the bathroom froze. Looking frantic, Percy

wrenched the stall door open and stared at the two figures inside—which meant everyone else watching the flashback got a look as well. A tiny pale baby lay in Ladonna's arms. It had the perfect face of an angel. Its skin, the color of a fluffy spring lamb, was covered with streaks of blood.

"Oh my God, Ladonna, what just . . . uh, I mean h-how . . . ," Percy muttered, her face softening. "Wow, look at those bright gray eyes!"

Ladonna stared at the child too, clearly shocked that it had just come out of her. "I don't know . . . *how*," she whispered. Then she looked imploringly at Percy. "Oh my God . . . help me. What do I do?"

"Shhh," Percy said. She grabbed the baby. "We'll figure something out." She removed the Sentura from her waist and gingerly wrapped the baby in the yellow fabric. The tiny thing cooed, comforted by the Sentura's warm embrace.

Boom. The door to the bathroom burst open. The Queen BellaDonna stalked across the tile, making a beeline for the last stall. She stared hard at Percy, then reached out her arms. "Give. Ladonna's child. To *me*."

Percy started to tremble but did not hand the baby over. There was a determined look in her eyes.

Ladonna cowered behind Percy. "But Mother, how did you know I was . . . ? Even *I* didn't know! I just thought I was sick! We don't get periods here, so how did *you* know? I didn't even *show*!"

The Queen BellaDonna craned her neck to glare at her daughter. "A mother always knows," she said icily. Then she shook her head. "This is from that common civilian, isn't it? That man in LaDorno?"

Ladonna's mouth dropped open. "He is not *common*! I'm in love with him!"

"What?" The Queen BellaDonna sucked her teeth. "You *love* him? Ladonna, there is no room for love here at Modelland. Not here. Not now. Not ever. DO YOU HEAR ME?" Then the Queen BellaDonna grabbed the baby from Percy's weak arms, glaring at it as though it were made of bile.

Tears ran silently down Ladonna's cheeks. "Wh-what are you going to do with my baby?"

"I will give the child to its father." Ladonna's mother held the baby at arm's length. "He will raise it. As for *you*"—she turned to Percy—"how *dare* you try to hide this from me? And you wrapped the baby in your sacred Sentura? Persimmon, your time at Model-land is now officially over. I am sending you back to where you came from, right now."

Percy's normally sunny expression turned to one of horror. "No!" she shrieked. "Please don't make me go home! I can't go back to that cult of Persequeshun!"

The Queen BellaDonna shrugged. "Well, you are aware of what your only other option is. Is it what you wish?"

Percy glanced at Ladonna as though waiting for her to explain what had happened. But Ladonna just continued to sob on the cold tile floor. Wilting, Percy turned back to the Queen Belladonna and quietly murmured, "But I didn't even know she was preg—"

"Quiet!" the Queen BellaDonna shrieked. "Is. It. What. You. Wish?"

A single tear formed at the corner of Percy's eye. "It is what I wish," she whispered.

Old Creamy's voice sliced through the flashback. "Ladonna,

you ruined Percy's life by making her a part of your problems. Percy was the number one Bella in our class. Better than all of us, a potential Triple7! You could have told your mother that Percy was innocent. You could have begged your mother to spare her! But what did you do? Thought only of yourself!"

"Defacake, do *not* try to pin this crap on me!" the BellaDonna yelled back. "Percy could have left Modelland forever and been free and kept her looks! Her fate was *her* choice!"

"I *had* no choice!" a third voice rang out.

Tookie looked up and saw Mannecant Persimmon cowering in the corner. Tears streamed down her face. "I couldn't have left!" she wailed. And then she stood, marched over, and loomed right in the face of her old Bella mate. "Ladonna, you *know* where I come from, and you *know* I couldn't go back there!" Spit flew out of her mouth as she spoke. The BellaDonna, usually unflappable, trembled.

"Moving on now," said the Flashback Females in unison.

The scene shifted abruptly, sweeping everyone into a quaint village that looked eerily familiar to Tookie. Cobblestones lined the streets. A windmill gently rotated in the sweltering breeze. Church bells sounded, and a man in a white chef's jacket unrolled the awning of his bakery. The air was torrid, baking their skin and drying out their mouths. This looked exactly like the bucolic environment on the OoAh's walls when Tookie and the others had first come in.

Ladonna's boyfriend opened the door of a small, quaint shop and stepped out onto the porch. Beads of sweat dotted his forehead. A statue of the Queen BellaDonna stood on the stoop, a stone basket at its feet. The boyfriend stared into the basket at the tiny creature inside, slowly shaking his head. Then, gracefully, he swooped down as though he was about to do a handstand and took the baby in his arms.

Suddenly, Tookie had a terrifying epiphany. The acrobatics. The grace. How he'd spun Ladonna around at the fashion show so effortlessly.

Was it possible . . . really possible . . . that this was Chris-Crème-Crobat, her father?

He turned away from the door, pulled out an object from a low shelf on his wall, and gingerly placed the baby inside. Curious, Tookie walked deeper into the room and waited for her vision to adjust. When it did, she saw a huge space full of leather, buttons, soles, laces, and shoes, shoes, shoes on every surface. She crept up close to the baby in the memory. The little bed the man had just laid her in was made of taut leather. An oval-shaped piece draped over the baby's body like a blanket. "There you go, little one," the father whispered. "Maybe you can cheer this sad sap up. There's quite a light that shines inside of you. Quite a light indeed."

A strange feeling came over Tookie. *Wait a minute.* The baby was cradled in a shoe. And she knew that shoe.

I know that man!

The BellaDonna's boyfriend—the father of her child—wasn't Chris-Crème-Crobat.

He was . . . Wingtip.

M

Everyone was whooshed out of the flashback once more, returning to the OoAh. Muffled sounds from the 7Seven stadium boomed through the walls.

Tookie stared at her mother, reeling from what she'd just seen. "You always t-t-told me to stay away from that man, Creamy. To n-not make eye contact. But you *knew* him all along?"

Ci~L clucked her tongue. "I see how it works. You tell Tookie to make no eye contact with the man, even though that's exactly the opposite of what *you* used to do."

Creamy scoffed and looked away. "That man is disgusting and always has been."

"That *man* has a name, and you *know* it!" the BellaDonna shrieked. "It's Ray Faye!"

"*We're entering another flashback now,*" one of the Females interrupted. Then she glanced at Tookie. "*Some of your questions just might be answered.*"

And with a swoop, they were all back in Modelland of the past.

The summer sun hung high in the sky. Bellas streamed around the courtyard, and the air had the same frenzied, expectant vibe to it as it did today. "Three more days," a green-uniformed Bella said to her friend as she passed. "Who do you think the seven are going to be this year?"

Then Tookie noticed Cremalatta and Ladonna standing at the base of the grand wall that surrounded the school. In this flashback, Ladonna looked pale and much thinner. "I can't sleep," she was moaning. "I can't eat. I can't think. I'm making myself sick." She looked at Cremalatta with hollow eyes. "I have to see my baby now. I can't wait."

"But the Tournament is only three days away, Ladonna," Cremalatta urged. "Then you'll become an Intoxibella and you'll be able to see the baby—and Ray—in secret all the time."

"Three days is too long," Ladonna moaned, wringing her hands. "And anyway, I can't compete in the Tournament feeling weak and sick like this. If I drop out or mess up, you know that's it for me—it doesn't matter *who* my mother is. If I can just see the baby for a quick second, I'll feel better. And strong. I'm nervous to go see the baby by myself, though. Come with me? *Please, Latta?* We'll be back so fast no one will ever know."

Cremalatta stared apprehensively at the wall. "What about the aging barrier?"

"I'm royalty, remember?" Ladonna insisted. "I can get it reversed. And we'll return in plenty of time for you to primp and put on that gorgeous brand-new 7Seven Tournament Jurk dress of yours, I promise."

"Okay," Cremalatta said. With that, the girls scaled the wall and jumped over into the Diabolical Divide. They took two steps and *snap!* Their skin dried and wrinkled. Their hair sprouted tufts of gray. Cremalatta's cheeks shriveled like a raisin. She looked much more like the Creamy Tookie knew. Even though Tookie knew what to expect from having watched Desperada's escape, the transformation was harrowing and unsettling; after all, this time it was happening to her mother.

Cremalatta felt her puckered face and screamed. "Ladonna! Do your royal thing! Make us young again!"

But Ladonna continued through the brush. "Latta, I got you, don't worry! Let's just get through the Divide first. It's deadly, so we gotta keep moving."

With a whoosh, the scene shifted back to the sweltering village where Ray Faye had his cobbler's shop. In the wee hours of that same night, Ladonna and Cremalatta were arriving at the front door of a house. As Tookie looked around, she spied a sparkling new state-of-the-art factory across the street. Several shiny delivery trucks were parked in a driveway. *Bangles, Baubles, and Beads,* the side panels said. Tookie's mouth fell open. It was B3 . . . her old school . . . when it was a jewelry factory. *No way!* Tookie thought. *Who knew the old dump had once looked so glorious?*

The sounds of a crying baby drifted under the door to the house. Ladonna rang the bell, then stepped back and peered at her aged face in the glass pane in the door, wincing at the sight.

The door opened and Ray Faye stood before them, a baby cradled in his arms. He looked back and forth from girl to girl, stunned at their aged faces. "Don't look at me," Ladonna blurted out, covering her face with her hands. "I know I'm hideous, but I'll change back as soon as I go back to Modelland."

Ray Faye lowered his shoulders. "Ladonna, I don't care what you look like. I've always told you that I love your voice more than your face anyway. Now come inside where it's cooler. Our baby is missin' Mama."

Ladonna slipped through the door. Cremalatta moved to go inside too, but Ray Faye gave her a sharp look and slammed the door in her face.

Some time later the sun rose. Ladonna drifted out of the house. "Ray honey, I'm going to run out and get some formula. I'll be back in a sec." She groped her way out the door, seemingly having trouble with her eyesight. "Damn age barrier," she muttered. "I think it gave me temporary cataracts!"

Moments later, just as Ladonna slipped out of sight, the wrinkly-faced Cremalatta tiptoed up the steps and silently turned the doorknob. The door was unlocked.

"Uh-oh," Ci~L whispered.

Cremalatta crept through Ray's modest home, stepping over baby toys and books. She stopped when she got to the kitchen, hopped up on the counter, hiked up the bottom of her skirt to show some extra leg, and waited.

"Ladonna?" Ray Faye called from the bedroom. "You back so soon?"

"Yes, I'm in the kitchen!" Cremalatta called in a disguised, high-pitched voice.

Ray's footsteps rang out in the hall. He entered the room holding the baby. As soon as he saw Cremalatta on the counter, he stopped short and placed the baby in a small cushioned basket. Cremalatta shot across the room, grabbed him by the collar, and threw him onto the kitchen table. She climbed on top of him, and start to moan. "I saw you looking at my body at that fashion show. You know you want this. A real girl, not some stiff royal one!"

"Get off of me, you nasty-ass, sick girl!" Ray screamed. He struggled to escape from Cremalatta's grasp, but Cremalatta was surprisingly strong. He wriggled out from underneath her, but she kneed him in his groin. He howled in pain, and the baby started to wail.

Cremalatta planted her lips on Ray's neck. Her hands worked the buttons of his shirt until he was bare-chested. "Tell me you love me, please, please, please . . . ," she murmured, the sagging skin on her face looking jaundiced under the harsh kitchen lamp. "Tell me I'm more beautiful than Ladonna."

The front door slammed. "They didn't have any more formula, so I bought milk instead," Ladonna's happy trill sang out from the front room. "I hope that's okay!"

"Get *off* me," Ray murmured quietly. He tried to push Cremalatta away.

"Ray-Ray, honey?" Ladonna called out, still oblivious. "Where are you?" Her footsteps came closer and closer to the kitchen. Suddenly, she was in the doorway.

"*Ray?*" she screeched, squinting hard at the figures on the table. The glass milk jug slipped out of her hands and exploded on the floor, which made the baby scream even louder.

Ray struggled beneath Cremalatta, but he still couldn't budge her. "Ladonna sweetie, it's not what it looks like! She has me in some sort of death lock!"

"What?" Cremalatta screeched, suddenly letting her limbs go slack and rolling so that *she* was beneath *him*. "*You* get off *me!*"

Ray scooted from beneath her, raising his hands in surrender. "She's crazy, Ladonna! I don't know what she's talking about!"

"Oh, *sure* you don't!" Cremalatta screeched. "Your girlfriend leaves for two minutes and you're all over someone else! What are you like when she's at Modelland?"

Ladonna moved very close to the two of them, trying to understand what was happening. She shook her head at Ray. "How. *Could.* You? And to my *best* friend! Cremalatta, I'm so sorry. You were right about him. I should have listened!"

Suddenly, there was a loud knock on the front door. "Modelland security!" a voice boomed. "Open up!"

Everyone froze. Ladonna's eyes widened. Wheeling around, she grabbed and shushed the baby and ducked into the bathroom. Seconds later, the guards broke down Ray Faye's flimsy door. One guard strode straight to the bathroom and dragged Ladonna and the baby out of the shower stall. The other pinned Cremalatta's arms behind her back.

"You two left Modelland without permission," the head guard said gruffly to the women. "Usually, we just leave your decrepit, wrinkled faces to rot, but since you're of royal descent, Ladonna, you must return to Modelland right now. All of you must. That means you too, sir." He glanced at Ray Faye, who was still shirtless in the middle of the room. "You know it is forbidden for civilians to be involved with Bellas. A sick and punishable offense."

"What about our faces?" Cremalatta touched her puckered skin. "What about turning them back, Ladonna?"

"I promised you I'd get us turned back, and I will," she assured her friend.

Once again the group felt a pulling sensation, and Tookie, Ci~L, Creamy, the BellaDonna, and Persimmon were whipped into another flashback. This time, Ladonna and Cremalatta stood in the grand crystal hall of the Bored at Modelland. The Queen BellaDonna, Ladonna's mother, stood and gravely shook her head. "You broke one rule too many, Ladonna," she said. "And this time, it was the *ultimate* rule. This is unacceptable. But because of your royal blood, you have a choice. You can leave Modelland and be with Mr. Faye and your child, where you can live together as a loving family. But you will have to relinquish all Modelland privileges. Never become an Intoxibella. And never see me again. And your face will remain aged."

Ladonna held her child tightly in her arms, her bottom lip trembling. Ray Faye shifted his weight behind her. He reached out to hold her hand, but Ladonna smacked him away. "Don't you dare touch me!"

Ray threw up his hands. "Ladonna, sweetie, please give me a chance to expl—"

"Or," the Queen BellaDonna went on, interrupting him, "you

can stay here in Modelland, have your youth restored, and become one of the 7Seven tomorrow, an Intoxibella. But you will never see your Ray again. You also can never admit that this baby is yours. And you will never see the child again."

"Never see my baby again?" Ladonna repeated, horrified. "Why can't I have both?" she asked her mother. "Why can't I have both my baby *and* my beauty?"

Her mother shook her head. "Those are the rules. Make. Your. Choice."

Ladonna looked from the baby to Ray to her mother to Cremalatta. All sorts of conflicting emotions washed across her face. Finally, she sighed. "I've made my choice." She slowly moved forward and handed the baby to her mother.

Tookie and Ci~L gasped. Ladonna's face instantly returned to its youthful splendor. She looked even more striking than before, as if her choice to relinquish her baby was a sacrifice that enhanced her loveliness.

"I have one request," Ladonna said, her eyes lowered. "I don't want *him* to raise my baby." She pointed at Ray. "If he does, he'll raise a heartless child. Please, Mother. Please. Please. *Please!*"

"Very well then," the Queen BellaDonna said. She turned to the guards. "Get him far away from here."

Security guards rushed in and grabbed Ray. He struggled against them. "Get off of me! This is my child too! Please! Please! Don't do this to me, Ladonna! My life will be over!"

The Queen BellaDonna just shrugged. "You heard Ladonna, the *love* of your life. The child does not belong to you anymore."

Ray's face crumpled. He planted his feet and fought to reach the tiny baby, but the guards dragged him away before he could give the child one last caress. His screams could be heard down the crystal corridor.

"What about me?" Cremalatta piped up.

The Queen BellaDonna gave her a cold, dark gaze. "What *about* you? Go away. And never come back here again. You are an awful influence on my daughter."

Cremalatta blinked so hard that her eyes disappeared into a bevy of wrinkles. "But what about my youth? Ladonna, you promised you'd restore everything! That's why I agreed to go down the mountain with you!"

"It's true," Ladonna said. She looked at her mother. "Please, Mother? Can you return her to—"

"No," the Queen BellaDonna decreed. "And that is final." She waved her hand, and security grabbed Cremalatta.

Cremalatta glowered at Ladonna. "You lying, selfish, royal bitch! You promised!" Then her face turned eerily calm. "Well, in that case, guess what, Princess? Ray *didn't* wrong you—you wronged him. I jumped *him*. I have no idea how he could resist me, but he did. He was fighting me off . . . the *whole time*."

Ladonna's jaw dropped. Her eyes searched Cremalatta's face. "But Cremalatta, you're my *best friend*!"

Cremalatta shrugged. "I am. And best friends share . . . *everything*."

Ladonna wheeled desperately toward the door of the grand hall. "Ray?" she screamed, her voice echoing. "Ray, baby! Are you still there?" There was no answer. Ladonna turned to her mother. "I've changed my mind! I want to be with him and my baby! I don't care about being an Intoxibella or about my face!"

"You've already made your choice," the Queen BellaDonna

said stonily. "You should have had better judgment in choosing your friends." She rose and handed the baby to a dead-eyed young Mannecant. "Seems the loyal one was the one you overlooked."

Tookie looked at the Mannecant, suddenly recognizing her. Ladonna let out a gasp too. The Mannecant was a transformed Percy—*Persimmon*. The surface of her once-soft skin was now hardened plastic. Dark creases lined every joint of her body. Her energetic bright blue eyes had been replaced with black voids. Present-day Creamy shouted out to older Mannecant Persimmon, "Lord have mercy, Percy. That Queen bitch sure did curse thee!"

Ladonna sank to her knees in front of Percy. "Percy, please! Give my baby to me! You and I are best friends, remember?"

Percy just stared at Ladonna, her face betraying nothing.

"Oh, so *now* she's your best friend?" the Queen BellaDonna said icily. "You should have stood up for her when you had the chance. It's too late. Persimmon's loyalty is to the BellaDonna throne now, Ladonna."

Ladonna made a pained noise at the back of her throat and rushed for the baby, but her mother thrust out her arm to stop her. "You have made your choice, my dear. You will go on to be a famous Intoxibella. And one day, you will rule this Land and be feared and adored by everyone in the world. You will uphold the principles of Modelland and redefine the face of beauty every five years. You chose correctly, Ladonna. And I know I will not *see* it, but I look forward to the day when you will be called BellaDonna."

"What about my eyesight?" Ladonna asked. "I can hardly see a thing!"

The Queen BellaDonna thought for a moment. "I think I'll leave your sight as is, so you always remember what you've done.

Your face as a future Intoxibella is for *others* to see and enjoy, after all—not you."

"And what about my baby?" Ladonna screamed, pointing at her pale child. "What will happen?"

"Your baby will be safe," her mother said vaguely. "But gone forever. You will never lay eyes on the child again."

"Please!" Ladonna cried as Percy took the baby away. "Let me hold my baby one last time! Just one more kiss!"

"Oh, Ladonna, stop being so dramatic," the Queen Bella-Donna scolded.

Ladonna sank to her knees as Percy vanished down the long hallway with her child in her arms. "Give her back to me! Give me my . . . Ci~L!"

44

Wicked Couture

Ci~L stared at the BellaDonna, the expression on her face a mixture of shock and terror. Her breath quickened into sharp, hyperventilating blasts. *In, out. In, out.* Her chest collapsed with each exhale as though an invisible assailant was stabbing her with a dagger.

"Hurts, doesn't it?" Creamy gave Ci~L a predatory smile. "Ladonna—now the BellaDonna—is your *mama*. And she gave you up. Traded you like a baseball card. For *face* value. Listen to this: Ladonna sacrificed you, a tiny baby, for her own face, even though she can hardly *see* herself because of those nasty cataracts. Ya gotta love the irony."

"But I have green eyes. That baby in the flashback had gray eyes," Ci~L said dazedly.

"Your eyes turned green later," the BellaDonna said in monotone, her gaze lowered to the floor. "A common occurrence with babies born with blue or gray eyes. Though I wasn't there to see it happen."

Ci~L's nostrils flared. "Because you threw me *away*."

The BellaDonna waved her hands helplessly. "Because *Cremalatta* tricked me!"

Creamy rolled her eyes. "Excuse me? What about how *you* ruined *me, Ladonna*? If it wasn't for you, I would have never trekked down that damn mountain!"

"Oh really?" The BellaDonna whirled around to face her. "Even though you were my best friend, I always knew you were jealous. But now I know just *how* jealous. It wasn't just that I was a royal, oh no. You couldn't stand that I had something else you didn't—*love*. But that's because no one could *ever* love you, Cremalatta. Your heart is black inside. It's a wonder you ever married—how did you convince someone to spend the rest of his life with you, with that nasty-ass face of yours? Is that why you carry around this pathetic doll? So you have total control over something, anything? So you have something to love you?" Then she snatched Bellissima from Creamy's hands.

"Give her back!" Creamy screeched. She grabbed the BellaDonna's shoulders, trying to shake Bellissima from her grasp. Clumps of dirt fell from Creamy and the doll to the pristine floor. When the BellaDonna shoved her away, Creamy kicked her in the chest with the soiled sole of her hiking boot. The BellaDonna staggered back, knocking over the Flashback Females.

Persimmon stepped between the warring women. "Cremalatta! Ladonna! Stop it!"

"This isn't your concern, Percy!" Creamy shrieked, shoving Persimmon hard and sending her reeling into the far wall. Ci~L ran to Persimmon and helped her up.

Creamy lunged for the BellaDonna once more. Just as their bodies clashed, a piercing scream rang through the air. Bellissima flew across the room. Droplets of something landed on Tookie's cheek. Then . . . dead silence.

Creamy and the BellaDonna huddled together for a moment, as though locked in an intimate embrace. But then Tookie saw a sharp, shiny metal object piercing her mother's gut and protruding clear through her back. The two women were skewered together with a spike from the BellaDonna's dress.

"Back together again," Persimmon muttered from the sidelines, rubbing the lump on her head.

Tookie wiped the moisture that had splashed her face, then looked at her hand. It was smeared with red. *Blood.*

"Creamy!" she screamed.

Blood gushed from Creamy's wound. The BellaDonna's olive complexion had gone pale from shock. Creamy writhed desperately to free herself from the BellaDonna's spike. Once she did, she spun around and staggered a few steps forward. Her eyes rolled back. Reddish froth spilled from her mouth. Blood trickled out of her nose. After a moment, she crumpled to the ground in a heap.

"Oh my God, Mommy!" Tookie tore across the floor, slid on the spilled blood, and dropped to her knees. "Oh, M-Mommy," she whispered, cradling the woman's head in her hands.

Creamy's eyes fluttered open and locked with her daughter's. "What did you just call me?"

"Mom—I mean, C-Creamy!" Tookie corrected herself.

Creamy nodded faintly, her face now ashen. Blood pulsed from her abdomen in time with the beat of her heart. Tookie could see her slipping away with each passing second. Creamy stared woozily at her daughter and then muttered, "Tookie . . . , "followed by something barely audible.

"Wh-what was that, Creamy?" Tookie asked gently, bringing her ear closer to her mother's lips. All the negativity she'd felt about her mother was instantly replaced by a fervent, protective love. Creamy may not have been the best mom in the world, but she was all Tookie had. If these were Creamy's last moments, Tookie wanted to be there for her. She wanted Creamy to know she loved her.

Creamy swallowed, as if mustering up her strength to utter her last words. Then, through cracked lips, she spoke:

"Tookie, get . . . me . . . my . . . Bellissima."

45

La Camara Brutta

Footsteps rang out in the hall. The heavy iron and concrete doors blocking off the Flashback room rose. Tookie thought it might be Myrracle, but Gunnero Narzz rushed in, followed by six Bestostero guards. "Cut the primping, BellaDonna. Your crowd has been sitting in their seats so long they're starting to stink like last year's trends." He gestured to the stadium scene projected on the wall. The acrobats had wandered off, and the jungle cats had been stuffed back into their cages because they'd become too restless and violent to be loose.

And then he eyed the grisly scene: The dirty, bloodied woman on the floor. The pool of blood around her, getting larger by the second. The bloodied spikes on the BellaDonna's gown. "What in knockoff handbag hell have you *done*?" he whispered to the Bella-Donna, and pressed his long, slender fingers to his mouth.

A muscle twitched in the BellaDonna's throat. "It was an accident," she croaked helplessly.

"No it wasn't," a voice piped up. Everyone looked over. It was Persimmon. Her face hard. Cold. "I saw the whole thing," the Mannecant said. "It was deliberate."

"Persimmon!" the BellaDonna cried, her expression full of horror and betrayal. "You know that's *not* true. Take it back now!"

Persimmon didn't move. For a moment, her face flickered between pure hatred and undying loyalty, but it settled on resentment. *You deserve it,* her expression seemed to say. And then she turned and walked silently out of the room.

The BellaDonna gazed around frantically, searching for anyone who might back her up. Finally, her gaze landed on Tookie. "Tookie!" she screeched. "You saw everything. You know I didn't mean to hurt your mother! *Help me!*"

A pang of guilt shot through Tookie. The BellaDonna had chosen Tookie to come to Modelland, after all. But Tookie knew it hadn't been for the right reasons. She knew that danger still lurked somewhere. She just wasn't sure where, or in what form. And honestly, Tookie couldn't tell if the BellaDonna had meant to stab her mother or not. It all happened so fast. Slowly, she shook her head. "I'm sorry, BellaDonna. But you hurt my mother really badly. I can't help you. I'm sorry."

"You can't pin-tuck your way out of this one," Gunnero giggled nastily. And then he dragged the screaming, writhing Bella-Donna out of the room by her seven-inch stilettos.

М

Finally, three hours, thirty-seven minutes, and twenty-eight seconds after everyone had gathered in the stadium, Gunnero Narzz walked onto the stage, his face drawn and serious. He conferred with the Bored for a moment. Every Bored member gasped. The huddle broke, and Narzz approached the microphone. "May I have your attention?" his voice boomed.

The crowd immediately went silent and still. No one breathed.

Narzz cleared his throat. "While you all have been sitting here in your seats like unwanted hemp-sewn ecofashion on a biodegradable shelf, something tragic has happened here on Modelland grounds. You don't deserve to know the details, but I will share with you one thing: the 7Seven Tournament is . . . postponed."

The crowd gasped.

"*Indefinitely*."

The upperclassBellas all screamed.

"And there will be no Day of Discovery discoveries tomorrow either," Narzz went on, looking pained. "Modelland is shutting down until further notice. *Merci* and *sayonara*. *Danke* and *zài jiàn*. *Gracias* and *arrivederci*."

M

Oh, this was a heavy day, dahling. In the history of Modelland—in the history of the world, I daresay—this was one of the most disastrous, devastating, disheartening days ever. Monsieur Narzz's message had reached everyone in the world at exactly the same time, the announcement flowing like lava down the mountain and incinerating everything in its wake. And dahling, the immediate effects of such a decree upon the world were, well, tragic.

Hospitals from Terra BossaNova to TooLip were flooded with vic-

tims who'd fainted from the hideous blow. Fashion designers fell into debilitating depressions, shocked that they would be given no new muses for inspiration. Some abandoned their showrooms. Others hurled themselves off their tall buildings in LaDorno, their bodies crashing to the street in front of tourists and children.

All of Metopia's fashion factories shut down—there was no need to produce new wares, after all, with no hope of new Intoxibellas to display them. Sure, there were existing Intoxibellas who were more than capable of rocking new wares. But this is fashion, dahling. And fashion is obsessed with the nouveau. Factory workers spilled onto the streets, angry and aimless. Some looted stores, breaking glass and stealing purses, shoes, dresses, suits. But Factory Dependents reveled in the madness, breaking free of their semi-enslavement and adorning their malnourished bodies with the glamorous goods they were forced to produce. Hoodlums in NorDenSwee, Cappuccina, and Oktoooberfest defaced the Intoxibella billboards that rose high above city streets, covering them with the words Liars and Betrayers and IntoxiHellas. Sidewalks that read WHERE THE HELL IS Ci~L? WE NEED HER now bore the answer WHO THE HELL CARES! Rioters rushed the Sapphire Esplanade in LaDorno, grabbing perfume bottles and hurling them at one another like missiles. Vicious fights erupted in the mall corridors—people tore at one another's clothes, gouged out eyeballs, and drowned one another in the fountains. Devastated girls dragged high, medium, and low fashions from the stores to the parking lots and lit them on fire. Another group knocked over a wheeled cart selling Modelland T-shirts, hats, and coffee mugs, throwing everything into the flames. A singed glossy photo of Ci~L slowly disintegrated to ash. A flag depicting the Modelland golden-eye SMIZE went up in a blue blaze.

Why all the bedlam, you ask? Well, the only thing certain in the *world, the only thing on which many people could depend, their single source of happiness and hope, had been postponed . . . indefinitely. What did that mean? One day? Two? Or . . . forever?*

Think about how you'd feel, dahling. Think about if someone suffocated you, strangled you, cut off your nose, held you underwater, for that is how the globe's population felt.

Guru Gunnero's announcement had cut off the world's oxygen supply, and they were desperately gulping for air.

Ж

In the depths of the stadium, Persimmon led Tookie through a dripping corridor and stopped at a heavy stone door with the words LA CAMARA BRUTTA etched into it. The artery-like dungeon walls were red and pulsing, like they were inside a giant organ. There was a bloodthirsty feeling in the air . . . as well as the unpleasant odor of human waste. Tookie recognized the eerie place as the location where she had first seen Ci~L abusing herself. But she had only peeked in. She had not entered.

Persimmon finally spoke. "The Ugly Room is a place for those who have committed vile sins. Sins far worse than the ones that send Bellas to the Catwalk Corridor."

"Ci~L spent some time here, didn't she?" Tookie asked, already knowing the answer.

Persimmon nodded. "Every mirror, every surface in this room, reflects the most repugnant version of the transgressor. Now close your eyes."

Tookie did as she was told, and Persimmon sprayed a fine golden mist around her face. "Anti-Repugnancy Spritz," Persimmon explained. "To make sure you don't experience the Ugly Room's effects."

Tookie opened her eyes once more. Persimmon still stood in front of her, as if she wanted to say something. Tookie thought of the memory that she'd just seen. "I'm sorry," she said in a small voice. "About . . . you know. You."

Persimmon lowered her head. "So am I," she sighed, then sharply turned and walked away.

A moment later, Ci~L stepped inside the Ugly Room. While Persimmon sprayed her, Tookie overheard Persimmon whispering in Ci~L's ear. "Do you realize that if you were never born, I'd be *you*—a Triple7. The day you took your first breath was the day my life ended." Persimmon took one last look at Ci~L and then left the room.

When Ci~L opened her eyes, she looked guilty, fragile, and naïve instead of confident and strong. She turned to go after Persimmon but stopped when she heard Tookie's voice.

"Ci~L, it's not your fault. Or Persimmon's. You're both victims. Are you . . . okay?"

Ci~L shrugged. "I have no idea." She sounded absolutely drained.

An ominous voiced boomed from above, as if the room itself was speaking to them. *"The gates will rise and you two can see your mothers now."*

Tookie and Ci~L walked together down the long dark-red corridor, and they were greeted with a new smell: the stench of rotting flesh, which grew stronger with every step. They stopped at a room that looked like a gaping red mouth, badly lit and filled with shadows and more rancid smells. The BellaDonna sat upright in a chair, dressed in a gray Ugly Room jumpsuit, similar to the one Ci~L had worn. Her body faced a wall of mirrors, which reflected not the lovely woman they had just seen in the flesh for the first time, but a pockmarked, scaly-skinned beast. She had entrails for hair, a twisted tree root for a nose, and millipedes for eyelashes. The BellaDonna writhed in pain at her hideous reflection, but she couldn't turn away: a restraint around her head forced her to face forward. Her wrists and ankles were bound to the chair, which was bolted to the floor. Metal clamps held her eyes open, making blinking impossible. A saline stream dripped into her eyes from a clear bag above.

"Ohhh," Tookie gasped, averting her eyes. The BellaDonna's face reminded her of a ghastlier version of her own at THBC.

Next to her, Creamy, also dressed in an Ugly Room jumpsuit, lay on a cot, her filthy feet splayed out, her dingy, wrinkled skin looking even more puckered and damaged than usual. Her soot-caked eyes were shut tight. Tubes protruded from her veins. Wires stretched from her nose. A bag was attached to her gut, draining blood. Bellissima lay on her back next to Creamy. Someone had kindly wiped the dirt from the doll's face.

Tookie studied Creamy carefully. "My mom doesn't look that much different from when she was in the Flashback room."

"I guess the Ugly Room figured she was already dirty and ugly enough," Ci~L said.

Tookie looked desperately at Ci~L. "Do you think my mom's going to die?"

Ci~L pulled out a chair for Tookie to sit, and read a medical chart at the foot of Creamy's cot. "It says here that no vital organs were hit, but that she's lost a lot of blood. It looks like it's touch-and-go. But if your mom survives, Tookie, she'll probably remain in the Ugly Room for a long time, possibly a life sentence. She broke a serious rule by invading Modelland. You saw the flash-back. She was banned for life."

Tookie inched closer to Creamy's cot. The woman looked so small, nothing like the Creamy Tookie knew back in Metopia. The flashback Tookie had just lived through swam through her mind, filling her with confusion, awe, and shame. Who *was* Creamy? How had she been capable of such terrible betrayal of a girl who was supposed to be her best friend? How was it that Tookie never knew about any of this . . . and yet she'd lived under her mother's roof for fifteen whole years?

The mysterious creature who lay before her had never uttered a word about being at Modelland, knowing the BellaDonna, or Wingtip—Ray Faye. But then again, would Tookie have wanted to know about any of it?

Tookie touched her mother's foot. It was ice cold. "C-Creamy. I—" She struggled to get the words out. "I l-love y-you. All I've ever wanted is for you to love me b-b-back."

Creamy didn't answer. All Tookie heard was the sucking sounds of her mother's blood in tubes.

Tookie glanced at Ci~L, who was slumped over, whispering her own plaintive, pent-up feelings to the BellaDonna's turned back. "I was raised in poverty, with barely anything. But a wonderful woman raised me and three other beautiful girls: Hendal, Woodlyn, and Katherine. Then I got chosen to come to Modelland and I had to leave them all. It was so hard . . . but never once did you acknowledge I was yours!"

The BellaDonna didn't respond.

"I—I know you l-loved me before," Tookie continued, her heart pounding. "I saw that one flashback . . . when I was a baby. Wh-what h-happened after that to make you h-hate me?"

"Did you *ever* want me back after you got your youth back?" Ci~L asked the BellaDonna. "Did you ever come looking for me after you became an Intoxibella?" Ci~L and Tookie were crying out in stereo, their own small chorus of pain and questioning. "Or were you happy to give me up in exchange for your beauty?"

"Why didn't you ever think I was special?" Tookie said. All of a sudden, she realized she wasn't stuttering any longer. "You should have, Creamy. Because . . . because I *am*. Even if I don't belong here, I'm still worth *some*thing. I know that now."

Ci~L wiped the tears from her cheeks and stared at the Bella-Donna. "When I went off message, when I dug up . . ." Ci~L paused, obvious in pain. Then she continued, "When I did what I did, why did you bring me back here? You should have just sent me away somewhere! Cut me loose! Been free of me for life! That's what you wanted!"

Suddenly, the BellaDonna wrenched her head, breaking free from the restraint. She turned and stared into Ci~L's eyes so harshly that Ci~L jumped back. "Listen to me, child, because I will only say this once: Gunnero was going to *kill* you for what you did! Your act threatened *everything* we stand for here, Ci~L! We all were livid! Furious! Disgusted by your actions. And I was embarrassed. But Narzz . . . oh, he was the worst. He put a price on your head! And even though I detested what you did and knew it was justifiable to punish you with death, I could not let that happen. Not to *my* child. Your Day of Discovery was so long ago, but I remember it like it was yesterday. I brought you here so I could spend every day with you, so that I could watch you grow and learn and *live* . . . close to *me*. I realize it was too little, too late. I realize it did not make up for giving you away. But it's the best I could do!"

"No it's not! You could have refused to give me up in the first place!" Ci~L roared, clutching the BellaDonna's arm. "You could have let go of your pride and your vanity and raised me! Kept me as your own!"

"I know that now. But you saw everything in that flashback. The difficult position I was in. The lies, the trickery. I was *confused*! But . . . what's done is done, Ci~L. The decision I made that day was the worst choice of my life! I've always regretted it. I've always wondered . . . *what if?* Yes, I've been hard on you this past year. But it's because I'm looking out for you. I'm trying to save you from harm. If you do not reform, Narzz has every right to execute you. You are my whole world, Ci~L. More than Modelland. More than anything." The BellaDonna erupted into violent sobs. "When I had you, I looked into your gray eyes and the first thing I said was, *I see love.* And Ci~L, every time I see you, even right now, I see love. That's how I named you. Ci~L . . . *see love.*"

Ci~L's mouth dropped open. Her chin trembled. She was trying desperately not to cry. "Really?" she whispered tenderly.

"Yes, baby," the BellaDonna blubbered. "Yes, my love."

Tears ran down Ci~L's cheeks. She tore away the leg and wrist restraints on the BellaDonna; the shackles fell to the ground. Ci~L then collapsed her head onto her mother's lap and the BellaDonna leaned forward, embracing her daughter.

The only sounds in the Ugly Room were the racking sobs of Ci~L and the BellaDonna, when without warning, the sound of heavy doors banging filled the space. Guards rushed in and surrounded Ci~L and the BellaDonna. Gunnero Narzz pushed to the front of the group. "Get up, Body Girl. You're coming with us." He grabbed Ci~L.

A look of fear flashed across Ci~L's face. Tookie recalled

what the BellaDonna had just said about Narzz wanting to kill her. The BellaDonna stood up. "Narzz. Get. Your. Hands. Off. My. Daughter."

Gunnero wrinkled his nose. "Oh, *now* she's your daughter." Then he looked at Ci~L with hatred. "Body Girl, you must pay for who you are and what the hell you have become."

Tookie jumped to her feet too. "Ci~L!" she cried.

"Shut up, Crazy Eyes!" Narzz screamed, and the guards dragged Ci~L out of the room. Tookie took one last look at her mother and then slipped out of the Ugly Room, following close behind.

46

With Perfect Execution

Beautification Boulevard was pandemonium. Bellas walked around in a daze, not understanding what was happening. The upper-classBellas, their fates suspended indefinitely, cried in protest. ZhenZhen lay in a heap outside the stadium, tears and makeup running down her face. "I can't believe this!" she wailed. "I held on to my no–Ci~L look for forty-eight whole minutes! I could have done it today! I could've become an Intoxibella!"

Mannecants rushed around, but without instructions from the BellaDonna, they were aimless and useless. Everyone knew something was up, but they didn't know what. A mob flanked Ci~L and Gunnero as they emerged from the Ugly Room. "Where is the

BellaDonna?" voices cried. "Why is she not showing herself? Why has she postponed the 7Seven Tournament? Why is she *doing* this to us?"

Narzz didn't answer, whipping past them without even giving them a second look. Then the girls noticed Ci~L, whom the guards were dragging by her hair. Horrible screeches emitted from Ci~L's mouth. "What are you doing to her?" the girls asked. Zhen-Zhen ran to the front of the crowd.

"Let Ci~L go! You're hurting us!" she shrieked.

Narzz shoved ZhenZhen aside.

Tookie breathed heavily to keep up with Narzz and Ci~L as they marched toward the M. When Narzz approached the building, the entrance slid open. The guards pushed Ci~L inside. Tookie slipped in just before the giant doors closed once more. The sounds of the angry mob were muffled once the doors banged shut. No one stopped her. No one saw her. If there was ever a good time to be a Forgetta-Girl, this was it.

Narzz led Ci~L down the glass corridor Tookie recognized from the last time she'd been in the M. Then he slapped a button on a wall and the large frosted-glass door split into two halves and swung open. Tookie blinked to adjust to the stark brightness of the room. Inside was the grand chamber she had seen before. Bizarrely shaped windows, some like triangles, some like trapezoids, some round portals, speckled the high walls. Tookie felt like she was entrapped in a surrealist crystal painting.

The three-dimensional tic-tac-toe board loomed at the front of the room, seemingly transported back from the stadium. A member of the Bored occupied each seat, staring down on Ci~L as the guards pushed her into a bright golden spotlight. For once, the eyes of the Bored members were wide open. Their faces were alert, interested. Maybe even nervous. Guru Applaussez's head-hand was chewing one of its own fingernails.

Tookie slipped behind a wall of glass that had just turned opaque, her heart pounding.

Ci~L peered at the waiting tribunal. Her hands shook by her sides. Her knees knocked. "What else do I have to do? I'm on message! Modelland is perfect, one type of beauty is the only beauty that exists! Blah, blah, blah! See?"

A loud gavel struck the glass table and shattered it, cutting Ci~L off. "I've had just about enough of you, Body Girl," Narzz growled. Then he signaled for the Bored. They rose in unison. Without a word, Narzz dragged Ci~L to a contraption and slammed her head into what looked like a crystal guillotine. "Guards!" he called behind him. "Let's hurry up and get this over with!"

Tookie's scalp prickled. Her stomach churned. They were going to behead Ci~L!

Two guards marched up to the guillotine, their faces grave. The other Bored members visibly quivered. Tookie could hear her pulse racing in her ears as one guard smoothed Ci~L's hair away from the back of her neck. The other adjusted the guillotine.

The first guard held Ci~L's shoulders still. "Please!" Ci~L screamed. "Just hurry up and do it!"

The diamond blade glimmered in the light, blinding Tookie, just like her mother's mirror had blinded Chris-Crème-Crobat on the tightrope many years before. She squinted for a moment, watching the blurry guillotine rushing toward Ci~L's neck.

Just as the blade reached it, red liquid gushed from Ci~L's neck, covering her body. And then an object appeared on Ci~L's head. A fashionable, off-kilter *crown*. The red liquid transformed into fabric, a stately red damask cape.

All at once, the other Bored members began to applaud. "To the new BellaDonna!"

The color returned to Ci~L's cheeks. She stood and looked around confusedly, then felt the crown on her head with the tips of her fingers. "Is this a joke?"

"Unfortunately, *no*, Body Girl," Narzz growled.

"You are ze BellaDonna's daughter, you are technically royalty," Guru Applaussez said. "And as you know, the mantle of la BellaDonna passes from one member of *la famille royale* to ze next. You, Ci~L, are ze only living heir. Once your Bella lineage was verified, we summoned you here.

"It was *almost* unanimous," it said, eyeing Gunnero, "but my extra hand in the air got us *les votes* we needed. But a vote was *très* unnecessary. Royalty always prevails. I flip ze bird to democracy!"

Ci~L scratched her head. "Me? The BellaDonna? Seriously?"

"*Oui oui, ma belle petite.* Come on, now. Take your rightful seat," Guru Applaussez said, gesturing to the middle throne on the risers.

Ci~L looked at it, a frightened expression crossing her face.

Gunnero raised his brows hopefully. "You can say no! It *is* an immense responsibility, after all, *Body*—"

Ci~L shot him a *don't you dare* look, cutting him off. "If you call me *Body Girl* one. More. Time. *Gunnero!* That is no way to speak to the newly crowned BellaDonna."

"Is that a yes?" the other Bored members said in unison.

Ci~L nodded. "I suppose it is," she said, smirking at Narzz.

Everyone except Narzz began to applaud.

"Yes!" Tookie screamed, forgetting she was in hiding.

The guards whipped around. They spied Tookie and lunged for her. Gunnero screeched, "What are *you* doing here?"

"Ze seamstress?" Applaussez said, confused.

"I—I'm sorry!" Tookie stammered. "I was just—"

Gunnero cut Tookie off, pinning her arms behind her back. "Princess BellaDonna, I will handle this crazy-eyed, shouldn't-be-a-Bella intruder!"

It took Ci~L a moment to realize that Gunnero was addressing her. Slowly, she descended from her throne and approached Tookie. "What are you doing here? What, did you follow me here? You are not allowed in the M building!"

"I just wanted to help you!" Tookie cried. "I was afraid you were in trouble!"

"I can take care of *myself*!" Ci~L spat.

Oh my God! Ci~L has turned into a demon again! Where can I run? Tookie thought, panicked.

Ci~L spun around and eyed Gunnero and the guards. "Release her immediately. I will punish her myself!"

Gunnero smirked, pleased.

The guards dropped Tookie's arms and Ci~L said, "*Psych!* Tookie, I was totally kidding. I was spooky, huh? Like before, when I was crazy, but I'm not crazy now but I feel crazy cuz I'm the frickin' BellaDonna. I'm so nervous and now I'm sweating again. You know how I sweat. Augh! Come here, girl!" And then Ci~L wrapped Tookie in a big hug.

"Ci~L, you totally freaked me out," Tookie said, giggling nervously. "I thought you were gonna kill me."

"Gunnero!" Ci~L called out to Narzz. "Don't you dare harm a curly, straight, wavy, or frizzy hair on her head. *Ever.*"

Gunnero grimaced like he smelled something foul, but reluctantly nodded.

"Thank you," Tookie whispered to Ci~L, dipping into a respectful curtsy.

Ci~L snickered. "Oh, get up. There's not gonna be any of that idiotic kowtowing during my reign." She looked at Narzz. "And you. If you have a problem with treating Tookie with the respect she deserves, you can *kiss my big fat Princess BellaDonna ass*!"

Gunnero just stared in shock.

"And speaking of kissing, I want you, Mr. Narzz, to bow down right now to Miss Tookie and kiss her feet."

Narzz blinked hard. "What?"

"That's right." Ci~L placed her hands on her hips. "I'm the Princess BellaDonna, baby. The head bee-yotch in charge. And from now on, you *will* do *Whatever.* I. Say."

Reluctantly, Gunnero took mincing steps up to Tookie. He fell to his knees, puckered his lips, and kissed Tookie's shoes, which were still soiled with Ugly Room crud.

And Tookie had to admit it felt pretty damn good.

47

La Lengua

Tookie emerged from the M building and started back toward the D, still numb with shock. Had it really happened? Was Ci~L truly the new Princess BellaDonna? Had Gunnero honestly kissed Tookie's dirty, oversized feet as though she were the Queen of Gowdee?

Pure, unfiltered happiness filled her from the tips of her toes to the top of her head. She couldn't wait to tell the Unicas what had happened. She could just picture Dylan almost fainting from glee, Shiraz doing a victory dance, and Piper smiling, hypothesizing how Modelland's conditions would improve under Ci~L's rule. The whole world around Tookie glistened as though it had been scrubbed clean. Many girls along Tookie's walk were still distraught, and some hysterical, over the abrupt ending of the 7Seven Tournament. Only Kamalini walked among the crowd unscathed and unbothered, bopping to her Headbangor. Tookie wanted to throw her arms around the girl—if Kamalini hadn't told her to run into the O on the first day there, Tookie might not be at Modelland today. But Kamalini was too far away. Tookie would have to thank her later.

Tookie was overflowing with delight and practically skipped down the path toward the D entrance. A rustling sound in the bushes made her stop short.

Zarpessa stepped out from behind the bushes, eyeing Tookie dangerously. Tookie froze, her euphoria suddenly fading away. She wasn't in the mood for a confrontation. "Look, Zarpessa, for the last time, I *didn't* tell anyone your secret, okay?"

"I know," Zarpessa said.

Tookie blinked hard. "You . . . do?"

Zarpessa thrust her chin into the air. "I went back to the FEDS and asked some questions. Dr. Erica told me everything that happened the night I . . . *you* know. She told me she asked around, seeing if anyone knew anything about my history, and no one did. Not even *you*." Her eyebrows arched. "*Why* didn't you tell? I mean, *I* would have, if I were you. Survival of the fittest."

"First you *want* me to keep it a secret, now you want me to tell?" Tookie threw up her hands in confusion. "Whatever happened to you is your business. But your harsh reality is still no excuse to be evil, Zarpessa. This is a place for all of us to start fresh. To forget what happened in our previous lives."

Zarpessa leaned back and examined Tookie in full, perhaps really looking at her for the first time. "Well, I guess this is where

I say . . . I don't know . . . thank you?" she said begrudgingly. "But if you think we're going to, like, *bond* now, you're sorely mistaken. I don't need a shoulder to cry on about my crappy family. Certainly not *your* scraggy-ass shoulder."

"Whatever, Zarpessa." Tookie shrugged, mad at herself for even thinking Zarpessa had changed.

Then Zarpessa stepped forward and stuck her finger in Tookie's face. "And what was all that in the OrbArena about my Theophilus?"

Tookie blinked. She'd forgotten what she'd said about Theophilus in the heat of the moment. "I just wanted to make Bravo jealous," she said in a small voice. There was no way she could get into the Theophilus argument with Zarpessa now. "His was the first name I thought of."

This seemed to satisfy Zarpessa, and she placed her hands on her hips. "Don't ever think Theophilus would be into you, you Unfortunate-Looking, big-headed, crazy-eyed, forgettable bitch. Stay away from him . . . and from me too. Because if you *ever* tell, I'll make your life a living hell. Worse than the hell I live in back home."

Tookie shrank back, her eyes wide. But even though she was trembling inside, she mustered a smile. "You're welcome, Zarpessa," she said as the girl walked away.

Tookie slumped down on a bench for a moment, trying to shake off Zarpessa's hatred. She heard the bushes rustle again and jumped up, prepared for the Wrath of Zarpessa, Round Two. Webb, Alexander, and O'Neil appeared from the bushes, surrounding her.

A knife of fear sliced through Tookie's chest. All she could think of was the lewd things Bravo's friends had probably said to him when the four of them had hatched the bet about Tookie. She rolled her shoulders back and tried to push past them. "Excuse me," she said tightly. *I'm better than they are,* she chanted again and again in her head. *Ci~L, the Princess BellaDonna, thinks so.*

"Tookie, wait," Webb said, grabbing Tookie's hand. And in a split second, all three boys stripped off their uniform shirts, revealing tan, mahogany, and golden skin and sharply defined pectoral and abdominal muscles.

Tookie recoiled and turned away. Now they were stripping for her? Did they want a piece of her too? "I'm not everyone's bet!" she shrieked. "Leave me the hell alone!"

But then she noticed there was something written on their chests in goopy red paint.

Tookie, Webb's chest said.

I'm So, Alexander's said.

And O'Neil's said *Sorry.*

Tookie read the words, frowning. She was seething. Was this some kind of joke?

She was about to turn away once more when the three boys jumped in unison, now showing her their backs. More words, in the same red script, were scrawled across their broad back muscles:

It Was

Never

A Bet.

"Yeah, right," Tookie sputtered. But when the boys turned back around, their expressions were plaintive and repentant, not teasing and disrespectful. From behind, someone grabbed Tookie's shoulder, and she turned to find . . .

Bravo. In a perfectly fitted velvet tuxedo.

"Thanks, y'all," Bravo said, slapping his friends' hands. "I owe you big-time." The three boys pulled on their shirts, gave Tookie a polite nod, and disappeared down the path, leaving Tookie and Bravo alone.

Tookie stared at him, still not sure if this was a joke. Bravo approached her. "So . . . ," he said nervously, "you're back."

"That's right," she said stubbornly.

There was a long silence. Finally, Bravo met her eyes. "What they wrote on their chests is true, Tookie. There was never a bet, I swear. I only told you that because I was mad you were leaving and I thought you used me. I opened myself up to you and I felt all vulnerable. Telling you that stuff gave you a lot of control over me. And then I regretted telling you when you said you were leaving, and I stooped really low and tried to hurt you more than I was hurting. I'm so sorry." He shifted his feet on the path. "But Tookie, I've never met anyone like you. I didn't want you to go. The architecture suddenly wasn't enough for me to want to stay here without you." Then he chuckled lightly. "I wanted to write *Tookie, you're the most amazing girl I have ever laid eyes on, I can't decide which to love more, your green eye or your brown eye,* but there wasn't enough room on everyone's chests. Believe me, we tried."

Tookie stared at him, her resolve crumbling a little. All at once, it made sense: The tuxedo. The writing on the chests. It was exactly what she'd told him she wanted during the ManAttack. All those crazy things she'd come up with . . . and he was executing them, one by one.

Then Bravo took her hand. "I want to show you something."

He started to pull Tookie across the O. They stopped at a garden Tookie had never seen before, right on the border between

Modelland and Bestosterone. It was filled with the most beautiful golden-yellow fabric flowers she'd ever seen, and they went on for a mile. "I just planted these today," Bravo said. "As soon as I saw you'd come back, me and my boys got on the job."

"You planted this . . . for *me*?" Tookie whispered, thinking again of her crazy first-kiss wish.

Bravo nodded. "Okay, confession time. We used special Modelland multiplying seeds." Then he grabbed Tookie's hands and began to sing a strange little tune slightly off-key.

"Oh, Tookie, Tookie, Tookie, I love you more than
Architecture and Lauro's oatmeal cookies.
Went to the FEDS 'cause my heart was failin',
The purse said, 'No, Bravo, De La Crème's got your pulse
*   sailin'."*

Tookie was trying with all her might to hold in her laughter. "You sound really bad, Bravo. You don't have to sing for me."

"This is what you wanted. And you deserve to get what you want."

"But you should be pissed at me," Tookie said. "Because I hit you. Because I left from *our* ZipZap. Because of . . . Theophilus?"

"But you came back," Bravo said. "And Theophilus . . . well . . ."

"Theophilus isn't my boyfriend," Tookie blurted out. "He's Zarpessa's, actually. I was kinda obsessed with him, but . . . nothing ever happened."

Bravo nodded, looking relieved. Then he continued his song.

"Oh, Tookie, I never wagered your lip nookie.
In your eyes is the only place I wanna lookie.
You've taught me 'bout loving and giving, I was a rookie.
You're so pure and sweet. And now I'm hookie
On Tookieeeeee."

Bravo then did a spin and tried to drop down in a half split but almost fell over.

Tookie covered her eyes. "Stop it," she said bashfully. But in truth, she kind of liked this. A *lot*.

Bravo lowered his face to hers. "I still wanna be your first, Tookie."

Tookie's blinked hard. *Oh my God . . .*

"Your special first," Bravo went on. He moved an inch closer and cradled her face in his hands. "Your *only* first."

Tookie shut her eyes. This was happening.

"How privileged I would be if you said yes," Bravo whispered, his lips puckered just so, looking extremely lush and bitable. "Will you?"

Tookie swallowed hard. In the distance, a couple of birds sang to one another. A peal of laughter rang from the O, but it all sounded very far away. "Privileged? For *real*?"

Bravo squeezed her hands. "For real, for real. Will you say yes?"

She could feel his breath on her face. Her heart rocketed in her ears. "Yes. But wait."

Bravo leaned back, staring at her.

"I have a story for you, just like the story you told me," Tookie said. "Once upon a time, there was this girl named . . . *Tookalatta*."

"*Tookalatta*?" Bravo said, amused.

"Shhh. Just go with it, 'kay? So anyway, nobody saw her—ever. She would lie on the floor of her school, waiting for someone to trip over her or kick her or *anything,* but no one ever did. It was like she was a piece of trash. Defective. Uncoordinated, unattractive, and unmemorable."

Tookie cleared her throat, her skin prickling. "Tookalatta wanted love," she went on. "She wanted affection. She wanted it so badly she collected a random item from a boy she liked." She touched the T O OKE pin under her flower. After a moment, she reached under the brooch, removed the pin, leaving the flower brooch where it was, and held the pin in her hand. Bravo looked at it, but didn't say anything. "And she practiced kissing that boy in her mirror when she thought she was alone," Tookie went on, twisting her mouth at the memory of how Myrracle had once caught her. "Tookalata was convinced that all she'd ever kiss for the rest of her life was a mirror. She was a Forgetta-Girl. A girl no one would ever want to kiss. A girl someone might bet on. Make fun of. Shun. Ignore."

"And how does the story end?" Bravo said, squeezing her hand. "Does Tookalatta live a miserable life, alone, afraid, not allowing herself to open up to anyone, running away? Or does she take a risk and realize that someone *does* want her—*really* wants her? And really *loves* her."

Tookie bit her lip, staring at the grass. "The second option," she whispered.

Bravo poked her playfully. "Hi, Tookalatta."

Tookie giggled, then looked up. "Hi, Deco," she said in a small, shy voice.

"Hi, Tookie," Bravo said, staring into Tookie's eyes.

"Hi, Bravo."

And then Bravo kissed her forehead. Then her cheeks. And then her nose. He sucked on her earlobe, sending a jolt of warmth all over her body, followed by an intense feeling of pleasure she'd never experienced before. Her back arched at his slightest touch. Tingles danced from the crown of her head down to her abdomen. She clenched her muscles, then let go. And then, at the same time, they both licked their own thumbs and smoothed the other's eyebrows.

"Close your eyes," Bravo said, and Tookie did as she was told. She heard the sound of a whipped cream can shaking and instinctively opened her mouth just in time for Bravo to shoot a cold stream of whip onto her tongue. The tingles continued down to her hips. She then heard Bravo squirt some cream into his own mouth. And then . . . slowly, gently, Bravo's soft lips touched hers. His lips parted and she felt something thick and slimy inside of her mouth. His tongue.

She pulled away, wide-eyed. "Uh . . . I don't like kissing that way."

Bravo looked surprised. "But you've never kissed before."

"I know I haven't, but . . . my mirror didn't have a tongue," Tookie said, smiling, tracing her finger across Bravo's cheek. "It just . . . *feels* weird. And this is about what *I* want, right?"

Bravo nodded, pulling his body slightly away from hers. "We can go as slow as you want, Tookie. You will set our pace . . . always."

And then he kissed her again, parting his lips only a little, his tongue remaining inside his mouth. He bit slightly on her bottom lip. Tookie grabbed on to the back of his neck, her body feeling hot and alive. They remained like that for a long, long time. And when they pulled back, they stared at each other as only two people who are enchanted with one another can do. A single tear fell from Tookie's brown eye. Bravo brought his lips to the wetness and kissed it tenderly. Modelland was bathed in joyful golden light. The corners of Tookie's lips felt like they might split from smiling. She wanted to prolong this moment for as long as she lived.

"Can we do it again?" she whispered.

And as they continued to kiss, Tookie opened her palm and let the defective, purloined T O OKE button fall to the grass.

She didn't need it anymore.

DO YOU *see her?*

The girl whose face looks, well, maybe not symmetrical, but still quite interesting. Yes, her eyes are still three centimeters too far apart and her mouth is four centimeters too wide, and yes, when you look at her face you might say something is definitely . . . off. But perhaps its unusual qualities draw your attention, making you linger.

Come on now, you see her. If you tilt your head up, up, way up, and stare at the mountain, she's standing outside on top of the M building, her gauzy Modelland nightgown waving in the breeze.

She's the girl whose hair still has multiple personality disorder and can't decide if it's supposed to be quasi-curly, silky-straight, frantic-frizzy, wet-and-wavy, or a "Power to the People" 'fro. But she's kind of okay with that. The girl whose feet are still the size of last winter's snowshoes. She's not okay with that. But her body is no longer hunched over—instead she stands tall, like she's sprouted an inch or two. And her stick-figure arms and legs are still fragile, yes, but there's something a little more filled-out about her than before. Even so, you still might hear her limbs pleading, "Feed me an entire vat of whipped cream, now!" But that's only because she fancies the delicacy so much.

Her head's still the size of a punch bowl, with a forehead that goes on and on and on, but she holds it high, like only someone whose big brain is filled with eloquent strings of words and brave, gutsy thoughts can do. And her eyes, though mismatched—one green, one brown—just add to her uniqueness. They almost look, dare I say, enchanting.

Do you see Tookie De La Crème up there?

I bet you do.

And I bet you'll remember her.

For a long, long time.

Ж

Our tale ends on a clear, starry evening, the most extraordinary of extraordinary evenings in the most extraordinary of places. And Tookie De La Crème, Modelland Bella, was not lying on the floor of B3, praying for students to trample her, but instead was standing outside atop the M building, wind in her hair, goose bumps on her bare arms.

She looked down at the expanse of Metopia's four distinct quadrants surrounding the mountain and prayed that Lizzie was still down there, still alive. Then she ran her hand over the wide stretch of skin above her eyebrows. All of a sudden, something ironic occurred to her: the adjective form of the word *Metopia* was *Metopic,* which meant, as she'd found in Dr. Erica's medical dictionary, "of or pertaining to the forehead." *It's a wonder I wasn't the* queen *of Metopia.*

Modelland was still anything but calm. Even though it was past midnight, Bellas still crammed Beautification Boulevard in protest, demanding answers about why the 7Seven Tournament had abruptly ceased. 7Seven contestants lay on the golden plaza, crying golden tears. Bestosteros stood guard among the crazed Bellas, trying to keep the peace. Purses circled and doctors skated around the crowd, scooping up the girls who were on the verge of nervous breakdowns. Then, from a corner of the plaza, Tookie heard a *meow!* followed by a scream. "Get away from me, you bitey-scratchy things! Creameeeeeee!" a ditzy voice whined.

Myrracle? Tookie thought, perking up. Was her sister still at Modelland, now trapped in Catwalk Corridor? *Well, at least she's here,* Tookie thought, stifling a giggle. *Modelland is where she belongs, after all.*

"Isn't the view amazing?" a voice said. Tookie turned, and there was Ci~L, wrapped in a gauzy jumpsuit with batwing sleeves. "I guess I'll get to see it all the time now."

"It's gorgeous," Tookie agreed. Earlier that evening, a note had been slipped under her door:

> Tookie,
> Meet me tonite at the south point of the M.
> Princess BellaDonna (Can you flippin' believe it? I can't!)
> Fierce & Love, Ci~L

Ci~L, who had not announced her reign to the Bellas yet—the Bored was still debating the most opportune time to do so—had given Tookie a special permit to get into the M building without setting off any alarms. Tookie had passed a few guards on her way up, but they'd just nodded at her like she was someone special.

Maybe she was.

Now Ci~L glanced at the large statue of the BellaDonna. It was covered with an enormous dropcloth. Next to it, a new statue was ensconced with scaffolding. Sculptors toiled away, carving the rock. Tookie knew this new statue would be of Ci~L. Princess BellaDonna of Modelland.

"This is all so freaky," Ci~L whispered. "It's kinda weirding me out."

Tookie looked at her. "What do you think will happen to . . . her? The old BellaDonna? Your . . ." She trailed off, unable to say *mother*. "Will she stay in the Ugly Room?"

"I may be the Princess BellaDonna, but that's not for me to decide," Ci~L answered, great sadness in her voice. "The Bored makes that decision based on a volume of rules and bylaws taller than you and thicker than me. I just hope they aren't too harsh on her. Yeah, she may have committed a crime, and she certainly did something insane that changed my childhood forever, but she's still my . . ." She bit her lip, unable to say *mother* either.

Then Ci~L looked out over the great expanse of the Land. "You've been at Modelland a whole year, Tookie. I spoke with the Bored. Despite your crazy mama's trespassing and the whole T-DOD switcheroo thingy, unfortunately, you're stuck here at Modelland." She winked at Tookie. "Yep, girl, they want you here. Well, most of us do."

"*Really?*" Tookie breathed out, her body filling with elation and relief.

Ci~L waved a finger at Tookie, her face stern. "But don't be putting ya celebration shoes on just yet. Applaussez still thinks you're a seamstress. Plus, when I was here, second year was crazy hard. Shoot, they're easy on you No-See Bellas."

"This year was *easy?*" Tookie sputtered in disbelief.

Ci~L nodded, moonlight dancing on her face. "But from here on out, it gets insane. Don't get me wrong, there's a new Triple7 sheriff in town, but I don't know exactly how I'll be changing things around here. I *do* know I'ma do things *Ci~L*–style, minus the crazy and spooky parts. And shoot, maybe I'll throw in some posing poetry slams and oh my God, who knows what else. But what I *do* know is that I wanna make this a place where girls like my sister-friends could have come." Her eyes watered with tears. "But that'll be an uphill battle with the Bored," she said, wiping her tears away. Then she looked at Tookie. "But mark my words, your *segunda* year will be like hell . . . in heaven. Think you can handle that? Plus a uniform change from green to violet?"

Tookie nodded shakily. "I want to try. I . . . I love it here. I feel like I almost belong."

"Because you do, girl." Ci~L's gaze was intense. "Look, Tookie, you've been underestimated your entire life, including here. The wind is in your face, it's blowin' harder than GustGape, and it ain't dying down anytime soon. But that's actually a good thing, because when people have low expectations, you're just constantly going, 'Ta-dah!' And they're like, 'Wow, I had no idea!' It doesn't take a lot to wow them when they don't expect much from you. You've got to go for your destiny now—that's how I became a

Triple7, girl. Dream big—bigger than you ever have, so big that people laugh in your face. You need to grab on to the handlebars of fierceness and not let go. Because you're *special,* Tookie. You might not know it yet, but you've got a beautiful light that shines inside of you."

Tookie's jaw dropped. "Someone else told me that exact same thing once," she whispered, remembering Wingtip's uplifting words from a year ago. It made sense that Ci~L had nearly echoed him: Wingtip—Ray Faye—was her father, after all.

Tookie breathed in, wanting to tell Ci~L something about her dad—that he was warm and tender, that he would have cared for her dearly, and that maybe he'd descended into melancholy because he'd lost her forever. Then Ci~L touched her arm. "Wanna fly with me?"

Tookie frowned. "Like on T-DOD? Like when you brought us back from LaDorno?"

Ci~L shook her head. "Naw, girl. Been there, done that. *Outside* the pouch." She lowered her chin, and her batwing outfit disappeared and a thousand glittering necklaces appeared all over her body. It was the same outfit she had worn on T-DOD. One of the necklaces stretched out like a tentacle and looped over Tookie's head. A warm light glowed. Tookie's nightgown lit up, revealing hundreds of strands of bejeweled necklaces.

Tookie gasped. Ci~L grinned. "Girl, if you want to fly with me, you gotta *look* fly. You dropped something after ManAttack. Thought you'd like it back." Ci~L placed her hands over Tookie's face.

An incredible, familiar feeling swept over Tookie. The SMIZE! This time she recognized the energy that pulsed through her, and just like before, power zipped through her veins.

Feelings like waves of intense ecstasy crashed into her, surrounding her with the most magnificent smells and tastes and sounds ever heard.

She felt tantalizing. Luminescent. Invincible.

Drop-dead . . . *beautiful.*

"Ready?" Ci~L reached out her hand to Tookie just as she had when they'd stood atop the car in LaDorno Square. Tookie grabbed it tight. She wasn't afraid this time, though—she was excited. She gripped Ci~L's hand with pride and conviction.

"Now climb on my back," Ci~L instructed.

And as they took off into the sky, Tookie thought about how much she'd changed since the day Ci~L had plucked her from her family in LaDorno on the Day of Discovery a year before. She was a different person now—confident, nervy. A friend who had friendSSSS. A leader. Suddenly, as the wind whipped through her multitextured hair, she thought of the letter she'd composed a few hours ago in her *T-Mail Jail.* The sentences flowed fluidly in her mind, just as they had done when she'd written them down on paper.

> This journey hasn't been easy for me. Every step of the way I've struggled, stumbled, doubted, cursed, and felt sure that I couldn't go on. But I feel stronger because of it, almost like I needed to go through it to get where I am now. I still don't know if Modelland is my place or if I'm meant for something else. Maybe I'll always doubt. But maybe it's the doubt that keeps me determined. Hungry. Always looking

to prove and improve myself, make myself better.

Every night, as I lie in my Lumière-less bed, I wonder how many other girls there are like me out there around the world.

Maybe, like me, your father abandoned you, or perhaps you never even knew him. Maybe your mom's a terror or you have no friends. Maybe you're not the best-loved or best-looking daughter. Maybe someone hurt you but you're too nervous to tell anyone. Maybe you hurt yourself and want to stop but don't know how. Maybe you give of your body freely, hoping to get love in return. Or maybe you look at everyone else's bodies and then compare them to and detest your own. Maybe people hurl angry, hurtful words at you, making you want to curl up and disappear. Maybe you hate your reflection, or everyone thinks you're the prettiest but you still feel ugly inside. Maybe you're under intense pressure that you think you can never overcome. Maybe someone tells you daily that you aren't smart or pretty or skinny or talented or good enough.

I know what you are going through. I've made a difficult journey to get here, and I have a lot farther to go. I must fight for my place every single day. It's easy to shine when everything is perfect. But when things are a little shaky, the best truly emerge to show it won't tear them down. That's when the struggle to succeed really starts. I pray you find that strength inside of you, that special inner light that shines extra-bright.

I want to dedicate my struggle and all my time at Modelland to you. Everything I've gone through, everything I'll continue to face, is all for you. And I want you to make me a promise: take all your pain, take all the hurt you're feeling and your bad memories and your darkest thoughts, and send it out to the universe ... to me. I'll be your vessel. I'll carry all of the hurt inside me so that you can be free. And every challenge I go through at Modelland will be for me and you. For us. We can do this. But I'm going to need you too. When I feel weak, scared, or like I want to give up, I need you to send your strength and power up to me on this mountain. I can't make it through this place alone. Okay? Promise?

I believe in you with all my heart—and I hope you believe in me. I just want us to get to the place where we believe in ourselves just as strongly. And besides, there's always room for you in the exclusive Unicas crew.

Fierce & Love,

Tookie ^{RG}

Tookie and Ci~L swept through the sky, circling within the Modelland borders. Suddenly, something invisible tugged at Ci~L's body, pulling her toward the mysterious cemetery within the Diabolical Divide. Ci~L glanced back at Tookie. "I'm getting the sensation that I'm about to teleportal," she yelled over the rushing air.

"Teleportal where?" Tookie yelled back, confused.

"I don't know," Ci~L answered. "Sometimes this happens— the universe tells me to teleportal, and even though I don't know where I'm going, I just go with it." She gestured to the six silvery gravestones directly below them. "If you let go of my hand, you'll float gently back to Modelland. You don't have to come with me. I don't know what we're in for."

Just months ago, Tookie would have dropped Ci~L's hand in an instant, too afraid to face the unknown. But now, the idea intrigued her. It would be an adventure. An experience. Better yet, an *experiment*.

She clutched Ci~L's hand hard. "I wanna go with you."

"Are you sure?"

"Hells yeah!" Tookie yelled.

"All right, girl! Let's do this!" Ci~L shouted. She arched her back and their bodies pivoted and shot toward the ground with breakneck speed. The wind snapped through Tookie's hair. She felt the skin of her cheeks pressing back as they gathered momentum. The cemetery loomed closer . . . closer . . . so close that Tookie could read the names on the graves: MUSE MELODIA, MUSE PRANCIA, MUSE CHROMIA, MUSE DRAMATIA, MUSE FABRICIA, MUSE CHITEC-TIA. Each stone glowed fiery gold as they approached. But instead of crying out in fear, Tookie let out an adventurous whoop. She thought again of the new letter she'd written for *T-Mail Jail*. Recalling how she had addressed it: *To every Forgetta-Girl in the entire world*. And how she had signed off: *Tookie*, dotting her *i* with *RG* for *Rememba-Girl*.

The Intoxibella and soon-to-be Segunda Bella shot like arrows toward the earth. A black hole opened up as their bodies approached. Just as Tookie and Ci~L entered, the hole magically, seamlessly swallowed them up . . . and the two of them disappeared.

A C K N O W L E D G M E N T S

The idea for *Modelland* came to me while I was in the car on the FDR Drive in New York City. I jotted it down on a piece of scratch paper and tucked it into my purse. Four years later, that scrap of paper has transformed into the book (*or digital thingamajig*) you now hold in your hands. And because of that, I have many people and places to say *merci, danke,* and *gracias* to.

From a scrap of paper, *Modelland* went to paper notebooks that I would write story beats in while sitting by the Hudson River. So thank you, Hudson, even if your water is not as blue as I would like it to be. The notebook material then made its way into my laptop, and I squatted at many cafés, for longer than the average dining period should last, and none of you complained (to my face). So thank you, NoHo Star, Caffe Falai (*"Ciao, bellos!"*), Balthazar, Delicatessen, Culina at the Four Seasons, Iris Café, Asellina at Gansevoort Park Avenue, the café at the Guggenheim Museum, and Andaz 5th Avenue—your hotel common areas and The Shop. And a special thanks to the Crosby Street Hotel restaurant. Sometimes I'd sit in one seat there for eight hours at a time, ordering breakfast, lunch, then dinner, only getting up for bio breaks. I know I abused the privilege of that corner window seat. You made me so comfy, though. You practically offered me a pillow and a blanket, and for that, I am forever grateful. Can't wait for the slumber party when I start *Modelland II*. Oh, I can't forget to thank my mom's and John's dining room tables. Thank you for letting me mar you with stacks of papers, computer cables, and coffee-mug rings. Mom and John, I send you each big, sloppy kisses.

My other life, being the chairwoman and CEO of The Tyra Banks Company, did not stop, and the pressure I was under was intense. At times, I had to get away so I could focus on *Modelland*. I went on a few kinda swanky retreats, camping out at hotels and doing nothing but writing. Terranea Resort, you helped produce a marvelous outline for *Modelland*. I might not have followed it exactly, but it was an amazing framework. St. Regis Monarch Beach, thanks for the love and golf cart trips to the restaurant right on the sand. And Montage Laguna Beach, thanks for not complaining when I asked for an extension cord for my battery-drained laptop and you snaked one from about a half mile away to my balcony table overlooking the shore. Speaking of the shore, much love to the Pacific Ocean. Your crashing waves crashed through my few bouts of writer's block.

Lake Como, thank you for providing me with a beautiful landscape in which to create and for inspiring the creation of Abigail Goode. As I gazed over your water, she popped into my mind. Hair? Water? Not sure what the connection is, but thanks anyway. (It didn't hurt that George Clooney lived a few doors down. . . .)

Morocco. The weeks I spent with you produced such superb material. Thank you to the Amangena resort for your candlelight and to Abdul for the verbena tea you kept pouring at three in the morning when I was on a writing roll with insane jet lag. Morocco, thank you for the architectural inspiration for the atrium in the FEDS. Thank you to the wonderful people of the Berber village I visited. It was a real treat for me to read a section of *Modelland* for half an hour to children who didn't speak English. I thought that if I could hold their attention that long, maybe my book had a chance at success. *Shukran.*

Greece. I polished my baby on your soil. I had to finally let her go while I was in your clutches. Hitting the Send button while staring at Crete waves was not easy. But all children must be launched into the world. It was time.

Yes, I have had the amazing privilege to write in some delicious places. But the place I am most grateful for is one that exists in some form around the globe, a place all have access to: the library. The majority of my time writing *Modelland* was spent in a library. A place where I feel at peace, at home. I can't believe the *bibliothecas* where I spent so much time working on *Modelland* will now house it. So with much humility, I thank the libraries—and the librarians in charge—where I spent so much valuable time: the Mid-Manhattan Library in the Stephen A. Schwarzman Building (goodness, you are GORGEOUS!), the New York Public Library for the Performing Arts at Lincoln Center, and the

Beverly Hills Library (especially for the BellaDonna Opera lyrics. And sorry for eating maple nut fudge—not chocolate—under the table. That BellaDonna songwriting worked up my appetite, and the fudge factory is right in your building!).

Cinemagic XM satellite radio, how do you know the exact score I need to hear when I am writing a particular passage?

Thank you to my Twitter and Facebook fam, who sent warm SMIZEs of encouragement as I struggled with carpal tunnel and my deadline.

Thank you to Harvard Business School and my marketing Professor Rohit Deshpande for schooling me on Hindi and Indian culture. Professor Robert Steven Kaplan, my leadership prof, thanks for suggesting I give the Unicas' richer, more vulnerable backstories. Columbia University, I cheated on Harvard with you and used your grand stairway as a post to write an entire chapter of *Modelland*. You are so unbelievably breathtaking, and I can't wait for our next tryst. Shhh . . .

Thanks to my agent, Nancy Josephson, for believing that Modelland was more than just a place in my head and for working diligently to make sure it came to life. To my book agent, Andy McNicol, for saying *supermodel* is an overused term and pushing me to come up with something else. Hence, Intoxibella! To Matt Johnson, my wonderful attorney (I know, you look nothing like Guru MattJoe and you have nothing in common with him, but I wanted to get your name in the manuscript somehow. Yep, yep.). To Brad Rose, my trademark attorney. You covered a very important Modelland detail for me. You rock!

Tama Smith, your business advice is my saving grace. Look for your name in *Modelland II*. Intoxibella Tama, maybe? Ken Mok, my dear partner on *Top Model*: you are an amazing cheerleader and an even more amazing father. And finally, you can visit Modelland, and not just in your sleepy awake-dreams! Michael Salort—can you believe it's a real book now? And there's no way in the world I could have done Man-Attack without you. For that and so much more, I am forever grateful. Joe, I could not have kept track of the *Modelland* story, backstory, front and side stories, and everything in between without you. Laura Brown, thanks for allowing me to hole you up in your *Harper's Bazaar* office while you schooled me on "low-flying duck" Aussie-speak. Madison, thanks for offering to read my crazy-long first draft. How the heck could you do that and study for "Ivy" exams? Miss Madison, I have read many of your school papers. You have a writing gift. Go for it, girl! Sydney, thanks for the two words in this book that you sometimes say that I HAD to put in. Oh, and Sydney, dance in your spirit AND your body. You really ARE good!!!

Janice Y. K. Lee, yours was the first author reading I've ever been to. Thank you for showing me that once the book is released into the world, it's no longer mine, that the readers own it. And thanks for the homemade Korean barbeque ribs. Yum! And Janice, I'm still hoping for a sequel to *The Piano Teacher* that I know you will never write. C'mon, Janice, just one secret MS for me. Please? Sara Shepard, we have experienced a few firsts together. A first novel for me, a first baby for you. You have no idea how my heart swelled when you told me I was a good storyteller! I only hope for a smidgeon of the success you have achieved with Pretty Little Liars. I can't wait to read the sequels that still live inside of that genius head of yours! Stephen King (it feels so good to even type your name, especially because people will assume we are friends!), I want to thank you for writing *On Writing*. Yep, I read it. Twice. I may have failed when it comes to your advice that one should not use too many adverbs and adjectives. But Modelland is so splendiferously, kaleidoscopically, out-of-this-world colorful, I couldn't help myself! Please forgive me!

Immaculate Heart High School, thank you for enriching my mind and making me an independent, freethinking woman. And thanks for having some of the best English teachers on the planet. Mr. Terry Vliet, if it weren't for you and your fabulous literature classes, *Modelland* might have never come to fruition. It might have remained a mere idea on scrap paper that just disintegrated in the bottom of my messy purse.

To L.A. Models, Elite Models (*¡Hola, Oscar Reyes!*), City Models (*Merci, Veronique!*), IMG Models, the city of Paris, and the fashion in-dustry worldwide: thank you for letting this big-foreheaded, flat-footed, skinny-calved, cellulite-dimpled-butt girl be a part of your world. You were the catalyst that gave me the voice to reach so many.

The Tyra Banks Company. My kick-ass team that keeps our company running, thank you for understanding that I had to check out for months at a time to work on my Modelland baby. EYE SEE YOUR BEAUTY! Hope, you Lioness of the Fierce Jungle (with great hair)! You miraculously managed my insane life, allowing me to focus on the completion of *Modelland.* Crotches! ;-) Sabrina, our Office Gypsy, thanks for your intense work ethic and keen eye. Your tireless help solidifying our *Modelland* cover, back cover, spine, and endpapers was a helluva task, girl! And Patrick, our Ringmaster. Wow, what can I say? Thanks for believing in, supporting, and understanding what *Modelland* means to me. Having you lead our team every day is a gift that keeps on surprising and giving. I appreciate you. Here's to all of us fighting to keep expanding the definition of beauty!

To my editor, Wendy Loggia. Thank you for taking my first thousand-page manuscript (I know, insane) and making it this. How the heck do you know how to do that and not sacrifice the story? It's a gift that is otherworldly. Are you human? Now that I think of it, your stunning eyes are kind of not really mortal. To Tribeca Flashpoint Media Arts Academy, the cover is slammin'! You know it, cuz y'all did it! I know it was lotsa work, but you all rocked it. Much love to sensational artists Perry Harovas and James "Red" Schmitt. Our hands-on sessions in Chicago were fun and inspiring. And Howard Tullman. You are full of passion for Flashpoint, its instructors and students. They are all lucky to have you as their leader! Hebru Brantley, the endpapers (the graffiti on the inner covers) are so much fun. There's so much amazing detail! But I can't find the fried chicken I asked you to put in there! To my publisher, Beverly Horowitz, I'm not sure if you knew how dedicated I would be to *Modelland* or that I'd also be a big pain-in-the-nitpicky-butt perfectionist, but you are a living legend, which means you've seen it all. I feel so blessed that Modelland has been anointed by you.

To you, the person reading this book. My first novel. What can I say to express my deepest gratitude? Releasing *Modelland* into the world, into your hands, makes me feel so excited, yet extremely vulnerable. I'm nervous and curious about how each chapter makes you feel, which characters speak to you. Which ones you love, hate, or love to hate. *Modelland* is no longer mine. It belongs to you. I hope you enjoyed reading her as much I did writing her. Thank you for spending your precious time with my baby.

To John. You make me smile. And laugh. And laugh. And smile. I'm smiling now as I write this. Your selflessness and patience are so rare. Thank you for the many mouthwatering meals you cooked while I typed away. Thank you for accompanying me on many of my odd (Columbia steps) writing excursions. Looking up and seeing you right there made me feel so special. Thank you so much for never complaining that I was writing too much. But thank you even more for telling me to go to bed when you knew what I was typing had to be gibberish because it was three in the morning. *Yo te quiero.* No, for real. ;-)

My brother, Devin, you are amazing. You serve our country and make me feel so safe when I go to bed at night. I know you always say how proud of me you are. You will never truly understand just how proud of you I am, Devy. That fact that you are my brother has me over-flowing with admiration. And our mutual love of all things Walt Disney has shown us that all dreams are possible. Thanks for exposing even more of Mr. Disney's life to me. You and Walt are my heroes. Luv, Whop.

Daddy, no matter how old I get, I know I will always be your little girl. Thanks for showering me with so much love. Thanks for taking me to Disneyland multiple times a year when I was young. Experiencing that magical place allowed me to dream up Modelland. Thanks for always calling to check up on me; you seem to have some SixxSensa for when I am stressed. Buster loves you, Daddy.

And Ma, thanks for snapping my author photo. You took my first modeling photos *and* first fiction-author pic. Cool! And thank you so much for carving out a huge block of your precious time to read every last word of that first thousand-page manuscript and giving me the harsh, unfiltered truth. You are truly the world's most lovely, most beau-tiful, most loyal and caring Intoxibella who ever was and ever will be. Long live the original Ci~L.

ABOUT THE AUTHOR

TYRA BANKS was fifteen years old when she started modeling, the same age as *Modelland*'s Tookie De La Crème. After establishing a supermodel career she could never have dreamed of, Tyra tackled the world of television, creating the hit show *America's Next Top Model,* which is seen in over 170 countries, and her two-time Emmy-award-winning talk show, *The Tyra Show,* to become the super businesswoman she always wanted to be. Tyra is a leading voice in empowering girls and is dedicated to expanding the definition of beauty worldwide.

Tyra invested five years in conceiving and writing *Modelland,* her first book of fiction. Her lifelong love of reading and storytelling is deeply embedded in every page. She was born in Los Angeles, lives in New York City, and has a vacation home in Modelland, where she is feverishly working on the next *Modelland* novel.

tyra.com